ARNALDUR INDRIDASON

Arnaldur Indridason worked for many years as a journalist and critic before he began writing novels. His books have since sold over 14 million copies worldwide. Outside Iceland, he is best known for his crime novels featuring Erlendur and Sigurdur Óli, which are consistent bestsellers across Europe. The series has won numerous awards, including the Nordic Glass Key and the CWA Gold Dagger.

The Shadow District – the first book in the Reykjavík Wartime Mystery series – won the Premio RBA de Novela Negra, the world's most lucrative crime fiction prize.

ALSO BY ARNALDUR INDRIDASON

ARNALDUR INDRIDASON

The Shadow Killer

TRANSLATED FROM THE ICELANDIC BY
Victoria Cribb

VINTAGE

1 3 5 7 9 10 8 6 4 2

Vintage
20 Vauxhall Bridge Road,
London SW1V 2SA

Vintage is part of the Penguin Random House group of companies
whose addresses can be found at global.penguinrandomhouse.com

First published in hardback by Harvill Secker in 2018
First published by Vintage in 2019
First published with the title Þýska húsið in Iceland by Vaka-Helgafell in 2015
Published by agreement with Forlagid www.forlagid.is

penguin.co.uk/vintage

A CIP catalogue record for this book is available from the British Library

ISBN 9781784704391 (B format)
ISBN 9781784704407 (A format)

This book has been translated with financial support from:

 ICELANDIC LITERATURE CENTER

Printed and bound in Great Britain by Clays Ltd, Elcograf S.p.A.

Penguin Random House is committed to a sustainable future
for our business, our readers and our planet. This book is made
from Forest Stewardship Council® certified paper.

MIX
Paper from
responsible sources
FSC
www.fsc.org   FSC® C018179

THE SHADOW KILLER

1

The *Súd* steered a careful course around the frigates and mine-sweepers in the approaches to Reykjavík harbour before finally coming alongside the docks. Shortly afterwards the passengers began to disembark, one after the other, many of them shaky on their legs and relieved to have dry land underfoot again. The voyage had been uneventful until they reached Faxaflói Bay, where the wind had veered to the south-west bringing squalls of rain and the ship had begun to roll. Most of the passengers stayed below decks, where a sour reek of wet clothes pervaded the cramped quarters. Several had been seasick during this last stage, Eyvindur among them.

He had boarded the ship at Ísafjördur, toting his two battered suitcases, and slept for most of the way, worn out from trekking round the villages and farms of the West Fjords. The cases contained tins of polish: Meltonian for shoes and Poliflor for furniture. He was also lugging around a sample dinner service that the wholesaler had imported from Holland just before the war.

Eyvindur had done quite well with the shoe and furniture polish, but in spite of his best efforts to sing the praises of Dutch tableware, it seemed there was no market for such goods in these treacherous times. His heart really wasn't in it, and he hadn't even bothered to visit all the places that normally formed part of his route. Somehow he couldn't summon the powers of persuasion, that almost religious fervour which, according to the wholesaler, all successful salesmen required, and so he had returned clutching only a handful of orders. Eyvindur had rather a bad conscience about this. He felt he could have made more of an effort and knew that the few orders he had secured would make little impression on the wholesaler's mountain of stock.

The trouble was that he had been in a bit of a state when he set out from Reykjavík a fortnight ago. That was one reason the trip hadn't gone as well as it should. Moments before he was due to leave he had made an accusation in his typically tactless way, which led to a row that had weighed on him throughout the trip. Vera had reacted furiously, calling him all kinds of ugly names, and he started to regret his words as soon as the *Súd* sailed out of Reykjavík harbour. He'd had two weeks to brood and find excuses for his behaviour, though to be honest he still wasn't convinced that he had been the one in the wrong. Yet her outrage had struck him as genuine when she retorted that she couldn't believe he would accuse her of such a thing. She had burst into tears, locked herself in the bedroom and refused to speak to him. In danger of missing his boat, Eyvindur had snatched up the cases of polish and tableware and run out of the door, wishing with all his heart that he had a different job, one that didn't force him to spend long periods away from home while Vera got up to goodness knows what.

These thoughts were still rankling as he leapt ashore and half ran towards the centre of town, hurrying as fast as his legs would carry him, plump, a little splay-footed and out of condition in spite of his age, clad in his trench coat, a case in either hand. The rain was coming down more heavily now and water trickled from the brim of his hat, getting in his eyes and soaking his feet. He took refuge under the porch of the Reykjavík Pharmacy and peered round the corner into Austurvöllur Square. A small troop of soldiers was marching past Parliament House. The Americans were in the process of taking over from the British, and you could hardly move these days for Yanks, army trucks and jeeps, artillery and sandbags – all the trappings of military occupation. The quiet little town was unrecognisable.

There was a time when Vera used to meet him off the ship and they would walk home together, she chatting about what she had been up to in his absence, he telling her about his latest trip, the characters he'd met and the goods he'd managed to shift. He had admitted that he wasn't sure how long he would last in this job. He wasn't really cut out to be a salesman. Didn't have the necessary gift of the gab. Wasn't that comfortable in social situations unlike, say, Felix, who positively radiated self-confidence.

That was true of Runki too. He sometimes sailed on the *Súd*, his cases crammed full of headgear from Luton. How Eyvindur envied Runki his nerve; he was always self-assured, even cocky, never had any trouble getting people's attention. He was a born salesman. It was all about confidence. While Eyvindur was getting his tongue in a twist over the Dutch dinner service, all over town people were donning Runki's new hats, in the smug belief that they had got themselves a bargain.

3

Too impatient to wait for the weather to let up, Eyvindur grabbed his cases again, ducked his head and ran across the square into the wind and rain, that cold, late-summer rain that hung like a low canopy over the town. He and Vera lived in the west end, in a small flat that belonged to his father's brother. Rents were astronomical these days with all the people flooding in from the countryside to the towns, especially Reykjavík, lured by the prospect of working for the army, for hard cash and a better life. His uncle, who owned several properties in town, was raking in the profits, though he charged Eyvindur a fair rent. Even so, Eyvindur found it steep enough and kept having to ask for more time when his self-confidence was at its lowest ebb and he failed to bring home enough in commission.

The flat was on the ground floor of a three-storey concrete building. He unlocked the front door, then the door to the flat, before hastily retrieving his cases from the step outside and carrying them in. As he did so he called out to his girlfriend, who he assumed was waiting for him inside.

'Vera? Vera darling?'

There was no answer. He closed the door, switched on the light and took a moment to catch his breath. He needn't have bothered to hurry over the last stretch: Vera wasn't home. She must have gone out, which meant he would have to wait a little longer before he could beg her forgiveness for his crass accusations. He'd been rehearsing what he was going to say – would have to say – if he was going to make things right again.

His outer clothes were sopping wet, so he took off his hat and laid his overcoat across a chair in the living room, then hung his jacket in the wardrobe by the door. Opening one of the cases, he took out a pound of genuine coffee that he had managed to get hold of in the West Fjords, hoping to give Vera a nice surprise. He was just about to go into the kitchen when he paused. Something wasn't right.

Turning back, Eyvindur opened the wardrobe again. His jacket was hanging there, along with a second, longer jacket of his and another coat. It was what was missing that brought him up short: Vera's clothes had gone. The shoes she kept in the bottom weren't there. Nor were her two coats. He stood for a moment, staring blankly into the cupboard, then walked into the bedroom. There was another, larger wardrobe there with drawers for socks and underwear and a rail for dresses and shirts. Eyvindur opened it and pulled out the drawers, to be confronted by the astonishing fact that all Vera's clothes had disappeared. His own things were still in their usual place but there wasn't a single feminine garment left.

He couldn't believe his eyes. In a daze, he went over to Vera's dressing table and opened the drawers and compartments: it was the same story. Had she left him? Moved out?

He sank down on the bed, his thoughts miles away, recalling what Runki had said about Vera when Runki thought he couldn't hear. The day he caught the boat to the West Fjords they had bumped into each other at Hot and Cold, a restaurant popular with soldiers. Runki had been there with a friend, shovelling down fish and chips, and as soon as he thought Eyvindur was safely out of earshot he had dropped that remark about Vera.

An absurd lie – he should have gone back and rammed the words down the bastard's throat.

The lie that had made Vera so angry, so hurt when he was stupid enough to fling it in her face.

Eyvindur stared into the empty drawers and thumped his fist

5

on the bed. Deep down he had been afraid of this. He was no longer so sure Runki's remark had been an outrageous lie – that Vera was mixed up in the Situation.

And then there was all that nonsense his old classmate, that dirty rat Felix, had been rambling on about when they ran into each other in Ísafjördur. Was there any truth to it? All that stuff about the school and those experiments. Or was he simply out to humiliate Eyvindur because he was drunk, and cruel, just like he used to be in the old days when Eyvindur had laboured under the foolish belief that they were friends?

2

Flóvent surveyed the flat but could see no signs of a struggle, despite the aftermath of violence confronting him in all its horror. On the floor lay the body of a man, shot through the head. It looked like an execution pure and simple; no sign that the victim had tried to run. No chairs had been overturned. No tables knocked aside. The pictures were hanging perfectly straight on the walls. The windows were intact and fastened shut, so it could hardly have been a break-in. The door of the flat was undamaged too. The man now lying on the floor with a bullet hole in the back of his head must have opened the door to his assailant or left it open, unaware that it would be the last thing he did. It looked as though the victim had just walked in when the attack took place, since he was still in his overcoat, the front-door key clutched in his hand. At first glance Flóvent couldn't see that anything had been stolen. The visitor must have come here to kill, and had carried out this intention with such brutality that the first police officers to arrive at the scene were still in shock. One had thrown up in the living room. The other was standing outside, protesting that there was no way he was going in there again.

The first thing Flóvent had done was shoo away those who had no direct role in the investigation: the policemen who had trampled all over the scene; the witness who had raised the alarm; the nosy neighbours who, when informed that a gun had been fired in the flat, were unable to say for certain if they'd heard a shot. The only people left inside were Flóvent himself and the district medical officer who had come to confirm the man's death.

'Of course he'll have died instantly,' said the doctor, a short, scrawny man whose prominent teeth were clamped on a pipe that he hardly ever removed from his mouth. 'The shot was fired at such close quarters that it could only end one way,' he continued, exhaling smoke with every word. 'The bullet has exited through his eye here, causing this God awful mess.' He contemplated the congealed pool of blood that had spread out over the floorboards. One of the policemen had carelessly stepped in the dark puddle, slipped and almost fallen. You could see the skid mark of his shoe in the blood. There were splashes on the furniture and walls. Lumps of brain on the curtains. The killer had shot through a thick cushion to muffle the noise, then tossed it back on the sofa. The exposed side of the victim's face had been almost entirely blown away.

Flóvent focused on trying to remember the protocol for examining a crime scene. Murders didn't happen every day in Reykjavík and he was relatively new to the job, so he didn't want to make any mistakes. He had only been with Reykjavík's Criminal Investigation Department for a few years, but he had also done a six-month stint with the Edinburgh CID, where he had learnt a lot about the theory and practice of detective work. The victim appeared to be in his twenties. He had thinning hair; his suit and coat were threadbare, his shoes cheap. He appeared to have been forced down on his knees, then fallen forward when he took the bullet to the back of the head. A single shot in exactly the right place. But for some reason this had not been enough. After the execution, the killer had stuck a finger in the wound and daubed the dead man's forehead with blood. What possible motive could he have had? Was it a signature of some sort? A comment that the perpetrator regarded as important, though its significance was lost on Flóvent? Was it a justification? An explanation? Second thoughts? Remorse? All of these? Or none? Or a challenge, intended to convey the message that the person who did this had no regrets? Flóvent shook his head. The clumsily smeared mark meant nothing to him.

The bullet itself proved easy to find since it was buried in a floorboard. Flóvent marked the spot before prising the bullet out with his pocket knife and examining it in his palm. He recognised the make, as ballistics was a special interest of his. This was one of the innovations in forensic detection that he was keen to introduce to Iceland. Fingerprinting too. And the practice of systematically photographing felons and the scenes of major crimes. Whenever necessary, he called out a photographer he knew who had a studio in town. Bit by bit his department was building up an archive, though it was still very rudimentary and incomplete.

'The person who fired the shot must have been standing behind him, presumably holding the gun at arm's length,' said the doctor,

9

removing his pipe for a moment before clamping it between his teeth again. 'So you ought to be able to get a rough idea of his height.'

'Yes,' said Flóvent. 'I was wondering about that. We can't assume the murderer was a man. It could have been a woman.'

'Well, I don't know. Would a woman be capable of this? Somehow I doubt it.'

'I wouldn't rule it out.'

'It was clearly an execution,' said the doctor, exhaling smoke. 'I've never seen anything like it. Forced to kneel on the floor of his own home and shot like a dog. You'd have to be a cold-blooded bastard to do a thing like that.'

'And smear his forehead with blood?'

'Well, I don't know . . . I've no idea what that's supposed to mean.'

'When do you reckon it happened?'

'Not that long ago,' said the doctor, looking at the congealed blood on the floor. 'Twelve hours, give or take. The post-mortem will give us a better estimate.'

'Yesterday evening, then?' said Flóvent.

At this point the photographer arrived, armed with his tripod and the Speed Graphic camera he had acquired before the war. Having greeted Flóvent and the doctor, he looked around the room, dispassionately appraising the scene, then went about his business methodically, setting up the tripod, removing the camera from its case, fixing it up and inserting the film holder in the back. Each holder contained two pieces of film. The photographer had come equipped with a number of these holders and extra flashbulbs as well.

'How many shots do you want?' he asked.

'Take several,' said Flóvent.

'Was it a soldier?' the photographer asked as he paused to replace the film holder then fixed the camera to the tripod again and changed the bulb.

'What makes you think that?'

'Doesn't it look like the work of a soldier?' The photographer was a world-weary man of about sixty. Flóvent had never seen him smile.

'Maybe,' said Flóvent distractedly. He was searching for clues to the identity of the gunman: any evidence he might have left behind such as footprints, clothing, cigarette ash. It looked as if the tenant had been in the kitchen fairly recently, fixing himself a snack. There was a half-eaten slice of stale bread and cheese on the table. Beside it was a cup of tea, partially drunk. Flóvent had fumbled in the victim's pockets for his wallet but couldn't find one on his body or anywhere else in the flat.

'I can't believe anyone but a soldier would be capable of a clean job like that,' said the photographer.

The room was briefly illuminated by his flash, then he recommenced the laborious process of setting the heavy camera up in another spot and inserting new film.

'It's possible,' said Flóvent. 'I couldn't say. You might know better.'

'An officer, maybe?' continued the photographer thoughtfully. 'Someone in authority? It looks like an execution, doesn't it? Betrays a kind of arrogance.'

'You two seem to be thinking along very different lines,' commented the doctor, tamping down his pipe. 'Flóvent thinks a woman did it.'

'No,' said the photographer flatly, studying the man on the

floor for a while before snapping another picture. 'No, out of the question.'

'Perhaps he was robbed,' suggested Flóvent. 'I can't find his wallet.'

From his inspection of the flat, he concluded that the man had lived alone. It was a typical bachelor's apartment, small and spartan, largely free from ornament, but clean and tidy. The only extraneous object was the cushion used to muffle the shot. Apart from that the flat was sparsely furnished, and what furniture there was showed signs of wear: the sofa and armchair in the living room, the two old wooden chairs in the kitchen. On the sofa lay an open suitcase containing hats, Lido cleansing cream and several packs of Kolynos toothpaste. The merchandise was spattered with blood.

The flash lit up the sordid scene one last time, then the photographer began to pack away his equipment. The doctor paused in the doorway to relight his pipe. Flóvent glanced back at the man on the floor, unable to comprehend the sheer violence that must have lain behind his killing: the implacable hatred, the anger, the utter ruthlessness.

'Did you take a picture of that mark on his forehead?' he asked.

'Yes, what is it? What does it mean?'

'No idea,' said Flóvent. After his initial examination of the corpse, he had kept his eyes averted from the man's shattered face. 'I can't make any sense of it. Can't begin to guess what it means or why someone would have smeared blood on his forehead like that.'

'Have you identified him?' asked the photographer as he was leaving.

'Yes, his landlady told me who he was, and there are bills here in his name.'

'So, who was he?'

'I've never come across him before,' said Flóvent. 'His name was Felix. Felix Lunden.'

3

The woman who found the body was a widow of around fifty called Ólafía. She had gone down to remind the man about his rent and walked in on what she described as the 'ghastly scene'. His rent had been due on the first of the month, she said, and he was never late. Admittedly, she hadn't seen him for a while but then he was often away for a week or two at a time, sometimes longer. She had gone down to the basement and was about to knock on his door when she noticed that it was open a crack. There was no reply when she called his name, so, after a moment's hesitation, she had gone inside to find out if he was all right and to ask why he hadn't paid his rent.

'Of course, it was mainly because I was worried about him,' she assured Flóvent, as if fearing he would doubt her motivation and suspect her of nosiness. 'The moment I walked through the door I saw him lying there on the floor. It was horrible, quite horrible, and I . . . I gasped, and, well, to be honest I screamed and ran back out again, slamming the door. The whole thing's a nightmare. A terrible nightmare!'

'So you found the door open, ma'am?'

'Yes, which was very unusual because he always kept it locked. In fact, he told me he wanted to change the lock because it was so old it would be far too easy to pick. Maybe he was right, but then we don't bother locking our doors any more than anyone else in this town. We're just not used to it. I suppose it's our old country ways that haven't kept up with the times. Not with the way things are these days.'

'Are you the only person with a key to the flat?'

'I beg your pardon?'

'Where do you keep your key?'

'*My* key? I hope you're not suggesting *I* was responsible. What a nerve.' The woman looked outraged.

'No, ma'am, of course not,' said Flóvent. 'I simply need to know who else could have had access to the flat in the last twenty-four hours – or in general. That's all. Is it possible that someone else could have taken your key, used it to enter the flat, put it back, then lain in wait for the man and attacked him when he came home? Or else picked the lock, as you mentioned? It must have happened yesterday evening.'

Ólafía's eyes still radiated suspicion. 'Nobody can have taken my key,' she said firmly, 'because Felix had it himself. He'd borrowed my spare to get it copied. Said he'd lost his own. Maybe that was why he was talking about changing the lock.'

'Did you see Felix at all yesterday evening?'

'No, not at all.'

'And you didn't hear any sounds from his flat?'

'No, I didn't. I was asleep by ten, as usual. That's when most

15

people in this house go to bed. I like my tenants to keep regular hours.'

'Had Felix been renting from you for long?'

'No. It was about six months ago that he enquired about the flat. I had to get rid of the previous tenants: a drunken lout and his wife, nothing but trouble. I have no patience with that sort of behaviour.'

'You say Felix used to go away for a week or two at a time? Why was that?'

'He was a commercial traveller, wasn't he? Used to make regular trips out of town.'

'And he'd always paid his rent punctually in the past?'

'Yes. But he was a week overdue this time and I wanted my money.'

The man's upstairs neighbours, a couple in their thirties, said they hadn't noticed any comings or goings or heard any raised voices in the night. But then they had been sound asleep by midnight. They'd been renting from Ólafía for two years, so they'd lived there longer than their neighbour. They didn't know him very well but both agreed that he had been a cheery bloke and easy to talk to – just as you'd expect a good salesman to be. They weren't aware that anyone had a bone to pick with him and couldn't imagine what it was all about or comprehend the shocking brutality of what had happened.

'I don't know if I'll be able to sleep in this house tonight,' the woman exclaimed, looking anxiously at Flóvent. As soon as she heard that their neighbour had been murdered, she had telephoned her husband, who worked as an overseer for the British, and he had come home early.

'I don't believe anyone else in the building is in danger,' Flóvent reassured her.

'Who could do such a thing – shoot a man in the head like that?' asked the woman.

Flóvent couldn't answer this. 'Did he have any dealings with the army?' he asked. 'Did you ever see Felix in the company of soldiers? Did any of them ever visit him, as far as you're aware?'

'Oh no, I don't think so,' said the woman. 'I never noticed any soldiers round at his place.'

The man said the same. After asking them a few more questions, Flóvent thanked them for their time, then went and knocked on the door of the third set of tenants, an older couple who had been renting from Ólafía ever since her husband died. They informed him, unasked, that the husband had been shipwrecked off the Reykjanes Peninsula in a storm.

Neither of them had heard a gunshot; they had both been fast asleep at the time Flóvent believed the weapon had been discharged. They couldn't tell him a great deal about Felix Lunden either. He wasn't there much and never caused any trouble, never had noisy visitors or threw parties, didn't seem to have many friends and wasn't involved with a woman, as far as they were aware. Or if he was, they hadn't noticed her visiting him. They knew nothing of his family circumstances.

'Do you know if he had any dealings with the army?' asked Flóvent.

'No. Are you asking if he worked for them?'

'Yes, or if he was acquainted with any soldiers.'

'No,' said the woman, 'that is . . . not that we were aware.'

Flóvent sat with the couple for a little while longer before returning to Felix Lunden's flat. The body had been removed and taken to the mortuary at the National Hospital. The district medical officer and photographer had left, but a uniformed policeman was standing guard outside to ensure that no one entered the flat. Flóvent was currently the only detective working for Reykjavík's Criminal Investigation Department. All his colleagues had been seconded to other, more urgent policing roles at the beginning of the war, but he thought he might have to recall some of them to assist him with this case, which promised to be both complex and challenging.

He studied the bloodstain on the living-room floor, then examined the spent bullet that had been buried in a floorboard. He rolled it in his palm, picked it up between his fingers and held it to the light. Every gun left signature marks on the bullet, as unique as a fingerprint. If he could only find the firearm, he could prove that it was the right one by comparing the marks on the bullet to those produced by the barrel.

He recognised the make and calibre of bullet. It belonged to a Colt .45 pistol, the standard-issue sidearm carried by American servicemen. His question about whether the neighbours had seen Felix Lunden in the company of GIs had not been an idle one. All the evidence suggested that he had been killed by someone connected to the military, and the message was clear: Felix had deserved nothing better than a cold-blooded execution.

4

The plane taxied to the end of the runway, turned and prepared for take-off. Thorson, driving after it at breakneck speed, could see no alternative but to block its path. He had no intention of wasting any more time on the entertainer if he could possibly avoid it.

The man had finally turned up when an elderly woman living on Öldugata had reported him to the police. They had been searching for him all morning. At first, when she found the man sleeping on the steps outside her house, she had taken him for a tramp. But then it occurred to her that he was the best-dressed tramp she had ever seen. After taking a closer look, she concluded that he must be a foreigner, here with the army perhaps – though he wasn't in uniform. When the police informed her that he was an American singer who had gone missing in town, and was quite the drinker to boot, she had laughed and said had she known she would have invited him in.

Thorson had wasted the entire day on that pain in the neck, all so he could shove him onto a plane and send him home. The singer was from New York. He had arrived in Iceland a week ago with a group of his fellow countrymen to entertain the troops, had been drunk more or less throughout his stay and had managed to get himself into a series of scrapes.

Thorson had been dragged into it when the man was beaten up after drunkenly insulting a bunch of soldiers after one of his shows. The US Military Police Corps was called in and Thorson had taken the man's statement when he was brought in to the sick bay to be cleaned up before being sent back to Hótel Ísland, where all the entertainers were staying. The singer had no idea who his assailants were; they didn't come forward and there had been no witnesses. All he could remember was that there had been three of them, they had found fault with his singing, and he had accused them of being rednecks. The incident had taken place behind the large barracks where the show, and a dance, had been held for the troops. The singer hadn't come out of it well. He had a split lip and a black eye and complained that his side hurt where he'd been kicked in the ribs.

Two days later, when all the performers were due to fly home, he failed to show up at the airfield. Thorson was given the task of finding him and getting him on that plane, no matter what. The singer wasn't in his hotel room and hadn't packed; the place looked like a bomb had hit it, with clothes, empty bottles and sheet music littering the floor. Thorson soon discovered that he had been playing poker in the kitchen with the cooks until the small hours. One of them told Thorson that the man had been ranting about getting even with a bunch of punks, and that he had last been seen, at the crack of dawn, heading in the direction of the harbour.

'Was he any good at poker?' asked Thorson.

'Had the shirts off our backs,' said the sleepy cook ruefully.

Thorson phoned the airfield and extracted a promise that the plane wouldn't take off until the singer turned up. After that, he called out several of his fellow MPs to join in the search, and they scoured the town, checking all the watering holes and guesthouses and even people's gardens. He also alerted the Icelandic police in case they got wind of the man's whereabouts. The singer hadn't been in Reykjavík long enough to acquire any regular haunts, so there was no telling where he might be. A man answering his description was seen trying to scrounge a bottle of *brennivín* at the seamen's hostel run by the Salvation Army; while customers standing outside Mrs Marta Björnsson's restaurant on Hafnar-stræti reported seeing an American weaving his way unsteadily towards the west end. Then a mature woman, wearing Icelandic national costume, reported that she had been accosted by a for-eigner who had started following her in the vicinity of White Star, a late-night bar on Laugavegur, and offered her money to sleep with him. There had been the odd incident of this kind ever since someone had started the rumour that women who wore *peysuföt* were prostitutes.

It wasn't until midday that the police heard from the housewife on Öldugata. The singer was delivered into the hands of Thorson, who drove him at high speed first to his hotel to collect his belong-ings, then out to the Reykjavík airfield where they learnt that the pilot's patience had run out. The plane was revving up for take-off. Without further ado Thorson stamped on the accelerator and raced down the runway. By then the entertainer was waking up to the realisation that his plane was about to leave and that he was in danger of being stranded on this remote island. He stood up in the jeep, waving his arms frantically and raising his fine tenor voice to bellow at the plane to stop.

The pilot sat watching their approach and for a moment it appeared that he was going to ignore them, then he threw up his hands in surrender and waited while Thorson pulled up alongside. The noise of the propellers was ear-splitting. A door in the fuselage opened and the singer leapt out of the jeep, grabbed his suitcase and was about to race to the plane when he remembered his saviour. Turning to Thorson, he drew himself up straight, raised a hand smartly to his brow in a salute, then climbed aboard. Thorson heaved a sigh of relief, swung the jeep out of the way, and watched the plane trundling down the runway, before lifting clumsily into the air and vanishing into the west.

On the way to the airfield Thorson had tried to find out how the hell the singer had ended up asleep on a doorstep in Öldugata. The man, who had only a hazy recollection of meeting Thorson before, said he had no idea what he had been doing there. But some women had approached him at Hótel Ísland and one of them had given him an address, so perhaps he had been trying to find their place.

'At least you've been keeping busy during your stay in Iceland,' remarked Thorson, looking the man over. The singer was Italian American: dark hair, sun-bronzed skin. When he smiled there was a flash of fine white teeth.

'Why are you staring at me like that?' he asked, catching Thorson's eye.

'Sorry, I was miles away. I guess I haven't been sleeping too well lately,' said Thorson. 'This place gets to you after a while.'

'It's the goddamn back of beyond,' the singer said flatly.

5

When Thorson eventually got back to base out at Laugarnes Point, he received a message that his commanding officer had been asking for him. It was the first time he'd had any dealings with Colonel Franklin Webster, head of the US Military Police Corps in Iceland. The colonel was attending an important meeting at Höfdi House, and Thorson was ordered to report to him there. He jumped into his jeep again and headed over to the handsome white Jugendstil residence that stood down by the sea, just outside the town. When he first arrived in Reykjavík the house had struck Thorson as one of the most distinguished buildings in the place, and his opinion hadn't changed. It had once belonged to a famous poet and was rumoured to be haunted. Shortly after the invasion on 10 May 1940, the British had purchased the house as a residence for their consul.

Thorson parked in front of the house, announced his arrival and explained who he had come to see, then was shown into a waiting room. There seemed to be a lot of coming and going: high-ranking men were conversing in low voices; British officers and their American counterparts hurried from room to room, and he recognised an Icelandic government minister striding briskly into the house and continuing straight up to the first floor, accompanied by two other men. There appeared to be some kind of flap on. A large photograph of the British prime minister, Winston Churchill, hung on the wall in the waiting room, and Thorson was standing contemplating it when he heard a deep voice address him.

'I hear you had a little trouble with one of our entertainers,' said the colonel, who had approached noiselessly from behind.

Thorson swung round and saluted. The colonel, who was at least thirty years older than him, looked amiable enough, but Thorson had heard from his colleagues in the military police that he was a tough customer.

'We handled it, sir,' said Thorson.

'Good. I understand you speak Icelandic fluently – that you have Icelandic parents, though you grew up in Canada. Have I got that right?'

'Yes, sir. I'm what they call a West Icelander. My parents emigrated to Canada and I was born and grew up there.'

'I see. How long have you been in Iceland?'

'I was posted here as an interpreter, sir, at the time of the occupation, along with some other Canadian volunteers. They transferred me to the military police right away. When the Americans arrived this summer I was seconded to your police corps. It helps to know the language when you're dealing with clashes between the troops and the local population.'

'Yes, I realise that. I happen to be on the lookout for a man who speaks Icelandic and understands the local character but has American interests at heart. Do you think you're that man?'

'Well, I speak Icelandic, sir,' said Thorson. 'But I wouldn't say I understand the local character yet.'

A smile tugged at the colonel's mouth. 'I don't suppose you know much about murder inquiries?'

'No, sir.'

'You'll learn fast. The request comes from the Reykjavík police. Anyway, I've got to leave now but your job is to give them all the help you can. I believe the officer in charge of the investigation is called Florent or some such name. You'll be working with him. He's expecting to hear from you.'

'What case is that, if I might ask, sir?'

'An Icelander, shot dead in his apartment,' said the colonel. 'They're claiming the bullet they recovered at the scene was fired from a US military pistol. In other words, they believe the crime was committed by an American. In my opinion that's bull, but naturally I can't . . . I expect regular reports on the progress of the investigation. If you need help, talk to me. If what they say is true and the trail leads to one of our men, it could be embarrassing. Not all the locals are happy about our presence here. Bear in mind that we don't want any trouble: we've got enough of that.'

Colonel Webster left the waiting room as suddenly as he had entered it. Thorson's eyes were drawn back to the portrait of Churchill, who frowned down at him as if to remind him of the gravity of the times they were living through. Then he turned on his heel and marched out of Höfdi House. On the steps he passed the Icelandic government minister and his two companions conferring in low voices, confident that no one could follow what they were saying. Thorson paused when he heard Churchill's name.

'. . . but they don't know yet,' said the minister, who was some-what older than his companions. 'Of course, it'll have to be kept hush-hush.'

'It seems highly unlikely,' said one of the other men. 'That he'll come here.'

'Well, they aren't ruling it out. There's no more information as yet, but they're hoping for the best.'

The three men glanced at Thorson, who smiled blithely as if he didn't understand a word they said, then continued down the steps to his jeep. As he drove into town, he wondered if he'd heard right. Could Winston Churchill really be planning a visit to Iceland?

6

By the time Flóvent arrived at the mortuary, the doctor who conducted most of the post-mortems at the hospital had finished his examination of Felix Lunden's body. There were two other bodies covered in white sheets waiting on nearby trolleys. The doctor, Baldur, a native of the Hornstrandir Peninsula in the north-west, lurched a little as he moved, his slight limp the legacy of an old tuberculosis infection in one foot. In front of him was a metal trolley bearing an array of bloodstained instruments – scalpels, forceps and small saws – of the type used to pry into the most secret places of the human body. He went over to the metal sink and started washing his hands.

'It can't have been a pretty sight,' he remarked, drying his hands on a towel. 'With half his face shot away like that.'

'No,' said Flóvent. 'It wasn't pretty.'

'No need to tell you how he died – a single shot to the head.' Baldur offered Flóvent some coffee from a thermos flask that he kept wrapped in a woollen sock. He poured out a cup of the still-warm liquid, handed it to Flóvent and asked if he'd like a drop of *brennivín* in it to improve the taste. When Flóvent declined, Baldur fortified his own coffee with a splash from a bottle that he kept in the cupboard under the sink. It was getting on for evening but he still had a lot to do; he'd told Flóvent he would probably be there until midnight. It was cold in the mortuary. Flóvent couldn't think of a less inviting place to be in the whole of Reykjavík.

'Did the post-mortem turn up anything interesting?' he asked.

'Nothing of real significance with regard to the body. The man wasn't very fit. He was probably a chain-smoker: you can see that from the tar on his fingers and the state of his lungs. He hadn't done any manual labour for a long time. His hands are soft, no calluses.'

'I'm told he was a salesman.'

'Yes, that would fit. Well, it looks like a professional job to me. A single shot did the trick.'

'As if it was the work of a soldier? Is that what you're implying?'

'Yes, perhaps. Though of course I can't say for sure.'

'Am I right in thinking that the killer then smeared blood on his forehead?' asked Flóvent.

'Yes, that's right.'

'With a finger?'

'Yes, he used his finger.'

'He stuck it in the wound?'

'Yes, unless he used blood from the floor. I expect there was quite a pool around the body when it was found.'

'Why would he do a thing like that? Why add insult to injury by smearing blood on the victim's forehead?'

'What did you say his name was – Felix Lunden, wasn't it?'

Flóvent nodded.

'I'm guessing he might be related to a doctor who once worked here at the hospital,' said Baldur. 'There can't be many people in Iceland with that surname. He had a surgery on Hafnarstræti for many years.'

'Who was he?'

'Rudolf, he was called. Rudolf Lunden. From a Danish–German family. He was forced to close his surgery following a riding accident. I don't think he's practised medicine since. But I didn't know him well. He had a reputation for being cantankerous. If I remember right, he was linked to the Icelandic Nazi movement in their heyday before the war.'

'Could this be his son then?'

'That would be my guess,' said Baldur. 'Given his name. And that mark on his forehead.'

'Oh? Were you able to decipher it?'

'Yes, I believe so.' The doctor took a sip of coffee. 'I believe the person who did this wanted to send a very specific message when he drew that symbol.'

'What is . . . What symbol?'

Just then the door of the mortuary opened to admit a young soldier. Over his uniform he wore an armband that identified him as a member of the US Military Police Corps. The young man looked from one of them to the other.

'I was told I could find Detective Flóvent of the Reykjavík police here?' he said diffidently. His Icelandic was fluent.

'I'm Flóvent.'

'How do you do, sir?' the young man said politely, and shook Flóvent's hand. 'My name's Thorson. I was told to offer my

29

services to the Icelandic police in connection with a man's death. I thought I'd better make contact with you as soon as possible. I hope this isn't a bad moment?'

'No, not at all. We were just discussing the post-mortem,' said Flóvent. 'You speak very good Icelandic. Are you an Icelander, by any chance? No need to call me "sir", by the way.'

'I'm a West Icelander,' Thorson explained, shaking hands with Baldur as well. 'From Manitoba in Canada. My parents originally came from Eyjafjördur. Is that the man who was shot in the head?' Flóvent noticed that he avoided looking directly at the corpse.

'Yes,' said Flóvent. 'Felix Lunden, a travelling salesman, from what we've managed to establish so far. Used to peddle hats, belts, a variety of face creams and toothpaste, that sort of thing.'

'Face creams?' said Baldur, adding another shot of *brennivín* to his coffee. 'Can people really make a living from that?'

'Apparently. He didn't have any dependants. Lived alone.' Noticing that Thorson was looking a little pale, Flóvent turned to him: 'I don't suppose you're used to seeing bodies in this sort of state.'

'No,' said Thorson. 'I . . . I've only served in Iceland. I haven't seen any action yet and the cases I've dealt with so far in the military police haven't . . . haven't been quite like this.'

Flóvent could tell the young soldier was making a great effort to appear professional. He wasn't doing too bad a job of it either. Indeed, Flóvent thought he detected an air of maturity about the young man despite his boyish appearance. Thorson was in his early twenties, fair, with a guileless face that hinted at a trusting nature. Perhaps too trusting, Flóvent thought. There was a look in his eyes that suggested people had been known to betray that trust.

30

'Do you think he was killed by a member of the US forces?' asked Thorson.

'You've probably heard that we found the bullet and that it comes from a Colt .45?'

'Couldn't an Icelander get hold of a weapon like that?'

'We're certainly not ruling out the possibility,' said Flóvent.

'If a soldier was responsible, and word gets out, my commanding officers are afraid it might lead to – how did they put it? – increased mistrust of the defence force. They're concerned that public debate about this crime could end up being a little one-sided.'

'And it's your role to prevent that?' asked Baldur. 'Bit young for politics, aren't you?'

'I'm not interested in politics,' said Thorson. 'What's that on his forehead?' he added, changing the subject. He had obviously plucked up the courage to examine the corpse's shattered face. 'Is that a letter?'

'I was just telling Flóvent when you came in,' said Baldur. 'It's not a letter, no; it's something else, and quite interesting too. You could say the body's been deliberately branded.'

'What with?' asked Flóvent.

'As far as I can tell, with the Nazi symbol.'

'The Nazi symbol? You mean the swastika?'

'Yes, the swastika,' said the doctor. He walked heavily over to the body and aimed a lamp at the head. 'It looks to me as if that's exactly what this mess on the man's forehead is meant to represent.'

Flóvent and Thorson stepped closer and examined the mark. The doctor was right. Clumsy and smudged though it was, when viewed under the powerful lamp it was clear that the body had been branded with the distinctive Nazi swastika.

7

There was a commotion outside in the corridor, caused, Flóvent guessed, by the arrival of Ólafía. He had sent for her to identify the body of her tenant. He went out to greet her and was told in no uncertain terms that she wasn't pleased about being dragged out to this horrible place. She was exhausted, she said. The day had been dreadfully difficult for her. A brutal murder had been committed in her house. Its reputation had been ruined. *Her* reputation had been ruined. She, who was always so scrupulous in everything, so very particular about selecting her tenants. Only respectable people. With no more than two children.

'I found the poor man lying on the floor, what more do you want?' she asked as Flóvent showed her into the mortuary.

'I'm afraid we need to take care of this formality as quickly as possible,' he explained. 'I don't know how clearly you were able to see him, ma'am, but I have to state in my report that you formally identified your tenant. We need to contact the man's family and —'

'Yes, yes, let's get it over with, then.'

'Did you get a good first impression of Felix when he started renting from you?'

'A very good impression,' said Ólafía. 'I have a nose for these things. Polite. Obviously well brought up. Nice manners.'

'You mentioned that he always paid his rent on time?'

'Always. He was very careful about that.'

'Did he pay in Icelandic krónur? Or did he use foreign currency? Dollars? Pounds?'

'Foreign money? No, he didn't have any foreign money. At least not that I was aware of. He paid in krónur like everybody else.'

'Did he ever mention his parents' names to you?' asked Flóvent. 'His father? Or mother?'

'No. Are his parents still alive?'

'We don't know. Nor do we know if he had any brothers or sisters. In fact, we hardly know anything about him yet. That's why it's so important for you to do us this favour.'

'Yes, well, I don't like it at all,' said Ólafía sourly. 'It's a terrible business altogether. Put yourself in my place. I don't know if I'll be able to rent out that flat again. Don't know if I'll have the heart to. Or if anyone will want to live there after something so . . . shocking. I haven't a clue what I'm supposed to do with the place. I'll have to pay some girls to clean it, and that won't come cheap.'

She entered the mortuary, where she greeted Baldur and Thorson. The doctor showed her to the table.

'I've tried to tidy him up a bit,' said Baldur, 'in case his relatives want to see him. But he's a bit of a mess, so I hope it won't give you a turn, dear. Let me know when you've seen enough.'

'I was the one who found him, you know,' said Ólafía. 'And I'm not your "dear".'

33

'Of course, I do beg your pardon,' said Baldur, shooting a glance at Flóvent as if amused by her testiness. He lifted the sheet back from Felix's head. Ólafía was visibly shocked by the disfigured face, the empty eye socket, the shattered cheekbone and jaw. But the man's features were still clearly visible on the other side, where the bullet hadn't done as much damage, and she focused her attention on this, appearing suddenly unsure. Her gaze swung from Baldur to Flóvent and back again, as though she was thoroughly confused.

'What? Has there been another murder?' she asked, her face taking on a forbidding expression, as though her patience had been tried enough. 'Just like the other one?'

'The other one?'

'Yes.'

'What do you mean, ma'am?' asked Flóvent.

'I thought I was here to identify my tenant, Felix Lunden. Wasn't that why you dragged me to this horrible place?'

'Yes.'

'Then where is he?' asked Ólafía, peering around.

'What do you mean?' Flóvent repeated. 'Isn't that him lying on the table in front of you?'

'Who?'

'Felix Lunden, of course.'

'This man?'

'Yes.'

'No. I've never seen this man before in my life.'

'But . . . ?'

'This isn't Felix Lunden, I can tell you that for sure,' said Ólafía firmly. 'I haven't the faintest idea who this man is.'

8

There was still a policeman outside Felix Lunden's flat when Thorson parked his jeep in front of the building. Flóvent drew up behind him, opened the door for Ólafía, then escorted her up to her house and thanked her once again for her help.

They had been completely wrong-footed when she said she didn't recognise the man on the mortuary slab and denied that it was Felix Lunden. It transpired that she had never actually got a proper look at the corpse, merely thought it must have been Felix since it was his flat. The man had been lying face down, shot through the head, his blood spattered all over the room, and she had drawn her own conclusions.

When Flóvent had asked if she was absolutely sure and tried to fish for more information, Ólafía had lost her temper and insisted on being taken home. On the way back she explained that she had simply assumed it was her tenant. She was furious with herself for being so unobservant.

Flóvent greeted the police officer on guard and reminded Thorson not to touch anything without letting him know. The sun was setting and he switched on all the lights as soon as they entered the flat. While Flóvent went into the bedroom, Thorson paused by the dark puddle on the living-room floor and studied the blood splashes on the walls, thinking about the symbol on the dead man's forehead. This was entirely outside his realm of experience, and he knew he would have to learn fast.

'Felix Lunden's not a very Icelandic name, is it?' he said when Flóvent returned from the bedroom carrying some books.

'No, it's not. He could be from a German family. I found some Nazi reading matter in his bedroom: Hitler's *Mein Kampf*, a book of photographs from the 1927 Nuremberg rally and a pamphlet about something called the Thule Society. He wasn't exactly advertising the fact he had them, though. I found them in a shoe-box at the back of his wardrobe. The books are all in German, so he must understand the language. He's obviously interested in Nazism.'

'And he drew a swastika on the body,' said Thorson.

'If he was the killer.'

'Didn't you have a home-grown fascist party here?' asked Thorson.

'Yes, the Nationalist Party they called themselves. They put up candidates for parliamentary and local elections but hardly got any support. As far as I know, the party dispersed when war broke out.'

'So they were inspired by German Nazism?' Thorson began leafing through the books.

'I believe so. They were opposed to racial "corruption", hostile to the Jews, hated communists and preached racist ideology, all the usual stuff the Nazis are known for. They called for a strong Iceland, whatever that means. For inviolable national unity. All that kind of propaganda.'

'Racial corruption?'

'The Germans sent over a consul called Werner Gerlach, a bit of a fanatic.' Flóvent took one of the blood-spattered hats out of the suitcase on the sofa and inspected it. 'He was supposed to be acquainting himself with Icelandic high culture and the pure Aryan race thought to live here.'

'The descendants of the Vikings?'

'Yes, the descendants of the Vikings, something like that,' said Flóvent. 'The Germans are well versed in medieval Icelandic literature. But, to his great disappointment, Gerlach found that the country was inhabited by a bunch of peasants and the Viking spirit was a thing of the past. He was arrested on the morning of the invasion and deported to Britain. They caught him making a bonfire of his documents in the bathtub at the German consulate.'

'This one's got an inscription,' said Thorson. He handed Flóvent the book containing photographs of the Nuremberg rally.

'"To Felix, with fond paternal greetings, from Rudolf, Christmas 1930",' Flóvent read.

'Rudolf?'

'Yes. So Rudolf Lunden *is* his father, then. He's a German doctor who used to practise in Reykjavík. Baldur knew him a little. Mentioned that he was a Nazi. We need to get hold of him and track down that son of his.'

Flóvent laid the hat on the sofa and inspected the suitcase more closely. It was evidently well travelled; the brown leather was scuffed and stained and worn at the corners as you would expect of a salesman's case. It was lined with linen that had once been white, and its owner had used it to tote around his samples – the cleansing creams, toothpaste and hats and belts – extolling their virtues. If Felix had been working as a salesman for some time, he would have crossed paths with any number of people. Visited the same places again and again, acquired loyal customers. According to Ólafía, he had been away a great deal, touring the country. Surely the suitcase was his?

Flóvent ran a hand over the samples, noting that they showed signs of having been taken out and hawked around. He pictured Felix sitting down in people's homes, catching glimpses of their lives, listening to their stories and trying to find a way in. Trying to convince them that they couldn't do without his products. He must have travelled to towns and fishing villages and even to remote farming communities. In some places the inhabitants would have set their dogs on him, in others they would have served him coffee while he relayed the news from the nearest town or even from as far afield as Reykjavík, before he produced a hat from his case for the housewife and another for her husband.

As Flóvent smiled to himself, lost in these scenes, his fingers encountered a bump under the lining of the case, near the handle. The bump was relatively small but it didn't feel like part of the suitcase. When Flóvent examined it more closely he noticed that the seam appeared to have been unpicked, then sewn up again. He pulled at a loose thread and a pocket opened in the lining, revealing a tiny capsule the size of an aspirin tablet. Thorson, from the sound of it, was in the kitchen, opening cupboards and drawers.

Flóvent took the capsule out, placed it on his palm and was just wondering what it could be when Thorson emerged from the kitchen with a telephone directory in his hands, saying that he couldn't find a Rudolf Lunden listed. Seeing that Flóvent was deep in thought, Thorson realised he hadn't heard a word he said. Moving closer, Thorson spotted the pill in his hand.

'Say, where did you find the cyanide capsule?' he asked.

9

Flóvent sat in his car outside the house, mentally rehearsing the visit, wondering how best to convey the necessary facts and elicit the information he was after. He hadn't been taught any special interviewing techniques when he became a detective, as there wasn't much call for them in the simple inquiries that tended to come his way. He usually relied on common sense, and it hadn't let him down so far.

Thorson had taken the cyanide pill for analysis by experts in military intelligence. One element of his training had been to recognise capsules of this type for the purpose of locating and removing them from German prisoners. He thought it was almost certainly German and could well be linked to espionage. The agents of the Third Reich were advised to carry such capsules at all times and use them rather than surrender and risk interrogation. It was all new to Flóvent. He had never come across anything like a cyanide pill before, to say nothing of Nazi spies.

'Of course, there'd be plenty to occupy them in Iceland,' he commented when Thorson had explained what he thought the capsule was. 'It's the largest Allied base in the North Atlantic.'

'Sure,' said Thorson. 'Military intelligence has a detachment here to keep an eye on any unusual activity. And also on individuals with longstanding connections to Germany, German nationals, any Icelanders who have ever studied in the country, that kind of thing.'

'So Felix Lunden's name is bound to have cropped up?'

'I'll make enquiries,' said Thorson. 'Do you mind if I take the pill and hand it over to our people for analysis?'

'No, you do that. Good idea. We'll see what they make of it. It looks to me as if this case concerns your people as much as ours.' He sensed a hesitation on Thorson's part. 'You don't agree?'

'Yes, it's just . . .'

'What?'

'Maybe you should get someone else to work with you,' said Thorson. 'I . . . I don't have a clue what I'm doing when it comes to this kind of investigation. I'll be straight with you. Before we go any further, I want you to know that I've never been involved in anything like this before.'

'To be honest, I'm in the same position,' said Flóvent. 'But maybe you're not so keen on this kind of work? I can understand that.'

'I'm worried about getting in your way,' said Thorson.

Flóvent wasn't used to such candour. 'You recognised the cyanide pill straight away,' he pointed out.

'Yes.'

'Let's see how it goes,' said Flóvent. 'It may actually be an advantage – to approach a case like this without any experience.'

Twilight hung over the town; the weather was bleak, with low

41

cloud threatening rain. Flóvent peered at the house in the grey light. It hadn't taken him long to discover where the doctor lived. The picture he was forming of him, based on what little information Baldur could offer, was still very sketchy. Rudolf had been born in Schleswig-Holstein, moved to Iceland in around 1910 and married an Icelandic woman with whom he had one child. Baldur thought the wife had died during the Spanish flu epidemic.

Flóvent and Thorson had agreed that Felix Lunden was the most obvious suspect, given that the body wasn't his. They were working on the assumption that he had fled and was now in hiding, perhaps even trying to leave the country. The police were going to issue an appeal on the radio and in the newspapers, and launch a nationwide search for him.

The dead man's identity remained a mystery. No one seemed to be missing a man in his twenties, who had ended his life in Felix Lunden's flat, shot in the head with a service pistol.

One thing puzzled Flóvent. The man had seemingly opened the door to Felix's flat using the key that he had been clutching in his hand when he was shot. Felix had mentioned to Ólafía that he had mislaid his own key, and she had lent him her only spare. So somehow the dead man must have acquired a key to Felix's flat. The logical conclusion was that their paths must have crossed recently and that the unidentified man had entered the basement flat without permission.

Unable to put off the evil hour any longer, Flóvent got out of the car and walked up to the house. It was an austere, single-storey building, clad in sombre pebble-dash and surrounded by a small garden. Carved in relief above the front door was the name of the house: *Skuggabjörg*, Shadow Crags. The door was opened by a maid, who wore a white apron over a black dress. Flóvent introduced himself and asked to speak to the owner of the house. She showed him in and requested that he wait in the hall. As the minutes ticked by without any sign of her returning, Flóvent began to edge his way further inside, examining the paintings on the walls and trying to read the spines on the crowded bookshelves. Then he just stood there listening to the silence. Order appeared to be highly prized in this house: the floors gleamed and there wasn't a speck of dust to be seen on the furniture, books or paintings. At long last the maid returned.

'He says he wasn't expecting you, sir,' she said apologetically. 'He'll be ready to see you in a few minutes. In the meantime, he asked me to show you into his study, if you would be so kind as to wait for him there.'

'Thank you,' said Flóvent and followed the girl into the study, where she left him. There he found still more bookcases, containing, as far as he could tell, German literature, academic works and medical texts. He noticed an edition of *On the Origin of Species*, in the original English, but he didn't recognise many of the other titles as he didn't know German. At the far end of the room was a large desk with papers, writing materials and piles of books neatly arranged on top. There was a pair of crutches propped against one of the bookcases.

'Do you see anything on the shelves that interests you?' a deep, German-accented voice asked behind him. Startled, he spun round to see a man in his sixties sitting in a wheelchair, observing him from the doorway with colourless eyes. Flóvent didn't know how long the man had been there but felt instinctively that he had been watching him for a while.

'It's a handsome library,' he replied, for the sake of saying something.

43

'Thank you,' said the man in the wheelchair as he propelled himself into the room. He had white hair, a thin face, and his eyes behind the round spectacles with their heavy black frames were severe, angry almost, as if he were a teacher faced with a class of recalcitrant pupils. He was wearing a dark jacket over a knitted jumper, and had a woollen blanket spread over his knees. 'I try to surround myself with a decent library,' he said in his carefully enunciated Icelandic. 'I understand you are from the police?'

'Yes, please excuse the intrusion,' said Flóvent, swiftly recovering his composure. 'Are you Rudolf Lunden, sir?'

'Yes, I am.'

'My name's Flóvent, and I'm a detective with Reykjavík's Criminal Investigation Department. I've come to see you about rather an unusual matter. Am I right in thinking that you have a son called Felix?'

'Yes.'

'You wouldn't happen to know where I might find him?'

'Find him? What for?'

'I –'

'What do the police want with him?' the man interrupted sharply.

'I wondered if I'd find him here with you.'

'Apparently you did not hear what I said: what do the police want with him? Would you be so good as to answer my question?'

'Of course. I –'

'Would you get on with it then,' the man interrupted again in a louder voice, his German accent becoming more pronounced. 'Please do not waste my time.'

Flóvent was thrown by the man's rudeness. Before knocking on the door he had sat in his car for a long while, trying to think of ways to mitigate the pain his visit was bound to cause. Now it seemed that he had been wasting his time.

'Sir, I came to see you in connection with a violent crime that was committed at your son's address,' he said. 'A man was murdered in his flat. Shot in the head. We thought at first that the victim was Felix himself – that he was the dead man. But it turned out to be somebody else. We're now looking for your son in connection with the murder. We believe he may be involved in some way.'

The man in the wheelchair regarded Flóvent as if he had never heard anything so preposterous in his life. 'Involved in a murder . . . ?'

'Yes.'

'What do you mean?' demanded Rudolf, and Flóvent saw that he had succeeded in unsettling him. But only for a moment. 'What are you talking about?' Rudolf went on angrily. 'I have never heard such . . . such a pack of nonsense!'

'Nevertheless, that is how the matter appears to us,' said Flóvent. 'The facts –'

'How could you allow such an absurd idea to enter your head?'

'I'm afraid those are the facts. I can understand that you're shocked. Naturally, it's not very pleasant news. Could you tell me where Felix is now, sir?'

'A murder, in Felix's flat?' Rudolf sounded stunned.

'I'm afraid so, yes. Do you know where your son is?'

'How the devil . . . ?'

'Do you know where he was yesterday evening, sir?'

'Who was the man?' Rudolf asked, ignoring Flóvent's questions as if he hadn't even heard them. 'Who was the man found in his flat?'

'We don't know yet,' said Flóvent. 'We haven't managed to

identify the body. But it's only a matter of time before we do, and then we'll be able to establish how the victim was connected to your son. I repeat, do you know where your son is?'

Rudolf was staring blankly, as if he had just been struck in the face.

Flóvent repeated his question. 'Do you know where your son is?'

The man in the wheelchair didn't answer.

'Do you think he could be on the run from the police?' Flóvent asked. 'Could he have gone into hiding?'

Evidently Rudolf had had enough of the visit. 'Was there anything else?' he snapped.

'Else?'

'That you have to say to me?'

'I think you misunderstand the situation, sir,' said Flóvent. 'I'm here on behalf of the police to seek information from you. Not the other way round.'

'Yes, well, I have nothing to say to you,' said Rudolf. 'Would you please leave me alone now.'

'I'm afraid that's –'

'I am asking you to leave,' said the man, raising his voice again. 'I have nothing more to say to you.'

'Do you have any idea of your son's whereabouts?' Flóvent persisted. 'Can you help us track him down? We need to speak to him urgently.'

'I insist that you leave my property!' Rudolf was shouting now.

'Is he here with you?' Flóvent went on doggedly. 'Is Felix here in your house?'

'You fool of an Icelander. You know nothing. Nothing! Get out of my house.'

'No, it –'

'Out of my house!' yelled Rudolf, rolling his chair menacingly towards Flóvent. 'Get out! Be off with you! I have nothing further to say to you. Out! Get out!'

Flóvent stood firm. The maid appeared at the door of the study. She had heard her employer shouting and was looking questioningly at Flóvent. When Rudolf became aware of her presence, he wheeled his chair round and ordered her to escort the policeman to the door: their meeting was over. He waved her away irritably when she tried to assist him, then propelled himself out of the room. Flóvent and the maid were left standing in awkward silence.

'I imagine he's not the easiest of people to work for,' Flóvent remarked after a moment.

The meeting hadn't gone at all as planned. He couldn't understand what had happened – whether it was his fault, or Rudolf's, or both. But it was clear that he would have to work out a different way of handling the doctor at their next meeting, and that this meeting needed to take place as soon as possible.

'He can be . . . He's had a trying time recently,' the girl said apologetically. She stood there in the doorway, large and sturdily built, her hair neatly tied back, waiting for Flóvent to leave. He guessed she was in her twenties and suspected that she had been hired not least for her strong arms. Rudolf would presumably require help with every aspect of his daily routine and, from the look of her, she would have no trouble providing it.

'Has he been in a wheelchair long?' Flóvent tried to appear outwardly calm as he recovered from the extraordinarily hostile encounter.

'I don't know . . . I don't like discussing my employer behind his back. Rudolf isn't a bad man, sir. He's always treated me with respect. I'd like to do the same for him.'

'Could you tell me something about his son, Felix, then?' Flóvent tried instead. 'Have you met him?'

'You'll have to ask my employer about him, sir,' said the maid in a low voice, then asked him to accompany her out to the hall. 'I've had no contact with his son.'

'Do you know where he could be staying, miss, if he's not at home?'

'No, it . . . You'll have to ask my employer,' she repeated.

'Yes, of course. I'll try again later. Has Felix been here recently? In the last few days? Is he here now?'

'No,' said the girl firmly. 'He hasn't been here for a while.'

'Do he and his father have a good relationship?'

'You'll have to ask them.'

'I see that Rudolf keeps a pair of crutches in his study,' said Flóvent, venturing a quick look back into the room where the crutches were propped against the bookshelves. 'Is he . . . can he . . . ?'

'He can get around on them, but it's very difficult for him.'

'Look, if there's anything you can tell me about Felix, I'd be very grateful. It needn't go any further. It's vital that we find him.'

'I'm sorry, sir,' said the girl.

'However trivial it might seem.'

'Yes, I understand, but I can't help you.'

'Have you noticed any unusual guests lately? Any strange phone calls?'

She shook her head, then escorted him to the front door and opened it. Flóvent emerged onto the step, thanked her and shook her hand in parting, and either because she felt she hadn't been sufficiently helpful or perhaps out of a desire to excuse her employer's rudeness, she didn't immediately release his hand.

'You must forgive him, sir. Rudolf . . . he isn't normally like that. He hasn't been himself lately. Not since his brother-in-law came round the other day. They had a row.'

'His brother-in-law?'

'The headmaster,' she whispered, her eyes anxious, as if she were afraid of being overheard. 'His late wife's brother. I heard them quarrelling and he sounded upset.'

'What were they quarrelling about?'

'I don't know . . . some boys, I don't know,' the maid whispered, then slipped back inside and quietly closed the door.

As Flóvent was retracing his steps to the car, he happened to glance back at the house and spotted a middle-aged woman watching him from the drawing-room window, her face stern. Even as he watched, she pulled the curtain and vanished from view.

10

US counter-intelligence had been given temporary quarters in one wing of the old Leper Hospital on Laugarnes Point. They shared it with their British colleagues who had requisitioned the hospital building shortly after the occupation. The few remaining patients had been sent to a sanatorium in Kópavogur, the settlement to the south of Reykjavík.

Although the United States was officially still neutral, within a few months American troops were scheduled to relieve the British garrison and take over responsibility for the defence of Iceland. First to arrive had been the Marine Corps and 5th Defense Battalion on 7 July with their anti-aircraft units, followed by the first land army contingent on 6 August, and more reinforcements were expected any day now to swell their ranks – thousands of armed men who had never even heard of Iceland before, let alone known where to find it on a map. In no time at all Reykjavík had become a seething mass of British troops preparing to withdraw, reinforcements from

America, incomers from the Icelandic countryside – seeking a better life in the suddenly prosperous city – and the citizens of Reykjavík themselves, young and old, who had yet to come to terms with the transformation their town had undergone in the last year.

As Thorson drove up to the imposing edifice of the old Leper Hospital on the northern side of Laugarnes, he found himself thinking about prejudice and ostracism, thoughts which were no strangers to him. Naturally the location was no coincidence: the patients had been segregated, kept at a safe distance from the town, or rather, more importantly, the townspeople had been kept at a safe distance from them. A second hospital, the Kleppur Asylum, stood down by the sea a little to the east, even further removed from the town. The Leper Hospital was the most impressive wooden building in the country. It consisted of two floors and an attic, with rows of windows the length of the building and two gables projecting from the front, one at each end. As he admired it, Thorson thought about all the disruption the military occupation had brought to this sparsely populated island and its simple society. On a calm spring day in 1940, the war had come knocking on Reykjavík's door, and transformed the lives of its inhabitants. Thorson, together with a handful of other Canadian volunteers, had been among the first to come ashore with the British invasion force, as a private in the Second Royal Marine Battalion. They had marched under arms to the country's main government offices and witnessed first-hand the look of bewilderment on the faces of the townspeople, who must have feared that life in Iceland would never be the same again.

Thorson's thoughts returned to the task in hand. Analysis of the cyanide capsule found in Felix Lunden's flat had confirmed his suspicions: it was a so-called suicide pill, manufactured in

Germany. If the user bit down on the capsule, or ampoule, the potassium cyanide it contained would theoretically kill him in a matter of seconds, though in practice it could take as long as fifteen minutes, causing indescribable suffering. It was the first time a capsule of this kind had turned up in Reykjavík, and the intelligence officer was demanding to know how it had come into the hands of the Icelandic police. He was a major, fiftyish, aggressive and gruff, with a pockmarked face and a black glove on one hand. It looked to Thorson as though he was missing two fingers. His name was Major Graham and he had served in the US Military Intelligence Division for many years. With him was his opposite number from British intelligence, who had been consulting the records for any mention of Rudolf Lunden in the period immediately after the invasion. He was somewhat younger than Major Graham and disfigured by a burn that extended from his neck up one side of his face, leaving only a stump of an ear. He had transferred to intelligence after sustaining serious injuries when his plane came down. His name was Ballantine – like the whisky, he said as he introduced himself, adding that he was no relation. The smile that accompanied this remark was more like a grimace. Thorson got the impression that the joke had grown rather stale.

'Why would an Icelander be carrying a suicide pill?' asked Major Graham. 'Hidden in a suitcase, you said?'

'Yes, we believe the owner of the case to be a travelling salesman, sir,' said Thorson. 'So the pill would be on hand whenever he was away from home.'

'Actually, that's not an uncommon cover,' said Ballantine, who also held the rank of major. 'And it's not a bad idea in this country. It would allow a man to travel wherever he liked without attracting any undue attention. And he could hide any equipment connected to his espionage activities in his suitcase. You did say you found samples of his wares in the case?'

'Yes, that's right, sir,' said Thorson. He had provided a brief report when he handed over the capsule for analysis. 'Are you confident that he's been spying for the Germans?'

'I wouldn't say we're confident,' said Major Graham, 'but this pill is a strong indication that he has been involved with the Germans in some way. After all, he's from a German family, if I understand right.'

'With the greatest respect, sir, that's not necessarily significant. We can hardly suspect all civilians with German roots of being spies.'

'I don't see why not,' retorted Graham.

'His father, Rudolf Lunden, was arrested two days after the invasion,' said Ballantine, opening a file that he had brought along to the meeting, 'along with other individuals who were on our list of people known to have close ties to Germany. He was detained for several days and interrogated at length. The plan was to deport him to Britain for internment along with thirty other German nationals, but nothing came of it, and in the end he was released. We have no information at all on his son Felix. He wasn't among those arrested.'

'Do you have any idea why Rudolf Lunden wasn't sent to Britain, sir?'

'The officer in charge is no longer in the country,' said Ballantine, 'so I'm not acquainted with the details. They must have concluded that he was harmless following his interrogation. His house was searched but nothing suspicious came to light. Besides, the man's confined to a wheelchair, which limits his activities. We kept his house under surveillance for a while, but he stayed at home for the most part and received few visitors.'

'He must have known he was being watched?'

'I don't believe he can have failed to notice.'

'Did any information about Felix emerge from the interviews?'

'No, he didn't mention his son, and it seems he was never asked about him. The interviews focused on trying to establish the nature of his relationship with the German consul, Dr Werner Gerlach. Apparently they were quite good friends. They used to meet regularly, according to Lunden, but mostly, if he's to be believed, because they were compatriots.'

'Was Felix a member of the Icelandic Nazi movement – the Nationalist Party?' asked Thorson. 'Do you have any information about that, sir?'

'No, nothing at all on Felix Lunden, as I said,' replied Ballantine. 'On the other hand, his father was listed as a member, and we confiscated the minutes of meetings, which we found at his house, together with a list of members dating from three years ago.'

'Hasn't the party been disbanded?' asked Thorson.

'It's ceased its activities, yes,' said Ballantine. 'Though that doesn't necessarily mean the party members have abandoned their Nazi sympathies. We keep an eye on a few of them, but the majority seem to have seen the error of their ways.'

'I assume there's quite a bit of information the Germans would want to get their hands on here in Iceland,' said Thorson.

'Indeed. Espionage flights from Norway aren't sufficient,' said Ballantine. 'They also need men on the ground watching our vessels, tracking our arms shipments and monitoring key positions like the naval base in Hvalfjördur. The Nazis are interested in all our activities in Iceland. If this Felix Lunden is collecting information for them, he must have access to a radio transmitter and possibly a camera as well. A transmitter can be concealed in an ordinary suitcase like the one you found at his flat. It would need to be powerful enough to communicate with the German U-boats that lurk off the coast, picking off our ships and Icelandic vessels too. If so, Felix must have a key to their codes, which would be worth getting hold of. It wouldn't be at all difficult for him to communicate with U-boats at a particular location – or locations, around the country – at pre-arranged times. These are probably points on the coastline where the U-boats can come in close to shore. We've already stepped up our patrols of some of these areas.'

'Is it possible that Felix could already have been picked up by a German submarine?' asked Thorson. 'Or that he might attempt to escape that way?'

'Yes, it's quite conceivable,' said Ballantine.

'So far we haven't caught any German agents in Iceland,' added Graham, scratching his chin. 'This Felix would be the first. Have you identified the dead man in Felix's apartment?'

'No, sir, not yet,' said Thorson. 'We don't have any leads. No one's asked about him. No one seems to have noticed that he's gone. At least, the Icelandic police haven't gotten any reports of a missing person his age.'

'I probably don't need to point out, er – Thorson, isn't it? – how important it is that you keep us informed of the progress of this investigation,' said Graham. 'I want you to deliver a verbal report on a daily basis, keeping us up to date with what the Icelanders have discovered. You'd better talk directly to me. The British are in the process of withdrawing and Ballantine here is no exception.'

'I'm afraid you'll have to discuss that with my commanding officer, sir,' said Thorson, careful to keep his tone courteous. 'Colonel Franklin Webster. I'm under orders to keep him informed about the inquiry. If he wants to make any changes to that arrangement, I'm sure he'll let me know.'

'Wouldn't it make more sense for us to take over the inquiry?' Graham asked, his eyes on Ballantine. 'Can we do that? Surely there's a risk the Icelanders will screw it up? Are they capable of dealing with an espionage case?'

'With respect, sir, we don't know for sure that the man's death is connected to spying,' Thorson pointed out. 'The detective in charge of the case seems reliable and he's very meticulous.'

'You're an Icelander yourself, aren't you? Do you speak the lingo?'

'Icelandic-Canadian, sir.' Thorson corrected him. 'I don't really know if I'm Canadian or Icelandic. Both, I guess. I don't believe the Icelanders need any –'

'Yes, well, regardless of that, if they don't come up with some results soon, we'll have to step in,' said Graham brusquely. 'That's the only way we'll get anything done. The bullet comes from an American weapon. That's enough for me. It's our business.'

'It would be problematic for us to interfere in the affairs of the Icelandic police, at least at this stage,' said Ballantine calmly. 'I'd advise holding back for the time being and keeping a close eye on them. I imagine that's your role,' he added, looking at Thorson. 'Do we have incontrovertible proof that the suitcase containing the cyanide pill belonged to Felix Lunden?'

'Who else could it belong to?' asked Graham.

'The dead man, for example,' said Ballantine.

They both looked at Thorson as if they expected him to have the answer, but he didn't, and neither did Flóvent. They had agreed that there was a strong chance the suitcase belonged to Felix, but Flóvent felt they shouldn't entirely rule out the alternative: that the unidentified victim had brought it with him to the flat. If Ólafía was to be believed, her tenant had sold various items of the type that had been found in the case, but that still didn't amount to proof that it was his.

'The police are analysing the fingerprints on the suitcase,' said Thorson. 'They may provide some more clues, but the odds are pretty good that it belongs to Felix.'

'This is our territory,' Graham repeated, scowling. 'We'll take over sooner or later. It's only a question of when.'

Shortly after this the meeting broke up, and Thorson headed back to his jeep. As he passed along the hospital corridors he caught glimpses of the old wards that had now been converted into offices for military personnel, and unconsciously he slowed his pace, his thoughts returning to the sick and the shunned, whose history still lingered in this building. He pictured the patients who had once occupied these rooms, afflicted by sores that couldn't be concealed, but also by other, invisible wounds, eating away at their minds: the wounds of the outcast. He felt a deep sense of kinship with the building's former residents. He was aware of his own inclinations, though he didn't fully understand them, and knew that they were no less reviled by society than the leprosy which people had held in such dread that they had built this handsome hospital to contain it. These were feelings that he tried to avoid thinking about and refused to admit even to himself, yet they persisted and he was finding it increasingly hard to control them, though he didn't dare breathe a word of them to anyone else for fear of exposure. He did his best to be on his guard, but sometimes he forgot himself, like yesterday when he'd narrowly avoided rousing the suspicions of the drunken singer.

Why are you staring at me like that?

11

Rudolf Lunden objected in the strongest possible terms to being brought in for questioning at the prison on Skólavördustígur. Two police officers had been dispatched to his home the morning after Flóvent's visit. Before bringing him in, they had carried out a thorough search of the premises in case Felix was hiding there, ignoring Rudolf's curses and threats that they wouldn't keep their jobs for long. He was still furious two hours later when Flóvent arrived at the prison to take his statement. Flóvent had been at a meeting with Thorson, who had brought him up to date with the results of his trip to the Leper Hospital. The wait had not improved the doctor's temper.

'Have you any idea how humiliating it is to be picked up by the police from one's home in this manner?' he hissed at Flóvent.

They were sitting in the small interview room to which Rudolf had been escorted when he arrived at the prison. There he had been left to stew – without explanation, without anyone deigning to speak to him or offer him water or coffee to drink – seething with rage all the while.

'You left me no choice, sir.'

'A police car outside my house!'

'You've shown absolutely no willingness to cooperate, sir,' said Flóvent. He had known that his heavy-handed methods would do nothing to mollify the German. 'You refused to answer my questions when I visited you at home, so I had no alternative but to bring you in. I assure you, sir, that I would much rather it hadn't come to this.'

'You are a fool!' shouted Rudolf. 'A damned, bloody fool!'

'I wish I could say the same to you, sir, but I'm afraid I don't know you well enough,' said Flóvent. 'All I know is that you're not making life any easier for yourself by shouting at me and refusing to answer my questions and throwing me out of your house. You can hardly have been so naive as to believe that this would deter the police. There is every indication that your son has committed a murder. I would have thought you'd want to find out the truth of the matter – find out what actually happened. We don't know where he is. If you're protecting him that would make you an accessory to the crime, and I have to say that your conduct, both to me last night and to the police officers who had to bring you here by force, suggests that you have something to hide. For your own sake, I hope that's not true, but I have to find out.'

Rudolf listened to this speech with a sober expression and for once didn't rudely interrupt. Flóvent thought briefly that he might have succeeded in pacifying him and persuading him to face facts. But as the rancorous pause grew longer, Flóvent began to wonder if Rudolf intended to protest by refusing to speak at all. He cast around for a new way of getting through to the doctor, though it galled him to have to humour the man.

'You're not under arrest, sir,' Flóvent said. 'Let me stress that. You've only been brought in for an interview. How we proceed now is entirely up to you – whether you're obliged to remain here longer or allowed to go home.'

'I regard that as a threat,' said Rudolf. 'You had better not try to threaten me.'

'It was no threat,' said Flóvent. 'But you have every right to know what your position is.'

Rudolf didn't bother to respond to this.

'I know that you're a widower,' said Flóvent. 'I'm told you lost your wife in the autumn of 1918. It occurs to me that it might have been during the Spanish flu epidemic. Am I right?'

'I fail to see what possible concern that is of yours.'

'I only ask because I lost my mother and sister to the Spanish flu.'

Rudolf didn't react.

'It does a child no good to watch his loved ones suffer and die. I suppose Felix had to go through something similar?'

'Felix does not remember his mother.'

'Ah, I see.'

'I demand to speak to your superiors,' said Rudolf. 'You are clearly not up to the job. You are making a serious mistake, and I wish to be sure that they are aware of the fact. Aware of how I am being treated. Of your disgraceful behaviour towards a man who . . . a man who has difficulty . . . a man who is handicapped.'

'I assume you're referring to Reykjavík's police commissioner,' said Flóvent. 'Would you like me to fetch him for you? There's nobody else. I'm the only detective in the Criminal Investigation Department at present. My head of department and my colleagues were assigned to other tasks following the occupation. Would you like me to call in the commissioner? I'm willing to do so.'

Rudolf vacillated, as though he couldn't tell whether Flóvent was in earnest or merely calling his bluff. He seemed unsure whether he should summon the highest authority in the police at this stage or if it was better to deal with the underling facing him for the time being.

'She gave birth to him shortly before she succumbed to the flu,' Rudolf said at last, grudgingly. 'There was little that could be done. Felix was . . . We do not discuss it.'

'My mother and sister are buried in one of the two mass graves in the cemetery on Sudurgata,' said Flóvent. 'I often visit them there. My father's keen to have them exhumed so we can rebury them in a family plot.'

'Why are you . . . ? Of what possible interest is that to me?' said Rudolf. 'I do not know why you are telling me this.'

'I'm finding it hard to understand your hostility,' said Flóvent. 'Is it directed at the police? At the Icelanders? The war? The occupying army? Or are you being obstructive in an attempt to protect your son?'

Rudolf shook his head. It was clear that he had no patience with Flóvent. The tiny chink that had opened in his armour had snapped shut again.

'I have been inside this building before,' Rudolf said through gritted teeth. 'You people do not frighten me. I have nothing to say to you. Nothing.'

'I wanted to ask you about that,' said Flóvent. 'Why did the British arrest you?'

'Because they are fools.'

'Wasn't it actually because you were a close friend of the German consul, Werner Gerlach?'

'It was outrageous how they treated him. Outrageous.'

'Were the British under the impression that you worked for him? Was that why they arrested you?'

'I refuse to answer that,' said Rudolf. 'I am no spy. I never have been. I . . . I object to the insinuation.'

'What was your relationship with Gerlach?'

'I do not see what concern that is of yours.'

'Did you have regular meetings with him?'

'We were close acquaintances.'

'What did you talk about?'

'That is none of your business.'

'About your son, Felix, perhaps?'

'Felix? No. Why should we have talked about him?'

'Did he accompany you to these meetings?'

'No, he did not. Why should he have done? What kind of questions are these?'

'I'm only trying to gather information about Felix,' said Flóvent. 'To find out who he is. Where he is. What sort of relationship you have with him. Whether you're protecting him. I hope you appreciate that it would be best if he turned himself in. If not, it could make your position very difficult – if you know where he's hiding, that is.'

'I do not know where he is.'

'Do you know the identity of the man found shot in the head in his flat?'

Rudolf shook his head.

'Does Felix own a gun?'

'He has never, to my knowledge, owned a firearm.'

'Do you think his life could be in danger?'

'Why should you think that?' asked Rudolf, and for the first time Flóvent detected a flicker of interest.

'We found something among his belongings that I'd like to ask you about,' said Flóvent.

'Among his belongings? What do you mean? What did you find?'

'A pill,' said Flóvent. 'A capsule, in fact.'

'A pill? What nonsense is this? What kind of pill?'

'No ordinary pill,' said Flóvent. 'It has a very specific purpose. We believe it originated in Germany, that it's what's known as a suicide pill.'

'A suicide . . . ?'

'It was hidden in a suitcase that your son uses for his samples, so he would have had it close to hand. A tiny capsule filled with cyanide. There are three questions I would like to put to you.'

'What . . . what questions?'

'Did you know about the cyanide pill?' Flóvent saw that Rudolf was looking badly shaken, but he pressed on remorselessly. 'Was it you who procured it for him? And was it agreed between you that he should use it in an emergency?'

12

Rudolf stared at Flóvent, his expression of astonishment slowly giving way to silent fury. The doctor had invited a tough response, and he had got one. It had proved so difficult to extract any information from him, about his son or himself, that the only tactic Flóvent could think of was to put pressure on him, shock him, knock him off balance. He had succeeded. Rudolf's knuckles whitened on the arms of his chair.

'Have you lost your mind?' he snarled, drawing himself up as best he could. 'How dare you ask such a question? Are you implying that I want my son dead? Is that what you think?'

'Were you aware of the cyanide pill?' asked Flóvent, feigning indifference to the rage he had provoked.

'No,' Rudolf exploded, then slumped in his chair again. 'I had no idea. Not the faintest idea.'

'Did you provide it?'

'No!'

'Did you urge Felix to use it if he was arrested?'

'I refuse to answer that.'

'Felix apparently thought it wise to keep the pill within reach. Do you have any idea why that might have been?'

'I refuse to answer that.'

'Did you acquire the pill from the consulate during Gerlach's time in office? Did you pass it on to your son?'

Rudolf clamped his lips shut.

'The British and Americans believe that enemy agents are active here in Iceland,' said Flóvent. 'That there are German spies transmitting reports on the build-up of forces and other Allied operations. Is your son one of these spies?'

Rudolf glared at Flóvent in stubborn silence.

'Are you a spy yourself?'

'I was compelled to answer all kinds of absurd questions when I was detained by the British,' Rudolf said at last. 'But they had to let me go because there was no evidence against me. And they were far better at this than you are. They were not amateurs who tried to wring sympathy from me by telling me self-pitying stories about themselves. They were professionals. You have a lot to learn.'

'Does Felix use his salesman's job as a cover?' Flóvent persisted. 'How did he come to be a travelling salesman in the first place?'

'I have no idea.'

'Has he been doing the job for long?'

'How should I know? He does not need a cover. He is not a spy. Try to understand that.'

'Does he travel to far-flung parts of the country on his sales trips? Or does he stay in and around Reykjavík?'

'I know nothing about that,' said Rudolf. 'You disgust me. Everything you say disgusts me.'

Flóvent halted his barrage of questions and sat there studying Rudolf. Eventually he continued: 'According to a list in the possession of the police, you were a member of the Icelandic fascist movement, the Nationalist Party. Is that correct?'

'I am not obliged to answer your questions.'

'What was your role in the party?'

'You will have to either arrest me or let me go. I refuse to answer any further questions. If you intend to arrest me, I insist on my right to a lawyer.'

'Was Felix a party member too?'

Rudolf didn't answer.

'What kind of relationship do you have with your son? Were you brought closer by the fact that he grew up without a mother? Or did that put a strain on your relationship? Are you close?'

Rudolf merely shook his head.

'Did he receive a normal upbringing? Was he a happy child? Did he have plenty of friends or did he spend a lot of time alone? What was he like as a boy?'

'I cannot begin to imagine what you are insinuating. Of course he had a normal upbringing. A respectable upbringing.'

'Does he stay in touch with his childhood friends?'

'I have no idea.'

'Did he attend his uncle's school? Your brother-in-law's school?'

Rudolf bestowed a withering look on Flóvent.

'You live close by, so I assume Felix must have been a pupil at his school. Did he get on well at school? Was he a good pupil? Obedient? How were his marks? I suppose it didn't hurt that his uncle was the headmaster? Was he in the top form? He can hardly have been in with the dunces.'

'The dunces? I should think not. He . . . What a load of non-sense. What kind of questions are these? I refuse to respond to such absurd questions.'

'No change there then,' said Flóvent. 'Are you and your brother-in-law on friendly terms? Do you have a good relationship with him?'

'I fail to understand what that has to do with you,' said Rudolf. 'I fail to understand these questions. They are nonsensical. Utterly absurd.'

'He came round to see you recently, didn't he? At your home?'

'What do you mean?'

'He visited you, didn't he?'

'Are you watching my house?'

Flóvent implied as much by his silence. Better for Rudolf to believe that than for him to suspect his maid of betraying his trust. Flóvent had been puzzling over her reference to boys. As far as he knew, Felix was an only child, so the boys in question could hardly have been Rudolf's sons. So who were they? And why had the brothers-in-law been quarrelling about them? He had tried unsuccessfully to get hold of the headmaster. When he phoned his house, he was told that the man was away in the countryside as it was the school holidays. He was due back in a few days.

'May I ask what you two were discussing?'

'Certainly not,' said Rudolf. 'Where did you get this information from? Why is my house being watched? I thought all that was over.'

'What happened at your meeting?'

'Meeting . . . ? Nothing at all,' said Rudolf. 'I have no idea what you are talking about. We are . . . my brother-in-law and I are on perfectly good terms. I do not understand why you are implying that there was something suspicious about our meeting. I . . . I simply cannot understand the nonsensical direction this conversation is taking.'

Flóvent hardly understood himself. He had leafed through the membership list for the Nationalist Party, a copy of which was held in the CID offices. There, the brother-in-law, whose name was Ebeneser Egilsson, was listed as an ordinary member. 'Was it about the Nationalist Party? Is it still in existence? Was that what you were discussing?'

'Of course not,' said Rudolf. 'What you are implying?'

'Did you discuss Felix?'

'No . . . Why do you keep harping on about this visit? What are you driving at? Would it not be simpler to ask me a straight question?'

'Were you discussing family matters, then?' Flóvent persevered.

'His family is none of my concern.'

'Or your brother-in-law's position at the school?'

'Why should we discuss that?'

'I wonder . . . was it something to do with the teachers perhaps? Or the boys at the school?'

Rudolf sat there without speaking, absently rubbing his chest, until at last he seemed to lose all patience with Flóvent's questions about himself, about Felix and, not least, about the headmaster's visit. 'Either arrest me or let me go,' he said, no longer sounding as sure of himself. There was a note of defeat in his voice. 'Do what you like. It is a matter of indifference to me. I will not answer any more of your questions.'

'I've probably taken up enough of your time. I only hope your brother-in-law Ebeneser will prove a little more cooperative,' said Flóvent, rising to his feet. 'I'm due to meet him shortly, which should clarify things.' He sensed that, beneath his fury and contempt, Rudolf was not in fact indifferent to the direction their conversation had taken. 'Would you like us to drive you home?'

'No, I would rather take a taxi.'

'Does your son know or associate with any American servicemen?' asked Flóvent casually.

The question seemed to take Rudolf by surprise. 'What do you mean?'

'It's a simple question: is Felix friendly with American servicemen?'

'No, not that I am aware.'

'What about you yourself?'

'What? Friendly with American soldiers? I should think not!'

'Then can you imagine how Felix might have got hold of a Colt .45 pistol of the type used by the US Marines?'

'I believe you are mistaken in suspecting him, and that this will soon become clear. So these . . . your foolish questions are completely irrelevant.'

'Yes, well, that remains to be seen. Before we finish, there was one rather odd detail about the body in your son's flat.' Flóvent paused to help Rudolf manoeuvre his wheelchair into the corridor. Getting it into the cramped interview room in the first place had proved quite a palaver. Rudolf curtly rejected his help and ordered him to summon a prison guard instead. 'We didn't get a proper look at it until the post-mortem,' Flóvent continued. 'We could easily have missed it altogether.'

'Missed what?'

'The swastika.'

'Swastika?'

'The killer took the time to draw a swastika on the victim's forehead, in blood. I have no idea what that means, why he should have done it, what message it's intended to convey. But it enables us to draw a few conclusions: that the killer's pretty ruthless, for example. Consumed with hatred perhaps. Or rage. The killing was more like an execution than an ordinary murder, which points to an unnerving singleness of purpose. No hesitation. No regrets. No mercy.'

Rudolf was staring at Flóvent in bewilderment.

'Does that sound like your son?' Flóvent asked. 'Would he be capable of such an act? Is he that sort of man?'

'My son . . . he would never do anything . . . Felix would never do anything like that.' For the first time in this gruelling encounter, Rudolf's manner betrayed anxiety, even alarm. 'Never,' he said. 'Never, under any circumstances would my son do anything like that.'

13

Salesmen came and went. The wholesaler had been a commercial traveller himself, so he knew first-hand how taxing the job could be and how meagre the rewards were at times. And for men who were engaged to be married or had a family, the long absences were no joke either.

Men from all walks of life ended up in the job. Some came to him as a last resort after circumstances forced them out of other professions. Drink was a common factor. Then there were the young poets and writers who were perpetually out of pocket. He welcomed them, despite knowing from experience that they wouldn't last. They had their uses and could generally be trusted – with a few notable exceptions – to be entertaining. They were always trying to scrape a bit of money together to bring out a volume of poetry or take some time off to write the novel that would make their name. Over the years he had employed teachers and lorry drivers, failed farmers and wastrels, and knew only too well that no one lasted long as a travelling salesman.

Not everyone had what it took. You had your chaps who were so cocky and bursting with self-confidence that it hardly mattered what goods they had to shift: they could sell almost anything to anyone. It wasn't the product they were selling so much as themselves: their confidence and their company, their friendship even, at least for a while. The best of them didn't even mention business until they were on the point of walking out of the door, when all of a sudden they would slap their foreheads and pretend to remember why they were there. By the way – they were almost embarrassed to mention it – but they had these coats and dresses for sale, hot off the boat. Almost as if it were a matter of indifference to them and they only opened their cases as a special favour to the present company. At this stage they would have had their coffee, complimented the shopkeeper or housewife on the refreshments and repeated the latest news from Reykjavík: the scandal, the amusing anecdotes, the gossip about politicians and other prominent figures about town. Tales of drunkenness and loose morals were always popular. In the case of farms that lay a little off the beaten track and received few visitors, this worked especially well, since the household was often starved of news and positively grateful for a visit from such an entertaining chap.

At the other end of the scale you had your non-starters who never managed to shift a thing. He knew even before he dispatched them on their travels that they would have an uphill struggle. They tended to be the gawky, timid ones, who had no faith in their own abilities. They doubted from the first that they would be able to sell anything but thought it wouldn't hurt to try.

73

He did his best to give them a boost. Despite their lack of promise, he knew that anything was possible and no one should be written off out of hand. These chaps usually made the mistake of starting with an apology when they knocked on a door, be it in a fishing village or on a farm, and no sooner had they finished stammering out their errand than they would find the door closing in their face. It wasn't that people weren't interested in the products they were selling; they weren't interested in them.

'That's the category this fellow falls into,' the wholesaler said, after regaling the policeman with his theory of the two different breeds of salesman. 'Though I'm not denying that he's secured some decent orders from time to time.'

They were sitting in the police station on Pósthússtræti, the duty officer listening patiently to the prattle of the wholesaler who evidently enjoyed the sound of his own voice. One of his salesmen had failed to return with the samples and proceeds from his trip. The wholesaler had tried to track him down, but he was nowhere to be found. The man looked worried as he said this. He took the matter seriously, though it wasn't the first time it had happened. His salesmen had tried to cheat him before. Yes, experience had taught him to keep a close eye on them and make sure they paid up.

'I sometimes ask them to collect payments for older orders and the odd outstanding debt,' he said, 'and the temptation can – well, it can prove too much for them.'

The wholesaler seemed eager to convey that he was a man of the world. He was overweight, with plump cheeks and heavy jowls, and reminded the policeman, to a distracting degree, of the caricatures of capitalists in *Spegillinn* magazine. To complete the picture, he was sucking on a cheap cigar that wreathed him in a cloud of thick grey smoke, and he held himself like a man of influence. Yet he displayed a sympathetic understanding of human frailty and a willingness to help 'those who are never going to conquer the world', as he put it. The implication being that he himself had achieved this in style.

'So you'd like us to find this man for you, sir?' said the policeman, who was young and inexperienced. He was eager to do anything in his power to help those who came into the station, whether they were wealthy wholesalers or down-and-outs.

'Yes,' said the wholesaler, 'that's exactly what I'd like. Before this gets out of hand, if you see what I mean.'

'By out of hand, you mean . . . ?'

'You obviously haven't been listening, my boy. Theft, of course,' said the wholesaler. 'I'd rather not have to accuse the man of being careless with my money.'

'You say you can't find him anywhere?' said the policeman.

'I've searched high and low,' said the wholesaler. 'He was supposed to report to my office as soon as he got back from his trip but he failed to do so. I drove round to his place the following day but it was locked up, there was nobody home and the neighbours hadn't seen him or the woman he lives with. She seems to have vanished off the face of the earth as well. I've been over there three times now but no one ever answers the door. He sometimes eats at Hressingarskálinn when he's in town, but the staff there haven't seen or heard from him lately. I have to admit, I'm worried.'

'Has he shown any sign of dishonesty before?'

'No, he hasn't, and I don't want to jump the gun and start accusing him of anything at this stage. But it's not like him to fail to get in touch. Not like him at all.'

'Are you concerned that something might have happened to him?'

'Well, I can't imagine what,' said the wholesaler, tapping his cigar in the ashtray on the policeman's desk. 'He's a harmless fellow. But I was wondering if you could perhaps enter his flat. On the grounds that he's missing. Disappeared. Vanished into thin air. He could be lying dead in there for all I know.'

'Has he worked for you long?'

'Yes, nearly a year,' said the wholesaler. 'His political views stop him from taking a job with the army. He's always ranting on about profiteering and capital and girls fraternising with the soldiers. He thinks everything's going to hell.'

'Really, does he support the Germans, then?'

'Good God, no. Quite the opposite. He's a communist. A damned commie. That's why I'm worried about him. I keep thinking that he might have heard the rumours about his lady friend and done something stupid.'

'Heard what? What about his lady friend?'

'She's moved out. Or so I hear. Got herself a soldier, taken to a life of vice. Not that I know anything about it. All I know for sure is that the fellow's back in town, because I spoke to the crew of the *Súd*. He always sails with her, so they know him well, and they say he was on board when she came home the other day. But now he's nowhere to be found.'

14

The German consulate stood empty and deserted in the gathering dusk. It was an impressive building with a large, round window in the gable facing onto Túngata. A few doors further up, the nuns of St Joseph's laboured to care for the sick, while across the road loomed the ungainly form of the Catholic Cathedral with its stumpy grey tower. Here on the hill, above the humble wooden shacks of Grjótathorp, the street was lined with handsome concrete villas, solidly built and blazing with lights, all except for the consulate that stood staring darkly from its single Cyclops eye.

A stiff northerly wind had sprung up, bringing with it a sharp chill, as Flóvent and Thorson let themselves into the consulate with a key acquired from US counter-intelligence. The Swedish embassy had taken over all consular operations, and now handled the affairs of German nationals in Iceland. The house had stood empty since the May morning the previous year when the consul general had been arrested. Flóvent didn't know what had happened immediately following his arrest, but a number of German citizens had been interrogated at Midbæjar School and detained there until they could be deported to Britain.

The light summer nights were drawing in now that it was August, and Flóvent had come armed with a torch. The two men found themselves in a hall with reception rooms opening off it and a staircase ascending steeply on the left-hand side. The building had clearly been vacated in a hurry. Almost everything had been removed, but there were still cupboards, tables and chairs abandoned here and there; and papers, empty boxes, old newspapers, items of clothing, tablecloths and torn curtains were strewn all over the floor. Amidst the mess was a framed photograph of Adolf Hitler, the glass broken as if someone had stamped on it. Two flags, with their black swastika on a red background, lay in tatters among the other rubbish.

They wandered through the ground-floor rooms in an eerie silence broken only by the odd car making heavy weather of the climb up Túngata. Charred scraps of paper still littered the passageways. Thorson had been allowed to see the documents that had been removed from Gerlach's residence by the British and subsequently handed over to US intelligence. Many of them had been translated into English, but he had found no references to Felix or Rudolf Lunden among them. Most of the documents concerned the consul's dealings with the Icelanders, including correspondence with members of the government, in which he complained that the Third Reich was being shown insufficient respect. All pretty inconsequential stuff, Thorson thought. He got the impression that Werner Gerlach's role had been to unite the German community in Iceland under the Nazi flag and to foment insurrection. None of the papers Thorson was permitted to see were singed or displayed any other sign of having been exposed to the inferno in Gerlach's bathtub. But they did include countless memos detailing the consul's views of the Icelanders, which were uncomplimentary, to say the least.

Entering the consul's office, Thorson and Flóvent saw two SS uniforms bundled in a heap in one corner and more framed photographs of leading figures in the Third Reich lying on the floor. Flóvent picked up a couple and showed them to Thorson. They were of Heinrich Himmler and Hermann Goering, personally signed with warm regards to the consul.

'I gather he and Gerlach are bosom buddies,' said Thorson, pointing at Himmler. 'I don't know about the other guy.'

They had come to this gloomy building in search of evidence linking the consul to the Lunden family, possible clues to the provenance of the cyanide capsule, and anything else that might help them with the investigation into Felix's disappearance. Beforehand, they had sat for hours in Flóvent's office in the large building at number 11 Fríkirkjuvegur, trying to work out how to proceed. In the end, the best idea they could come up with was to take a look around the German consulate. There was no news of Felix's whereabouts as yet, and they still didn't know the identity of the dead man. The most plausible theory was that Felix had shot the man himself and was now on the run, possibly even making arrangements to flee the country. The suicide pill pointed to links with Germany and could conceivably have reached him via the consulate. They had no other leads. Flóvent told Thorson about his trying encounters with Rudolf Lunden and how almost nothing had seemed to rattle the doctor until Flóvent mentioned the swastika on the victim's forehead. Only then had he been lost for words.

'There's one thing about Rudolf Lunden that puzzles me,' said Flóvent, putting the pictures of Himmler and Goering down again. 'I've been wondering why he wasn't deported with Consul Gerlach and the other German nationals who the British saw urgent reason to arrest. How did he slip through the net? The purges the British carried out were pretty extensive, yet they allowed him to stay.'

'He's an Icelandic citizen, isn't he?' said Thorson. 'And he's lived here for thirty years.' He set off upstairs to the first floor, with Flóvent on his heels, then continued up to the attic. They found themselves in the room with the round window facing the street.

'In addition to which, he's getting on in years and is confined to a wheelchair,' said Flóvent.

'Is there any other explanation? The intelligence guys told me they'd made a point of checking out his background and questioning him thoroughly. But they left it at that. They didn't find any evidence to suggest he was a threat. Nothing to justify internment in Britain.'

'Even though he was friends with Gerlach and an influential member of the Nationalist Party?' said Flóvent, flashing his torch around the attic. 'Something doesn't add up, if you ask me. The way I see it, he should have been deported along with all the rest.'

'This Werner Gerlach's quite an interesting character,' said Thorson. 'They gave me a brief summary of his career at the meeting in the old Leper Hospital, but maybe you're already familiar with the details?'

'No, actually. I don't know much about him.'

'He trained as a doctor and was professor of anatomy at the University of Jena,' said Thorson. 'He came to this country just before the war broke out, in April of '39. They believe he was sent to Iceland on the direct orders of Himmler, who, like many Nazis, is particularly interested in this country.'

'Yes, apparently they believe it's been home to some kind of pure Nordic, Germanic race ever since Viking times.'

'Whereas in reality you're just a bunch of degenerate weaklings?'

'Yes,' said Flóvent and smiled.

'Speaking of which, there's one rather noteworthy fact about the University of Jena. Related to this interest in racial purity.'

'What's that?' asked Flóvent. 'I've never heard of the university before.'

'I'm not familiar with it either,' said Thorson, 'but apparently they do research there on eugenics and genetics, including studies of criminals. The university's top in its field in Germany. The Nazis are obsessed with the idea that criminal traits are hereditary, and they've set up major research programmes to prove it. Graham and Ballantine are aware of similar studies being carried out in German concentration camps. They mentioned the camp at a place called . . . what was it again? Buchenwald, I believe. Apparently the Germans are performing genetic experiments on the prisoners there.'

'Isn't that a load of nonsense? That criminal traits are hereditary?'

Thorson shrugged. 'Well, the Nazis think they've found a solution to the problem.'

'Which is?'

'Castration,' said Thorson. 'They know of no simpler or more effective method of preventing criminals from breeding than to geld them.'

'Isn't that . . . is there any truth in this?'

'Well, it's what our friends at the Leper Hospital claim is going on,' said Thorson, kicking a balled-up newspaper. It fell open to reveal some scraps of paper. Thorson bent down to take a closer look and discovered two charred pages, obviously ripped from a book. There was no sign of the book itself but clearly it must have come into contact with the flames in the consul's bathtub. The pages, which had been singed top and bottom, appeared to come from a guestbook. Thorson picked them up gingerly and saw a date that looked like 1939. There was handwriting on both sides of the pages and although it was mostly illegible he could discern a few names and other words that the fire hadn't managed to destroy.

While Flóvent trained his torch on the fragments, Thorson did his best to decipher them, as he had a smattering of German. He managed to pick out a few of the names. They were German and some were accompanied by greetings or comments like *With grateful thanks for your hospitality* or *Thank you for an enjoyable evening in the company of friends.*

'Do they tell us anything useful?' asked Flóvent, frowning down at them.

'No, probably not,' said Thorson.

'What's this?' asked Flóvent, taking hold of one of the pages. 'What does it say there?' He drew Thorson's attention to a signature that was very hard to read. There was no date by the name or any information on the purpose of the visit.

'What's the surname?' he asked, staring hard at the writing. 'Isn't it Lunden? Doesn't it say Lunden?'

Thorson peered at the almost illegible name. The first letter was an *H*. It was followed by something unreadable, then an *n* and finally a letter that looked like an *s*. The surname began with an

L. Then there were a couple of unclear letters, then a *d* and an *e*, and finally another letter that was impossible to read. *H_ns L_de_*.

'Could it be Hans or something like that? Hans Lunden?' said Flóvent. 'The surname's definitely Lunden, isn't it?'

'Yes, it looks like it.'

'Yet another member of the Lunden family?'

'That's certainly a possibility. Though it could say something different. I'm not very good on German names.'

'If it is Lunden,' said Flóvent, 'wouldn't he be . . . what? Felix's brother? I thought he was an only child.'

'Or Rudolf's brother. Or a cousin, perhaps. Whoever he was, he must have known Werner Gerlach well enough to have been invited here.'

'Felix and Rudolf and now Hans?'

'Who are these people?'

'What's that in front of his name? More letters?'

Thorson struggled to decipher the scrawl. 'Impossible to read. Unless . . . could that be a capital *D*?'

'*D*, and what's this?'

'Could it be *D . . . r*?'

'Doktor Hans Lunden? Yet another doctor,' said Flóvent thoughtfully, shining his torch into the corner where the fragments had been lying tangled up in the newspaper. Then he directed the beam back at the pages and raised his eyes to Thorson, repeating the words under his breath. 'Yet another doctor.'

15

They watched a man of about sixty collect a bundle of fishing rods from his car, with a calm, unhurried air, then put them away in a shed. Flóvent had decided they should pay a visit to Rudolf's brother-in-law, the headmaster, just on the off-chance that he had returned from his trip. Spotting the figure with the fishing rods, Flóvent parked in front of the drive, and he and Thorson got out and walked over.

'Ebeneser?' said Flóvent.

The man had noticed them parking outside his house but behaved as if it was of no consequence. He was dressed for salmon fishing, and wore a green waterproof over a traditional knitted *lopapeysa*, and a pair of waders. He looked as if he had come straight from the riverbank.

'Do I know you gentlemen?' he asked.

'Are you Ebeneser Egilsson, sir?' asked Flóvent.

'Who's asking? Who are you?'

'My name's Flóvent and I'm from the Criminal Investigation Department. My partner here is Thorson, from the military police. I don't know if you've heard, sir, but we're investigating a case involving your nephew, Felix Lunden.'

'Felix? Really?' The man sounded puzzled. 'I . . . I haven't heard anything about that. Is Felix all right? Is he in some kind of trouble?'

'We're not sure,' said Flóvent. 'But we're keen to talk to him. Do you have any idea where he might be?'

'Where he might be? Whatever's going on? I've been out of . . . I've been fishing and . . . I don't know what this is about. Why are you looking for him?'

'So you haven't heard from your brother-in-law, Rudolf?' asked Flóvent.

'Rudolf? No. Is anything the matter with him? Is he all right?'

'Yes, we spoke to him earlier today. I take it you are Ebeneser Egilsson, sir? Headmaster of . . . ?'

'Yes, I am. I'm Ebeneser. Look, what's this about Felix?'

'We need to speak to him urgently.'

Flóvent asked if they might step inside as they had a few questions they would like to put to him. Ebeneser objected at first, pleading exhaustion after spending all day driving on bone-shaking roads. But when he saw the determination on Flóvent's face, he clearly thought it would be better to get it over with, and besides he seemed curious to know what sort of hot water his nephew was in. The house bore all the signs of a cultured home. Tightly packed bookshelves had been fitted in wherever there was space, paintings by some of Iceland's leading landscape artists graced the walls, and there were magazines and academic journals scattered across the tables. Many of the books were on genealogy. When Flóvent enquired about these, Ebeneser explained that he was an enthusiast and enjoyed tracing people's family trees.

Flóvent gave him an account of the case, starting with the moment the police were notified about the body in the basement flat, but was careful not to give too much away. He described the scene but omitted the details about the American firearm and the symbol on the victim's forehead. He said only that the police had yet to identify the body but that they had spoken to Rudolf.

Ebeneser reacted with incredulity and seemed to have difficulty taking in what they were telling him. Little by little, though, the shocking news sank in. He kept asking about Felix. Did they think he was dead as well, or in some sort of danger? Who was the man in his flat? Was Felix suspected of murder? But there were no answers to be had from Flóvent and Thorson.

'I presume you were away at the time, sir?' said Flóvent, who had done most of the talking.

'I've been away for a week,' said Ebeneser. 'Fishing. My two companions came back to town the day before yesterday. Do you mean . . . Are you asking me for some sort of . . . alibi?'

'Just a formality,' said Flóvent. 'I'll need the names of anyone who can back up your statement.'

Ebeneser provided these, though he added huffily that he wasn't happy about being required to do so. His word ought to be more than sufficient.

Flóvent assured him there was no need to worry and repeated that it was a formality. The man was not as aggressive as the brother-in-law, but beneath his aggrieved air Flóvent sensed some of the same reactions Rudolf had shown: defensiveness, unwillingness to cooperate, dissimulation, impatience. From Ebeneser's unkempt appearance and hoarse voice, he got the impression that the man had been holed up in a hut with a bottle.

'I can't believe Felix . . . would be capable of anything like that,' said Ebeneser. He cleared his throat. 'He's bound to come forward sooner or later to provide an explanation. I don't doubt that for a moment.'

'Well, we'll see. Have you any idea where he might be?'

'No, none at all. The last I heard, he was working as a travelling salesman, out of town for longer or shorter periods. Are you sure he isn't on one of his sales trips?'

Thorson caught Flóvent's eye. He'd detected a hint of contempt for Felix in his uncle's voice, as if being a salesman was an unworthy occupation for a young man of his background. He wondered if Felix had been a disappointment to this family of schoolmasters, doctors and academics. But he kept his thoughts from his face and couldn't tell if Flóvent had picked up on it as well.

'It's possible,' said Flóvent. 'Do you happen to know if he's familiar with the German consulate on Túngata?'

'No . . . The consulate?'

'Was he a frequent guest there?'

'No, I . . . I wouldn't know. Why should . . . ?'

'Do you own or have access to a firearm?' asked Flóvent, keeping up an unrelenting flow of questions.

'No, I don't own a gun, nor do I have access to one,' said Ebeneser sharply, as if the questions were getting on his nerves. 'I sometimes cast a line for salmon. That's the nearest I come to hunting for sport. I don't use firearms and, frankly, I find it hard to understand why you should think it necessary to ask me if I own a pistol.'

'These are merely routine enquiries we're putting to everyone connected to Felix. You shouldn't read too much into them, sir.'

'Well, I'm not sure I appreciate your . . . your tone or your questions. It's almost as if you take me for a common criminal.'

'On the contrary,' Flóvent assured him, and ploughed on unperturbed. 'May I ask if you're on friendly terms with any American or British servicemen?'

'No, I can't say I am. Naturally I've had dealings with them. They've made use of some of the school buildings, for example, but I'm not personally acquainted with any of them.'

'What about Felix? Do you know if he spends much time around members of the occupation force?'

'Not that I'm aware. But I wouldn't know.'

'How's his relationship with his father?' asked Flóvent. 'Are he and Rudolf on good terms?'

'I think you had better ask them about that.'

'Yes, of course. When did you last see Felix?'

Ebeneser couldn't say exactly. He frowned, apparently trying to remember when their paths had last crossed, and finally said he thought it had been earlier that summer, about a month ago perhaps, when Felix had returned from one of his sales trips. Ebeneser had run into him in the centre of town, on Pósthússtræti, and Felix had told him he'd just arrived on the *Súd* after a stint in the West Fjords. He had been his usual ebullient self. Felix had always been an outgoing character and found it easy to meet people. Doubtless that helped him peddle his wares to them. That's to say, he had mentioned how well the trip had gone, but they'd only exchanged a few words before Felix had to dash off.

'Did you notice if he was carrying a suitcase?'

'Yes, I daresay he was,' said Ebeneser. 'Though I didn't pay any particular attention to it.'

'Do you know what a cyanide capsule is?' asked Flóvent.

'A cyanide capsule?'

'Would it come as a surprise to you that we found a cyanide pill in Felix's suitcase and that analysis has revealed that it was manufactured in Germany?'

The headmaster stared dumbly at Flóvent. He appeared not to understand the question.

'Would it come as a surprise to you?' Flóvent repeated.

'I've never even heard of such a thing,' said Ebeneser. 'A cyanide . . . ?'

'A capsule of the type we found is known as a suicide pill,' Flóvent explained. You bite it and death follows in a matter of seconds. Can you imagine why Felix would have wanted to keep a pill like that close to hand?'

'No, I have to admit . . . I have to admit I've absolutely no idea. I'm astonished, frankly. Why would Felix have a . . . a pill like that in his possession? Surely there's been some mistake?'

'Did you meet Dr Hans Lunden when he visited the country a couple of years back?'

'Hans?' repeated the headmaster in surprise. 'What about him?'

'Did you meet him? Do you know him?'

'Well, I . . . no, not very well. He's . . .'

'Yes?'

'He's Rudolf's brother. But perhaps you already knew that. He lives in Germany.'

'Is he there now?'

'As far as I'm aware. But I'm not sure why you're asking me. What has he got to do with this?'

'I understand that Hans Lunden visited Iceland in '39,' Flóvent went on, as though he hadn't heard the question. 'Am I correct?'

'That sounds about right,' said Ebeneser. 'Shortly before the war. During the spring, if memory serves.'

'So you've met him?'

'Yes, once. At a party given by my brother-in-law. Look, I feel as though I'm being subjected to some sort of interrogation. Have I committed an offence? Why are you bombarding me with questions like this? Could it not wait until tomorrow? I . . . It's been a long, hard day and, as I've already explained, I'm really rather tired.'

'Of course,' said Flóvent. 'We won't take up any more of your time. There are just a couple more points I'd like to clear up. Do you think it's plausible that Hans Lunden could have provided Felix with the cyanide capsule? Or does the notion strike you as absurd?'

Ebeneser looked from one of them to the other, his face registering surprise and suspicion.

'Is it possible that he brought more of these pills to the country, do you think?' Flóvent asked, when it became evident that the headmaster wasn't going to answer. 'Do you have any inkling?'

'I can't imagine what you're insinuating,' said Ebeneser. 'I don't know what Hans Lunden did or didn't bring to Iceland. It's a mystery to me why you're asking me all these questions. Are you trying to incriminate me by linking me to some . . . some suicide pill? I simply can't work out where all these questions are leading. I'm completely at a loss and can't think what you expect me to say.'

'No, that's hardly surprising,' said Flóvent. 'Please believe me when I say that this is as new to me as it is to you, but I hope you

90

understand that I'm compelled to ask. Please bear with me just a little longer. I gather you and Rudolf were members of the Nationalist Party. Did Dr Hans Lunden come to Iceland under their auspices? Under the auspices of the Nationalist Party, I mean?'

'I don't believe so. But I wasn't a very active member and know little about their arrangements, so I'm afraid I can't answer that.'

'Are you still a Nazi sympathiser?'

'Certainly not,' said Ebeneser, flicking a glance at Thorson. 'Not that it's any of your business. I simply can't work out what it is that you want from me. Besides which, it's extremely late . . .'

'I suppose Felix had direct links to Germany, to his relatives there,' said Flóvent, changing tack. He didn't want to alienate the headmaster, as he suspected that their paths would cross again, sooner rather than later.

'Actually he's spent more time in Denmark. Perhaps you're aware that his grandmother's Danish?' said Ebeneser, sounding weary. 'Look, I'd be grateful if we could wrap this up now. If you don't mind.'

'Of course. It's late, as you said.' Flóvent made as if to leave. 'Thank you for seeing us at such an inconvenient time. We only dropped by on the off-chance that you'd be home. Has he been in Denmark recently? Felix, I mean.'

'Actually, it's not that long since he came home,' said Ebeneser. 'Felix was trapped there when the Nazis . . . when the Germans invaded last year, and he stayed on in Copenhagen until he was able to get a ship back to Iceland.'

'Really, so he was in Denmark fairly recently? Do you know what he was doing there?'

'He was there almost two years. And no, I'm not sure what he was up to.'

'All right, thank you very much. We won't keep you any longer. You've been most helpful. Oh, just one last thing. Have you seen Rudolf at all recently?'

'No,' said Ebeneser emphatically. 'I haven't seen Rudolf for a while.'

'You haven't visited him? Haven't seen him at all?'

'No. No, I haven't seen him.'

They shook hands in parting, and Flóvent smiled amiably to hide the fact that he knew better.

16

Thorson asked Flóvent if he could give him a ride down to Hótel Borg. He sat in the passenger seat, nursing the charred pages they had found at the German consulate and trying to decipher more names by the light of the torch. It was almost impossible given the state of the pages and the jolting of the car. They discussed what Rudolf's maid had whispered to Flóvent about the headmaster's visit. They couldn't imagine what possible reason Ebeneser could have for covering it up.

'I doubt we could have got any more out of him this evening,' said Flóvent. 'But I need to sound him out further about the Lunden brothers' friendship with the German consul. I'll talk to him again tomorrow. Perhaps it would be better if I went to see him alone. Having a representative of the defence force in his house seemed to put him more on his guard.'

'What was the maid talking about?' asked Thorson. 'Who are these boys?'

'Goodness knows,' said Flóvent. 'They were quarrelling about "some boys". That's all she said. I need to talk to her again as well.'

'Well, he is the headmaster of a school,' said Thorson.

'Yes, but I find it unlikely that they were arguing about school-children,' said Flóvent. 'What I can't work out is why Ebeneser would lie about something as natural as going to see his brother-in-law. Why doesn't he want us to know that they met recently, that they had a bust-up? What's he got to hide?'

'We might be able to make out this part too,' Thorson interrupted. He was pointing at an almost illegible name on the same page as the German doctor's. While they talked he had been squinting at the writing, shining the torch on the burnt pages and holding them at every imaginable angle, even over his head, in an attempt to decipher them.

'What does it say?' asked Flóvent. 'Who is it?'

Thorson tried to read the letters, guessing at the gaps. The first name was less damaged and he thought he could work out what it was.

'It looks to me as if it could be a long name like . . . Bryn . . . hildur. And . . . what's this? Some family name rather than a patronymic . . . *H* . . . *e* . . . or *o* . . . is that an *l*? Hel . . . ? Not Helena. Or . . . could it be Hólm? Could that be it? Brynhildur Hólm? Is that an Icelandic name?'

They had reached Hótel Borg. Flóvent parked in the street in front of the revolving doors and switched off the engine. Town was busy, as it was Friday night and the dance halls were open. Young people walked along Pósthússtræti hand in hand; some-times a girl would wander by with a soldier on her arm. Flóvent watched a pair of lovers disappearing into the hotel and wondered if Thorson had a date there, but he wouldn't have dreamt of asking. Although he liked what he'd seen of the young Canadian, they didn't know each other at all.

'Yes, could be,' he said. 'But I haven't heard the name before. Does it look as though she was there on the same occasion as Hans Lunden?'

'It's hard to tell,' said Thorson. 'But we should see if we can track her down. She might be able to tell us something about Dr Hans Lunden if she was a guest of the consulate at the same time.'

'Yes, good idea,' said Flóvent. 'Are you off for a night out?' he asked on a lighter note, nodding towards the hotel.

'Yes, no, I'm billeted here at the moment – I've got a small room on the top floor,' said Thorson. 'But I might look in on the dance later. In the Golden Room. Isn't that what they call it? The ballroom?'

'Yes, that's right. The Golden Room,' said Flóvent, glancing at his watch and realising how late it was. 'Have fun. We'll talk in the morning.'

Thorson said goodnight and was about to get out of the car when he paused and closed the door again. There was something he'd put off discussing with Flóvent, despite the fact that it might be significant. He'd been trying to figure out whether it was connected to the case, but he hadn't come up with anything. The thought wouldn't leave him alone, though, and he felt he had to share his concerns with the Icelandic detective.

'Something is bothering me, but I don't know if I should even be talking about it.'

'What's that?'

'It's probably nothing, but I've been thinking about this case we're working on and its links to the German consulate and German nationals living here, to Nazis, and . . .'

'What are you worried about?' prompted Flóvent, studying the young soldier who spoke the Icelandic of his emigrant parents with a hint of a northern accent. He looked troubled.

'I happened to overhear something as I was leaving the meeting with my commanding officer at Höfdi,' Thorson continued after a long pause. 'When I was assigned to work with you – with the Icelandic police, that is. Some men from the government were talking on the steps outside. Of course they assumed I didn't understand. From what I could hear, they were discussing . . . Winston Churchill.'

'Churchill? What about him?'

'It sounded to me like he might be planning a visit to Iceland. He's got a conference scheduled with Roosevelt in the Atlantic somewhere off Newfoundland, and they said there's a chance he might stop off in Iceland on his way home. Were the Icelandic police briefed about it?'

'Well, this is the first I've heard about a visit, but that doesn't necessarily mean anything,' said Flóvent. 'I'm usually the last to hear what's going on. Did you recognise the men you saw at Höfdi? Have you any idea who they were?'

'At least one of them was a government minister,' said Thorson, who took an interest in Icelandic domestic affairs. 'I believe he was there specifically to discuss the visit, but that's only a guess. I've been thinking it over and felt I had to tell . . . to tell you. In case there's a connection to our case.'

'You mean to Felix Lunden?'

Thorson nodded. 'I think we should make it a priority to track him down,' he said. 'Just to be on the safe side. In case there's anything to this rumour of a visit.'

'Are you implying he might be some sort of threat?' asked Flóvent. 'Isn't that a bit far-fetched?'

'I'm not sure. We know there are German agents operating here. The occupation must have made things harder for them, but we're assuming that spies are still active in the country, just as they are elsewhere in Europe. Iceland's no exception.'

'Yes, but we have no rock-solid evidence to link Felix to that type of activity,' said Flóvent. 'And nothing to link the incident in his flat to this visit.'

'Well, I thought I ought to mention it,' said Thorson. 'In case we uncover any leads that point that way. After all, where is Felix? What's he up to? Is he armed? We don't know. Since there's a pretty good chance he's the killer, we have to work on the basis that he could be armed with a Colt .45. The question is, do we need help with this investigation? I can talk to Ballantine and Graham. Though, come to think of it, they're . . .'

'What?'

Thorson recalled Graham saying that it was their affair and sooner or later they would have to step in and take over the investigation. In the meantime, he had ordered Thorson to provide a daily report on their progress.

'Nothing,' said Thorson, 'I just wondered if you might need more help from us.'

'But this is an Icelandic matter,' said Flóvent. 'You're involved because the murder weapon is almost certainly a military one and we need easy access to the occupation force if the trail leads us to a soldier. If we need any further assistance from your people, I'll let you know.'

'Yes, of course, I just wanted to mention the Churchill angle.'

'Thank you. But I don't believe there's any cause for concern. Nothing like that would ever happen here. Not in Iceland.'

Thorson was taken aback by his assertion. Two years ago Flóvent could have said something like that without a second thought, but a great deal had changed since then. Iceland was no longer a remote island, cut off from the rest of the world. The country had been dragged into the maelstrom of world events and plenty was happening here now that would have been inconceivable before. Had Flóvent not yet woken up to this new reality or had he temporarily forgotten it? There were no longer any grounds for such misplaced optimism. Flóvent was deceiving himself. It wasn't the first time Thorson had come up against this mindset. Perhaps it was the Icelanders' innocence that had been the first victim when the British invasion force marched into town on 10 May last year. Thorson remembered a buddy of his asking if he'd be interested in settling in Iceland after the war. Thorson had used his leave to go hiking in the mountains in the mild summer weather. He'd come back waxing lyrical about the beauty of the landscape and the silence that had enveloped him as he slept out under the midnight sun. Thorson admitted he hadn't given it any thought, and then his buddy had made a remark that stayed with him: 'I guess you'd have to learn to think like an Icelander if you wanted to live here.'

'You shouldn't underestimate the seriousness of the situation,' he said to Flóvent now. 'I think we should still bear the possibility in mind – maybe try to get confirmation of whether he's actually coming. If measures need to be taken. You see, Graham and co., they don't trust . . .'

'Who don't they trust?'

'I shouldn't have opened my big mouth . . .'

Thorson hesitated again. He hadn't meant to say any more, but he wasn't happy with the dilemma he found himself in. On the one hand, he was accountable to his commanding officers and wanted to fulfil the task he had been entrusted with; he didn't want to work against the interests of the occupation force or his comrades in arms. On the other hand, he felt a lot of sympathy for the Icelanders. His parents had taught him to consider them his own people, however distant. He had heard his fellow soldiers poking fun at the locals, sneering at them, and had tried to make up for their behaviour. It hurt him to hear people deriding the country and its inhabitants. And now he felt he was being forced to choose sides, forced into a thankless position. He hated not being able to speak honestly to Flóvent.

'What's on your mind?' Flóvent asked, picking up on his hesitation. 'Is everything all right? Who don't they trust? What do they want? Is there something you can't share with me?'

'They want to take over the case,' Thorson said at last, with a sigh. 'And sooner or later they'll do it. They have no faith in the Icelandic police. They don't trust them – you, the Icelanders – to do it right.'

Flóvent gave Thorson a searching look. 'Because of the visit?' he asked at last.

'No, at least I don't think so. Well, that didn't actually occur to me. They believe the killer has to be a member of the occupation force because of the gun. They may have even started their own inquiry.'

'Are you aware that they have?'

'No.'

'Well, thank you for telling me. You didn't have to.'

'I don't want to be a . . . some kind of a sneak. To do anything underhand. I felt it was right to come clean with you. That way at least everything's straight between us.'

'Not many men in your position would have behaved as honourably,' said Flóvent.

'I'm pretty sick of their attitude to the locals. And I don't want to get caught up in some kind of double game . . . '

He was going to phrase it differently but could think of no other way of saying it. If anyone was playing a double game, it was him.

But Thorson said nothing about that either.

17

They parted company shortly afterwards, and Flóvent drove back to Fríkirkjuvegur prior to heading home. There was a message waiting for him at the office: a policeman from Pósthússtræti had been asking to speak to him in connection with the Felix Lunden case. He put through a call to the station but learnt that the officer in question had gone off duty. After that, he rang the Reykjavík commissioner's right-hand man, an old acquaintance from his days with the regular police, to sound him out about Churchill's visit. His contact, it turned out, was completely in the dark. Astonished by the suggestion, he immediately wanted to know where Flóvent had picked it up. Flóvent merely said he'd heard it on the grapevine. He was reluctant to mention Thorson in case he got the young man into trouble.

Until the rumour had been substantiated, he felt it was premature to link Felix Lunden's disappearance to a possible visit. So far he had not one shred of evidence to suggest that Felix was involved in a plot connected to Churchill or that he was a German assassin. Even supposing the suitcase did belong to him, and the cyanide capsule too, that wasn't sufficient grounds for such a conclusion. Admittedly the pill was an indication that there was more to Felix Lunden than met the eye and that he might be working for the Germans, but it revealed nothing about an actual Nazi plot in Iceland.

Flóvent's acquaintance, Arnfinnur, a man somewhat older than him, said he would make enquiries and get back to him shortly. Then he asked if Flóvent was making any headway with the murder investigation and whether the occupation force was playing ball. Flóvent said it was progressing, slowly, and complained, not for the first time, about a lack of manpower. The Criminal Investigation Department needed more men. Up to now his requests had fallen on deaf ears, but he thought the murder at Felix's flat might prompt his superiors to remedy the situation. Arnfinnur said he would see what he could do but hinted that since the military police were willing to assist, and the Icelandic force was desperately understaffed at what was after all a difficult time, Flóvent would probably have to make the best of things. Flóvent had heard that one before.

He had no sooner replaced the receiver after his conversation with Arnfinnur than the phone rang. It was his father, wanting to know if he'd be home soon. Flóvent told him not to wait up, but knew it wouldn't do any good. His father, who worked on the docks, seldom retired for the night until Flóvent came home. He kept supper warm for his son when Flóvent was held up at work, and made sure he never went to bed hungry. They usually spent their evenings chatting or companionably listening to the wireless, and Flóvent knew that his father treasured these moments.

He was a family man who had lost half his family in one fell swoop when his wife and daughter died of the Spanish flu. He and Flóvent bore their sorrow in silence. He had never gone out looking for another woman after his wife died. He was a member of the last generation of Icelanders to experience true hardship, having lived through war, depression and epidemic – all without uttering a word of complaint.

Flóvent said he was on his way, but as he was hurrying out of the office the phone rang again. He paused in the doorway, then strode back and snatched up the receiver.

'Is that Flóvent?' said a man's voice.

'Yes?'

'I know it's late but I tried to reach you earlier. My name's Einar. I'm a police officer, and I was on duty at Pósthússtræti this morning when a man came in, a wholesaler. I've been thinking about it ever since he left, because of the man you found murdered in that basement flat.'

'Oh? What about him?'

'The wholesaler's looking for one of his salesmen,' said the policeman. 'He thinks he's made off with his samples and all the cash.'

'Is his name Felix, the salesman in question? Hasn't the wholesaler heard our appeal for information about him?'

'No, actually, it's not Felix.'

'Who is it then?'

'I wondered if he could be the man who was killed. The salesman, I mean – the one who's been reported missing.'

'Can you get hold of him quickly? The wholesaler.'

'Yes, he left a telephone number and –'

'Ring him and tell him to meet me at the National Hospital

mortuary in twenty minutes. Tell him it's urgent. If necessary, we can send a car for him.'

Thorson didn't know exactly what he was looking for when he left Hótel Borg, not long after saying goodbye to Flóvent. It wasn't the first time he had embarked on one of these forays into Reykjavík's nightlife in an attempt to explore his longings and desires, to find answers to the questions that preyed on his mind. He knew he was unusually inexperienced – perhaps because he was so oddly un-interested. His comrades in the military enjoyed their fair share of attention from the local women and some took full advantage of it, while others were more circumspect, put off by the whole sordid Situation. He'd heard stories from his fellow soldiers, some as tragic as they were extraordinary. Stories of questionable morality. Of bizarre pride. Passing through the camps, he would often think of the freezing night when he had stopped to help an inadequately dressed woman who had fallen into a snowdrift. As he drove her home she confided in him that earlier that evening she had slept with three marines in their barracks. But she had refused to take any money for it, she assured Thorson, saying proudly: 'I wouldn't want them to think I was some kind of whore.'

He was headed for Hótel Ísland, a very different, far less classy place than Hótel Borg, consisting of a hotchpotch of wooden buildings that lined the street from Austurstræti to the corner of Adalstræti. The crowd was spilling out into the road outside the dance hall; it was made up mostly of soldiers, a few with women on their arms. When Thorson arrived, a doorman was throwing out a sorry-looking Icelander in shabby clothes, telling him he had no business in there. Thorson hoped it was because he was drunk and not just because he was a local. Recently the Icelandic police had formed the Morality Committee for the Supervision of Minors, and two of its representatives were busy ejecting young girls from the premises despite their protests. Inside, a small jazz band was playing and people were dancing close together in a sweltering fug of cigarette smoke, aftershave and sweat. The noise was deafening, a cacophony of shouts and roars of laughter vying with the music. Thorson edged his way to the bar and bought himself a drink. A drunken sergeant bashed into him. A new consignment of American troops had recently arrived, and he thought their numbers now equalled those of the British and Canadian troops in the dance hall. The local women had already begun to transfer their affections to the Yanks and he soon saw why. The Americans had a lot more money to throw around. They were better groomed. Had broader grins. They were Clark Gable to Britain's Oliver Twist.

Thorson looked around the room, where the booze was flowing and the dancers' feet thundered in time to the music.

Hótel Ísland. *Hotel Iceland.*

It hadn't occurred to him before just how appropriate the name was. Here you truly got the sense that Iceland was nothing more than a staging post.

A night's lodging.

A one-night stand.

She was here, as she had been on previous weekends, with a group of marines, but when she spotted him she came straight over and asked if he was going to buy her a drink. He ordered a gin: she had said it was her favourite tipple. They clinked glasses.

She was grateful that he spoke Icelandic because she barely knew a word of English. It was a shame he was practically an Icelander, she said, because he looked very dashing in his uniform. Then she laughed because she had a sunny disposition and was easily amused, and he felt comfortable with her. He had learnt quite a bit about her, as she didn't mind talking about herself, though he put no pressure on her to do so. She was at least ten years older than him, dark-haired, with thick ringlets snaking down to her shoulders, and a curvaceous figure. Her face had lost some of its bloom, which he put down to a fast lifestyle, but her eyes were still beautiful and almost completely round. They grew impossibly wide whenever she repeated, or heard, something she found odd or interesting. A friend of hers had met ever such a nice British soldier from Brighton, she told him, and they were head over heels in love. Of course Thorson knew that Hótel Ísland also had its heart-warming tales: love blossoming across oceans, fairy tales where men and women found their soulmates while war raged on in the outside world, and that this love could be pure and innocent.

'Have you made up your mind?' she asked, once they had drained their glasses.

'Yes, I think so.'

'Got the money?'

He put his hand to his pocket but she stopped him.

'Not here, darling. Come on.'

Baldur was annoyed at being phoned so late at night and initially refused to meet Flóvent at the mortuary, before eventually giving in. Flóvent was waiting for him outside and apologised profusely when the doctor, who lived near the hospital, emerged from the darkness on his bicycle. At that moment a lorry drove up with a roar and out stepped the wholesaler. He asked which of them was Flóvent.

'What the hell is going on?' he asked, shaking both their hands. 'The cop who rang said he'd have to arrest me if I didn't get over here straight away.'

'Thank you for coming, sir,' said Flóvent. 'I understand you're missing one of your salesmen.'

'Yes, that's right,' said the wholesaler. He had lit one of his cheap cigars on the way over and was sucking on it avidly. 'Let's drop the "sir", shall we? Do you think he's in here?'

'Let's go and see, shall we?' said Flóvent. Baldur opened the door for them and they followed him inside. He pulled the trolley out of the cold storage unit and rolled it under the unforgiving lights of the mortuary.

'I warn you,' said Flóvent. 'The man was shot in the head and he's not a pretty sight, though Baldur here has done his best to tidy him up, so –'

'Don't worry about me,' interrupted the wholesaler. 'There's no need. I used to work in an abattoir when I was younger.'

'This is no abattoir,' boomed Baldur.

There was a white sheet covering the corpse. Baldur lifted it back, and they saw the instant recognition on the wholesaler's face.

'Yes, that's him. No question. Hardly surprising I couldn't get in touch with him, is it?' He seemed to feel compelled to lighten the atmosphere.

'Who is he?' asked Flóvent. 'What's his name?'

'Eyvindur,' replied the wholesaler. 'I knew he'd come back to town on the *Súd*, but I had no idea he'd ended up here with you.'

'Eyvindur?'

'Yes, the poor chap,' said the wholesaler. 'One of the worst sales-men I've ever had,' he added, inadvertently showering the body with ash from his cigar.

She got up off the mattress and wriggled back into her knickers, put on her bra, slipped her dress over her snaking locks and smoothed it down, then looked at him with those large, quizzical eyes that missed nothing but suspected so much.

'It happens to everyone, darling,' she said, but she didn't sound very convincing. 'Don't worry about it. This place doesn't exactly help. I wish I could have offered you something better.'

Thorson glanced briefly around the shed, then buttoned up his trousers and pulled on his shirt, wishing the floor would swallow him up. He mumbled something and tripped over a pile of nets as he slunk out into the August night, then hurried back to his room at Hótel Borg.

18

Flóvent saw at once that something was missing from the flat. He realised what it was when he opened the wardrobe in the bedroom and noticed that all the clothes were gone from one side. Then he remembered what the wholesaler had said about the woman Eyvindur lived with: that she hadn't been home either when he called round. He checked the cupboard in the hall. Same story. Only men's clothing. He surveyed the flat. From all the small touches that were absent, it was plain that there wasn't a woman living there now.

Apart from that the wholesaler hadn't been a great deal of help. He knew little about Eyvindur, though he was able to tell them that his patronymic was Ragnarsson and that he had worked for him for nearly a year, undertaking numerous sales trips during that time. The fruits of these trips had been pretty meagre, though the wholesaler admitted that he hadn't always given Eyvindur the best or easiest goods to shift. He believed the man was honest, though he had admittedly suspected him of theft when he hadn't shown up after his latest trip. He also told them that Eyvindur lived with a woman – Vera he thought her name was – but she hadn't been home in the last few days when he had gone round to their flat. He'd heard a rumour that she'd left Eyvindur.

They weren't married, as far as the wholesaler knew, and had no children. But Eyvindur never used to speak about himself, except when he complained about the presence of the occupation force and said there was no way he would ever work for British imperialists. Still less for American capitalists. Mind you, he hadn't been any better disposed towards the Germans. The wholesaler had heard him roundly cursing the Nazis too.

There had been nothing out of the ordinary about Eyvindur's last sales trip, or any of his other trips, for that matter. He generally sailed with the coaster *Súd* and went ashore at selected destinations; he would stay for a few days before returning with the boat and reporting back with the proceeds and orders, if there were any. So his employer couldn't begin to imagine who would have possibly wanted him out of the way. He had been an innocent soul, as the wholesaler put it – never hurt a fly, to the best of his knowledge. Why he should have been round at Felix Lunden's flat was a mystery to him. Of course they were both commercial travellers, but he wasn't aware that they knew each other outside work. The wholesaler knew who Felix was, but only by reputation. He worked for another company, he explained and supplied a name, which Flóvent committed to memory.

Too impatient to wait until morning to examine the victim's flat, Flóvent went straight from the mortuary to the address, which the wholesaler had given him, in the west of town. He saw no need to bring in Thorson at this stage, but called out a locksmith who worked for the police when required. The man picked the lock in no time, then went home again, leaving Flóvent alone in the flat. Sparsely and shabbily furnished, it consisted of a small living room and kitchen, a bedroom and a WC. Nothing new, nothing modern. Clearly the couple who lived there had been hard up. There were three photographs on a chest of drawers, two of them portraits of old people, the third a picture of a young couple that was a little out of focus – Eyvindur and Vera themselves, Flóvent guessed.

'Why did you jump to the conclusion that Eyvindur had stolen from you?' Flóvent had asked the wholesaler as they were saying goodbye outside the mortuary. 'Had he ever done that before?'

'Good God, no. But I was owed some money by a client in the West Fjords and I'd asked Eyvindur to call in the debt. I know for certain that he received the money, so, when I couldn't get hold of him, naturally the possibility crossed my mind. But as far as I know Eyvindur was as honest as the day is long.'

'Would he have been carrying money, then?'

'Well, it wasn't a large amount,' said the wholesaler. 'Perhaps he spent it. But you'll let me know if you find anything among his possessions, won't you?'

Flóvent found Eyvindur's wallet on the kitchen table. It contained nothing but small change. He searched the flat for the wholesaler's money but couldn't find it. There hadn't been any cash on the body either, and he wondered if Eyvindur could have been murdered for a handful of krónur from the West Fjords. The notion seemed far-fetched. He had no reason to suspect the wholesaler – the man seemed honest enough – but Flóvent knew he shouldn't eliminate him from his enquiries. Could he have killed Eyvindur over a paltry sum like that? Was his concern for the salesman a front? He could have reported Eyvindur to the police with the intention of putting them off the scent. Such a ploy wasn't unheard of. Sometimes the best place to hide was in plain sight.

The only interesting discovery Flóvent made during this preliminary inspection of the flat was a small crumpled brown envelope, half hidden under the battered sofa in the living room, as if someone had chucked it there. When he smoothed it out, he realised what it was; he'd come across that sort of thing before, and tried but failed to understand the writing on it: *Individual Chemical Prophylactic Packet.* The envelope had contained what was popularly known by the soldiers as an EPT kit. This one was empty but there should have been a sheet of directions, a soap-impregnated cloth, a cleansing tissue and five grams of antiseptic ointment for application to the genitals. The kits, which were issued to the troops on a regular basis, were intended to provide protection against venereal disease.

Flóvent pocketed the envelope and searched for further clues about the woman who had been living with Eyvindur but seemed to have vanished from his life. He studied the blurred photo again and was just hunting for any letters or messages when he heard a noise outside in the hallway. He went out to see what was going on and found a man wrestling with the door of the flat opposite. 'Damn it,' he heard the man say with a sigh, and saw that he was trying, rather ineffectually, to free the key that had jammed in the lock. The man nearly jumped out of his skin when he saw Flóvent emerging from Eyvindur's flat.

'Wh ... what ... Who are you?' he stammered, gaping at Flóvent in alarm.

'I'm from the police. Do you live here?'

'Well . . . yes, I . . . I'm having a bit of trouble with the key,' said the man, turning back to the lock. Flóvent reckoned he was drunk, too drunk to open his own front door without a struggle. 'I had a new key cut,' the man explained, 'but it sometimes gets stuck in the lock. Are the police looking . . . looking for Eyvindur, then?'

'Have you seen him recently?' asked Flóvent, deliberately withholding the news of Eyvindur's fate. A reek of spirits filled the hallway.

'No, I haven't a clue where he is. You should talk to his uncle. He owns the flat. He might know something.'

'Has he been round here looking for him? Have people been asking after him, that you're aware?'

'No, only the fellow with the cigar. Said he was a wholesaler. I haven't seen anyone else.'

'What about the woman who used to live with him? Vera, wasn't it? Have you seen her at all recently?'

'Oh, no, I haven't seen Vera for a while.'

'Do you know anything about her?'

'No more than anyone else who lives here. Poor old Eyvindur was at his wits' end . . . asking all the other tenants in the building about her, if we'd noticed when she moved out. He was a bit . . . a bit down in the dumps about it, as you might expect. *She* knew – the woman who lives above me, that is. She told him. Saw the whole thing . . . saw a black car outside late at night. Vera threw her belongings inside and then she was gone. Without a word to anyone.'

'You don't happen to know where she went? You, or any of your neighbours?'

'No, well . . . no, not really . . . but . . .'

'Yes?'

113

'I thought maybe poor Eyvindur had gone to the camps to look for her. That was my first thought.'

'The camps? You mean the military camps? Why would he have done that?'

'I thought maybe she'd left him on account of those soldiers who've been prowling around here . . . around the house,' said the man. 'I didn't tell Eyvindur about that. Didn't think . . . didn't think it was any of my business. I reckon they were visiting her, though. I assumed they must be. Saw them . . . saw them mooning up at her window.'

'What did they want from her?' asked Flóvent.

'A good time, I expect,' said the man. 'You used to hear gramophone music.'

'Were they British? American?'

'The ones I saw? One was British.' The man sounded sure of himself. 'A British soldier but . . . but there were others as well . . . I don't know any more about it, you understand. Only, she told us – the woman who saw Vera sneaking out like a thief . . . like a thief in the night – that the man who picked her up was British. A Tommy. Obviously one of her soldier friends. Some soldier she'd bagged herself.'

When Flóvent finally got home around midnight he found his father asleep on the sofa in the living room. Flóvent tried not to wake him but, sensing his presence, his father opened his eyes, sat up and asked wryly if he was trying to work himself to death. They ate the reheated meal at the kitchen table and chatted quietly for a while before going to bed. Flóvent shared the details of the case with his father because he trusted him to keep a secret and knew that the old man liked to hear about the more complex investigations that came his way. He had often proved a helpful listener, though he worried at times that his son pushed himself too hard. He knew how conscientious Flóvent was and how he took much of the ugliness he saw in his job to heart – but never spoke of it, a habit he had learnt as a boy during the harrowing days of the Spanish flu.

'Travelling salesmen?' he said, after listening to his son's account.

'Yes, travelling salesmen.'

'Could they have fallen out, this Felix and what was his name . . . Eyvindur?'

'It's possible.'

'And the upshot was that this Felix shot the other man in the head?'

'Maybe. We simply don't know.'

'What did they quarrel about? Their turf?'

'It has to have been something more important than that,' said Flóvent. 'Something that really mattered.'

'What really matters?' asked his father.

'Well, women, I suppose.'

'Yes, can't deny that.'

'We're told that the woman who was living with Eyvindur was no better than she ought to be. Her neighbour mentioned that she'd been hanging around with soldiers. That she was seen leaving in a car with one.'

'Is she mixed up in the Situation, then?'

'Looks like it.'

'Her boyfriend can't have been too happy about that.'

'No, I don't suppose he was,' said Flóvent, picturing the body of the salesman in the the mortuary. 'I don't suppose he was.'

'What about you?'

'Me?'

'Are you looking around at all?'

The question was tactfully phrased, prompted not by a desire to pry but by the loneliness the old man had endured ever since his wife had died, a loneliness he wouldn't wish on his son.

'No time for that.' Flóvent smiled.

'I hope you're not worried about me. I can look after myself. You know that.'

'Of course.'

'I wouldn't want to get in your way.'

'You're not.'

'The woman from the shop that you . . . are you still interested in her?'

'I'd rather not discuss it.'

'All right, son.'

19

Eyvindur's neighbours spoke well of him. He was a quiet, sober tenant who kept himself to himself, polite but unsociable, and they were deeply shocked to hear that he was the man who had been murdered. To be sure, he had been away a fair amount because of his job and hadn't lived there very long, but they had only good things to say about him. It was a different story with Vera. They didn't know where she was now, but they had noticed some funny goings-on during Eyvindur's absences: visitors who came and went under cover of darkness, stones thrown at windows, muffled voices in the early hours, doors slamming and quick footsteps retreating along the pavement outside. She could be touchy too, that Vera, and had a sharp tongue, so no one had dared to speak to her about it. None of them had breathed a word to Eyvindur about the night visitors until after she'd gone.

The woman from upstairs claimed that the couple had had a violent row just before Eyvindur left for his last trip, and Vera had walked out on him. The woman had witnessed the incident, seen Eyvindur leaving the flat, his face scarlet. He had managed a flustered greeting, then hurried off, carrying his two suitcases, in the direction of the harbour. Although she didn't know what the quarrel had been about, she suspected it might have had something to do with the guests who came round while he was away. Vera had done most of the shouting; there had only been the odd peep out of Eyvindur – then he was off.

'They weren't even married,' the neighbour said, tutting. 'She's no better than a slut, that girl.'

'So you don't approve of her, ma'am?' said Flóvent.

'She's such a little madam,' said the woman, her voice thick with disgust. 'Like she thinks she's better than other people, that . . . that soldier's whore.'

'You say you saw him leave, ma'am?' said Flóvent. 'Were you in the hall outside their flat at the time?'

The woman hesitated just long enough for Flóvent to suspect that she had been listening with her ear to their door. She looked as if nothing that happened in the house, night or day, got past her. Nosy. Censorious.

'I . . . happened to be passing,' she said after a pause.

'Did you hear what they were arguing about?'

'No, that is . . . how was I supposed to do that? I was on my way upstairs to my flat. I couldn't hear anything. Not a thing. Just the noise she was making. But I couldn't make out a word.'

'So you didn't hear them mention the name Felix?'

'No, didn't I just tell you that all I heard was shouting? Not what it was about.'

'I understand Vera entertained guests, soldiers perhaps, while Eyvindur was away,' said Thorson. He had accompanied Flóvent

118

on this second visit to the flat, and heard all about the wholesaler's identification of Eyvindur's body and about Flóvent's visit the previous evening.

'You can say that again.'

'It wasn't always the same men?'

'No, it wasn't always the same men that I saw. I told her – told her I wouldn't put up with sordid goings-on like that in this house.'

'Sordid goings-on?'

'It was obvious,' the woman said, her face tightening oddly.

'What was?'

'Well, you can see for yourself – the girl was working as a whore! She had the barefaced cheek to turn these premises into a soldiers' brothel. Why else would they have come round to see her? To drink tea? Do you think she was hosting little tea parties?'

'You believe she was working as a prostitute?'

'Yes, what else would she have been up to? She's sex mad, that girl, and she finally found a way to make some money out of it.'

Flóvent and Thorson exchanged discreet glances. The woman had worked herself up into quite a state and made no attempt to disguise the violent antipathy she felt towards her former neighbour. Flóvent had shown Thorson the small brown envelope he had found under the sofa. Thorson wasn't surprised that one of these should have turned up if it was true that Vera was providing services for soldiers.

'What did she say when you accused her of this?' asked Flóvent.

'*Accused* her? Do you think I'm lying?'

'No,' said Flóvent. 'Of course not. But didn't she protest? Or . . . ?'

'She didn't say a word. Apart from telling me to shut my

face – that it was none of my business what she chose to do in her own home. I said I'd see to it that her den of vice was closed down. Next thing I knew she'd moved out – in the dead of night.'

'Can you describe the man who came to pick her up?' asked Thorson. 'We understand that you saw her go out to the vehicle.'

'No, it was dark, but I could tell he was in the army,' said the woman. 'I reckon he could have been British but he never got out of the car, so I didn't get a proper look at him. He didn't lift a finger to help her.'

'And she was carrying clothes and other belongings from the flat that she loaded into the car?'

'Yes, that's right, made two or three trips, then took off with him.'

'Did you see what kind of vehicle it was? The model? Or licence plate?'

'No. I know nothing about cars. It was black.'

'Not a military vehicle, then?'

'No, I don't think so. But I wouldn't know. I hear she's started doing their washing for them. The soldiers, I mean. Opened a laundry.'

The woman told them how several days ago Eyvindur had returned home only to discover that Vera had moved out. He had taken it very hard and gone round asking everyone in the house about Vera's movements. Well, he'd learnt from her what his girlfriend had been up to, though of course she'd tried to break it to him gently – it wasn't her job to interfere in their private life. It wasn't easy having to tell him about Vera's visitors. Eyvindur hadn't believed her. He'd called her a liar and sworn that Vera wasn't like that. Then he'd locked himself away and wouldn't speak to anyone else in the building. And to make matters worse, the landlord, his uncle, had come round and told him, out there in the hallway where everyone could hear, that he would have to move out.

'Apparently he owed him several months' rent,' said the woman. Her tone made it clear that her sympathies lay with Eyvindur. 'He was always having some kind of money trouble. Never had a króna to his name.'

'When did you last see him, ma'am?' asked Flóvent.

'It must have been when the landlord was giving him a piece of his mind,' said the woman, counting up the days that had passed. Flóvent guessed this must have been the day before Eyvindur's body was found.

They thanked her for her assistance and returned to Eyvindur's flat. There on the floor, in plain sight, was the answer to one of the many questions that had been troubling them since the discovery of the body: two suitcases, labelled with Eyvindur Ragnarsson's name. They turned out, on closer inspection, to contain samples of the wholesaler's wares: shoe polish, Poliflor, and a dinner service, but nothing untoward. No pills hidden in the lining. Both cases were battered, one of them held together only by two pieces of string.

'So the suitcase you found in the other flat definitely belonged to Felix?' said Thorson.

'Yes, I think we can safely assume that,' said Flóvent. 'Which means the capsule's his as well.'

After they had searched the flat thoroughly for any clues that might explain why Eyvindur had been murdered, Flóvent turned his attention to some papers that Thorson had dragged out of a small store cupboard next to the kitchen. The papers were brown and brittle with age, tied together with string. The cupboard was full of all kinds of other junk, including two pairs of skis and a trunk, which proved to be unlocked. When Thorson opened it, he found old clothes and books, including two dog-eared hymn-books, and a photograph. Thorson picked up the photograph carefully. It was an old studio portrait of an elderly couple in their Sunday best, the man sporting a full beard. They stared back at Thorson from the depths of time, solemn and a little mistrustful. Underneath the photograph was an anniversary publication from Ebeneser's school, a four-page pamphlet containing two photographs. One was taken outdoors and showed four adolescent boys with two men and a woman standing a little behind them. Three of the boys were rather shabbily dressed and two of them were wearing caps pulled down over their eyes. The men wore dark suits and one of them had a hat on. The woman stood out because she was wearing the uniform of her profession, a nurse's costume with a starched white cap on her head and a cape over her shoulders.

Thorson could have sworn he knew one of the men, though he looked considerably younger in the picture. He was the one without a hat, and his features were instantly recognisable. Thorson peered at the boys' faces, trying to see if any of them could be Eyvindur, but the picture wasn't very clear, and his only point of comparison was the badly disfigured face in the mortuary.

'What have you got there?' asked Flóvent, sticking his head into the cubbyhole.

Thorson handed him the photograph and the pamphlet. Flóvent studied the picture of the old couple, who stared solemnly into the lens as if the camera were some incomprehensible magic box. Then he examined the photo of the boys with the adults standing behind them.

'Recognise him?' asked Thorson.

'Isn't that the headmaster?' said Flóvent. 'Isn't that Ebeneser, who we met yesterday?'

'Looks like it to me,' said Thorson. 'A little younger, of course. Could the picture have been taken at the school? You can only see the corner of a building, but it certainly looks pretty large.'

Flóvent didn't seem to have heard. He was staring at the picture.

'Could it be her . . . ?' he muttered to himself.

'Who? Do you know the other people in the photo?' asked Thorson. 'And the old couple?'

'I could have sworn I'd seen that woman before,' said Flóvent, pointing at the nurse. 'I'm sure it's her.'

'Who is she?' asked Thorson.

'I wonder,' Flóvent muttered. 'I only saw her for a second but . . .'

'Who? Who is she?'

'I saw her at Rudolf's house. She was watching me from the drawing-room window but quickly pulled the curtain. It's definitely the same woman. I don't know her name but she was at Rudolf Lunden's house.' Flóvent studied the photograph again. 'I'm positive it's the same woman.'

He peered at the boys' faces. 'Do you suppose one of them's Eyvindur?'

'He must have had some reason for hanging on to the leaflet,' said Thorson.

'She might have a better idea of what Ebeneser and Rudolf were quarrelling about,' said Flóvent, brushing his finger over the woman's face.

'When they were arguing about the boys?'

'Yes. When they were arguing about the boys. Perhaps she could shed some light on that.'

They both got the shock of their lives when the door of the flat suddenly opened with a bang and a man appeared in the doorway. On catching sight of two men in the living room, he stormed towards them with a face like thunder.

'What the hell are you doing in here?' he demanded, glowering at Thorson. 'I won't have any soldiers in this house. Did Vera send you? Are you looking for her? Is it that slut you're after?'

20

For a moment they didn't know what had hit them. Then Flóvent set about trying to placate the man, explaining repeatedly that they were policemen investigating Eyvindur's murder, and that Thorson was there on behalf of the military police. The man turned out to be Eyvindur's uncle, the landlord. He wanted to rent the flat out again immediately. 'No reason to wait,' he said, a little shamefaced. He had only just learnt of his nephew's death and all he seemed to care about was finding a new tenant. The demand for housing in the city was growing by the day, he explained apologetically, and he didn't want to waste any time – although of course it was shocking news about his nephew. 'But life goes on. What can I say? There's no point letting the place stand empty – as long as you don't object? The police, I mean.'

Flóvent told him they saw no reason why he shouldn't rent out the flat again as soon as he liked. The uncle explained that he was going to put Eyvindur's possessions in storage and perhaps try to sell some of them to make up for the rent he had owed.

'Eyvindur always had trouble keeping up with his payments,' the uncle said. He was a tall man in his fifties, with a deep voice and a no-nonsense manner, who knew his own mind and clearly didn't suffer fools gladly. His name was Sigfús. 'If it had been anyone but my boy Eyvindur, I'd have thrown him out long ago,' he added, as if to show belatedly that he had cared a little for his nephew.

Flóvent told him that the police had tried to contact Eyvindur's next-of-kin but despite their best efforts to track down his family, they hadn't managed to find any other relatives. The uncle confirmed that there weren't any. Eyvindur had no children and that wretched woman had walked out on him. He didn't have any brothers or sisters either, and his parents had both passed away.

'Are you any closer to finding out who killed him?' asked Sigfús, adding that he had been stunned when he'd heard that his nephew had been murdered. Eyvindur was the last person he would have expected to suffer such a violent fate. 'A harmless lad. I wasn't aware that he had an enemy in the world,' he said.

'No, the motive's not clear,' said Flóvent.

'He was always rather alone in the world, poor lad. Had a tough time of it. I let him live here for a song, considering what I could have charged these days. If I'd known what she . . . what that Vera was up to while he was away, carrying on her sordid trade here, I'd have thrown her out.'

'Do you by any chance know where she is, sir?'

'No need for formality, young man – and no, I don't, and I don't want to. She can go to the devil, for all I care. Isn't she behind this whole thing? I never liked her. Never. Wasn't this just her way of getting rid of the boy? They said on the wireless that he'd been shot with a soldier's pistol.'

'Yes, but –'

'Isn't it obvious then?' asked the uncle, addressing Thorson now. 'Wasn't it one of you lot? Isn't that . . . so-called army of yours nothing but a parcel of murderers and good-for-nothings? She must have talked one of them into shooting my nephew. It wouldn't have been difficult. She wanted to carry on her whoring in peace. Eyvindur must have been pestering her, begging her to come back, so she egged on some soldier-boy to get rid of him. Isn't that the most likely story?'

'Do you know if your nephew had any dealings with the military?' asked Thorson, ignoring the man's conjecture. It was obvious that he had a grudge against the occupation force. This was nothing new.

'As far as I know, he had nothing to do with them. But Vera, on the other hand . . . She seems to have been busy keeping them happy and earning a bit of money on the side.'

'Did Eyvindur ever mention this? That he was afraid of Vera? Of what she might do to him?'

'No. Eyvindur would never have done anything to upset her. She had him completely under her thumb. Bit of a doormat, he was. Let her push him around. Hardly drew breath without asking her permission. I reckon it was her that persuaded him to go in for this sales racket. Ordered him, more like. I could tell from the way he talked about it. She wanted him out of her hair, said he was smothering her. Of course, she only did it to get him out of the way, so she could carry on with her whoring in peace. Eyvindur was no salesman. He said so himself.'

'When did he say that?'

'Not that long ago. He was paying me part of the rent he owed, and said he didn't have much money and that Vera was always complaining. There was all sorts of stuff she wanted. I felt a bit sorry for the lad as he was already months behind with his rent. None of my other tenants would have got away with that. I thought of using him as a rent collector, but I knew he'd be hopeless. People would laugh in his face. Strange, that. They wouldn't have laughed at my brother.'

'At Eyvindur's father, you mean?'

'Ragnar Ragnarsson. You ought to recognise the name if you're not a complete greenhorn.'

'Ragnar Ragnarsson? You don't mean . . . ?'

'Spent years behind bars. You ought to know who he was.'

Flóvent did indeed recognise the name and remembered having to deal with the man in his early days with the force. Recalled an ugly, powerfully built thug with tattoos up both arms. An arrest after a violent brawl at a drinking hole. A charge for assault. Ragnar had gone berserk when the police arrested him. His victim, a younger man, had been in a state of shock, more dead than alive when they reached the scene and got him to a doctor. He hadn't known his assailant from Adam. Flóvent also remembered other occasions when Ragnar Ragnarsson had come to the attention of the police. Smuggling, burglaries, beatings. Then suddenly he was gone. Fell ill while serving a lengthy sentence. There had been a delay in calling out a doctor and by the time they got him to hospital he was dead. Flóvent heard later that it was a blood clot in the brain that had killed him.

'I remember him well,' he said, unable to hide his surprise. 'You mean *he* was Eyvindur's father?'

'You wouldn't exactly say Eyvindur was a chip off the old block,' said Sigfús. 'I've never met two men more different than Eyvindur and his father. I'd swear that boy didn't have a drop of his blood. And the lad paid the price for that.'

'Of course, Ragnar was a bully and a jail—'

'Careful how you talk about him. I know he was no angel, but he was still my brother.'

'No angel?' Flóvent repeated. 'He was a vicious brute. No one shed a tear at the station when they heard he'd kicked the bucket. It just meant one less thug on the streets.'

'Well, say what you like,' said Sigfús, 'I'm not going to argue with you. What have you got there? Are those Eyvindur's photographs?'

Flóvent passed him the photograph they had found in the trunk, and Sigfús said it was of his own parents, a farming couple who had only visited Reykjavík once in their lives and had the photograph taken as a souvenir. The school anniversary booklet was new to him, though, and so was the photograph it featured, though he immediately identified Eyvindur as one of the two bareheaded boys.

'We believe one of the adults is the headmaster, Ebeneser,' said Flóvent. 'Do you have any idea who the other people are?'

'No, I . . . Isn't that a nurse?'

'We think so.'

'I seem to remember Eyvindur talking about a nurse at his school. I used to have him to stay when . . . when things were difficult at home.'

'What did he have to say about her?'

'Oh, only that there was a woman there who was kind to him,' said Sigfús. 'No more than that. I have a feeling it was the nurse.'

'Do you remember her name?'

'No, I don't. Don't recall if he ever told me her name. Only that she treated him well. Was kind to him. They weren't all kind. I expect that's why he talked about it. It wasn't what he was used to at home, poor lad. Totally neglected, he was. Crawling with lice the times I looked after him.'

'What about his mother?' asked Thorson.

'She died before he was confirmed. Didn't take much notice of him when she was alive, mind you. She was a drunk. But then the wretched woman didn't have an easy time of it with my brother.' Sigfús looked back at the picture. 'This boy here . . . ' he said thoughtfully, pointing at the other bareheaded pupil.

'Yes?'

'He used to knock around with Eyvindur a bit. If I remember right, they used to play together sometimes when the lad was living with me. A foreigner, or he had a foreign sort of name, at any rate.'

'Could it have been Lunden? Felix Lunden?'

'Felix? Yes, damn it, that was it.'

'You mean he and Eyvindur were at the same school?'

'I think so, yes. As far as I can tell, that's him – the Lunden boy.'

'Have you heard where your nephew's body was found?' asked Flóvent.

'Yes, in some flat here in town. I was going to ask you about that. Round at some other salesman's place, wasn't it?'

'It was at the home of a man called Felix Lunden.'

Sigfús stared at Flóvent as if he couldn't believe his ears. 'What are you saying? Is it . . . was it him who shot Eyvindur?'

'We don't know.'

'Isn't it as plain as day? Where is he? Where is this Felix?'

'We don't know that either.'

'Is he . . . has he gone into hiding? Damn it to hell! It was him, wasn't it? He was the one who killed Eyvindur!'

21

There was no answer when they knocked at Rudolf Lunden's door. Flóvent pressed his face to the windows but couldn't see any movement inside. Thorson did a circuit of the house but saw no sign of life. The place was locked up and lightless, as if no one had ever lived there. Not even the mild August sun could soften the cold, dark pebble-dash of its walls.

Having drawn a blank, they headed over to the headmaster's house, only to be told that he was at the school. His wife smiled at these two policemen who had come to see her husband, her eyes flickering towards Thorson's uniform. In spite of her friendly manner she couldn't conceal her surprise. It appeared that Ebeneser hadn't told her about their visit the day before. She made polite but determined efforts to discover why they wanted to see him, but they gave nothing away.

Eyvindur's uncle had been unable to tell them any more about his nephew's friendship with Felix Lunden. Eyvindur hadn't had many friends, he said, and it was rare for anyone to come round to see him. And Eyvindur hadn't wanted them to anyway. He was ashamed of his home and afraid of his father.

'Ragnar used to raise his fist to the lad,' Sigfús had said as they were parting, and they sensed his growing reluctance to talk about his brother. 'Nothing serious, as these things go,' he continued, 'though I suppose that sort of thing's always serious. Eyvindur was, well, he was scared of Ragnar. That's another reason why I let him stay with me.'

'Were they good friends, Eyvindur and Felix?'

'I expect so, good enough,' said Sigfús. 'At least, I remember they used to knock around together.'

'Did Eyvindur ever mention Felix again after they left school? Recently, for instance? Do you know if they kept in touch?'

'No, I never heard Eyvindur talk about him.'

That was all they could prise out of the man. Following this encounter, Flóvent was keen to speak to the woman he'd caught sight of in Rudolf's window, to ask her when the photograph had been taken and why, and he wanted to hear about her dealings with Eyvindur as a boy. He and Thorson both felt that Eyvindur and Felix's old friendship could hold the key to the mystery – why Eyvindur had been murdered in the flat of 'the Lunden boy', as the uncle called him, and why Felix had fled.

'Why was a doctor's son playing with a lice-ridden boy from a bad home?' asked Thorson after they had taken their leave of Ebeneser's wife. 'The son of a violent convict and an unfit mother?'

'It's not so unlikely in this town,' said Flóvent. 'We're a small community, and people are connected in a variety of ways, though the class divisions here are bigger than many are willing to admit.

Their paths are bound to have crossed later on as well, as adults. Especially once they both started working in the same business.'

'And it all ends with Eyvindur getting shot in the head?'

'Yes, it ends in disaster.'

'Surely the most likely explanation is that Felix shot him?'

'Yes, I think that's very likely.'

'Eyvindur must have got hold of a key to his flat.'

'Maybe.'

'And Felix caught him in the act . . . ?'

They finally located Ebeneser in a classroom at the school. He was bending down behind the teacher's desk and nearly jumped out of his skin when the two of them walked in without warning. The classroom was on the small side; all the furniture was designed for the youngest boys, and the three men were out of all proportion to the tiny desks and chairs.

'You . . . you here?' stammered Ebeneser, hurriedly straightening up. 'I thought . . . I thought I'd answered all your questions?'

'Yes, I just need to run a few more things past you,' said Flóvent, shaking his hand and noticing, as he did so, that the other man's palm was clammy. The headmaster didn't look much better than he had on his return from his fishing trip. His hair was still tousled, he was unshaven and his suit could have done with a clean. At that moment a bottle of *brennivín* rolled out from under the teacher's desk and came to a halt against one of the legs with a loud clunk.

'Aha . . . there . . . there it is,' said Ebeneser quickly, as though he had caught somebody out. 'That sort of thing has no place here.' Hastily he stooped to pick up the bottle. 'We can't be having that. Unfortunately . . . I knew he kept it here, you see . . . or I . . . that is, I suspected him . . . of having it, and yes, here it . . . so

134

that's clear then.' He placed the bottle on the desk. Then, thinking better of it, shoved it in a drawer.

Flóvent didn't think Ebeneser had been drinking. If he had, he hid it well. But they had obviously walked in on the headmaster at an awkward moment. Flóvent behaved as if he hadn't noticed anything: he wanted to keep Ebeneser sweet. Thorson adopted the same approach. They allowed him to stage this little play without comment; after all, it was none of their business.

'We're trying to, er . . . trying to get to grips with the problem,' said Ebeneser, pulling himself together. 'I'm sorry you had to witness that. The master in question . . . he . . . well, never mind, I wasn't . . . really wasn't expecting to see you here, to be honest. You've a knack of taking one by surprise.'

'We heard you were here,' Flóvent explained, suddenly remembering that he hadn't had a moment to check Ebeneser's alibi. He reminded himself to remedy this the first chance he got.

'Was Felix a pupil at this school?' asked Thorson.

'Felix was here, yes.'

'You taught him yourself, maybe?'

'Yes, on occasion.'

'Was he a good pupil?'

'He was an exceptional pupil.'

'He had a promising future, then?'

'Yes, that's fair to say.'

'Yet he ended up as a travelling salesman?'

Ebeneser hesitated, unsure how to take this comment.

'Weren't people expecting a little more from him?' asked Flóvent. 'With all due respect to salesmen, of course. His occupation must have been rather a disappointment to his family. Wouldn't you agree?'

'I imagine his father expected more of him, yes, probably. If that's what you mean.'

'But it didn't do any good?'

'Felix tried to continue his education but didn't seem to . . . er . . . have what it took any more. He left Reykjavík College without taking his exams and went abroad. To Denmark. To his father's family. I thought I'd already told you that. He didn't complete his education there either.'

'Do you remember a pupil of yours called Eyvindur?' asked Flóvent. 'Eyvindur Ragnarsson? He would have been about Felix's age.'

Ebeneser thought. He was recovering his composure. 'Eyvindur Ragnarsson? Yes, I remember a boy by that name. He was a pupil here about ten years ago, if memory serves. At the same time as Felix. He had a tough time of it, the poor boy. A difficult home. His father –'

'Yes, we know all about Ragnar,' said Flóvent.

'He was a nasty piece of work,' Ebeneser went on. 'An out-and-out criminal. From what I recall, Eyvindur had to be taken away from his parents – temporarily, at least – on more than one occasion. There was always trouble at home. The child welfare authorities had to be brought in. They were forever having to intervene. His mother wasn't fit to look after him.'

'Do you remember her?'

'Not really. She was never around for Eyvindur. Nor was his father, of course. Appalling neglect, I'm afraid. One of the worst cases we've seen at this school.'

'Forgive me for jumping from one thing to another, but why did you say that Felix no longer had what it took?'

'I'm sorry?'

'You said Felix had tried to continue his education at Reykjavík College but didn't have what it took *any more*. What did you mean by that? Did he have what it took before? If so, what changed?'

Ebeneser said he didn't follow. He eyed the drawer containing the *brennivín* bottle as if he wished they would go away and leave him to carry on where he had left off. He was afraid he couldn't help them, he said. He was due at a meeting. If they wanted to discuss these matters further – though why they should was a mystery to him – it would be better if they called and arranged an appointment. He could receive them at the school or at his house at a time that suited them. But now, alas, he was busy, if they would be so kind . . .

Ebeneser prepared to leave the room. Although the man's discomfort was plain, Flóvent still hadn't obtained the information he was after. 'But we haven't discussed the boys yet,' he said.

'The boys?' said Ebeneser confused. 'What boys?'

'I don't know,' said Flóvent. 'I was hoping you could enlighten me.'

'Which boys are you referring to?'

'The boys you were arguing about with Rudolf Lunden.'

22

Ebeneser stared at Flóvent without saying a word. As Flóvent waited patiently for an answer the silence in the little classroom grew more and more oppressive. The three of them seemed to be the only people in the building. There were still a few weeks left before term began and the corridors filled again with children, sunburnt and boisterous after their long summer break. At this time of year the building was cold and silent. It gave Flóvent such a strange empty feeling, walking through the echoing corridors of a school during the summer holidays.

'I . . . I'm afraid I'm not with you,' said the headmaster eventually, folding his arms.

'You said you hadn't seen Rudolf lately but we happen to know that's not true,' said Flóvent. 'We know you went to his house recently and we'd be grateful if you'd tell us more about your meeting.'

'I . . . as I said, I can't help you with that . . .'

'You did meet?'

'Well, since you're so determined to have an answer,' said Ebeneser, who seemed to have finally made up his mind about what to say, 'we did meet briefly the other day. I didn't think there was any need to mention it because . . . he . . . It concerned a private matter that I don't believe is any of your business. I don't know where you got your information from, but it's not unusual for me to talk to Rudolf. He's my brother-in-law. Did he tell you about our meeting?'

'Is it unusual for you to avoid talking about it?' chipped in Thorson. 'You seem very reluctant to do so.'

'No, it's not that I'm reluctant. To be frank, it's simply none of your business,' said Ebeneser, on a firmer note. 'Look, can we bring this to a close? I'm extremely busy.'

'In a minute,' said Flóvent. 'What did you two discuss? Your nephew Felix? Who were the boys you were talking about?'

'There must be some misunderstanding,' said Ebeneser. 'We weren't talking about any boys. Would you mind telling me if you heard that from Rudolf himself? Not that I understand why he would have said such a thing. Where did you get your information?'

'What *did* you quarrel about then?' asked Flóvent, his patience wearing thin. 'Your mutual enthusiasm for Nazism? I don't suppose there was much to argue about there. The party meetings you attended?'

Ebeneser looked affronted, as if such questions were unworthy of an answer. Flóvent contemplated hauling him in for questioning at the prison on Skólavördustígur if he remained obdurate, but abandoned the idea. He was probably making a mountain out of a molehill, and anyway it would attract unwelcome attention if news got out that a headmaster and former member of the Icelandic Nazi party was being held by the police in connection with

Felix Lunden's disappearance. Something more substantial than a refusal to cooperate would be required before he could justify resorting to such measures. Still, he decided to test the headmaster's patience a little further and pulled the school anniversary publication out of his pocket.

'Are these the boys you were quarrelling about?' he asked, pointing to the photograph.

Ebeneser took the pamphlet from him, his face impassive. He studied the people in the picture for a while before eventually asking where they had come across it. Flóvent explained that it had turned up in a trunk belonging to one of the boys in the photograph. He had recently died in a tragic incident. He was the man who was found dead in Felix Lunden's flat – shot in the head. 'It was Eyvindur,' he said.

'Eyvindur?' whispered the headmaster.

'Yes.'

'Was it him? He was the man found dead at Felix's place?'

'We finally managed to identify the body,' said Flóvent.

'But . . . Felix? Where is he?'

'We were hoping you might be able to help us answer that.'

'Was it Felix who shot him?' asked the headmaster.

'We have no other suspects at present,' said Flóvent.

Ebeneser continued to stare at the photograph. He appeared to be casting around in vain for the right words, and Flóvent sensed that he was growing increasingly flustered.

'Do you think something might have happened to Felix too?' Ebeneser asked, finding his voice at last.

'There's no evidence of that. Do you mean has he been murdered as well?'

'No, I'm not . . . I know nothing about Felix,' said Ebeneser, 'if you came here to ask me about him. I've no idea where he is. I have to say I find it unlikely that he would have committed a crime like that, but how would I know? Felix and I haven't had any contact for . . . for a long time and I don't know what he's been up to in recent years. You should ask Rudolf about that. I really don't think I have anything to add.'

'About the photograph . . .'

'I'd rather be alone now, if you don't mind. This isn't . . . this is bad news . . . terrible news for us. For our family, you understand. I'm . . . naturally I'm very upset about this. If what you say is true, if it's true that Felix is . . . guilty of an appalling crime like that, it's a dreadful shock for those of us closest to him.'

'We understand that,' said Flóvent. 'Could you tell us when the picture was taken? We need the names of the other people in the photo. And to know what the occasion was. If you could –'

'Do you think he's made a run for it? Felix, I mean?'

'Yes, it looks like it. At least we don't know any better. About the picture . . .'

'I'm afraid I can't be of much help,' said Ebeneser.

'Isn't that the school building we can see in the background?' prompted Thorson.

'Yes, it looks to me as if the photo was taken in the grounds here, for the anniversary publication,' said Ebeneser. 'Are you absolutely sure that Felix killed Eyvindur?'

'All the evidence points that way,' said Flóvent. 'Clearly they were at school together,' he said, taking the leaflet back from the headmaster. 'Do you know if they were friends?'

'No, I don't.'

'We have reason to believe that they were close at one time, whatever may have happened later.'

'Yes, it's possible. I simply don't know.'

'Could you tell us the names of the people in the picture?' Flóvent asked, holding it up to Ebeneser's face.

'Well, that's me, obviously, and that's Felix in front of me. Next to him is Eyvindur. Then there's the school nurse . . . and a teacher, who died several years ago. I don't recall the other two boys. I remember Eyvindur because he was . . . well, we had so many problems on account of his background. He was badly bullied. He couldn't stand up for himself in the playground. Are you absolutely sure it was him you found in Felix's flat?'

Flóvent nodded and supplied the additional detail that Eyvindur had been killed with the kind of pistol used by the American military, though the trail didn't seem to lead in that direction at present. He wasn't sure if he should mention the swastika drawn in blood. Few were aware of this detail as yet. But in the end he decided he might as well chance it. Ebeneser listened to what he had to say in horrified amazement, then replied that he couldn't imagine Felix doing such a thing. Or anyone else, for that matter.

'Do you think it's because they knew each other as boys?' Ebeneser asked tentatively, as if afraid of the answer. 'If it *was* Felix who shot him?'

'It's possible,' said Flóvent. 'Can you think why he would have done it? Were they good friends when they were young? They're standing side by side in this picture. They must have been fairly friendly.'

'I'm afraid I couldn't say.'

'What can you tell me about the nurse?' asked Flóvent, pointing at the picture again. 'Did she work at the school for long?'

'She worked here for several years, yes, and at other schools too.' Ebeneser fell silent.

'You must remember her well,' said Flóvent, 'but maybe you know her better from another context.'

Ebeneser coughed. 'I do, actually. She's been working for Rudolf Lunden for the last few years.'

'Quite,' said Flóvent. 'What exactly does she do?'

'Everything really,' said Ebeneser. 'She nurses him. Takes care of him. She's his housekeeper.'

'Does she live in?'

'Yes.'

'But they're not married or anything?'

'No, they're not married.'

'But they have a close relationship?'

'You'd have to ask them about that. Was it her who told you about the meeting? About my meeting with Rudolf?'

'No,' said Flóvent. 'By the way, I don't even know her name. Could you enlighten me?'

'Brynhildur,' said the headmaster. 'Her name's Brynhildur Hólm.'

23

The bandleader announced that they would be taking a twenty-minute break after the next tune, then launched into a jazz number with a lively trumpet line and an increasingly manic drumbeat that drove the dancers wild. When it ended, they poured off the dance floor, back to their tables. There was a new crush at the bar – soldiers mostly, shouting to each other, barging through the crowd, drinks held high, through the heat, the cigarette smoke, the roars of laughter.

The dance floor at Hótel Ísland was so packed that the doormen were turning newcomers away, Thorson among them. He had to resort to showing his police ID before they would let him in, along with two Icelandic girls who had been waiting ages to get in. He saw no sign of the Morality Committee. Thorson let himself be swept along by the press of people to the bar, and because he wanted a drink and was in no particular hurry, he stood there patiently, waiting for a bartender to notice him. The staff couldn't keep up.

He saw young women – their hair done up in elaborate victory rolls – in the company of soldiers, glimpsed red lips emitting infectious peals of laughter, sensed happy excitement shining from beneath tinted eyelashes. Thorson scanned the room but couldn't see his friend anywhere. She had told him she was from the sticks, from Keflavík, on the other side of the bay. When she was growing up she used to gaze across at Reykjavík casting its glow into the night sky, and tell herself that all life's adventures awaited her there, under that sea of lights. As soon as she was old enough, she left home, sailed across the bay and never looked back.

Thorson finished his drink and left. He bumped into a few acquaintances on his way out and they dragged him back to their table and tried to pour more booze down his neck, but he made his excuses, explaining that he was working, kind of. Someone pushed a glass of rum towards him. 'Come on, be a man, drink up!' He slipped away as the band started up again with a popular number. As everyone streamed back onto the dance floor, he disappeared outside into the darkness.

He headed for the net shed down by the harbour. It was at Hótel Ísland that their paths had first crossed. She had confided in him that Reykjavík hadn't turned out to be quite the fairy tale she had imagined. She was disenchanted. Yes, there were nicer shops, bigger buildings, more cars and more going on, but it still had the same suffocating small-town atmosphere as Keflavík. She had arrived during the Depression and taken a job as a maid for a large family, slaving away for demanding employers and earning a pittance. After two years she left her position and worked sporadically at fish-processing factories or doing odd jobs that she picked up here and there, working from dawn to dusk whenever she got the chance. She didn't mind the long hours. What mattered was that she was her own mistress, didn't have to answer to anyone. She moved in with a divorced bar owner but their relationship was on the rocks by the time the invasion force landed and the town filled with cheerily singing soldiers. Before long she started getting friendly with the British troops, one thing led to another, and she found herself earning money from these encounters. Her new friends paid for her nights out and her drinks as well. She wasn't ashamed of that. She was down-to-earth and honest. Thorson ventured to ask why she did it. He didn't want to hurt her feelings, let alone judge her; he just wanted to know what was going through her mind. His friend merely smiled, her expression strangely faraway and empty, as though she had never quite managed to catch hold of that tantalising new world that she had glimpsed in the city lights across the bay.

Thorson knew that plenty of women were the exact opposite. He was acquainted with a girl who worked at Hótel Borg, and even though he came from an Icelandic family and spoke the language fluently, he had found it hard to get to know her. His uniform was the problem. She wanted nothing to do with him or any other serviceman. Recently he had run into her outside the Ísafold printworks and stopped for a chat, only to notice that she seemed on edge and kept glancing around almost fearfully at the passers-by, before abruptly breaking off the conversation and scurrying away. Thorson knew it was because she didn't want to be seen talking to a soldier in the street, however briefly, and risk tarnishing her family's reputation. Gossip spread like wildfire in this town, none of it charitable.

Thorson reached the shed and peered in through a dirty windowpane but couldn't see anything. The door was locked. He was just turning away when he heard a rustle behind him.

'Want to try again, darling?'

Looking round, he saw that his friend had stolen up behind him. She blew out a cloud of cigarette smoke. Usually she was well groomed. Now the lipstick on her upper lip was smudged and her mascara had run down to mingle with her rouge. She was wearing nylon stockings and a flimsy dress, a khaki military jacket slung over her shoulders and a white sailor's cap on her head.

'No,' he said with an embarrassed smile.

'What are you doing here then?'

'I wanted to talk to you,' said Thorson. 'What are *you* doing here?'

'Waiting,' she said.

She burst out laughing and he realised she wasn't her usual self. He had never seen her in this state before. Never seen her so drunk.

'Are you OK?'

'Don't worry about me, darling,' she said. 'Why are you here? What do you want? To talk to me? I can't help you. You know that. You aren't that way inclined.'

'I'm looking for a woman,' said Thorson, anxious not to be reminded of their last encounter. 'I thought you might know her. Her name's Vera. I wanted to ask if you recognised the name.'

'What made you think I'd know her?'

'Because you're both . . . She may be involved with soldiers . . .'

'Do you find it difficult to say? You can say it. I am what I am. I've never tried to hide it.'

'Yes, well, she . . . she's said to be on friendly terms with soldiers.'

'On friendly terms with soldiers. What a polite way of putting it. And that's why you think I might know her?'

'I thought of asking you. In case you recognised the name.'

'Vera?'

'Yes. She left her boyfriend. Used to entertain guests at night when he was out of town. Soldiers.'

'I don't know her.'

'Maybe you could ask around about her? Ask your friends? It looks like she's taking in laundry for the troops. We're making enquiries, but that sort of thing takes time because there are so many women offering that kind of service.'

'Maybe you should talk to the ladies at Landakot Hospital.'

'Ladies . . . ?'

'The French nuns. We all end up there sooner or later.'

Thorson stared at her blankly.

'You've never had the clap, have you, darling?'

Just then, three US Marines appeared round the corner and headed in their direction. They were carrying beer and bottles of vodka and one of them had a carton of cigarettes.

'Were you waiting for them?' asked Thorson.

'They told me about a Nissen hut over at Melar that's kind of like a nightclub.'

The men greeted Thorson, and he replied in English. Since he wasn't in uniform, they reacted with surprise, saying they'd taken him for a local. They laughed. One of them put his arm round Thorson's friend and started pawing at her. Thorson had never seen them before. They were enlisted men, a little younger than him, not yet twenty, and exceptionally foul-mouthed. They lit up and swigged from their bottles. Thorson heard one mention Chicago. Maybe that's where they were from. His friend was also listening to their conversation, but he suspected she hardly understood a word.

'Were you fucking her?' one of them asked bluntly.

'There's no need to be crude,' said Thorson.

'Well, excuse me. I didn't mean to be *crude*. I just wanted to know if you were done so you could get lost and leave us to it. Capeesh?'

His friends broke into ugly, jeering laughter.

'I don't think she wants to go anywhere,' said Thorson. 'She was just saying she didn't feel like hanging around with you. Maybe because you're such pimply little jerks.'

The three men exchanged glances. The one who had his arm round his friend let her go, and they all squared up to Thorson. He considered taking out his police ID but wanted to keep that as a last resort. Besides, he didn't know if it would have any effect on the men at this stage. His friend looked on without making any move to intervene.

'So you're a wise guy,' said the marine.

'I don't want any trouble,' said Thorson. 'Just back off and leave her alone.'

'You think you're going to stop her coming with us? What's it to you? Are you her pimp?'

'No, I'm not her pimp.'

'Then can't she decide for herself?'

'What are they saying?' asked his friend. 'Is everything all right?'

'Well, it's your choice, of course, but maybe you shouldn't go with them,' Thorson said to her. 'Maybe it's not such a good idea.'

'Don't be silly,' she said. 'They're nice boys.'

'They're not talking about you very respectfully.'

'I don't know anyone who does, darling. Except you, maybe.'

'What are you two jabbering about?' said the marine, eyeing Thorson. 'You understand that gobbledegook?'

Thorson was going to ignore them and carry on trying to talk his friend round, when one of the men stepped forward menacingly. His friend, sensing that he had put himself in danger and wouldn't stand a chance against the three of them, slipped between them, took the marine by the arm and pulled him away with her. The other two backed off and Thorson watched the group disappear round the corner.

He wished he hadn't met her under those circumstances. Tried not to think about what went on in the Nissen hut over at Melar that they'd said was kind of like a nightclub.

24

The wholesaler who had employed Felix Lunden was none too pleased to receive a visit from Flóvent so late in the evening. He was getting on in years, set in his ways and very protective of his reputation. And quite unused to visits at this hour of the night, as he told Flóvent after he had finally relented and invited him in. The wholesaler lived alone; his wife was dead and his three sons had left home years ago. One of them worked alongside him and was gradually taking over the reins.

Flóvent explained the reason for his visit, telling him about the murder committed in Felix's flat, which he had no doubt heard about in the news. The wholesaler acknowledged that he was aware of the case. But he hadn't heard from Felix for a while and had no idea where he might be. It was about six months ago that Felix had approached him about a job. He had been so keen that when the wholesaler told him he wasn't hiring at present, Felix had offered to work for free to begin with, until he had proved himself. It was an unusual offer, to say the least, one that was too good to refuse.

Felix had made an excellent impression on him. The young man radiated self-confidence and was extremely polite and cultivated. A born salesman. Shortly afterwards he had set off on his first trip and the results had exceeded all expectations. Once he joined the company, sales had taken a big leap and the goods flew out of the warehouse. Everything from protective clothing to overcoats, as well as a range of cosmetics for the ladies. Felix had a certain quality that people trusted: it was there in his smile, his firm handshake, his infectious laugh. He knew how to take advantage of the various situations a commercial traveller might find himself in, and, perhaps most valuable of all, he knew how to talk to people on their level.

Having said that, the wholesaler hadn't got to know Felix particularly well; he had no reason to, didn't make a habit of socialising with the men who worked for him. It was evident to Flóvent that Felix had been quite reticent when he applied for the job. He hadn't mentioned, for example, that he had studied briefly at Reykjavík College or that he had been in Denmark when it fell to the Germans. As far as the wholesaler was aware, Felix didn't have any strong views on the war, the Nazis, the Allies, Hitler or Churchill. Flóvent had asked Ebeneser the same questions but had learnt nothing of any value. He asked specifically whether Felix had said anything about the British prime minister, but neither the headmaster nor the wholesaler could recall his views on current affairs: he didn't seem to have aired them at all, or not in their hearing anyway.

'Do you know why he was so keen to work in sales, sir?' asked Flóvent. 'Why he was so determined to secure a job with you?'

'No. He just said he'd like to try his hand at selling, and I seem to remember he also wanted a chance to travel around the country. But he didn't mention anything else. The men who go into this business are often single. Bachelors. Some have had enough of being cooped up in town and are looking for a change of scene.'

'Were there any particular places he was keen to visit? Did he go to some areas more than others?'

'Felix was free to decide his own itinerary, within reason. He often took the western route, covering the west coast and the West Fjords. He covered the south-west as well, from fishing villages on the Reykjanes Peninsula to the inland districts around Selfoss. He was a hard worker, I'll give him that. No sooner back in town than he was dashing off again. Made an effort to cover even the least rewarding places.'

'The least rewarding?'

'Yes, places where there wasn't much hope of any orders. That's especially true of the West Fjords. He went to every last backwater, every isolated farm. He was very conscientious.'

When asked about Eyvindur Ragnarsson, the wholesaler said he didn't know him. He'd never employed anyone by that name, and he wasn't aware that Felix and Eyvindur were acquainted. Felix had never spoken of him.

'It's a bit of an odd coincidence that they should both be salesmen, don't you think?' the man said. 'Doesn't it suggest a connection to their work? Some kind of falling out?'

'Can you imagine what it might have been about?' asked Flóvent, keeping quiet about the fact that the two men had attended the same school as boys.

'Well, money, I suppose. Or women, maybe? Or perhaps they quarrelled about the territories they were covering. It's always tough when there are a lot of salesmen working the same patch, though it would be absurd to murder someone over something like that. Quite absurd.'

'You're not aware of anything like that? Of fights between salesmen?'

'No, certainly not.'

Flóvent asked him more about how Felix's trips were organised and how often he took them, where he put up in the country-side, and where he would get on and off the coasters. He also asked about all the characters who worked in the commercial travelling business and if any of them, including Felix himself, displayed any noticeably eccentric behaviour.

'Well, now you come to mention it, I've been wondering a bit about a name Felix was using recently,' said the wholesaler. 'Per-haps it's nothing new. I wouldn't know.'

'Oh?' said Flóvent, making a move to leave. He glanced at the clock, reluctant to detain the man any longer.

'I don't know if it was something he used often.'

'The name he was using?' Flóvent didn't quite follow. 'You know his surname's Lunden, sir? His full name's Felix Lunden. Did that strike you as odd?'

'No, of course not. That's his name, but I don't think Felix always used that surname. I'm not sure he always called himself Lunden.'

'What did he call himself then?'

'Rúdólfsson.'

'Felix Rúdólfsson?'

'Yes. Goodness knows why. I didn't ask him. Didn't feel it was any of my business.'

'How did it come to your attention?'

'I needed to get hold of Felix recently and rang a guesthouse I knew he always patronised. But when I asked to speak to him, they said did I mean Felix Rúdólfsson? I wasn't quite sure what to say. I'd asked for Felix Lunden but the woman on the phone said they only had one Felix staying with them, a Felix Rúdólfsson. So I asked to speak to him and shortly afterwards Felix came on the line.'

'So Felix was using a false name on his travels around the country. Any idea why?'

'Well, I don't know if you can go as far as that,' said the wholesaler. 'On this particular occasion he was calling himself Rúdólfsson. That's not in doubt. But I can't speak for the rest of the time. I was a little taken aback, but I didn't say anything about it. Didn't interfere. As far as I was concerned it was his business.'

'Where was he at the time?'

'The West Fjords. In Ísafjördur. As a matter of fact, that was his last trip for us. He came home, delivered his orders and settled up. The next time I heard of him was when I read in the papers that he was suspected of murder.'

'So he was going by the name of Felix Rúdólfsson?'

'If he didn't want to use the surname Lunden, that was his affair, of course, but it did strike me as a little odd, especially after that poor man was found dead in his flat.'

'Of course, Lunden's a German name,' pointed out Flóvent. 'That wouldn't necessarily go down well with people nowadays.'

'No, of course, that would be understandable. But it occurred to me to wonder if . . . if there could be another reason. If he was travelling incognito or something.'

25

For the second day in a row Flóvent found Rudolf Lunden's house empty. He knocked on all the doors and peered in the windows but could see no sign of life. It occurred to him that the neighbours might know where Rudolf was. He was in luck: a middle-aged housewife came to the door of her house and was able to enlighten him. In the early hours of the previous morning she had heard an ambulance in the street and watched as Rudolf Lunden was carried out on a stretcher and driven away. She didn't know what was wrong but said this wasn't the first time it had happened; he was in poor health and had to be admitted to hospital from time to time. She'd heard somewhere that he had a weak heart but couldn't guarantee that this was true. The woman turned out to be quite chatty. She stood on her doorstep, wearing a pair of horn-rimmed glasses and an apron over her day dress, and told Flóvent she was fairly sure it was because of his heart problems that Rudolf hadn't been deported like so many other members of the German community. Her husband worked for one of the ministries and he'd heard it said that the British thought it unlikely Rudolf would survive the journey. 'Humanitarian considerations,' said the woman, her tone indicating that she didn't think these should be wasted on the likes of Rudolf Lunden.

Flóvent thought of how he'd hauled the man down to the prison to grill him about Felix, and felt overwhelmed with guilt. He had resorted to that course of action because he had been riled by the doctor's manner, by his arrogance, his hypocrisy. Flóvent's conscience had been bothering him ever since, not only because the man was handicapped but because he hadn't applied for a warrant and privately doubted the legality of his action. The news that Rudolf might have a weak heart, on top of everything else, left him feeling doubly perturbed. He wondered if the doctor was in hospital because of him.

The housewife could tell him less about Brynhildur Hólm, though she was aware that Rudolf employed a housekeeper as well as benefitting from the services of a maid twice a week – unlike her and her husband: they'd lost their household help to the British. The woman had been forced to do all the chores herself ever since. She knew nothing about Rudolf's housekeeper, not even her name. This was the first time she'd heard it. But then, she remarked, Rudolf and that Brynhildur Hólm weren't ones for mixing with their neighbours – they didn't so much as give you the time of day in the street. And they didn't have many visitors, though she'd noticed a few comings and goings, usually in the evening, and the visitors in question stayed late, at least until long after she herself had retired for the night. It seemed to Flóvent that the housewife kept a remarkably close eye on everything that happened in her street, but he kept his thoughts to himself.

He thanked the woman for her help and had just got back into his car when he spotted the maid walking up to Rudolf's house. He had been meaning to talk to her again but hadn't had a chance. She was closing the door behind her when he called out to her. The girl recognised him immediately. There were a couple of questions he needed to ask her, he said. Would that be all right? She was a little taken aback but opened the door halfway and informed him that Rudolf wasn't in.

'Yes, I know. It was you I came to see, miss,' said Flóvent. 'Last time I was here you said something about a row between Rudolf and his brother-in-law Ebeneser. Do you remember?'

The girl shook her head.

'You said you'd heard them arguing about some boys. Do you know who the boys were?'

'No, I don't.'

'Could they have been schoolboys?'

The girl shook her head again.

'Friends of Felix, perhaps?'

'I'm afraid I can't help you, sir. I really shouldn't have mentioned it. I don't know why I did.'

'It was out of a sense of loyalty, wasn't it, miss?' said Flóvent. 'You wanted to explain Rudolf's behaviour. Is he always that difficult?'

'His health has gone downhill recently,' said the girl. 'He's not well and he's not happy about . . . I'm sorry, I can't help you any more. Please excuse me.'

She pushed the door to and was about to close it when Flóvent put out a hand to stop her.

'Does he employ a housekeeper?'

'Yes, Brynhildur,' said the maid. 'Maybe you could talk to her, sir, but she's not here at the moment. I've really got to go now. Good day.'

'Do you know where she is, miss?'

'No, I'm afraid not.'

It turned out that Rudolf Lunden had been admitted to the Department of General Medicine at the National Hospital, but Flóvent was told that it should be safe to speak to him as long as he kept his visit short. When he arrived, he found Rudolf asleep in a double room in the large hospital building on Hringbraut. He was alone; the other bed was empty. Flóvent wasn't sure how to occupy himself while he waited for Rudolf to wake up. The last thing he wanted was to disturb his sleep. The wheelchair was nowhere to be seen and there were no personal items on his bedside table, only two periodicals that belonged to the hospital: *Andvari* and the literary journal *Skírnir*. After Flóvent had paced up and down the corridor and in and out of the room for a while, his curiosity got the better of him and he picked up the copy of *Skírnir*, which was lying open on top of the other journal. The issue was from 1939 and featured articles on a variety of literary and ethnographic subjects. Rudolf seemed to have put it down in the middle of a piece on the origin of the Icelanders, in which the author advanced the theory that they were descended from the Heruli tribe, who had originated in an area near the Black Sea and moved north during the Migration Age.

Hearing Rudolf groan and seeing that he was stirring, Flóvent quickly replaced the journal and got to his feet. The doctor recognised him the instant he opened his eyes.

'What . . . what are you doing here?' he asked hoarsely. 'I do not want you here.' Plainly Rudolf had not forgiven Flóvent for the way he had been treated. His gaze was contemptuous, his tone uncivil.

'I was sorry to hear you'd been admitted to hospital, sir,' said Flóvent politely, choosing his words with care. He had rehearsed them out in the corridor while Rudolf was sleeping. 'I'd just like to ask you a few more questions, but I'll try to be brief. I don't wish to disturb you. We've uncovered one or two things in the course of our inquiry that I feel it's only right to put to you. I'm afraid the matter's rather urgent. I know your situation's difficult, but I do hope you'll have patience with me.'

'I insist that you leave this instant,' whispered Rudolf, sending Flóvent a ferocious look. 'Have you come to arrest me? To carry me out of the hospital by force?'

Flóvent shook his head. Making an effort to be respectful, he explained that he had tried to visit him at home, but had only just learnt that he was in hospital.

If he thought Rudolf would be at all mollified by his meek tone, he was mistaken. The doctor's eyes flashed with animosity and when Flóvent asked again if he might put a few questions to him, Rudolf's response was a flat refusal. He added that he had hired a lawyer who was preparing a formal complaint about the way the police had treated him, and that Flóvent would be hearing from him shortly. He'd had no grounds for forcibly conveying the doctor to the prison and no legal right either.

'I felt I had no alternative, sir,' said Flóvent. 'You refused to speak to me. In my experience, a trip to the prison tends to make people more cooperative. I'm afraid I wasn't aware of your . . . condition. I wish you had said something.'

'You are a fool,' snapped Rudolf. 'An uneducated fool, with no manners.'

It was on the tip of Flóvent's tongue to retort 'Which reminds me, I wanted to ask about your son', but he thought better of it. The temptation to ask whether Felix was a disappointment to him was almost irresistible. He was burning to ask this and more questions in the same vein, but couldn't risk giving the man a heart attack. He doubted the doctors would have sanctioned his visit if they had realised that he was from the police, so he thought he'd better make it quick.

'You are being extraordinarily difficult, sir,' Flóvent remarked instead.

'You are simply not up to your job.'

'Aren't you the least bit worried about Felix? About where he's hiding? Or about his state of mind?'

'Whatever worries I may or may not have are none of your business. I am asking you to leave!'

'Unless, of course, you know where he is. Do you, sir?'

Rudolf didn't answer.

'Are you aware that Felix sometimes goes by the name of Felix Rúdólfsson rather than Lunden?'

'That's the first I've heard of it. Why should he do that? What a load of nonsense. Is that all you've come here to tell me?'

'Are you familiar with the name Eyvindur Ragnarsson?'

Again Rudolf didn't answer.

'He's the man we found in your son's flat. Do you recognise the name?'

Rudolf shook his head. 'Will you please leave me in peace,' he said.

'So you don't know why he was found murdered in your son's flat?'

'No.'

'And you don't know where your son is hiding?'

'How often do I have to tell you that I have no idea of his whereabouts?'

'Do you have any reason to believe that something might have happened to your son?'

'What do you mean?'

'That he might have suffered the same fate as Eyvindur, for example?'

'That he is dead – is that what you are implying?'

'You must have considered the possibility. Now that you know about the cyanide capsule we found in his suitcase. Aren't you afraid he might have killed himself?'

'I cannot tell you anything about Felix. As I have repeatedly told you, though you are apparently too dim-witted to understand.'

'Aren't you the least bit worried about him?'

'I will not dignify that with an answer,' said Rudolf. 'I will not dignify anything you say with an answer. I insist that you leave me alone.'

'Felix must have been remarkably free of prejudice as a child,' Flóvent remarked. 'Did you know that he and Eyvindur were friends, or at least played together, as boys?'

Rudolf ignored this.

'I mention that he must have been free of prejudice because there was a huge gulf between them socially. Eyvindur came from an appallingly rough home. His mother was a drunk and his father a violent criminal, forever in and out of prison. Yet Felix was from a bourgeois family; his father was a doctor. Did he ever talk about Eyvindur? Were you aware of their friendship?'

Again he was met by silence.

'Why would a boy from such a prominent home befriend a lad

who lived in conditions like that, with a dangerous convict as a father? Wouldn't Felix have had to seek your permission to associate with him? Did you give it? Or did Felix do it to defy you? Was that when he stopped living up to his father's expectations?'

'Get out,' snapped Rudolf. 'I have nothing to say to you.'

Flóvent took out the four-page pamphlet that he and Thorson had found at Eyvindur's flat, held the photograph up to the doctor and asked if he recognised the people in it. Rudolf seemed to have made up his mind to behave as if Flóvent wasn't in the room. Flóvent asked again if he recognised the people. When he received no response, he began to describe what the picture showed, naming Ebeneser and Brynhildur and the boys Felix and Eyvindur, and asking if Rudolf knew the others. The doctor didn't even deign to look at it.

'I understand that Brynhildur Hólm works as your housekeeper nowadays,' said Flóvent. 'Am I right?'

Rudolf said nothing.

'Can you confirm that?'

'What do you want with her?' Rudolf asked at last.

'I'm afraid I'm not at liberty to tell you that,' said Flóvent as politely as he could. He had a degree of sympathy for Rudolf, under the circumstances, but the doctor's withering scorn undeniably grated on his nerves. 'At present, anyway,' he added, noting that the man's face had turned even darker red. 'Could you tell me where I can get hold of her? We've established that she used to rent rooms on Njálsgata until a few years ago. My colleague is going to speak to her landlord –'

'That is no concern of mine. You can invent whatever nonsense you like,' said Rudolf. 'Leave me alone. I have nothing whatsoever to say to you.'

'All right,' said Flóvent. 'There's just one more question I'm obliged to put to you.'

'I have no desire to speak to you. You seem incapable of grasping the fact.'

'Who's Hans Lunden?' asked Flóvent. 'Who is Dr Hans Lunden?'

Rudolf shot him a glance, visibly startled by the name. 'Why do you ask?'

'He was in the country shortly before the war, and it's possible he's visited on other occasions too. Perhaps you could enlighten me. Who is he and what was he doing here?'

Rudolf said nothing.

'He's your brother, is he not? How did he come to know the consul, Dr Werner Gerlach?'

He wasn't really expecting Rudolf to answer any of his questions, given how uncooperative he had been up to now. And his instinct was correct. The doctor lay there in stubborn silence, waiting for Flóvent to take himself off. But the visit hadn't been a complete waste of time. Flóvent had no idea what it all meant, but he had made it clear to Rudolf that he knew about Hans Lunden and his links to the German consul. If this information was significant, Rudolf was bound to wonder how he had found out and, more importantly, whether Flóvent knew more about what Hans and Gerlach had been up to. Before he left, there was one more thing he wanted the doctor to think over.

'What is the nature of the relationship between Brynhildur Hólm and Hans Lunden?'

There was a long pause.

'What do you think you know?' Rudolf finally retorted with a sneer. 'You know nothing. You are an ignorant fool.'

'What is it that I don't know?' asked Flóvent. 'Do enlighten me. Why can't you be straight with me? Don't you feel the slightest concern for your son?'

Rudolf turned his head away.

'I want to ask you again about your quarrel with Ebeneser,' said Flóvent. 'You had a row about something to do with some boys. To do with Felix, I would guess. Can you confirm that?'

Rudolf didn't react.

'Would you care to tell me about that?'

The silence dragged on and Flóvent gave up. Clearly it was futile to keep pressing the doctor on these points. His eye happened to fall on the copy of *Skírnir* lying on the bedside table, and, changing the subject, he asked the doctor about his interest in the origin of the Icelanders and this new theory about the Heruli. Rudolf continued to snub him, staring silently out of the window.

Only as Flóvent was leaving the room did Rudolf finally turn to him.

'To think they believed that Iceland was home to such a remarkable race,' he said. 'That this was the ancestral heritage . . .'

'Who? What heritage?'

'These peasants.'

'What heritage?'

'These . . . damned peasants.'

Rudolf could not be persuaded to explain, so Flóvent took his leave, wishing him a quick recovery. He walked out of the hospital feeling intensely frustrated. He lingered for a while outside, letting the hot August sun warm his face and trying to make sense of Rudolf's parting comment. Eventually, he set off and was heading west, alongside the hospital, when a woman suddenly emerged from the building. To his astonishment, it appeared to be Brynhildur Hólm. He was about to call out to her but checked himself and instead began to follow her at a discreet distance as she walked briskly up towards Skólavörduholt. She strode purposefully past the military barracks on top of the hill, looking neither right nor left, wearing a long black coat and black lace-up shoes, and clutching a small black doctor's bag.

26

Brynhildur Hólm's former landlord was eager to assist the police, especially when he heard that Thorson was Icelandic-Canadian. He had relatives in North America himself, he said: two maternal uncles who had emigrated to Winnipeg just after the turn of the century, with their entire families, and still kept up with their relatives back in Iceland. He was very interested in Thorson's life out west, so Thorson told him a little about Manitoba, about the farming conditions and a few of the well known figures in the Icelandic community, poets and others who had made their mark. In spite of the landlord's curiosity, he was deliberately vague about his own circumstances.

The man remembered Brynhildur well. She had rented rooms from him on Njálsgata for several years and always paid on time; he had no complaints about her as a tenant. She had been single, and he suspected she might have been a little lonely as few people came to see her and she made no effort to get to know her neighbours. Having said that, she had been helpful with their minor injuries and ailments once they learnt she was a nurse. He didn't think she had ever been married, but her manner had discouraged personal questions, so he couldn't be sure.

The landlord asked what the military police wanted with Brynhildur since he couldn't imagine her ever breaking the law. Thorson dodged the question by explaining that he was merely assisting the Reykjavík police with a minor matter involving relations between the armed forces and local civilians. Brynhildur was a possible witness to the incident, he lied.

The man hadn't heard from Brynhildur Hólm since she moved out. He had seen her about town but didn't know where she might be lodging now. He had never come across Rudolf Lunden but knew of the headmaster, Ebeneser, by reputation. The rooms Brynhildur had rented were now occupied by a family from the East Fjords; the husband made a decent living working for the British at Nauthólsvík Cove.

As Thorson was thanking the man and about to leave, the landlord said that, come to think of it, he had been meaning to get in touch with Brynhildur Hólm for quite some time because she had asked him to look after two boxes of books for her when she moved out, but had never come back to fetch them. They were still in his storeroom and although they didn't take up much space, naturally he would like to restore them to their rightful owner. Speaking of which, he wondered if Thorson would be seeing Brynhildur any time soon. Thorson said he assumed so, that it was only a matter of time before he managed to track her down.

'You couldn't possibly remind her about the two boxes she left with me?' the landlord asked.

'Sure,' said Thorson.

'They're in here,' said the man and beckoned Thorson to follow him, adding that honestly he would be grateful to be rid of them sooner rather than later. 'There's nothing valuable in there,' he said. 'I checked. Just some old books that she's obviously not that bothered about.'

The storeroom was down in the cellar. The man showed Thorson inside and pointed to two small boxes protruding from a shelf among a lot of tools and pots of paint.

'It needs a tidy-up in here,' the man said, apologetically surveying the room. 'I'm always meaning to clear it out but never find the time. No one uses the room but me. I expect most of this lot could be taken to the tip. But there you go.'

He lifted down one of the boxes, opened it and said he had sometimes thought of taking the books to an antiquarian to find out if they were worth anything – and selling them if they were. 'It costs money to store these boxes, you know,' he said. 'Nothing in life comes for free. Nothing comes for free.'

As he rattled on, he showed Thorson the contents of the box. There must have been about fifteen books, mostly Icelandic children's titles, including the Nonni books, some of them in German translations. When the man picked one up and flicked through it, Thorson noticed that Brynhildur had written her name on the flyleaf. The man put the books back, taking care to make it look as if they hadn't been disturbed.

The other box contained German and English works on nursing – textbooks, Thorson thought. When the landlord handed him one, a small pamphlet fell out onto the floor. Picking it up, Thorson discovered that it had been translated from German to English and published in London five years ago. It consisted of no more than twenty pages and had a cheap grey paper cover, which featured the title and the author's name. Thorson wouldn't have given it a second glance were it not for the name that caught his eye when he picked it up from the floor. The author was one Hans Lunden. The title also aroused his interest. It was couched as a question: 'Can crime rates be reduced by selective breeding?'

'What've you got there?' asked the landlord. 'Anything of interest?'

'Not really,' said Thorson, leafing through the pamphlet.

'Would you like to take it away with you?' asked the landlord, seeing that Thorson was absorbed in the text.

'No, thanks. No need,' said Thorson, handing it back. He recalled what Graham and Ballantine had told him at the Leper Hospital. About the genetic research the Nazis were conducting on prisoners in an attempt to prove that criminal traits were hereditary. Experiments in German concentration camps, they'd said. The name Buchenwald had come up.

'So, that's all there is in these boxes. Probably not worth anything, like I say,' said the landlord with a sigh, tidying away the pamphlet and putting the boxes back on the shelf. 'Not surprising the lady has never got round to fetching them, really. Mind you, it's not like her. She was always so neat and tidy when she lived here. Took good care of her belongings, from what I could see. Always punctual with her rent: I never had to ask. Not once. You'll remind her when you see her, won't you? About the boxes?'

Thorson promised. They went back upstairs, and he said goodbye to the landlord, and thanked him for being so helpful. As Thorson was driving away he regretted not having taken the pamphlet with him to show Flóvent. Especially the short paragraph about the author, which stated that Hans Lunden had been born in Schleswig-Holstein, graduated in medicine from the

University of Stuttgart and subsequently worked as a lecturer at the University of Jena's Pathological Institute, specialising in genetics.

Thorson was sure he remembered hearing that the German consul, Werner Gerlach, had carried out research in genetics at the same university.

27

Flóvent wasn't sure what to do. As he shadowed Brynhildur Hólm over Skólavörduholt, he debated whether he should keep going or abandon this game and order her to stop. He didn't even know why he had decided to follow her instead of approaching her and introducing himself. She must have been visiting Rudolf, shortly before Flóvent himself had arrived, and then lingered at the hospital for some reason. Perhaps she had stopped to speak to a nurse she knew and had slipped out of the back exit just as he happened to leave. She appeared to be heading for the centre of town, walking briskly, as if her errand couldn't wait.

It was on top of Skólavörduholt that the British had erected the first barracks in Reykjavík, christening it Camp Skipton after a small town in Yorkshire. Some seventy Nissen huts now colonised the crown of this hill, where there were plans to raise a splendid church one day in honour of the poet and clergyman Hallgrímur Pétursson, author of the *Hymns of Passion*. The main route out of town had once led this way, passing Steinka's Cairn, where way-farers had customarily thrown a stone for good luck. In 1805, an unfortunate woman from the West Fjords had been found guilty of a crime of passion and died in prison. Denied the right to lie in consecrated ground, she had been buried on the hill under a pile of stones like an animal. Flóvent glanced in passing at the place where her cairn had once stood. A large Nissen hut now occupied the spot.

Looking ahead again, he saw Brynhildur threading her way between the puddles in the road that ran past the camp. Although she was no longer young he heard the odd wolf whistle from the soldiers who were lounging in the sunshine, playing cards, smoking and exchanging banter. Brynhildur didn't so much as glance at them, but marched on in her tightly buttoned coat, clutching her black bag, heading towards Skólavördustígur.

She followed the street down to where it joined Bankastræti, then at the bottom turned right towards the harbour. In no time at all she had entered Hafnarstræti where she slowed her pace, then without warning darted into an alleyway. Seeing her vanish round a corner, Flóvent hurried after her. As he drew near to the entrance, he slowed down, then cautiously entered the alley. It ran between two buildings, a few doors down from Mrs Marta Björns-son's restaurant, and ended in a courtyard. Flóvent couldn't see a soul and had no way of telling where Brynhildur had gone. But it stood to reason that she must have entered one of the buildings, because there was no obvious route out of the yard apart from the alley.

Flóvent guessed that she had noticed him and deliberately slipped into the alley to shake him off. He ran back out to the street in case she had crept into one of the houses and out of the front door, but he couldn't see any sign of her. Returning to the yard, he began trying the back doors, one after the other. They were all locked. He reasoned that Brynhildur must have the key to one of them and decided to see if he could get through the front.

As he stepped back out onto Hafnarstræti, he almost ran into a group of US Marines and had to wait for them to pass. Then he scanned the front of the buildings and noticed a small, easily missed sign in one window advertising Hermundur Fridriksson's Clinic. It was then that he remembered Rudolf Lunden had once had a medical practice on Hafnarstræti.

So that's where Brynhildur Hólm had been heading in such a hurry.

Not knowing the address of Rudolf's surgery, he decided to try the house with the sign on it. The front door was unlocked. It was a three-storey stone building with a high attic and a steep staircase that creaked beneath his feet. He knocked on two doors on the ground floor, and, when no one answered, continued up to the next floor. Again he started knocking on doors, and the second was answered by an elderly woman who said she remembered Rudolf Lunden well and that his surgery had been on the top floor of the house next door. The buildings had once contained both apartments and offices, including two doctor's surgeries, but then old Hermundur had died and Rudolf had closed his practice. As far as the woman knew, both surgeries were standing empty.

Flóvent rushed back down the stairs and tried the front door of the neighbouring house. It was also unlocked and, on entering, he found himself in a dark hall with the same kind of staircase. He wondered how Rudolf had managed to get up all those steps.

He didn't know how long the doctor had been confined to a wheel-chair, but he could see why he would have had to close his practice after the accident. Flóvent found the surgery at the top of the stairs. Although the door was locked, it rattled when he tried the handle and he thought it shouldn't be too difficult to force. He put his shoulder to it and shoved hard until he heard a snap and felt the lock giving way and the door opening.

Immediately inside was a small waiting room with three chairs, a framed photograph of the Alps hanging on one of the panelled walls. The curtains were drawn, leaving the place in semi-darkness, and the air was thick with dust. Another door led from the waiting room into the consulting room, where a small parti-tion screened off the examination area. Flóvent pressed a switch on the wall, but no light came on. He went over to the window and pulled back the curtains, admitting enough light to see by. There were dusty medicine cabinets and optometry instruments, a desk, a filing cabinet, an examination table and half-open draw-ers containing dressings and hypodermic needles. The surgery looked as if it had been a busy, thriving practice when it was aban-doned. As if Rudolf had walked out at the end of an ordinary day's work and never returned.

But somebody had been there recently, because the dust had been disturbed in places, particularly around the desk and exam-ination table. When Flóvent inspected the room more closely, he also discovered the remains of a meal, two milk bottles and a cof-fee thermos. Picking up the thermos, he sniffed at it. There was no question. Someone was holed up in the old surgery.

For an instant he stood stock still, listening, but all he could hear was the noise from the street below.

'Felix!' he called out. 'Are you there? Felix Lunden!'

His words echoed round the rooms but there was no reply.

Flóvent returned to the little waiting room and this time noticed another door in the back wall. From the window he saw that it seemed to open onto a narrow fire escape. He guessed that Brynhildur Hólm had come up that way and fled as soon as she heard him outside on the landing, rattling the door. Perhaps Felix had been with her. At any rate somebody had recently been inside Rudolf Lunden's surgery. Flóvent was about to race down the stairs after her but changed his mind, deciding it was too late now.

He returned to the consulting room, and when his eyes had adjusted once more to the gloom, he spotted the black doctor's bag that Brynhildur had been carrying when she left the hospital. On opening it, he found it contained not medical equipment but essential supplies: a razor, soap and newspapers, a packet of coffee and a few slices of bread.

He picked up the razor, hearing, as he did so, a faint creak from one corner of the room. Flóvent jerked his head round towards the sound and noticed a large wardrobe built into the wall.

'Felix?' he called.

He listened.

'Brynhildur?'

When no one answered, he tiptoed over to the wardrobe.

'Felix?' he called again.

He received no response and was about to yank open the door when, without warning, it flew towards him. A man he had never seen before leapt out and took a swing at him. Flóvent saw something gleam in the man's hand and felt a searing pain, first at his temple, then in the back of his head. The man had struck him twice before Flóvent could even raise a hand to defend himself. As Flóvent reached out to grab his attacker, he felt his strength rapidly dwindling, his body becoming a dead weight, incapable of obeying his commands. Then he blacked out and wasn't even aware of his head hitting the floor with a crack.

28

The notification landed on Thorson's desk just as his shift was finishing. Things had been fairly slow, so he had spent the evening trying to establish the location of all the laundries that took in washing for the military. Since the invasion, they had sprung up like mushrooms, as local women saw a chance to earn good money by working for themselves. He had also tried several times to reach Flóvent on the phone, eager to tell him about the pamphlet he had found among Brynhildur Hólm's books.

A while ago Thorson had agreed to take a half shift as a favour to a colleague who wanted to go fishing with some friends at Lake Hafravatn, ten miles east of Reykjavík. Thorson had cast a line there himself from time to time. It was a beautiful place, with plenty of trout, a popular spot among his friends in the military police to relax on their days off.

The notification concerned a minesweeper currently moored in Reykjavík harbour. The man who reported the incident was part of an American delegation in town for a few days, who had gone for an evening stroll down by the docks. He had daughters that age, he said, and hated to see that kind of thing. He wanted the military police to intervene immediately. When Thorson was assigned the task he was told it might be an idea to alert the Icelandic police, particularly the Morality Committee, but if he wanted backup, he would have to wait because everyone was busy.

The phone rang on his desk just as he was dashing out of the door and he paused to grab the receiver. It was Major Graham from the Leper Hospital. Thorson explained that unfortunately he couldn't talk right now as he had to respond to an incident.

'Are you any closer to finding this . . . this Felix Lunden?' asked Graham, as if he hadn't heard a word Thorson had said.

'We're optimistic that he'll be found soon, sir.'

'I need to be briefed so that we can get our hands on him before the Icelandic government can muddy the waters. You got that, Thorson? If you catch him alive, that is. We could be dealing with espionage here. Any idea what he's been up to? Have you uncovered anything about the man who was found in his apartment?'

'Yes, we . . . He was a travelling salesman as well.'

'You don't say? You think it could have been personal, then? Did they know each other?'

'Probably.'

'What was the other guy doing there?'

'We don't know yet.'

'This Lunden must be dangerous. Is he armed?'

'Not as far as we know.'

'You'd better assume that he is,' said Graham.

'I'm afraid I can't talk . . . I have to respond to an incident right away. Could we discuss this later, sir?'

'Keep us briefed about what's going on, Thorson.' Graham said a curt goodbye and hung up.

Thorson knew he had to act fast. He decided not to alert the Morality Committee until he had found out exactly what was going on down at the harbour. The committee had been set up in an attempt to deter underage girls from consorting with soldiers. Thorson had worked with them before but didn't like the way they operated, spying on the girls and even sending them out of town. Somehow he doubted that a spell at a reform school in the countryside would do the girls much good.

So Thorson was alone as he drove at breakneck speed down to the harbour and along the docks to where the minesweeper was moored. He braked by the gangway, jumped out and bounded up it in a few strides. Two guards stepped out as he arrived on deck and ordered him to halt. He flashed his police ID and asked to speak to the officer in charge.

'I'm the officer of the deck. What do you want?' asked one of the guards suspiciously. He was older than the other one and showed no desire to cooperate.

'Are there any other men on board besides you?' asked Thorson.

'Most of the crew went ashore,' said the younger guard. 'All the officers apart from the lieutenant, but he's asleep and we're under orders not to wake him.'

'Not for any reason,' repeated the older guard.

'I need to inspect the ship,' said Thorson. 'It shouldn't take long.'

'Inspect the ship?' echoed the suspicious guard. 'What for? Inspect what?'

'We received a notification. It's my job to make sure there's nothing to it. Have you two been on watch here all evening?'

'Yes, sir.'

'Have you allowed any civilians on board?'

The guards exchanged a look.

'I don't know if we're required to answer that,' said the older man.

'Are you going to let me on board?'

'We need permission from our commanding officer,' said the older guard stubbornly. He looked Hispanic: pitch-black hair, brown eyes. Thorson wondered if he came from New Mexico or somewhere like that. 'Nobody comes aboard without his say-so.'

'Then wake the lieutenant.'

'No can do.'

'Are there Icelandic civilians on board this ship?' asked Thorson.

'Not that I'm aware.'

'They were spotted around here less than half an hour ago.'

'Do you have papers?'

'Papers?'

'A warrant to come aboard. Signed and stamped.'

'Stop fooling around,' snapped Thorson, losing patience. 'I don't have time for this. Either you let me on board and we solve this business nice and quiet, no fuss, or I call out all available MPs and we launch a joint operation with the local police to search this vessel for Icelandic civilians. And who knows what else we'll find. It's bound to lead to arrests, maybe detentions – the kind of trouble I know we'd all like to avoid. Unless, of course, you want to explain to your captain exactly what happened and how it could have been avoided. Is that what you want? It's your call.'

The guards' eyes met as Thorson's words sank in. He could tell that they were no longer so sure of themselves. His speech seemed to have had the desired effect, because after a moment the older man silently moved aside and allowed him to board.

He hurried below decks, ran along passages, banged on doors. The guards hadn't lied when they said most of the crew had gone ashore: the minesweeper was like a ghost ship. Unfamiliar with the layout of naval vessels, Thorson opened all the doors he encountered, revealing one compartment after another; he barged into the mess room where a lone crew member sat peeling potatoes, burst into the WC, then jumped down a companionway to the deck below, then down to the level below that, until he was deep in the bowels of the ship, next to the engine room, and the smells of oil, metal, glycerine and sweat were overpowering. He opened one more door and there at last were the two girls that the man from the American delegation had spotted boarding the ship in the company of some sailors.

The girls couldn't have been more than fifteen, the man had said, just kids. He had been right about that, Thorson thought. The three men with them were playing cards in a stinking haze of cigarette smoke. They were visibly drunk and there was more alcohol and tobacco on the table. One girl was sitting half-naked in the arms of a sailor. The other lay stretched out on a bunk, smoking a cigarette, her legs bare under her thin dress. Two of the men were stripped to the waist, the third was in his undershirt. They were all different ages; the oldest looked to be about fifty.

'Who the hell are you?' asked the sailor who was fondling the girl. He jumped to his feet and almost dropped her on the floor. His thick fingers were black with grease.

Engineers, thought Thorson.

'I don't want any trouble,' he said.

'Trouble? What trouble? Who's making trouble?'

The other two crew members gaped at Thorson, then put down their cards and got to their feet, startled by the disturbance.

'The girls need to come with me,' said Thorson.

'Says who?'

Thorson produced his military police ID, but it didn't seem to have any effect on board this ship, far from home. The engineer knocked it out of his hand without even looking at it. Thorson ordered the girls to come with him immediately. They seemed surprised to hear a soldier speaking Icelandic, but, their wits dulled by drink, they didn't budge. They were both blonde and could well have been sisters. The make-up they had used to redden their girlish lips and cheeks only made the whole situation seem sadder.

'They ain't going anywhere,' said the engineer who was doing all the talking.

'Girls!' shouted Thorson, regretting now that he hadn't called for backup. 'Come with me. This minute!'

They flinched and prepared to obey him, but by now the engineer had had enough. He charged at Thorson, sending him stumbling out into the narrow passage. The man tried to punch him in the face, but Thorson dodged the blow and it connected with his shoulder instead, throwing him against the wall. As he backed away down the passage, the engineer grabbed a heavy wrench and came after him. Thorson saw his buddies emerge from the berths. The girls tried to slip past them, but only one of them got through. She turned back and shouted at her friend to hurry, but the sailor wouldn't let her go.

'Where do you think you're going?' said the engineer who was following Thorson, brandishing the wrench at him. 'Ain't you going to come talk to us?'

'Let the girls go, then we can talk,' said Thorson.

He had reached the companionway and was just debating whether to leave the girls behind and run for help, when he heard footsteps overhead and the older guard from the deck started climbing down towards him, stopping halfway down the ladder.

'Don't do anything stupid now, Rick,' he said to the engineer who was poised to beat Thorson to a pulp. 'Leave them alone.'

'Stay out of this, Cortez. It's none of your business.'

'Cut it out!' barked Cortez. 'He's a cop, you moron. Do you want the whole goddamn police corps on your back? I told you they were too young. What did I tell you?'

The man called Rick paused and squinted up at the guard. Clearly he was damned if he was going to back down. During their stand-off, Thorson called to the two girls again. The sailor let go of the girl he was holding and they both fled towards Thorson, who ushered them up the ladder, then started climbing up behind them. Cortez and Rick were still eyeballing each other as Thorson shoved the girls ahead of him to the next deck and hurried them up another companionway until they were out in the open. Having found the gangway, they raced down it onto the dock.

29

One of the girls was a lot tougher than the other and made it plain that she had no intention of going home. She refused to give Thorson her address and complained that he had spoiled their fun. At first she claimed not to have any family at all, but in the end she admitted that she'd left home – and nothing would make her go back. The other girl wasn't nearly so angry and seemed, if anything, grateful to him for rescuing them from the bowels of the ship. She lived with her father and two brothers near Camp Tripoli and wouldn't mind if Thorson gave her a lift home, so long as he let her out at a safe distance, because her father hated the soldiers and had repeatedly forbidden her to fraternise with them. Thorson didn't ask why she had defied her father. No doubt she had her reasons, and anyway he was tired. He said nothing more about it but did as she asked and let her out by Vatnsmýri, an expanse of marshland near the airfield, once she had wiped most of the make-up off her face and promised Thorson that she would never go on board a naval vessel again, and that she would stay away from soldiers.

She and her friend said goodbye to each other, and Thorson watched the girl stumbling home over the tussocky ground. He wondered if he should have handed her over to the Icelandic authorities. She had said her father would kill her if he discovered that she'd been fooling around with soldiers. He'd thrashed her for much less – her brothers too – when he'd been drinking. And he drank most of the time. Thorson told her in parting that if she ever needed his help, she shouldn't hesitate to ask for him at the military police headquarters.

The tougher girl asked him twice if he had any cigarettes and informed him that she'd already run away from the reform school the Morality Committee had packed her off to. She knew she'd be sent back the moment they caught her, but she'd only run away again. When it dawned on her that Thorson was going to keep his promise and drop her off where she wanted to go, her hostility faded. Up to that point she had responded to all his questions with insults, but now she relented and admitted that she had an older sister she could stay with. She told Thorson the name of the street. Although she claimed to be eighteen, he guessed she was fifteen at most. He tried to tell her that although many of the sailors and soldiers in the town were good guys, there was always the odd rotten apple. Women had to be very careful, and kids like her should steer clear of them altogether.

She protested that she'd never had any trouble. All the guys she knew were good to her and gave her money, cigarettes and sweets. He tried to make her understand that though they might be nice to her and offer her booze and cigarettes, they'd want a lot more in return, and she didn't belong in that world, not at her age, especially if it led to the depths of a warship in Reykjavík harbour.

He couldn't tell if he'd got through to her and guessed she'd heard it all before anyway. Yet her defences seemed to be giving way a little. She was beginning to sober up now and sat silently in the front seat of the jeep, a small, vulnerable figure, her skimpy dress revealing slim white legs, dirty white knee socks slipped down around her ankles, and childish buckle shoes that didn't even touch the floor. Without warning she broke down and started sobbing. Thorson pulled over, switched off the engine and put his arm round her, trying to comfort her as she sat hunched up next to him.

'Don't cry, honey,' he said.

'I don't want to go back to the reform school,' she sobbed. 'Don't let them send me away. They drag you off, lock you up, then send you to this horrible place in the middle of nowhere.'

'I'm not taking you in for questioning,' said Thorson. 'But you have to understand that what you're doing is incredibly dangerous. You can't carry on like this. What about your mother, can't you . . . ?'

'She . . . she's . . . she's happy as long as I bring her booze and cigarettes.'

'What about your dad?'

'My dad?' The girl sounded puzzled.

'Yes, is there . . . is he . . . ?'

'Mum thinks my dad was some bloke from the Westman Islands.'

'You don't know who he is?'

'No.'

'How did you meet those men, those sailors you were with? I hope you're not getting . . . too familiar with them.'

'In town. At the bars. At Ramóna and White Star. Anywhere, really. I haven't done anything with them.'

'Well, keep it that way,' said Thorson.

'I know what they're after. Do you really think I haven't met their type before? There's a man in our street who pays me to watch him while he . . . you know. All I have to do is watch –'

'For Christ's sake,' Thorson exclaimed. 'You should stay away from men like him. They can be dangerous and you shouldn't . . . shouldn't be doing that . . .'

'My sister's . . . she's bagged herself a Tommy. She's engaged. He's from London and she's going back with him after the war – going to live there, and become English.'

She made it sound as if her sister had hit the jackpot.

'So what are you saying?' asked Thorson. 'Are you hoping to follow her lead?'

'She says it's much better to find yourself a soldier than some Icelandic bloke. She went crazy when they first arrived . . . the Tommies. Was out partying with her girlfriends every night. They're always having a good time. One of them's married and all, but that doesn't stop her.'

'No,' said Thorson, 'I bet it doesn't.'

Now that the girl had recovered, he started the engine again and continued on towards her sister's house. It was getting late and when he stopped the jeep they could hear the sound of car horns and shouting from the centre of town. The girl didn't say as much but Thorson sensed that she was grateful, though he didn't know whether it was for rescuing her from the minesweeper or for keeping the Morality Committee out of it. Both, maybe.

Her sister turned out to be a young woman of twenty-five, who was busy getting ready for a night out and was apparently livid with her younger sister for something that had happened earlier that day. She looked Thorson up and down as he stood at the door in his uniform, but when he explained, in Icelandic, that he was a West Icelander, a light seemed to go out. 'Uh-huh,' she said, indifferently. He told her to take better care of her little sister in future.

'Better care?' she said, searching for a cigarette, looking a little the worse for wear. She found a packet and a lighter of a type Thorson knew was popular among the soldiers. Sucked the smoke deep into her lungs. 'What's she done now? I can't control her. She's completely off the rails.'

'She's done nothing wrong,' said Thorson. 'But she was in bad company.'

'The committee's picked her up twice already,' said the sister. 'They packed her off to the countryside. Like that did any good.'

'I'm not going back,' said the younger girl.

'Oh, why don't you shut up?' said her big sister, exhaling smoke. 'Was there anything else?' she asked Thorson irritably.

'No. Just take better care of her. She's a good kid.'

'Uh-huh,' said the sister and shut the door in his face.

Thorson shook his head, having second thoughts now about whether he had done the right thing by bringing the girl here. As he turned to leave, he heard the woman tearing a strip off her kid sister.

'What the hell were you up to? Where have you been?'

Thorson felt sorry for the girl.

'Don't tell me you've been on the ships! Go on, answer me! Are you completely off your rocker? Are you a bloody navy whore now?'

Thorson didn't hear a reply, just a light crack as if the girl had been slapped in the face.

'Why couldn't you go to Vera's, you little tart? She's been asking for you all day. Why couldn't you go round to hers like I told you?'

A moment later there was a knock at the door and the Canadian policeman was standing on the step again, handsome but a little too sensitive-looking. The woman couldn't work out what it was about him that she found so irritating.

'Yes, what, are you still there?' she barked at him. 'What do you want?'

'Excuse me, did you say Vera?'

30

It took Flóvent quite a while to come to his senses. His head ached, especially at his temple; why, he didn't know. He had a hazy recollection of following Brynhildur Hólm from the hospital down to the town centre, of climbing a steep staircase and entering a doctor's surgery. Putting a hand to his head, he encountered something sticky in his hair and on his clothes too. He was lying on his side on a hard floor, enveloped in darkness, though the window let in a bit of light from the street outside. He felt both sick and hungry at the same time, and couldn't for the life of him work out where he was.

He lay there for a while, wondering dully how he had come to be lying on the floor.

Eventually, Flóvent eased himself into a sitting position, feeling groggy and unbelievably tired. Peering around in the gloom he saw the outlines of an examination table and a filing cabinet, a desk and a chair, and realised that he must still be in the doctor's surgery. He struggled to his feet and immediately doubled up, coughing and retching. He leant against the examination table for support and happened to glance over into the corner where the wardrobe was standing open. It all came flooding back: how the door had been flung open and a figure had leapt out and hit him over the head. He ran a hand gently over his sore skull, realising, as he did so, that the sticky stuff was blood.

'He hates his father.'

Flóvent spun round, and without the support of the examination table almost fell flat on the floor again. Straining his eyes in the direction of the waiting room, he saw, as if through a mist, a woman rising from a chair and coming towards him. He could barely make out her face in the gloom but knew at once who it must be.

'Brynhildur? Brynhildur Hólm?'

'You must have followed me. I didn't notice until too late that I'd led you here.'

'It wasn't hard to follow you . . . ma'am. Then I remembered that Rudolf Lunden used to have a surgery on this street.'

'There's no need to call me "ma'am", is there? We heard you coming up the stairs but didn't think you'd break in. You were supposed to chase me out of the back door and down the fire escape, but you can't have seen me. I had no idea he was going to attack you like that. He thinks he's in danger. But you should be safe now.'

'Felix?'

'He was gone by the time I came back,' said the woman, stepping out of the shadows into the faint light. She spoke in a weary monotone; her face was drawn. She still had on the long black coat and stout black lace-up shoes that she had been wearing earlier.

'Where is he?'

'I don't know.'

'You're lying,' said Flóvent, trying to shake off his wooziness.

'You don't have to believe me if you don't want to. But I am worried about him. Felix is in a bad way. He's frightened and confused, says he can't trust anyone.'

'Why should I believe a word you say?'

'Have it your way. I thought I'd try talking to you, seeing as you're here. Felix should never have attacked you. I want you to know that I condemn that sort of violence. I knew you wouldn't have any trouble catching . . . What I mean is I have no interest in playing cat and mouse, so we might as well talk now. Are you all right? How are you feeling?'

'You're an accessory to his crime,' said Flóvent. 'But then you know that.'

'Accessory?'

'He shot Eyvindur.'

'No, he didn't. He says he didn't.'

'And you believe him?'

'Yes, I do. I see no reason to doubt Felix. I can understand that others might, but I don't.'

'If he's innocent, why doesn't he turn himself in? Why play the fugitive? He must be guilty of the murder. It's the only reasonable explanation.'

'He refuses to say a word. All I can think of is that something's happened that he'd rather his father didn't know about. Felix thinks I'll go straight to him with the story. Their relationship's a little tricky.'

Flóvent pointed at the black bag. 'You've been taking care of him.'

'I didn't know what else to do. He asked for help. I couldn't turn my back on him. Enough people have done that already.'

'Forgive me if I don't believe a word you say.'

'Look, he rang scared out of his wits, and begged me to help him. He said he had nowhere else to turn. Something dreadful had happened. He wouldn't confide in me at first, but in the end he told me about the body in his flat. I've tried to get him to explain what it is he's afraid of but he refuses. Says the less I know, the better it'll be for me. I don't understand what he means but he's been talking that way ever since the night Eyvindur was killed.'

'I know they were at school together and used to be friends,' said Flóvent. 'Was that why he killed Eyvindur? Did it have something to do with the past?'

Brynhildur Hólm regarded Flóvent for a moment without speaking, then said patiently: 'Listen to me: he says he didn't shoot Eyvindur.'

'Yes, you've already told me that.'

'Of course I urged him to talk to the police. I've been begging him to do that ever since he went into hiding. But he says it's not safe. He needs to wait. I don't know what he's waiting for. I can't get any sense out of him.'

Brynhildur hadn't heard from Felix for several months, then late one evening the ringing of the phone shattered the silence in the pebble-dash house. Rudolf had gone to bed. She was the only one awake, and she knew at once that something serious had happened to him. Felix was in such a state he could hardly string a sentence together. Once she had managed to calm him down a little, he had started babbling something about the basement flat he rented. That he'd arrived home to find Eyvindur lying on the

194

floor in a pool of blood. Felix lost his head, had a sort of nervous breakdown – he didn't know how else to describe it. He was convinced the police wouldn't believe him; they'd arrest him and something would happen to him while he was in custody. He implored her not to tell his father what had happened until he himself could find out what was going on. Brynhildur believed what he said, so when Felix begged her to meet him, she immediately thought of the old surgery. She knew where the keys were kept and told him to meet her outside the building. He'd been holed up there ever since. She had tried to make him understand that things couldn't go on like this; the police would come looking for him, and hiding from them would make things harder for him in the long run. When the police mistakenly thought he was the man who had been shot, Felix was relieved: it would give him a breathing space to consider his options. But his options had turned out to be limited. Brynhildur didn't believe he had been in contact with anyone else or dared to leave the surgery at all.

'You can decide whether or not you believe me,' she said, once she had finished her tale, 'but I don't think Felix has killed anyone. I don't think he could, don't believe he's capable of it.'

'Who does he think shot Eyvindur, then?'

'Felix says he doesn't know.'

'A soldier?'

'Well, of course Felix was upset and fled the scene straight away, but he got the impression that whoever did it had acted with ruthless efficiency, like a soldier or a trained assassin. The killer hadn't hesitated. That's why he's inclined to believe it was a foreigner rather than an Icelander, though he says he can't be sure.'

'Why's he scared that something will happen to *him*?' asked Flóvent. 'What's he frightened of?'

'Isn't it obvious?'

'No.'

'Felix is convinced that Eyvindur was killed by mistake. He's sure that he himself was the target and that the people who want him dead are still after him. That's the whole point. That's the problem. They're still after him and he believes they want him dead.'

31

Brynhildur had kept her promise not to tell anyone where Felix was hiding, not even his father. She had meant to tell Rudolf before he heard the news from the police, but she didn't get a chance. Only after Flóvent's visit had she come clean. She admitted that she was sheltering Felix at the old surgery and explained why his son wouldn't go to the authorities. Rudolf was absolutely livid that she had failed to tell him straight away and insisted that Felix should turn himself in.

The whole episode had proved a great strain on the doctor, who had a weak heart, and being forcibly dragged in for questioning by the police had been the final straw. That night he'd developed pains in his chest and had been rushed to hospital. When Flóvent followed Brynhildur earlier she had been on her way to tell Felix that things couldn't go on like this.

'You expect me to believe that?' said Flóvent.

'Yes, I'm telling you the truth.'

'What about Felix? Has it not occurred to you that Felix might have fabricated the whole story to con you into helping him? That it's very gullible of you to swallow this stuff about him being the victim?'

'Of course it has. And I accused him of exactly that. Said I found his story preposterous. I threatened to go to the police if he didn't tell me what was really going on. I've no interest in taking the rap . . . as an accomplice or accessory to the crime or whatever you call it, for him or anyone else.'

Flóvent was now able to stand without leaning against the table for support. He still felt a little dizzy, though, so he dropped into the chair by the desk. Brynhildur remained where she was, her back ramrod straight, not giving an inch, as if she would stand by her word whatever the consequences.

'Where's Felix now?' Flóvent asked.

'I don't know,' she said. 'He was gone by the time I came back. I've no idea where to.'

Flóvent couldn't suppress a smile. 'It's time to stop protecting him,' he said.

'I . . . I decided to give him the benefit of the doubt,' she countered. 'When he said his life was in danger. I think you would have done the same in the circumstances. A man had been shot dead in his flat and that man should have been him.'

'Did you also believe him when he told you about the cyanide pill we found in his suitcase?'

'Cyanide pill?'

'So Rudolf didn't tell you either?'

'What cyanide pill?'

'I informed Rudolf that we'd found a capsule in Felix's suitcase and sent it for analysis. According to military intelligence, it's a suicide pill, manufactured in Germany. Are you telling me that you weren't aware of its existence? That neither of them let you into their confidence?'

Brynhildur didn't reply.

'What was it for?' asked Flóvent. 'Why was he carrying it around with him? When did he intend to take it?'

'I don't know anything about a pill,' said Brynhildur after a pause. 'Felix hasn't told me the whole story, I do realise that. I told you – he doesn't want to drag me into it.'

'I wonder what else Felix has failed to tell you. What else Rudolf has decided you don't need to know. What else you aren't sharing with me. Why don't you stop lying and tell me the simple truth? Where is Felix? And don't claim you don't know. He comes running to you as soon as anything goes wrong. You're like . . . like a mother to him. Where are you hiding him now? Tell me!'

'I don't know where Felix is,' said Brynhildur. 'And I don't know anything about a pill.'

'German spies carry pills like that. Was Felix sending information to Germany?'

Brynhildur didn't answer.

'Is he just waiting to leave the country? Is that why he's not turning himself in? Are the Germans coming to pick him up?'

'I don't understand what you're talking about. Leave the country? Where would he go?'

'To Germany?'

Brynhildur stared at Flóvent without speaking, standing quite still, her expression unreadable. He felt his strength gradually returning and pulled the school anniversary pamphlet from his pocket.

'What's that?' she asked as he handed it to her.

'Perhaps you can tell me.'

Brynhildur went over to the window and held up the picture to the light from the street. There was a long pause before she turned to look at Flóvent. 'Where did you get this?'

'It was among Eyvindur's things,' Flóvent replied. 'Ebeneser said the photo was taken at the school. I gather he and Rudolf had a row recently about some boys. Who were these boys they were arguing about? And why are you in that picture with Felix and Eyvindur?'

'Have you talked to Ebeneser?'

'Yes.'

'What did he say?'

'Nothing. Rudolf won't discuss it either. Eyvindur's uncle tells me that he and Felix were boyhood friends. Yet they came from very different homes. Eyvindur's father was . . . he was a vicious thug and persistent offender. His mother was an alcoholic. I wouldn't have thought Felix would be allowed to associate with a boy from that sort of background. But all I got out of my visit to Rudolf was something about heritage. That the ancestral heritage was supposed to be here in Iceland. Do you have any idea what he meant? What he could have been referring to?'

Brynhildur was staring at the photograph.

'Why were they quarrelling about the boys?' asked Flóvent, returning to the attack. 'Who were these boys?'

She raised her eyes, then handed the pamphlet back to him. Flóvent couldn't tell what she was thinking.

'Where did you hear that?' she asked finally. 'Who told you they'd quarrelled?'

'That's beside the point,' said Flóvent. 'Do you know what they were quarrelling about?'

'You'll have to ask them,' said Brynhildur. 'The picture was taken in the school grounds on the occasion of some anniversary or other. Eyvindur and Felix were at school together – as you've already said. But that's all I know. It was a long time ago. One forgets so quickly.'

'There are two other boys with them.'

'Yes, I don't remember their names.'

'And the man with you and Ebeneser?'

'I don't recognise him. He must have been one of the teachers, I suppose.'

'All right, let's leave that for now. Clearly there's something here that none of you are willing to discuss. You all turn evasive, feign ignorance.'

'Yes, well, you can think what you like.'

'Is that why Eyvindur's forehead was marked with a swastika? Is it something to do with this picture?'

'Swastika? What swastika?'

'You didn't know? Felix – or the unknown killer, if he's to be believed – dipped a finger in Eyvindur's blood and drew a swastika on his forehead. Can you imagine why? Or what it's supposed to mean?'

Brynhildur was visibly shocked. 'That's horrible. I didn't know.'

'Didn't Felix tell you? I wouldn't have thought he'd forget a detail like that.'

'Perhaps he didn't notice,' said Brynhildur. 'Perhaps he couldn't bring himself to take a closer look at the body. I don't know. He didn't say a word about it.'

'Why would someone draw a swastika on Eyvindur's forehead? What message were they trying to send?'

'I simply don't believe that Felix did it,' said Brynhildur staunchly.

'The swastika must be linked to Nazism, surely?'

'I don't know . . . It would appear so.'

'Tell me about Hans Lunden.'

'Hans?'

'Yes, Dr Hans Lunden. How do you know each other? What business did you both have with Werner Gerlach at the consulate shortly before the war?'

'Business? I went there once – I was invited to dinner. But I wasn't a regular guest. Hans Lunden is Rudolf's brother. It was, well, before the war and . . . Where did you get this information, if I might ask?'

'What brought Hans Lunden to Iceland? What business did you both have at the consulate?'

'He came to see his brother as far as I'm aware. Rudolf would know more about that than I would. You should ask him. The dinner was given in Hans's honour. He's a well-known physician in Germany. Or scientist, rather. I was invited to accompany them.'

'Tell me about you and Rudolf.'

'What is there to tell?'

'What's the nature of your relationship?'

'We . . . we get on well. If you're implying that our relationship goes beyond that of a housekeeper and employer, you're mistaken.'

'In other words, you simply work for him?'

'Yes.'

'Not for anyone else?'

'No. Honestly, what is this all about? I don't appreciate the tenor of these questions. I don't appreciate it at all.'

'What did you mean when you said that Felix hated his father?' asked Flóvent, changing tack. He got the impression that he wasn't going to get much more out of her tonight. He would have to take Brynhildur into custody for further questioning.

'I beg your pardon?'

'Earlier, when I'd just recovered my senses, you said he hated his father. I presume you meant Felix?'

'Their relationship has been ... strained ... for a long time,' said Brynhildur. 'I think strained is the right word.'

'Why is that?'

'You'll have to ask them,' said Brynhildur evasively.

'You have no idea where Felix could have gone?'

'No.'

Flóvent stood up, still a little unsteady on his feet.

'You'll have to come with me.' he said. 'You must have realised that.'

Brynhildur studied him for a while, then asked: 'Is that really necessary?'

'There's every indication that Felix has committed murder. You helped him to hide from the police. You chose to cover up for him. I'm afraid there's no alternative.'

'You don't believe his story.'

'No. I have no reason to believe a man who fails to come forward immediately when a man is killed in his home.'

Later that evening Flóvent unearthed the documents.

He had left Brynhildur in custody, cleaned himself up as best he could, then decided he was sufficiently recovered to take another look around Rudolf's surgery before heading home. Brynhildur had offered no resistance and had accompanied him without a word to the police station on Pósthússtræti, from where she was escorted to the prison on Skólavördustígur. The only thing she asked was whether she would be locked up for long. He was unable to answer that.

With the aid of a torch he had borrowed from the police station, Flóvent walked slowly through the surgery, opening drawers and cupboards. He didn't know exactly what he was looking for. Clues to where Felix might be hiding, perhaps.

Since he was intending to conduct a more thorough search of the premises in the morning, he suddenly decided, halfway inside the wardrobe from which Felix had leapt out earlier, that he'd had enough for now. The wardrobe was empty. As he was backing out, he accidentally bashed the torch against the door. As it hit the floor he heard a hollow thud. Flóvent tapped the wooden base. There was no mistaking it. He got down on all fours and ran his fingers along the floor of the wardrobe until he felt a slightly raised edge. With the help of the pocket knife he always carried, he managed to prise up one of the boards. Underneath was a small bundle of papers and some envelopes that turned out to contain specimen jars. Some of the papers showed tables of what appeared to be height and weight measurements, others featured lists of questions. He leafed through them quickly. At first glance, some of the questions seemed to relate to personal matters such as family circumstances, sleeping habits and diet, while others were intended to assess cognitive development and intelligence.

Flóvent stared down at the hiding place in the base of the wardrobe, the maid's words – about Ebeneser and Rudolf quarrelling over some boys – echoing in his mind.

32

The woman stared at Thorson in confusion, having just been interrupted while bawling out her younger sister. Either she hadn't heard his question or she hadn't taken it in.

'Vera,' repeated Thorson. 'You mentioned her name. Could you tell me which Vera you mean? Who is she?'

'Vera?' echoed the older sister of the girl Thorson had rescued from the minesweeper – an effort for which he had received precious little thanks. The girl herself was standing behind her sister, cradling her red cheek and glaring at him as if it was all his fault. Him and his meddling.

'Yes.'

'What do you want with her?'

'She . . . knows a friend of mine,' Thorson improvised. 'I just wondered if it was the same woman. It's not a very common name,' he added, 'Vera.'

'An army friend of yours?'

'Yes.'

'She takes in washing for the soldiers,' said the woman. 'Billy helped her get set up. Is his name Billy? Your mate?'

Thorson nodded. 'Does she run a laundry?'

'Hardly a laundry, but Billy fixed her up with a washing machine, and she's got a wringer and some washing lines. She's run off her feet. My sister,' said the woman, giving the younger girl a dirty look, 'sometimes helps her out and Vera's obviously earning enough to pay her a bit.'

Thorson continued to quiz the woman about Vera until his prying made her first puzzled, then suspicious. But by then she had told him about Vera's relationship with Billy, a sergeant in the British Army, who had been instrumental, if Thorson had understood correctly, in finding her a steady stream of customers. She had left her Icelandic boyfriend, who was a bit of a deadbeat, and started a new life; she was standing on her own two feet and had broken free from a relationship that wasn't going anywhere. Billy had opened her eyes to a world of possibilities and she had no intention of missing out on them.

The woman confirmed that the man Vera used to live with was called Eyvindur, but she had no idea what had become of him. She'd heard about a murder but didn't know the identity of the victim or whether anyone had been caught yet. As far as she knew, Eyvindur was off on a sales trip. That's what Vera herself had told her. Vera was planning to break the news to him, about Billy, as soon as she got the chance. Really, she should have moved out ages ago.

'Are they planning on getting married?' Thorson persisted, ignoring her question. 'Billy and Vera?'

'Yes, I think so.'

'I hear from her neigh . . . I hear she used to entertain soldiers.'

'What . . . Why are you so interested in Vera?' The woman sounded indignant on her friend's behalf. 'Are you spying on her? Who did you say you were? How do you know Billy? You did say you knew him?'

Deciding he had all the information he needed, Thorson asked the woman to excuse him: he had to get going as he was on his way to answer a call. Then he hurried back to his jeep and drove off. Late though it was, he felt he had to speak to Vera as soon as possible; it couldn't wait until morning. She had a right to know about Eyvindur.

After ascertaining that Flóvent wasn't in his office on Fríkirkjuvegur, Thorson drove towards Pósthússtræti. He spotted him crossing Hafnarstræti with heavy steps, heading in the direction of the police station, a bundle of papers under his arm and a preoccupied look on his face.

Thorson greeted him with the news that he had found out where Vera was living and was hoping Flóvent would come along to meet her. Flóvent asked to him to hang on a tick while he put the papers into safe hands. A few minutes later, they were driving to the west end, towards Vera's laundry. On the way there Flóvent shared the news of his own adventure and the latest twist: that Felix was claiming Eyvindur had been killed by mistake and that he himself had nothing to do with the murder.

'Brynhildur believes him and swears she doesn't know where Felix is now,' said Flóvent, 'but I don't believe a word she says.'

'Why's he in hiding? Who's supposed to be after him?'

'She says she doesn't know that either because Felix won't tell her. She's spending the night in a prison cell. Perhaps she'll be more forthcoming in the morning.'

The house stood on its own, not far from a small cluster of buildings to the west of Camp Knox. It was an old concrete house with a small ground floor and an attic, and behind it was a patch of grass where a number of washing lines had been erected. White sheets, uniforms and vests were flapping in the wind. There were tubs lying here and there on the grass and the air was full of steam and the smell of soap powder. The laundry appeared to take up at least half the ground floor, and they assumed Vera must live upstairs in the attic.

Light spilled out into the darkness. They could see the silhouette of a figure inside, unloading a machine and dumping a pile of washing on the wringer, then picking up a tub and carrying it out into the garden. There she began to peg up the wet clothes by the light from the laundry door. They could now see that the woman was wearing a large apron and military boots. Although she was having to lug a heavy tub on her own and could hardly see what she was doing in the darkness, she was happily humming a popular new tune as she worked.

They walked over and said good evening. She glanced at them both before carrying on with what she was doing. 'Have you brought washing?' she asked.

'You look pretty busy,' remarked Flóvent.

'It never lets up,' she said. 'How can I help you?'

'Are you Vera?' asked Thorson. 'We're looking for a woman called Vera who takes in laundry.'

'Yes, that's right,' said the woman, spreading out a large white sheet on one of the lines. 'What can I do for you? I can't really take on any more washing. As you can see, I'm already working half the night as it is, even though I've got two girls helping me out.'

'It's about Eyvindur,' said Flóvent. 'Eyvindur Ragnarsson. You two used to live together, didn't you?'

The woman paused in the act of lifting another sheet from the tub and turned to face them. She had an attractive figure but didn't flaunt it. In the light from the house they could see that she was tanned from the summer sun, with thick blonde hair down to her shoulders and a slight cleft lip, very faint, just enough to make her mouth look a little uneven, almost lascivious. The blue eyes regarded them with a questioning look.

'What about him?'

'Haven't you heard?'

'Heard? Heard what?'

'He's dead,' said Flóvent.

'What?'

'I'm sorry to have to tell you like this but we've only just found out where you live. We had hoped to inform you without delay, but it hasn't been easy to track you down.'

'Dead? Eyvindur?'

'I'm afraid that's not all,' said Thorson. 'He was shot dead here in Reykjavík. Have you really not heard?'

'What do you mean "shot"? What are you saying?' Vera looked stunned.

'It's true. I'm sorry,' said Flóvent. 'We're from the police and we're in charge of the investigation. Thorson here represents the defence force. The gun used to kill Eyvindur was almost certainly a military weapon. We haven't managed to trace it yet. Or the killer.'

As Vera listened, she reached under her apron and fumbled in the pocket of her dress for a packet of cigarettes. She lit one, silent and preoccupied, as the news gradually sank in.

'You didn't know?' asked Flóvent.

'I . . . no, I walked out on him,' said Vera. 'I always meant to talk to him but . . . he was away in the West Fjords when I moved out. I kept meaning to go and see him but . . . there's been so much to do.' She gestured at the washing. 'All I knew was that a body had been found in a basement flat. It didn't occur to me that . . . that it could be Eyvindur. Never entered my head. I thought he was away. Is this some sort of joke?'

'I'm afraid not,' said Flóvent. 'His body was discovered in the flat of a man by the name of Felix Lunden. We don't know what he was doing there. Perhaps you might have some idea?'

'No,' said Vera. 'I recognise the name, though. Eyvindur used to talk about Felix. He was a salesman too, and they'd known each other a bit in the old days. I don't understand – was it Felix who did it?'

'We don't know for certain, I'm afraid,' said Flóvent. 'He's lying low and we haven't managed to find him yet.'

'But why? Why should he have done it? Killed Eyvindur? It's . . . it's absurd. He was . . . he was completely harmless. He'd never have hurt anyone. He was so inoffensive, was always going on about how useless he was. He found everything so daunting. And now he's been shot? Oh my God, I didn't know. I can't believe it. Just can't believe it.'

Vera stared at them, her astonishment at Eyvindur's fate plain on her face.

'No, I don't believe it,' she repeated. 'It's ridiculous. You can't just come round here, making up stuff like that.'

'It's always difficult to be the bearer of bad news, especially in situations like this,' said Flóvent. 'But I'm afraid it . . . it's a fact.'

'You moved in with him in spite of all that,' remarked Thorson.

'I'm sorry?'

'He seems to have been a bit of a wet blanket. So what did you see in him?'

'He was . . . I just got fed up with him,' she said. 'I didn't get to know him properly until after we'd moved in together. I'd recently arrived from the countryside. Didn't know my way around. He knew the ropes, and I liked him. He invited me to come and live with him and I was desperate for somewhere to stay, so . . .'

Vera broke off, distracted.

'We understand that you vanished from his life with about as much ceremony,' remarked Flóvent.

'What do you mean?'

'You ran off in the middle of the night with a soldier,' said Flóvent. 'Threw your things in his car, took off and never looked back.'

'Have you been talking to that old bag upstairs?' asked Vera. 'She hates my guts. Everything she says about me is a lie. You shouldn't take any notice of her.'

'She told us about the men you entertained,' said Thorson, 'while Eyvindur was away on his sales trips. She says it was more than just a couple of soldiers.'

'Yes, I bet she did.'

'She's not the only one who mentioned it.'

'What, am I on trial here?' asked Vera, grinding her cigarette under her heel. 'Do you think I'm the only woman in Reykjavík who's friendly with soldiers?'

'Was Eyvindur aware of that fact?' asked Flóvent.

'Why are you asking me that? You don't think I did anything to him, do you?'

'We're just making routine enquiries,' said Flóvent.

'He'd heard a rumour in town – gossip,' said Vera. 'Flung it in my face, but did it in his usual way – hesitating, stammering, insinuating things. I don't know why I didn't just tell him the truth. I suppose I felt sorry for him. Perhaps I wanted to protect him. I should have told him it was over between us – what little there was. I pretended to be terribly hurt and offended that he'd listen to gossip like that. Somehow I didn't feel ready to tell him the truth – that I was planning to leave him. Maybe I should have told him straight away. It would have been the honest thing to do, but I couldn't bring myself to say it out loud. Anyway, I'm not sure he'd have wanted to hear the truth. He said we should talk about it properly when he got back. I didn't say anything but I knew it was over. When he left, I took my chance. I moved out here, started working for the army, started supporting myself. I suppose it wasn't very nice of me to disappear like that. But it wouldn't have changed anything if I'd done it differently. I'd still have left him. I know that sounds callous, especially now that he's . . . that he's dead, but that's the way it is.'

'Did you ever see Eyvindur again after that?' asked Thorson.

'Yes, once. He came round here – he'd found out where I was – and showed me some money he'd got hold of. Begged me to come back to him.'

'Where did he get the money?'

'I don't know. It was nothing to boast about. I suppose he must have had a good trip. I didn't ask. After that he left.'

'It doesn't seem like you had much time for him,' said Flóvent.

'Yes,' she said, 'I did, actually. Look, I just wanted you to know how things were. Eyvindur isn't . . . wasn't a bad man, far from it, but I knew our relationship was never going to work out. He wasn't willing to admit it. I had tried to talk to him about it but he didn't want to hear.'

'Was Billy the one who helped you move?' asked Thorson.

'Yes.'

'In the middle of the night?'

'I couldn't face the neighbours and their prying eyes, so I bolted. There wasn't much to take. My clothes. That was about it. We didn't own a lot. I left the rest behind.'

'What about the other soldiers?'

'Other soldiers? What do you mean?'

'According to the neighbours, you used to have visitors at night. There were quite a lot of soldiers hanging around your place.'

'They can say what they like. It was only Billy and . . . well, his mates. They sometimes came with him.'

'And partied all night?'

'Is that against the law? And it wasn't all night. The stupid old cow. You shouldn't take any notice of her. Was she saying I was some kind of tart? She can talk. I sometimes see her daughter hanging around the camp here and she's not washing their clothes, I can tell you that. The old bitch. The bloody old busybody.'

33

They asked if she lived in the house where she worked and she said yes, she slept in a little room in the attic. She invited them in, and as they entered the laundry, Thorson and Flóvent offered their apologies and said they wouldn't take up much of her time. They just had a few more questions concerning Eyvindur and Felix. For example, did she have any idea what Eyvindur could have been doing at Felix's flat? She busied herself with the washing and said no, she didn't, but she did remember how astonished Eyvindur had been to bump into Felix aboard the *Súd* and discover that they were in the same line of work. Their paths hadn't crossed for donkey's years before that, not since they were at school. They hadn't been in the same form because they came from such different backgrounds, but in spite of that they had been friends once. Their friendship had ended when Felix just lost interest in Eyvindur one day.

Though Eyvindur didn't talk much about the past, Vera gathered

that he'd had a rough home life and few friends, so his relationship with Felix had meant a lot to him. Eyvindur's mother might
never have existed for all he mentioned her, but he'd spoken
briefly about his father after he and Vera lost the rooms they were
renting and he was forced to throw himself on the mercy of his
uncle. Only then did she learn that his father had done time for a
variety of offences, including assault, which had come as quite a
surprise to her since Eyvindur himself wouldn't have said boo to
a goose.

The encounter on board the *Súd* had not been a particularly
cordial one, according to Eyvindur. He and Felix had very little to
say to one another. Eyvindur had wanted to ask him why their
friendship had ended so suddenly when they were boys. Vera
understood from Eyvindur that he kept going round to the doctor's house to ask after Felix and had been told each time that he
wasn't home, until finally Felix himself had said he wanted nothing more to do with him and that he was to stop bothering them.

But Eyvindur didn't like to talk about it and changed the subject whenever Vera asked about his old friend. He wasn't one for
reminiscing, but he would chat about his sales trips, though
mostly he just harped on about his failures. It had rankled that
Felix was far more successful than him, and that had got him
started on Runki, another salesman whose feats Eyvindur could
only dream of.

Now that she came to think of it, Eyvindur had mentioned one
thing that had struck him as very odd. Felix had taken great pains
to cover as wide an area as possible on his sales trips. He would
trek to the most out-of-the-way places where only a few souls
scratched a living. Other salesmen knew they weren't worth the
trouble, yet Felix had been determined to visit them. Eyvindur

couldn't imagine it was worth his while, however gifted a sales-man he was.

'It may sound like a strange question, but did Eyvindur happen to mention where any of these places were?' asked Thorson. 'Were they close to any military facilities, for example?'

Vera shook her head. She didn't think he'd mentioned that. Now that she had got over her indignation at the gossip they'd had repeated, she was friendly and willing to chat despite the late hour. She answered their questions thoughtfully and sensibly, and, at their prompting, tried to search her memory for anything she might have forgotten. Yet Flóvent's thoughts kept returning to her upstairs neighbour, who had called her sex mad and accused her of being a soldier's whore. And then there was the brown envelope he had found on the living room floor. She had cheated on Eyvin-dur, then walked out on him, straight into the arms of a British soldier. When Flóvent looked for traces of sorrow or remorse, for any kind of emotional turmoil, he could see none. The news didn't seem to touch her at all, now that she had got over her initial sur-prise. Either she was more heartless than he had thought or the news hadn't truly hit home yet.

'Why do you ask about military facilities?' she said. 'Was Felix interested in them for some reason?'

'We don't know,' said Thorson.

'Are you suggesting he was some kind of spy? Eyvindur did say his father was a Nazi.'

'We have no proof that he was spying,' Flóvent corrected her. 'Did Eyvindur imply that he was? Did he see Felix taking photo-graphs on his trips, for example? Or expressing an interest in troop movements or military instillations?'

'No, I don't remember anything like that, but . . .'

'Yes?'

'It's so strange you should mention spying because Felix . . . Eyvindur told me once that he thought Felix only wanted to be his friend so he could spy on him.'

'How do you mean?'

'Apparently, Felix was always asking Eyvindur about his father, insisted on going round to his house to play every time, and seemed very curious about his family – downright nosy in fact. Eyvindur found it very odd.'

There was a knock at the laundry door. A British soldier appeared and smiled at Vera, simultaneously casting a suspicious glance at Flóvent and Thorson. Returning his smile, Vera put down the washing and began to tell the man that they were from the police, but soon faltered as her English wasn't up to the task. Thorson chipped in, explaining that they had come to see Vera in connection with Eyvindur's death. The man turned out to be Billy Wiggins, Vera's boyfriend, a rather stocky British sergeant of around thirty, with red hair and a ruddy complexion, who was clearly none too pleased to find his girlfriend in the company of other men so late in the evening.

'You all right, love?' he asked Vera. She nodded. He walked over and took her in his arms and they kissed. The news of Eyvindur's death didn't seem to faze him in the slightest. Flóvent caught Thorson's eye, then asked Vera to step outside with him. When Billy made to follow, Thorson blocked his path, saying that he'd like to ask him a few questions; it would only take a minute. Billy looked set to push past him, but Thorson was firm, repeating that he didn't want any trouble but he had a few questions. When Billy continued to ignore him, Thorson informed him that he would have to accompany him to police headquarters. The sergeant gave in and Thorson began asking him about his relationship with Vera and whether he had ever met Eyvindur.

'What's it to you?' asked Billy Wiggins, with an uneasy glance out of the door to where Flóvent and Vera stood talking. 'Why don't you leave me alone?'

'Did you know him, sergeant?'

'No, I never met him. Never laid eyes on the man.'

'Are you sure?'

'Sure? Of course I'm sure. What do you take me for? You don't think I had anything to do with his . . . with his death?'

'I didn't say that. Are you concerned about that?'

'About what?'

'About being implicated in the murder?'

'No, I'm not. Because I didn't do anything to the bloke. Vera's a great girl and . . . and we get on well together. She'd made up her mind to leave him ages ago. She was just waiting for the right moment.'

'How did you meet Vera?'

'How? At Hótel Ísland. She was out having fun.'

'Was she there with Eyvindur?'

'No,' said Billy with an ugly laugh, raising his eyebrows at Thorson's naivety. 'He wasn't there.'

Flóvent was standing outside, watching the washing fluttering in the evening breeze. Vera had taken out another cigarette. She inhaled, her eyes on the door of the laundry where Thorson was talking to Billy.

'So you can't imagine why Eyvindur would have gone to see Felix after all these years?' Flóvent asked.

'No, I . . . nothing comes to mind.'

'Could it have been something to do with his sales trips? Or their school days? Something he wanted to ask him about? Had they started meeting up again? Renewed their friendship?'

'I simply can't help you,' said Vera, blowing on the glowing tip of her cigarette. 'Eyvindur sometimes talked about Felix, but he never had anything good to say about him. Only that when they were boys he'd suddenly dropped him and refused to have anything more to do with him. Eyvindur felt used. That's how he talked about Felix. He said it hadn't been a real friendship after all.'

'It's possible Felix was no longer allowed to see him,' said Flóvent. 'To associate with him. That's the sort of home he was from. His father was very strict, I'd imagine. A snob.'

'Yes, anyway, Eyvindur was still wondering about it. About what really happened.'

'Did he ever mention taking part in any experiments at his school?' asked Flóvent.

'What kind of experiments?'

'I'm not entirely sure,' said Flóvent. 'I just wondered if he'd said anything. A series of tests – to do with his health, perhaps. Or his development.'

'No, I don't remember him talking about that. Though he did once mention a school nurse, whose name I've forgotten. He showed me a picture of her. Felix was in it too.'

Flóvent took out the school pamphlet from Eyvindur's flat and showed it to her. Vera confirmed that it was the same picture. She held it up to the light from the laundry door and peered at it.

'I wonder if it could have been him?' she mused, as if to herself.

'Who?'

'Him,' she said, pointing to the boy standing next to Eyvindur and Felix in the photo. 'I have a feeling he was the one Eyvindur was talking about. I can't remember his name but he had a similar story to tell.'

'A similar story? How do you mean?'

'It was like he'd experienced the same thing,' said Vera. 'Eyvindur ran into him one day and they started talking about Felix and it was exactly the same story. Felix had gone out of his way to get to know the boy at school and was close friends with him for a while, spent a lot of time with him. Then he suddenly dropped him, never spoke to him again.'

'Do you think that could have been why Eyvindur went to see Felix?' asked Flóvent. 'To ask what was going on?'

'I suppose it's possible.' said Vera. 'I just don't know. Haven't the foggiest. He was always . . . always trying to sort something out, always saying that things were about to get better. He claimed he was about to come into a load of money. I gave up on him in the end. Couldn't take it any more.'

'Where was this money supposed to come from?'

'He never said. I expect it was all talk, as usual.'

34

Brynhildur Hólm told Flóvent she had hardly slept a wink, but then she'd never had to spend a night in prison before. He could tell she was badly shaken by the experience. She complained bitterly about being locked up, protesting that such treatment was quite uncalled for. She had demonstrated a willingness to cooperate with the police: there was nothing to be gained from throwing her in jail. Flóvent explained, as he had the night before, that she had admitted to aiding and abetting a man suspected of a serious crime and that it would be irresponsible of the police to allow her to remain at large. There was a risk she might destroy evidence, and she might well continue to assist the suspect.

The plan was to isolate Felix and force him to give himself up, or at least smoke him out of his hiding place. A formal warrant had been issued for his arrest and members of the public were being urged to inform the police if they had any information about his movements over the past week. His photograph had been published in the papers and circulated to police stations up and down the country, as well as to the military police.

At midday, Flóvent sat down with Brynhildur Hólm in the interview room at the prison. She had been officially detained in custody for several days. Flóvent brought out the papers he had discovered under the wardrobe in Rudolf's surgery and spread them on the table. Her expression didn't change. Flóvent began by remarking that so far none of the people involved in the case had told him more than a fraction of the truth, it seemed to him. And that what he had been told was implausible at best. All the facts had been twisted with the express purpose of misleading the police.

'I don't know what game you're all playing,' he said, 'but it's a distasteful one. Don't you think it's about time you started working with us?'

'What are those?' Brynhildur asked, glancing at the papers.

'Documents I found at the surgery after you'd left. I had a doctor take a look at them for me this morning, and he found them very interesting for various reasons which I intend to discuss with you in a minute.'

'Rudolf's expecting me at the hospital. He'll be worried if I don't turn up.'

'That'll have to wait. What concerns me is this business with the boys. Eyvindur and Felix were friends at school. Then, out of the blue, Felix didn't want to know him any more. And we've heard about another, similar, case involving one of the boys in the photograph I showed you yesterday.' Flóvent pulled the anniversary pamphlet from the pile of papers. 'This one here – the boy standing next to Felix and Eyvindur. We're trying to get hold of him, but, in the meantime, maybe you can tell me a little about him?'

Brynhildur lowered her eyes to the documents and the photograph, then sat there without speaking, her mind evidently working hard. Flóvent supposed that she was trying to decide whether she had reached the end of the road. Whether it was time to come clean.

'You've had a while to think about it,' said Flóvent. 'Your situation could hardly be worse. You must see that. If you continue to withhold information it will only make your position more difficult and provide us with more ammunition.'

'I thought he'd got rid of all that,' Brynhildur said, her eyes fixed on the papers. 'I didn't think he'd kept any of it. He . . . he no longer holds the same views. Rudolf's changed. Unlike his brother.'

'The same views? On what? The Germans, you mean? The Nazis?'

'He renounced his faith,' said Brynhildur. 'I suppose you could put it like that. He stopped believing the relentless Nazi propaganda.'

'And Felix? Has he renounced his faith too?'

'You think Felix is a spy,' said Brynhildur after a long pause. Flóvent thought he detected a new note in her voice.

'That's one theory.'

'Well, you could say he's had experience in watching people. He used to do it for his father when he was a boy. Around the time that photo was taken. You could regard that as a kind of spying, I suppose. Quite different in nature, but still . . . I suppose it all amounts to the same thing.'

'I'm not with you,' said Flóvent. 'What kind of spying? When he was a boy, you say?'

'Rudolf received a threatening letter recently,' Brynhildur said.

'Someone must have slipped it through the letter box because it didn't come by the regular post. There was no postmark. No stamp. It contained a typewritten letter. We don't know who sent it, but we suspect it was Eyvindur. It was unsigned and full of spelling mistakes. The writer was incensed by something Rudolf and Ebeneser had done, which, admittedly, I was involved in as well. They were both named in the letter. The sender had discovered the truth. How, I don't know. I thought we could keep it a secret but apparently not. The writer knew about the study and the experiments; he believed that a crime had been committed against him and threatened to expose the whole affair unless certain conditions were met.'

'The experiments?'

'Yes.'

'What experiments?'

Brynhildur hesitated.

'Were these papers part of it? Part of this study?'

'It looks as though they were,' said Brynhildur eventually. 'I thought Rudolf was going to destroy all the records but . . .'

'When did he receive this threatening letter?'

'A few days before Eyvindur was killed. But no one told Felix. He and Rudolf are estranged. And anyway the threats weren't directed at him, and we didn't even know whether to take them seriously. So you can imagine my shock when Felix told me it was Eyvindur who'd been murdered. As soon as Rudolf heard, he was convinced that Felix was responsible – that it was Eyvindur who sent the letter, that he'd been planning to get even with Felix. It wasn't . . . the idea wasn't that far-fetched. Felix had helped his father with his research. And Eyvindur was one of the subjects.'

'So Rudolf believes his son is capable of murder?'

'I don't know. They haven't spoken for years.'

'Why not?'

'Felix swears he didn't kill Eyvindur and claims he has no idea what he was doing in his flat,' said Brynhildur, dodging the question. 'He insisted he stumbled on Eyvindur's body. Then again, Eyvindur was involved in the study, so . . .'

'Are you saying you don't believe Felix either?'

'I want to believe him. His version would be . . . easier to bear, though the whole thing's a tragedy. A terrible tragedy.'

'Why didn't you and Rudolf take the letter to the police?'

'Because then we'd have had to tell them about the study and . . . Rudolf flatly refused to do that. He still thinks he can hush it up. He can't bear the thought of anyone knowing what we did, not now we're at war with Germany and the Nazis are jackbooting all over Europe. He's renounced his faith. When Hans came over hoping to conduct research with the support of the Icelandic government and grants from the German Reich, Rudolf refused to work with him. If he'd done so, it would have been impossible to cover up his earlier study.'

Brynhildur heaved a sigh. 'My fear is that Eyvindur wrote the letter, then went to see Felix and their encounter ended in disaster. But Felix won't admit it. I think he's trying to avoid facing up to what he's done by inventing all these stories about spying and being in mortal danger.'

'But yesterday you said Felix was incapable of killing anyone.'

'Yes, I know. I've tried but failed to get him to confess, and I find it hard to picture him shooting anyone, but . . . but you never know.'

'Is that why you say he hates his father? Because of the study?'

'It's a long story, but that's certainly part of it.'

'So someone shooting Eyvindur by mistake – is that a complete fabrication?'

'I simply don't know. I think we're all in the same boat, Felix, Rudolf and I; we're all trying to work out what happened. Felix is desperate and keeps coming up with conspiracy theories. Yesterday he started saying that Eyvindur must have been the target after all. That the murderer might have been sent by the woman Eyvindur used to live with. Apparently she was carrying on with soldiers. Vera. Is that right? Could her name be Vera? Felix had heard a rumour that she was mixed up in the Situation, and he thinks maybe she wanted Eyvindur out of the way. He thinks a soldier might have gone after Eyvindur and killed him for her.'

'At Felix's flat? Isn't that . . . Does Felix have any idea why Eyvindur was in his flat?'

'No,' said Brynhildur. 'He swears Eyvindur had never visited him before.'

'Eyvindur couldn't understand why Felix suddenly broke off their friendship when they were boys,' said Flóvent.

'Yes, well, by then Felix had provided his father with all the information he required, and after that Eyvindur was of no more use to them.' Brynhildur hesitated, then added, with obvious reluctance: 'He takes after his uncle a bit too much at times. He has a very cruel streak. The poor boy.'

35

Thorson stepped out of the jeep and surveyed the farm. There was a new-looking two-storey house with small windows and raw, unpainted walls, which looked as though it had been thrown up in a hurry. A little way off stood a traditional turf farmhouse, which appeared to serve as a cowshed and barn nowadays. Two of its three gables were leaning drunkenly into the yard, and the walls were so overgrown with grass that the layers of turf were all but invisible. Part of the roof had fallen in, reminding Thorson of a story his father had once told him. When he was a boy in the north of Iceland, a dangerous bull had climbed onto the low, grassy roof of a farmhouse and stamped right through. There it had hung, thrashing and bellowing, its legs dangling down into the living room. His father had never forgotten the sight of the magnificent beast in such a ridiculous plight.

Thorson was worn out after six hours of jolting over rough roads. He had set off from Reykjavík that morning, headed east over the mountains, and stopped for lunch at Tryggvaskáli in the village of Selfoss. There was a military airfield not far from the village and he had watched as one plane landed and another took off. They were engaged in air-defence patrols around the island. Ever since the war broke out there had been occasional sightings of German reconnaissance or fighter planes flying along the coast. They took off from Norway with fuel tanks specially adapted for long-distance missions over the North Atlantic, but so far they hadn't caused much damage in Iceland.

The British also had a unit stationed in Selfoss to defend the bridge over the River Ölfúsá. Thorson had been studying engineering back in Canada before he joined up and bridges were a particular interest of his, so he had taken this opportunity to examine the structure. It was a fine suspension bridge, spanning the point where the river narrowed between two cliffs, and he had paused to draw it in the sketch pad he always carried. This had attracted the attention of a British sentry, and he had been forced to show the man his ID before he could allay his suspicions.

He knocked at the open door of the farmhouse, then stepped inside, rather diffidently, calling out to ask if anyone was home. He hadn't seen a soul around the yard or by the outbuildings. The day was hot, sunny and dry as a bone, and when he had looked out over the fields it seemed as though the entire household was hard at work on the hay harvest. In the kitchen, he found an ancient-looking woman sitting in one corner. A little boy of not quite two was playing on the floor nearby, tethered to her chair leg so he couldn't wander off and get into trouble. The old woman, absorbed in replacing the broken teeth of a rake, didn't hear him come in, but the little boy looked up and grinned at him, then rose, tottering, to his feet. The tether was too short, however, and he plumped down on his backside again before he could take more than a step. At that the old woman glanced up and, seeing Thorson, removed a pair of battered round glasses from her nose and wished him a good afternoon. She was deaf, and he had to raise his voice to make himself understood. He had come from Reykjavík, he explained, to see the farmer, but of course he must be busy with the haymaking in this fine weather. Yes, he was, she said, and asked what he wanted to see him about. Thorson had worn a brown moleskin jacket instead of his uniform. People wouldn't be used to receiving visits from soldiers out here, and he was afraid the uniform would put them on their guard. He explained that he was here to make enquiries about a young woman called Vera, to find out if this was the farm she had grown up on and if her parents still lived here.

'Vera?' exclaimed the old woman.

'That's right.'

'What about her? Is she in some kind of trouble?'

'Why do you say that, ma'am?'

'I've no idea where she is,' the old woman went on. 'The lass moved to Reykjavík a few years back and hasn't been seen since. Her parents don't live here any more. They gave up farming a couple of years ago and moved east over the sands, all the way out to Höfn.'

'Oh, so –'

'Yes, my son farms here now. He built this house. We're from the neighbouring property, you see. Little Vera lived here, right enough, but her whole family's left the area.'

Thorson looked around the kitchen. A coffee pot stood on the hob, the sink was full of crockery and the stove was stacked with dirty pots and pans, because on a dry day like this every able-bodied person on the property was needed to bring in the hay. Outside the window he glimpsed the crumbling turf building that had until recently served as the farmhouse. Under that grassy roof Vera must have entered the world.

When he and Flóvent had spoken to her in the laundry, it had struck Thorson as interesting that she had come from the countryside and known nothing of Reykjavík when she met Eyvindur. He had pressed her for more detail about her background, but she had seemed flustered and had resorted to deliberately vague answers, giving the impression that she would rather not discuss it. At this point Billy Wiggins had lost patience and said he was fed up with this bloody interrogation.

As early in the morning as could be deemed considerate, Thorson had phoned the woman who used to live upstairs from Eyvindur and Vera, and asked if she knew where Vera came from. She was as quick to answer as she had been before. Eyvindur had once mentioned a farm in the shadow of the Eyjafjöll mountains, but it was clear that he had never been there himself. He wouldn't have minded visiting the farm, he'd said, but Vera wasn't keen and had very little contact with her family. This had struck their neighbour as odd. She'd concluded that Vera must be lying about her origins, perhaps to cover up the fact that she'd been messing around with soldiers ever since they'd first set foot ashore. The slut.

'So you haven't had any news of her at all, ma'am?' asked Thorson loudly, standing there in the farm kitchen, phrasing his question as politely as he could, anxious to show the old lady his respect.

'No, none at all. We haven't once heard from her or seen her since she left.' The little boy had now climbed onto the old woman's lap, where he sat staring curiously at Thorson.

'Were they good neighbours, her parents?'

'Who did you say you were again?' asked the old woman, squinting at him. 'Should I know you? My eyes aren't what they used to be.'

'No, you don't know me, ma'am,' said Thorson. 'I'm acquainted with Vera from town and just happened to be passing. I knew the man she was living with. I don't know if you –'

'Oh, really? Has she got married, then?'

'No, they weren't married.'

'Well, I don't know why I should have heard anything about her. We're not in touch with her family. Was it a soldier? The man she was living with?'

'No,' said Thorson. 'His name was Eyvindur. He died recently.'

'Oh, poor girl. Still, it won't take her long to find herself another. She's no better than . . . Can I offer you a coffee, young man? Have you come all this way from Reykjavík just to ask about the girl?'

'I'd gladly accept some coffee,' said Thorson, 'but please don't trouble yourself, ma'am. I'm sure I can fix it myself.'

The old woman laid down the head of the rake and gave directions from where she was sitting with the child on her lap. She told him which tin he would find the coffee in, where they kept the chicory, how to rinse out the coffee pot and how many spoonfuls of coffee to put in. The farm had electricity, supplied by a diesel generator, and a modern electric cooker had replaced the old coal range that Thorson had noticed standing outside in the yard, already looking obsolete. The aroma of coffee filled the air. The old woman asked Thorson to give the little boy a flat-cake and told him where to find it. The child climbed back down to the floor and sat there chewing happily. The woman drank her coffee black, and Thorson followed her example, assuring her that he didn't want anything with it. She asked him to stop calling her 'ma'am': that sort of civility was nothing but an affectation introduced by Danish merchants; why, she'd never called anyone 'ma'am' in her life, despite being so terribly old. She was fond of a bit of snuff, though. Taking out a small tobacco pouch, she offered some to Thorson who sniffed a few grains off the back of his hand and immediately sneezed. This tickled the old lady. She took a pinch of snuff, placed it daintily in each nostril, then wiped her nose with a red handkerchief.

They chatted about the weather for a while; they'd had an outstandingly good summer in this part of the country, resulting in a bumper hay crop, and everyone had been so busy with the harvest that almost nothing else had got a look-in. She asked for news from Reykjavík, particularly about the Situation: about local women consorting with soldiers and whether it was very blatant and how such a thing was possible and why didn't the government step in. Thorson told her that while there was a certain amount of courting going on between the soldiers and Icelandic women, it was perfectly harmless for the most part, though of course there were exceptions, and the so-called Morality Committee had been set up to keep an eye on underage girls. The old woman tutted a great deal at this and said she'd heard it was a disgraceful state of affairs, and of course it was only going to get worse now that the country was being flooded with Yankees.

She helped herself to another pinch of snuff. Thorson noticed a stubby, much-smoked pipe in an ashtray beside her and guessed that it was hers as well. Her gums were almost completely toothless, and she whistled as she talked. Her long grey hair hung in two plaits, on either side of her face, and her skin was as wrinkled as a crumpled paper bag. Her whole appearance, from her gnarled fingers to her bent back, bore the stamp of the long years of toil that had been her lot in life.

'What about Vera? Is she in the Situation then?' she asked.

Unwilling to spread gossip, Thorson merely repeated that her boyfriend had died very recently.

'Well, since you're asking about her . . . I was going to say that Vera was one of those women who always attracts trouble. Man trouble, I mean. Of course she had looks on her side, no question, and she knew how to flaunt them. The local lads used to swarm around her like flies. She had them all eating out of her hand. And there was a bit of bother about something that happened . . .'

'Oh?'

'. . . which may have been why she moved away.'

36

Brynhildur Hólm coughed and asked for a drink of water. Flóvent went to the door and ordered the guard to fetch a jug. Then he took his seat opposite her again and picked up where he had left off, asking her to clarify what she had said about Felix: that he took after Hans Lunden rather than his own father, that he had a cruel streak. Brynhildur refused to elaborate: Flóvent could interpret her words as he wished. The guard returned with a jug of water and two glasses.

'All right. Then tell me about Rudolf's research,' Flóvent said, pushing the papers towards her. 'What exactly was he studying?'

Brynhildur looked at the pages in front of her. 'If I tell you what I know, will you help Felix? Perhaps it was wrong of me to say he had a cruel streak. Because my heart bleeds for him, you know. Felix is in a bad way. He's frightened, backed into a corner, and I'm afraid he'll do something foolish if this goes on any longer. Afraid he'll do something terribly foolish.'

'I'm not sure what it is you're asking of me,' said Flóvent. 'Naturally, I'll do what I can for Felix within reason, but he'll have to turn himself in.'

'I'm not sure he will.'

'Do you think he's really in danger? Assuming Eyvindur wasn't the target.'

'He's convinced of it. I want to help him but I don't know how.'

'Would you begin by explaining the significance of these papers?' asked Flóvent, tapping the pile.

Brynhildur said nothing for a while, as if weighing up her choices and not liking any of them.

'It all started with their interest in criminals,' she said at last. 'Rudolf knew he'd never get permission from the government to conduct this type of research. It was Hans who urged him to do it anyway, privately. Ebeneser and Rudolf were committed Nazis in those days and thought they could get away with it. I was persuaded by their theories myself, but actually . . .'

She broke off for a sip of water. 'I wish we didn't have to talk about this,' she said. 'We never spoke of it again. Not until . . .'

'Not until the letter arrived?'

Brynhildur nodded.

'So what was the study? What is all this?' asked Flóvent, gesturing at the pages.

'The idea actually came from Rudolf's brother. Hans had been doing some research in Germany, and during his time as a lecturer at Jena he had published a short pamphlet setting out his ideas. Rudolf believed he could carry out a similar study here. No one would need to know. Iceland was the ideal place. Up here in the remote north. An isolated society. The brothers agreed about that. They were still on good terms at the time.'

'Isolated?'

'Yes. You see, Nazism was a growing force in Germany, and it gave rise to a variety of theories, including the notion that criminality – amorality, I suppose you could call it – is passed down from generation to generation. In other words, that criminal traits are inherited. Rudolf told me that Hans was very interested in this idea. He was familiar with existing studies on the hereditary aspect of human abnormalities such as alcoholism, homosexuality, violence, incest and so on but criminal traits were of particular interest to him because he believed it might be possible to reduce or even eradicate them. Through measures like the castration of criminals, he believed it would be possible to cut their numbers from one generation to the next. That was the gist of Hans's theories.'

'And?'

'And Rudolf was convinced. He persuaded Ebeneser to join him, which wasn't difficult. Ebeneser would have done anything for him, and at the time he worshipped almost everything that came out of Germany. I myself . . . Rudolf and I have . . . that is . . .'

'Go on.'

'After his wife died he employed me to help him with the housekeeping. I had just completed my training and was also working as a nurse, and over time we became – how shall I put it? – close.'

'Lovers? You denied that when I asked you earlier.'

'I . . . I don't like discussing . . . our private life. After his accident he needed me more than ever.'

'What happened?'

'It was a riding accident. Out on Laugarnes Point. His horse took fright and bolted. Rudolf was left paralysed from the waist down and became terribly depressed. Understandably. He says I saved his life. That if I hadn't stood by him through that awful time, he wouldn't have seen any reason to go on living.'

'I see. Tell me about the study.'

'As headmaster, Ebeneser was in a unique position to provide Rudolf with information about his pupils' backgrounds. He could check up on their family history and select boys for the study. Ebeneser's a keen genealogist as well, so he was able to trace the ancestry of the offenders in question. Since I was the school nurse, I handled the questionnaires, took measurements and obtained samples. We were looking for developmental markers – both mental and physical – as well as physiological traits. Rudolf prepared the tests. We carried out our observations as unobtrusively as possible. I incorporated them into the boys' usual check-ups. I simply increased their frequency, since it was perfectly natural that I should pay more attention to boys from broken homes, or the homes of convicted criminals.'

'Boys like Eyvindur?'

Brynhildur nodded. 'I don't believe they ever realised what we were doing. Rudolf came to the school from time to time to examine them. He processed the data we provided him with and passed on reports to his brother. Hans was very enthusiastic about our work, as you can imagine, since he was engaged in the same sort of research himself. Nazism was gaining a foothold in Germany, and our observations were supposed to lay the groundwork for a larger study into the Aryan race that Hans dreamt of conducting in this country: the search for the origin of the Icelanders, of the Viking temperament.'

'As I said, I asked a doctor to take a look at these,' said Flóvent, tapping the papers, 'and he told me that they are indeed physical measurements, very precise ones. Hands, feet, head shape, bone structure. Even the gap between the eyes. What exactly was it that you were looking for?'

'The brothers were familiar with the theories of Cesare Lombroso, but Rudolf wanted to go further. I don't know if you ... You see, Rudolf wanted to study both the individual and his environment. He felt Lombroso's theories on heredity were insufficient when considered in isolation. He wanted to understand the influence of environmental factors on heredity.'

'Lombroso's theories?'

'About the links between criminality and physical characteristics,' Brynhildur explained. 'His theories are based on genetics and relate to the physical characteristics and physiognomy that distinguish criminals from the general population. By taking precise measurements and making careful observations, scientists believe they can predict whether the individual in question is predisposed to become a criminal later in life.'

'Physical characteristics?'

'Well, for example, Rudolf was looking out for a gangling frame, or a particularly powerful torso. For distinctive facial features: the position of the eyes, the dimensions of the skull, a specific head shape. A variety of these characteristics have been identified by scientists. Rudolf wanted to extend the study beyond physique and look at the influence of environmental factors on the children of criminals. That is, the influence of their upbringing and living conditions. Limited though it was in scope, he was convinced that our study would produce significant results. If we're brought up in a certain environment, in certain conditions, isn't there a possibility that we will behave in a certain way?'

'You mean we learn from what's in front of us?'

'You could put it like that, yes. Rudolf considered these questions alongside Lombroso's theories about physical anomalies. Felix was . . . Felix, he . . .'

'Go on. What about Felix? Was he complicit in all of this?'

'Yes, I'm afraid . . .' Brynhildur left the sentence unfinished.

'What did he do?'

'Rudolf got him to befriend some of the subjects,' said Brynhildur, and for the first time in their conversation she showed signs of shame at what she had done. 'Felix used to report back to his father on their living conditions, family make-up and the relations between the different family members. He'd tell him what children like Eyvindur felt about their parents and their own futures, their attitudes to crime, alcohol, even sex. Some of them had already started smoking and drinking. These were boys of twelve or thirteen. Fifteen of them in all.'

'It's our understanding that Eyvindur was fond of Felix. He probably didn't have many friends, so their relationship was important to him, and he could never understand why Felix had suddenly turned his back on him,' said Flóvent. 'Why he suddenly wouldn't talk to him any more. He suspected that it had all been an act, their friendship. In the end he came to the conclusion that Felix had simply been using him. And, from what you say, it seems he was right: the friendship was only on his side. Felix was indeed using him. Abusing his trust.'

Brynhildur lowered her gaze to the papers and Flóvent sensed her reluctance to discuss the subject.

'As I said,' she went on, after a moment, 'Felix can be very cruel when he wants to be. He was quick to gain a hold over the other boys and exploited his mental superiority over them. He knew his father had chosen them as the subjects of his research because they came from bad homes, and he picked on the weakest of them.

The most vulnerable. But he managed to dominate those who were stronger than him too.'

'How did he do that?'

'In various ways. The goal was to see how far he could go. How easily influenced the boys would be. How they would react to his dominance and how he could manipulate them . . . Rudolf was . . . Felix was supposed to . . .'

'What?'

'It doesn't matter.'

'What were you saying about Rudolf and Felix? Who set him this goal?'

Brynhildur hesitated.

'Felix didn't come up with the idea, did he?' said Flóvent. 'Was Rudolf orchestrating all this?'

Brynhildur nodded. 'Halfway through the study, Rudolf began to consider Felix's role among the boys,' she admitted. 'The role of the strong leader. It was a popular concept in Germany at the time. Rudolf realised that Felix had a hold over the other boys and he . . . Well, he encouraged his son. Conspired with him. Even put words in his mouth. Rudolf's a very thorough man.'

'What happened?'

'Inevitably, it ended in disaster.'

'How? Between Rudolf and Felix, you mean?'

'Yes, between them and . . . I'd rather not go into it. Rudolf abandoned the study, dropped it altogether and forbade us ever to mention it again.'

'And so you two thought it had been safely swept under the carpet?'

'Yes, until that letter came through the door and stirred everything up again.'

'And it threatened to expose Felix's role and the experiments unless, what did you say, certain conditions were met? What were they?'

'The writer wanted a specific sum of money for keeping his mouth shut. Quite a large sum.'

'And you two believe Eyvindur wrote the letter?'

'We think it's possible. Felix . . .'

'Yes?'

'Felix . . . Felix may have blurted something out on one of his sales trips,' said Brynhildur. 'He says he was drunk and came out with a lot of stuff that he ought not to have said. About Eyvindur. And the experiments. It made Eyvindur angry. Understandably, I suppose.'

37

Thorson had been driving for about five minutes when he came to the turn-off the old woman had told him about. The road was blocked by a gate. He got out and opened it, drove through and closed it behind him. Two black dogs, of some indeterminate mongrel ancestry, greeted him at the gate, fawning over him and wagging their tails, ecstatic to receive a visitor.

He parked the jeep in front of the farmhouse, took off his jacket and laid it on the back seat. The temperature had risen during the course of the afternoon, and he was sweltering. The old turf farmhouse was sandwiched between a small concrete house, built tight against one side, and a modern outbuilding, consisting of a cowshed and barn, which was now packed with fragrant, newly harvested hay. Thorson surveyed the meadows that stretched far into the distance. It looked as if the haymaking was over.

There was no one at home in the concrete house, but Thorson

noticed a wisp of blue smoke rising from the old turf building; he was about to head over there when he spotted a third dog, sitting a couple of yards from the door, watching his every movement without stirring from its place. It was a big, powerful-looking beast, with a red-gold coat and a dark stripe on its back, and it wore a collar, unlike the other dogs. As Thorson approached, the animal emitted a low growl, baring a fearsome set of fangs. Taken aback by this greeting, Thorson halted in front of the dog and warily held out the back of his hand, but the growling only intensified, and the dog showed its teeth again. The other two dogs watched, no longer wagging their tails. It was as if the animal was guarding its master, warning Thorson to leave him alone. At the foot of the turf wall lay the carcass of a lamb, badly hacked about, as if the ravens had got at it.

Thorson wasn't keen on dogs. He scanned the surroundings for help but couldn't see a soul. He was unwilling to abandon his errand at this stage, but he had nothing to bribe the beast with, so he decided to see what would happen if he gave the dog a wide berth and approached the door from the side. The animal let Thorson pass, though it kept up a constant growling. Thorson heaved a sigh of relief, wondering what an earth he would have done if the dog had gone for him.

Once inside, he caught the strong earthy smell of the walls and floor, and then a powerful reek of smoke, as if from burning peat. He thought he could hear classical music, punctuated by the ringing of metal on metal. As he made his way along the passage, his eyes adjusting to the gloom, he wondered if the old farmhouse had been converted into a smithy. He received his answer when he entered what would have been the living area and saw a man standing in the middle of the room, beating out a scythe with a heavy sledgehammer, then cooling it in a bucket of water, sending up great clouds of steam. A lone light bulb hung over the man's head. The music was coming from a big wireless that had been set up on an old workbench. Strung from the rafters were large fillets of salmon, joints of smoked lamb and what looked to Thorson like a flayed guillemot.

The man had his back to him and was so engrossed in his work that he didn't notice his visitor until Thorson coughed and said good afternoon. He hadn't meant to startle him, but the blacksmith jumped and whipped round. Then Thorson saw that, just as the old woman had said, the man wore a patch over one eye.

'I'm sorry,' Thorson said hastily, 'I didn't mean to give you a shock.'

'Who are you?' asked the blacksmith, reaching over and switching off the music.

'My name's Thorson and I've just driven all the way from Reykjavík. I wondered if I might have a quick word. I won't take up much of your time.'

'Thorson?' said the man with the eyepatch. 'What kind of name is that? From Reykjavík, did you say? To see me?'

'Yes.'

'Are you a politician? Or the tax man? If so, you can get lost. I've nothing to say to you.'

'No, I'm neither. I'm from the police. The military police, in fact.'

The man regarded him, baffled, with his one eye. The old woman had told Thorson that he was a recluse who lived here with his dogs, a few cows and a herd of sheep. He was hard-working but unsociable, and took little interest in the doings of his neighbours, let alone in the course of the war. According to the old woman, a number of the local farmers' daughters had set their caps at him, but to no avail. She blamed Vera for that. You'd have thought she'd cast a spell on the poor man.

Thorson apologised again and started to tell the blacksmith about himself – the usual spiel about coming from an Icelandic family in Canada, which was why he spoke the language. He was working with the Icelandic police in connection with a recent incident in Reykjavík. The smith might have heard about it on the radio.

'I only listen to music,' the man said, still unsure of the reason for this unexpected visit. 'I don't follow the news much.'

Thorson told him that a man's body had been found in a basement flat in Reykjavík, shot in the head with what the police believed to have been a US military pistol. The victim's name was Eyvindur, and he had been living with a woman who came from around here. Although she had moved away to the city, Thorson gathered that the blacksmith had known her well at one time.

Thorson's explanation was met by a long silence. The man stood there watching him, the big sledgehammer in his hand, and although the question hung in the air between them, he seemed reluctant to voice it, as if he was afraid of the answer. Thorson waited, and after a while the man laid down the hammer and adjusted his patch, pulling it down more firmly over his eye.

'What woman?' he asked at last, though Thorson could see that he already knew the answer.

'Her name's Vera.'

The man regarded his visitor without speaking. Thorson thought he detected a combination of distaste and surprise in his manner. A complete stranger, all the way from Reykjavík, had popped up out of the blue and was standing here, on his beaten-earth floor, telling him about a serious crime in the capital. Bringing up a name the smith had never expected to hear again. No wonder he was speechless. Thorson guessed that in his position he would have been pretty shaken himself.

'Why . . . What do you want from me? Why are you here?'

'I understand that you used to know Vera rather well.'

'Is she involved?' the blacksmith asked after a pause. 'In what happened to that . . . that . . .'

'Eyvindur? It's not out of the question,' said Thorson.

'Why do you want to talk to me?'

'To find out more about her,' said Thorson. 'I've been talking to some of the locals, and they advised me to speak to you. Said you knew her best, though you might not speak very highly of her. Was that a fair comment?'

'You'd better leave,' the man said, picking up the hammer again. 'I've nothing to say to you.'

'Would you at least think about it?' asked Thorson. 'I'd be grateful if I could ask you a few questions.'

'You shouldn't listen to what the people around here say. They think they know a lot more than they do. Good day.'

'Is it true that she –?'

'You'd better leave now,' said the man, his manner starting to turn threatening. 'I don't want to talk to you. I never want to hear another word about that . . . that woman. Just leave me alone. Do you hear me? Leave me alone!'

'All right,' said Thorson. 'I hear you. I won't take up any more of your time. There's just one thing I wanted to say before I go.

She's with a soldier now, a British sergeant. I don't know if you've heard. She started seeing this soldier while she was still living with the man who was murdered. Does that surprise you? That she was cheating on him?'

'Get out!' The man raised his voice and stepped towards Thorson, clutching the hammer. 'I don't want to hear about it. Get lost. Get out of here!'

Thorson retreated along the passage, out into the open air. The man followed and stood in the doorway, watching him sternly with his one eye, a powerfully built figure, with black hair and beard, in a frayed work shirt and worn braces, his face covered in soot.

The moment Thorson stepped outside he encountered the red-gold dog with the dark stripe down its spine. It snarled at him, and Thorson stumbled away in the direction of his jeep. The other two dogs that had frisked around him earlier were standing a little way off, watching, but suddenly they started barking like crazy. He had only a few yards left to go when the savage dog – foaming at the mouth now, its growling giving way to ferocious barking – sprang at Thorson and knocked him to the ground. As Thorson rolled around in the dirt, frantically trying to stop the beast from ripping his throat out, his thoughts went to the pistol in his glove compartment. If he'd had it to hand, he would have used it without a moment's hesitation. He felt the dog's jaws close over his forearm, and he punched its nose as hard as he could, but it was too strong. Thorson yelled with pain and groped for a rock to bring down on the animal's head. Then a dark figure loomed over him. The dog loosened its grip and went flying into the air with a yelp, landing several yards away on its back. It slunk off behind the turf farmhouse, its tail between its legs.

'Are you all right?' he heard the man ask and felt strong hands helping him to his feet. 'I'm afraid he's old and cussed. I've been putting off shooting him. He attacks anything that crosses his path. Don't take it personally.'

Despite what he said, Thorson sensed that the blacksmith wasn't particularly sorry about the attack. Thorson made as if to continue towards his jeep but there was blood oozing from his arm where he had been mauled, and the man asked him to wait a minute; he couldn't leave in that state.

'Let me bind the wound,' the blacksmith offered. 'It shouldn't get infected, but you never know. I've got some antiseptic in the house. And I can lend you another shirt, if you like.'

Thorson examined the bleeding tooth marks and realised that it would be sensible to accept the man's assistance. His shirt was ruined: the dog had shredded the sleeve.

'Is that his lamb?' Thorson asked, gesturing at the carcass lying by the wall of the turf building.

'I expect so,' said the man, and Thorson noticed that most of the hostility had left his voice. 'There are foxes prowling around here too, but it was probably the dog. I was about to bury the thing when you arrived. I usually try to keep the place a bit tidier,' he added apologetically.

Thorson followed him inside the modern concrete house, and the blacksmith offered him a seat in the kitchen, then began searching in the cupboards and drawers for something to use as a dressing. He found iodine and the antiseptic cream, tore some rags into strips, then washed the wound with water.

'I could put in a few stitches if you'd let me,' he said, examining the two largest toothmarks. 'But I've got nothing to use as an anaesthetic. Except *brennivín*, maybe.'

'There's no need. Just bind it up tight, and I'll see how it looks when I get back to town.'

'At least we can stop the bleeding. I'm sorry about the dog. He's old, and I just haven't been able to bring myself to shoot him. I'm too soft. He was a very good dog once.'

'You hear stories about their loyalty,' remarked Thorson, 'but he seems to be taking it to extremes. It's the first time a dog's attacked me like that. And hopefully the last.'

'Yes, he's been faithful to me all right.'

'More faithful than certain others?' said Thorson.

The man cocked his good eye at him, tilting his head as if to see Thorson better. 'I don't want to hear about her,' he said. 'I hope you understand. I don't care what she's up to over there in Reykjavík. I don't give a damn.'

'It's OK,' said Thorson. 'I'll back off. I just wanted to know who she was. If she has a history of stirring up trouble, I'll have to find that out from someone else. I understand if you don't want to talk about her. It's just a shame that she may get away with murder because you're protecting her.'

The blacksmith paused. He had washed the wounds on Thorson's arm and bound them with a clean rag, which he was fastening with two pins he'd fetched from his bedroom. He had also brought out a clean shirt for Thorson. The day had turned to evening, and the sun was glowing pink on the walls of the kitchen. There was a smell of stewed coffee, antiseptic and work-worn hands, and despite the dog attack and his injured arm, Thorson felt oddly contented. The man's manner was quite different now. He seemed genuinely concerned about Thorson and ashamed of his dog, keen to make up for the hostile reception this Canadian visitor had been given on an Icelandic farm.

'Protecting her?' he echoed. 'I'm not protecting her.'

'I'd be able to put more pressure on her if you told me what happened between you. I have so little to go on. I don't really know anything about her, and there aren't many other people I can talk to. All I know is that she wasn't well liked by her neighbours in Reykjavík.'

'I can't help you.'

'What happened between you?' asked Thorson.

'Nothing, except that I lost an eye,' said the man, and Thorson sensed that he was about to flare up again.

'All right. I didn't mean to . . .'

The man finished binding his arm. 'Maybe . . . Sometimes I think it was a fitting punishment for having been so blind to her true nature. I closed my eyes to what she was really like.'

'What she was really like?'

'I thought I knew her. But it turned out I didn't.'

'Did you grow up with her?'

'Partly. I'm not from round here originally. I was sent here after my mother died, and I was raised on this farm by some distant relatives, a fine couple who are both dead now. I've tried to get on with the locals, but perhaps I was . . . Yes, in answer to your question, I've known her a long time.'

'What happened?'

'She started dropping by . . .'

'And?'

'I'd rather not talk about it.'

'It's OK. I understand.'

The man watched as the setting sun painted the kitchen wall

red. 'It was an evening like this one,' he said at last. 'In August. After a good summer. I never suspected . . .'

'What?'

'What she was . . . really like. She made a fool of me. Everyone round here knows about it. She turned out to be . . . two-faced . . .'

38

He remembered the first time she visited him on her own. This was after he had heard about their engagement. Previously, she'd always come with her boyfriend, but this time he spotted her walking up the path alone. He'd been hard at it in the smithy all day, so he hurriedly washed his hands and tried to scrub the worst of the soot off his face before she reached the door. An interest in ironworking had prompted him to start the smithy not long before. He'd set up his forge in the old turf farmhouse, where he also did a bit of woodturning, a skill he had picked up at a workshop during a visit to Reykjavík.

He asked where her fiancé was, and she explained that he had gone into the next village and wouldn't be back until late that night. The three of them knew each other quite well as they had all grown up in the area, though he himself hadn't moved there until he was nine years old. Admittedly, he had sometimes cast an appreciative eye in her direction, but that was all. He was unusually timid around women and had never dreamt that he had any chance with Vera; she had never shown the slightest interest in him, after all. And now she was engaged and, as far as he knew, would be married soon. She had once had a reputation for being able to twist men round her little finger, but her engagement had put an end to all such talk. Her fiancé farmed the neighbouring property, and he regarded him as a friend.

'Aren't you going to invite me in?' she asked, standing at the door and smiling, though the smile didn't reach her eyes.

'Of course. Is everything all right?'

'I just felt like a walk,' she said. 'I'm bored.'

She took a seat at his kitchen table, her skin attractively tanned by the summer sun. He set about making coffee and tried to keep up a flow of conversation but sensed that she was distracted and not really listening as he rambled on about the weather and the hay harvest and how he had run an electric cable from the diesel generator to his new smithy in the old turf farmhouse, so now he could listen to the radio in there and have a bit of light to work by.

'He doesn't want to move,' she announced, when he finally ran out of things to say, running her tanned hand over the tabletop. She had beautiful hands, with slim, delicate fingers, one of which sported a ring.

'Move?'

'He promised me, but then he started making all kinds of excuses: he wouldn't get enough for the farm, didn't know how to make a living anywhere else. Now he says he's changed his mind and can't face leaving. He's dreaming of extending the hayfields, draining the marshes, constructing new outbuildings. I doubt he'll actually go through with any of it, though. He promised me we'd go away, move to Reykjavík. He promised.'

She looked disconsolate and he remembered how she had often talked of Reykjavík as though she were dazzled by the very idea of the city, how she used to declare that she had no intention of rotting away in the countryside. He recalled that her fiancé hadn't been averse to the idea either and had even talked of selling him the farm if he'd give him a good enough price for it.

'Perhaps you'll be able to get him to change his mind,' he said, for the sake of saying something.

'I doubt it. I even . . .'

'What?'

'I actually threatened to leave him. To go to Reykjavík alone. Break off our engagement.'

'How did he take it?'

'He didn't. He said I'd get over it and see that he was right. That we were country folk and the city was no place for the likes of us. Can you . . . Have you ever heard anything to beat it? He never used to talk like that. I think . . . I feel as though he's betrayed me and now he's forcing me into a life I don't want. I always meant to go south, to the city.'

Tears were sliding down her cheeks, and he didn't know what to do. In the end he went over and sat down beside her in an attempt to comfort her. She took his hand, then put her arms around his neck and cried into his shoulder. He was conscious of her breasts pressing against him. Then she loosened her embrace and abruptly announced that she had to go. She thanked him, and before he knew it she had vanished into the dusk.

A few evenings later he saw her walking up the road again, and he came out to meet her in the yard, worried that someone would spot her visiting him alone and unchaperoned, in the evening. He hastily invited her into the house, though his conscience was clear. He hadn't done anything wrong except think about her ever since she'd stopped by, about her relationship with her fiancé, which didn't seem without its problems; about her beautiful, tanned hands and her soft breasts pressing against him. Perhaps it was guilt about these thoughts. They were lustful. Impure.

Instead of going inside she asked if she could see his forge, and he took her into the old turf building and switched on the light bulb hanging from the ceiling. She switched it off again immediately, and they stood in the semi-darkness, talking softly. At that stage he didn't realise how brazen she was, how unwavering of purpose. She was wearing a woollen jumper over her dress, and her legs were bare. She wanted to thank him for the other evening, she said. There was no need, he replied; he hadn't done anything, and she smiled and asked if he ever thought about her. Said she sometimes thought of him, which surprised him. He admitted that he had been thinking about her ever since the other night. 'And before that?' she asked, and he answered with silence. She came closer, but he didn't move, and then she was standing pressed against him, kissing him gently on the lips. He let her do it, and only then did he realise that he had been yearning for that kiss, yearning to feel her lips on his, and that perhaps he had wanted her for a long time, longer than he'd realised. She kissed him again and he kissed her back, flung his arms around her, crushed her against him. She drew his hand under her dress, and he discovered that she was naked underneath and felt a hot shiver run through his body. She kissed him hungrily, pulling him against her and reaching for him, then leant back against the old workbench. He lifted her up and felt the hunger, heat and lust overwhelm him as she undid his waistband and thrust herself against him, her slim, brown fingers guiding him in.

They met twice more in the smithy, and on both occasions she pulled him to her and hoisted herself onto the bench, where she thrust herself against him, sending him to new heights of pleasure each time.

Then one evening he noticed that the light was on in the smithy. He hadn't seen her for several days and hadn't spotted her walking up to the farm. He hurried across the yard. He was going to tell her that he wanted to stop meeting in secret like this; they should talk to her fiancé and come clean. She could break off her engagement, and they could be together. He had thought about it and was prepared to leave the farm and move to Reykjavík with her; he could find something to do in town and she would be free to earn her living in whatever way she liked. He couldn't wait to see her reaction to this plan as he ducked into the old passageway and walked towards the light in the smithy.

He gasped when he saw her fiancé bending over the hearth, prodding at the embers with a poker.

'Did you do it in here?' the other man asked, straightening up.

He was too stunned to speak.

'Not on the floor, surely. Where then? Where? On the workbench?'

'I . . . I . . .'

He could see there was no point denying what had happened, so he tried to say that they had meant to talk to him: she was unhappy and wanted to leave him; they were even thinking of moving to Reykjavík. He was going to explain all this, to make a clean breast of things, but the words wouldn't come.

'Well, she got what she wanted,' said the fiancé. 'I can't live with a woman like that. The engagement's off. I wouldn't dream of marrying her now. Not after she's been here. Not after she's been with *you*.'

'I didn't mean to . . . we were going to talk to you.'

'We?'

'Yes.'

The man laughed. 'You don't really think she's interested in you?'

'We . . .'

'When are you going to wake up?' jeered Vera's fiancé, with all the fury of a man who has been betrayed. 'She was only using you to get back at me. She knew exactly what she was doing. I expect you knew too. I bet it amused you, bet you enjoyed thinking about me as you screwed her. I thought we were friends . . .'

'How . . . how did you know . . . ?'

'We had one of our fights – she's always picking fights with me. And she told me about you. About your . . . your love nest. That she'd screwed you in here. She flung it in my face. That you'd fucked her in the smithy!'

The man's fury was mounting with every word until, beside himself with rage, he snatched the hot poker out of the embers and struck the smith in the face. The glowing end caught him full in the eye, searing his eyeball.

As Thorson listened to the story the sun sank lower in the sky and the shadows lengthened and deepened in the kitchen. The blacksmith instinctively stroked his eyepatch as he concluded his tale. Thorson could tell that he was still suffering.

'I yelled in agony and stumbled down the passage, out into the yard and into the kitchen, where I tried to cool the wound with water. The pain was unbearable and I knew . . . I knew at once that I'd lost the eye. That there was no way it could come through something that painful unharmed.'

'Was her fiancé right?' asked Thorson after a long pause. 'Was she just using you to get back at him?'

'She never spoke to me again. Next thing I heard, she'd broken off her engagement and left for Reykjavík. In hindsight, I suppose I was easy prey and she knew it. Knew I'd be easy to seduce. She used me to punish him, then threw me away like a piece of rubbish.'

'And you haven't seen her since?'

'No. Of course it was tough losing my eye, but I'm not sure it was any worse than being made a fool of. That was the most painful part, really. Being taken in by her wiles.'

His words betrayed such deep suffering that Thorson was filled with pity.

'So has she got herself into trouble in Reykjavík?'

'We don't know,' said Thorson. 'It didn't take her long to find a new man in town and move in with him. He was murdered, like I said. But by then she'd already started seeing a British soldier.'

'And you think she was involved?'

Thorson shrugged. 'Impossible to say.'

The blacksmith gazed out of the kitchen window at the sunset, as if weighing up whether he should add something else. Thorson waited patiently, and after a long interval the man cleared his throat.

'Is there more?' asked Thorson.

'No, it's just she said something that you probably ought to know about. It's only just come back to me. I thought nothing of it at the time, because she was obviously messing around. I don't even know if I should be telling you because you're bound to take it too seriously. Read too much into it.'

'What did she say?'

'There was an accident. A man drowned in a trout lake up on the moors near here. And she said I could go fishing with her fiancé and come back alone. That accidents happened. Then she laughed. She said it light-heartedly. I don't think she meant anything by it, but . . .'

'Now you're wondering if she was only half joking?'

'No, like I said, I didn't think anything of it at the time.'

'But now her boyfriend in Reykjavík has been found dead.'

'I just wanted you to know. I'm sure she didn't mean anything by it.'

Shortly afterwards the blacksmith accompanied Thorson out to the jeep. The dogs were nowhere to be seen. Thorson offered him his moleskin jacket in return for the shirt, as they were about the same height, but the man flatly refused to take anything from him.

'There's something about her, something that draws men to her, though I can't put my finger on it' the man said in parting. 'Some kind of spell that makes you do anything she wants. I wouldn't trust a word she says, but whether she'd go so far . . .'

'Well,' said Thorson, 'we'll see.'

They shook hands.

'She disappeared,' said the blacksmith. 'She couldn't leave fast enough. I gather she did a midnight flit and didn't say goodbye to a soul.'

Thorson climbed into the jeep.

'The strange thing is . . . It probably sounds crazy, but . . .'

'Yes?'

'I miss those evenings,' said the man, his gaze straying towards the smithy. 'She was . . . I still think of her sometimes, in spite of everything.'

39

Flóvent paused the interview to ask Brynhildur Hólm if she wanted to speak to a lawyer, but she repeated that she had committed no crime. He sensed that to her taking such a step would seem like an admission of guilt. He tried to persuade her otherwise, and she said she would think about it, then asked if she would have to stay in prison much longer. Flóvent couldn't answer that but repeated that she should let him know if she wanted a lawyer present during the interviews and he would arrange it for her. She said she would like to get this over with as quickly as possible. Her conscience was clear and Flóvent must understand that there was absolutely no need to keep her locked up in prison.

'So Felix told Eyvindur about your experiments at the school?' Flóvent prompted, once they had resumed their seats in the interview room. 'Told him about the part he had played in the whole thing. And afterwards Eyvindur wrote that letter with the intention of blackmailing you.'

'He really got on Felix's nerves,' said Brynhildur. 'On those sales trips. Felix tried to keep his distance, but Eyvindur hounded him, perhaps because of the way Felix had treated him in the past. He must have held quite a grudge against Felix. He wouldn't leave him alone, wanted to know why he was going to places that none of the other salesmen bothered with, kept dropping spiteful remarks about his German roots. Referring to Nazis. Going on about how the Nazis would be thrashed. Saying that Felix should go back to Germany. Then one day, Felix had had too much to drink, and he snapped. Told him they'd never been friends, that he'd been nothing but a guinea pig, or words to that effect. He deliberately humiliated him, didn't pull any punches. Said they'd proved that he was no better than his crook of a father. He must have said a little too much because after that Eyvindur started digging around . . .'

'How? Who did he contact?'

'Well, we know he spoke to Ebeneser. According to him, Eyvindur rang him, then turned up at the school one day, demanding to know what had been going on in his final year. Judging by the questions he was asking, Felix must have given him quite a good idea of the work we were doing, though it's possible he'd been talking to other boys from the school as well.'

'Eyvindur told his girlfriend that he was expecting to come into some money, but she didn't take him seriously. Said he was always making plans that came to nothing. Where's the blackmail letter now?'

'Rudolf . . . he was so upset that I think he burnt it. He wants to forget about the whole affair. Can't bear to hear any mention of it.'

'So you believe the letter has been destroyed?'

'Yes. It was very amateurish. Mostly abuse, levelled at us. Calling us Nazis and threatening to expose us. Saying that we'd be made to suffer, and so on. Then there were instructions about the money Rudolf was to pay and where he was to leave it.'

'And where was that?'

'By one of the gates of the graveyard on Sudurgata.'

'Did Rudolf discuss the letter with Felix?'

'No, not that I'm aware. But I suspect that when the letter had no effect, Eyvindur must have got in touch with Felix – although Felix won't admit it – and tried to force him to pay up or to put pressure on his father. I suspect that's why Eyvindur was in his flat.'

'And?'

'And it ended in disaster. For some reason Felix left Eyvindur in the state you found him in. I have asked him again and again, but he won't budge from his story: Eyvindur was already dead when he found him. He can't tell me who it was who attacked him or why. But Felix keeps coming back to the possibility that the attacker may have mistaken Eyvindur for him – that he himself was the intended victim.'

'Which brings us back to the same question: why would anyone have wanted to kill Felix?'

'He has some ideas about that, but he won't share them with me.'

'Related to spying?'

'I don't know.'

'Or the experiments? To how he behaved as a boy?'

'He refuses to discuss it.'

'If he's to be believed, surely the only reasonable conclusion is that the person who shot Eyvindur didn't know what Felix looked like. If he killed Eyvindur by mistake?'

'Yes, and that makes Felix all the more convinced that he must have been the target – the possibility that they brought in some outsider to do the deed. Those were his words. I don't know what he meant.'

'Isn't he contradicting himself? Earlier you told me that he was also claiming Eyvindur was the intended victim.'

'I think he's struggling to work out what's going on. Felix doesn't know what to think any more and the same applies to me. I really don't know what to believe. I'm utterly confused.'

'These experiments . . . Do you know what happened to your subjects? Did your predictions come true? Did they end up as criminals?'

'I've tried to find out – casually, you understand, not in any methodical way. I remember most of the names and try to keep up with what's happened to the boys when I get the chance.'

'And?'

'I believe most of them have turned out quite well,' said Brynhildur. 'One became a teacher, for example, though two of them are in a sorry state, no better than vagrants, and a couple more have spent short spells behind bars for burglary or assault.'

'What about this one?' asked Flóvent, pointing to one of the boys standing next to Eyvindur in the photograph. 'You didn't answer me before.'

'I've told you, I don't recognise the other two boys with Felix and Eyvindur.'

'It's our understanding that he was another of Felix's "friends".'

'It's possible.'

'That Felix befriended him and passed on information about his family?'

'I really couldn't say.'

'You mean you don't know if he was involved in the study? I thought you remembered the boys' names? Knew what had happened to most of them?'

Brynhildur stared at the picture. 'He may have been called Jósep,' she said at last. 'If I'm not mistaken. Jósep Ingvarsson.'

'What's he doing now?'

'He's a vagrant,' said Brynhildur. 'I've seen him loafing about in Hafnarstræti and wandering around the centre of town. His father was always being sent to prison; he was very violent.'

'Do you think Jósep could have written the letter?'

'Felix believes it was Eyvindur.'

Flóvent gathered up the papers on the table. He had decided to draw the interview to a close for now.

'You say you want to help him. Well, if Felix is in danger, as he claims, we could help him.'

Brynhildur remained silent.

'Think about Felix. About the danger he believes he's in. You don't have much choice. You must see that. Besides, you yourself are mixed up in this affair, and it could improve your own position if you're straight with us. You ought to –'

'He worshipped his uncle,' said Brynhildur suddenly. 'Felix is a fanatical Nazi. He'd have gone to Germany and joined the army if Hans hadn't persuaded him that he could be of more use here at home.'

'Be more specific. Of more use how?'

'When the Germans invaded. But when that didn't happen . . .'

'Yes?'

'It's possible that Felix is in fact a German agent – thanks to Hans – and that Eyvindur blundered into the firing line by accident.'

'All right. Let's go back to Hans Lunden. What exactly does he do?'

'He came over shortly before the war, full of the plans he had for Iceland following the German occupation. Hans wanted his brother to run an anthropological research programme based on his earlier work, but Rudolf had turned his back on Nazism by then and they fell out over the matter. Hans was furious and left without even saying goodbye to Rudolf. I don't think they've been in contact since. Hans believed that the Nazis should take Iceland as a model, since it was home to a uniquely pure, ancient Nordic stock that was superior to other races.'

Brynhildur took another sip of water, then explained that Hans was an admirer of the sagas with their descriptions of warriors and feats of great prowess and daring. He had immersed himself in the country's medieval texts, including the Eddic poems, with their Norse myths and tales of the ancient Germanic past. To him, the heroic forebears of the Icelanders were supermen by modern standards, and he dreamt of recreating them. He conducted anthropological research into Nordic racial superiority at an institute set up by Himmler in Berlin, as part of the Ahnenerbe, or Ancestral Heritage Group. That was why he had come to Iceland in '39. Hans had been confident that when war broke out, the Germans would occupy Iceland and then it would be possible to embark on serious genetic and anthropological studies of the Icelandic population, of their ancient Germanic heritage and

Viking blood – the very origins of the Icelanders. Hans had intended to direct the project himself: Rudolf was to be his right-hand man.

'But then the German invasion didn't happen,' said Flóvent.

'Which must have been a great disappointment to Hans.'

Rudolf had ultimately drawn the conclusion that the ideas Hans and other Nazi intellectuals had about Iceland were based on a misconception. Werner Gerlach had told Hans the same during their meetings at the consulate. In their view, modern Icelanders were no better than peasants and had nothing in common with their warlike Viking ancestors. There had been a great deal of interracial mixing on the island ever since the earliest settlement in the ninth century. In support of this argument, Rudolf referred to the observations he had made in the course of his study, suggesting that his findings could, instead, provide the basis for further research into the degeneration of the pure Nordic stock. They demonstrated that the descendants of the Vikings were anything but noble Aryans. But Hans Lunden wouldn't listen. It ended in a bitter quarrel. Then the British occupied the island and their plans came to nothing.

'Do you have any idea where Hans Lunden is now?' asked Flóvent.

'The last Rudolf heard was that he had abandoned the Nordic project and started conducting genetic studies on prisoners. On criminals.'

'So, what you're saying is that all this happened long after he and Rudolf had collaborated on their secret study at the school?' said Flóvent, indicating the documents. 'And that these papers date from much earlier.'

'That's right,' said Brynhildur. 'The school study was quite different in its aims, but it was instrumental in awakening Hans Lunden's interest in Iceland.'

'And you believe that Hans set Felix up as a German agent?'

'Yes, and that Eyvindur was shot instead of Felix.'

40

Thorson spent the night at the RAF barracks in Selfoss. He had reached the village long after midnight and didn't dare continue to Reykjavík, exhausted as he was from the drive, the dog attack and from trawling from farm to farm in search of information. He had tried to speak to Vera's former fiancé but learnt that he was away travelling in the north of the country. Twice Thorson had nodded off at the wheel, and he was afraid of tackling the mountain road over Hellisheidi in the dark, without any sleep. He decided to ask if they'd let him bunk down at the British camp. The officer in charge was still awake, sitting up smoking in front of his hut, and was happy to oblige. They conversed in low voices; then the officer showed Thorson to an empty bed. He fell asleep the moment his head hit the pillow.

The following morning he breakfasted with the airmen, thanked them for their hospitality, then went on his way, reaching Reykjavík around noon. He immediately set about discreetly gathering information on Billy Wiggins. After making a few phone calls he discovered that the previous week Wiggins had been involved in a punch-up with a private from a British artillery regiment. Apparently he was so drunk he had been compelled to sleep it off in the detention camp at Kirkjusandur. The fight had not been considered serious enough for any charges to be brought, however, and the cause of the altercation was not recorded in the military police incident book.

Thorson was on the point of heading over to speak to the private involved when the phone rang and he was informed that Major Graham wanted to see him immediately at the Leper Hospital. Thorson was conscious that he had failed to keep Graham briefed about the inquiry, in defiance of his orders. He had twice provided his own commanding officer, Colonel Webster, with a telephone report on the progress of the investigation and the possible link between the murder in Felix Lunden's flat and enemy espionage. Colonel Webster had taken the information seriously and ordered him to contact counter-intelligence, but Thorson had been dragging his feet out of a personal dislike for Major Graham.

After a few more phone calls he managed to track down Flóvent at the prison. Flóvent brought him up to date with the interrogation of Brynhildur Hólm and his growing conviction that Felix had been spying on military operations in Iceland at the instigation of his uncle, Hans Lunden. Thorson, in turn, gave him a brief account of his journey east to the rural farming community where Vera had grown up, of the stories circulating about her among her former neighbours, of the farmer she had seduced and the violence that had ensued.

'Are you saying she did it purely in order to break off her

engagement?' Flóvent asked when Thorson had finished. 'To get back at her fiancé?'

'It looks like it.'

'She set the two men at each other's throats?'

'And wasn't really interested in either of them.'

'So, on this basis, you believe she may have taken measures to get rid of Eyvindur once and for all?'

'It's possible. I'm going to check out Billy Wiggins. Take a closer look at their relationship. I'll let you know what I find out.'

'Right you are,' said Flóvent. 'We should meet. I need to fill you in properly on what Brynhildur confessed to me about the experiments she and Rudolf were conducting – and their impact. I'll see you shortly.'

There was no sign of Major Ballantine when Graham received Thorson in his office at the old hospital and immediately began by reprimanding him for failing to report back. Thorson tried to excuse himself on the grounds that he had been rushed off his feet with the investigation, and had been out of town following up a lead, but Graham was fuming and didn't calm down until Thorson reminded him that his commanding officer was Colonel Franklin Webster and that if Graham had any complaints about him, he should raise them with the colonel.

'Are we dealing with spies?' asked Graham irritably. 'Can you tell me that?'

'We still can't say for sure whether the murder's directly related to espionage. But we have found evidence to suggest that Felix Lunden, who rented the flat where the body was found, has been working as an enemy agent. We believe he's been travelling to places of strategic importance in the guise of a salesman. Although we still have no confirmation of that. His uncle, a doctor who lives in Germany, recruited him as a spy, if the testimony of a family friend can be trusted.'

'And this Felix is still at large?'

'He was hiding out at his father's old doctor's office. The Icelandic detective I'm working with tracked him down there, but Felix managed to give him the slip. We'll catch him soon. I'm convinced of that. He doesn't really have anywhere to turn.'

'Well, I don't care what you're convinced of,' said Graham. 'As far as I can see, the Icelandic police haven't achieved a thing. My opinion, as I said, is that we should take this out of their hands if they can't even solve a straightforward case like this one.'

'It may not be that easy, sir. The victim was an Icelander and –'

'Yes, well, I don't give a damn about that,' said Graham. 'Have you found any papers belonging to this . . . this Felix? Do you know where he's been? Who his contacts are? His collaborators? Have you found out anything useful about the man? Such as how he gets the information out of the country? Or exactly what information he's been gathering?'

'We've found out quite a lot,' said Thorson, 'but it doesn't relate directly to his activities here as an agent, rather to his family affairs and –'

'Right, in other words you've made no progress,' said Graham with a heavy sigh, and Thorson was at a loss to why he seemed so irritated about their collaboration with Flóvent. 'I'll recommend to Colonel Webster that Intelligence take over the case. You'll be hearing from us. That's all. Good day.'

'But there's no call –'

'Good day!'

* * *

The soldier who had got into a punch-up with Billy Wiggins was one Private Burns. He was on guard duty with two other men at a small searchlight station on the tip of the Seltjarnarnes Peninsula to the west of Reykjavík. There was a fine view over the great sweep of Faxaflói Bay, from Keflavík and the lighthouse at Gardskagi on the Reykjanes Peninsula in the south, to Hvalfjördur in the north, and the mountainous Snæfellsnes Peninsula in the north-west. When Thorson introduced himself and asked to speak to Private Burns, a lanky, fair-haired boy of barely twenty stepped forward, his face a picture of bewilderment at this visit by a US military police officer.

Thorson took him aside and explained that he wanted to know more about his fight with Billy Wiggins, and if it was really true that he didn't want to press charges. Burns nodded. He had a rifle over one shoulder and a large pair of binoculars hanging from a strap around his neck, for spotting enemy vessels. That was right, he said, it had only been a minor scuffle. Wiggins outranked him, and Burns was keen to let the matter drop. In fact, he'd all but forgotten about it when Thorson appeared and insisted on bringing the whole thing up again.

'What exactly happened?' asked Thorson.

'I managed to offend him somehow, sir. I don't really know what I did,' said the young private. 'Mind you, apparently he's always flying off the handle. And he's crazy with jealousy. But I didn't know that at the time.'

'Jealousy?'

'Over that woman who takes in washing,' said Burns, who had brought out a packet of cigarettes and a lighter.

'Which woman?'

'The one with the laundry up by Camp Knox. She works for the garrison. I don't remember her name . . . but the boys told me Billy Wiggins helped her get set up and pulled a few strings so she had plenty of work. He's her boyfriend.'

'Is her name Vera, this woman?'

'That's right.'

'What about her? What happened?'

'It was no big deal. I didn't know she was Wiggins's girl. He just went for me and started beating the living daylights out of me. Me and my mates, we'd been talking about the Yanks – how they're overrunning the place and swaggering around like they own it . . . Sorry, sir.'

'Don't worry about it, private. I'm Canadian.'

'Oh, anyway, we bumped into Wiggins outside Hótel Ísland. He was drunk and in a nasty mood. He knew a couple of blokes from Camp Tripoli who were there with us. We were having a laugh, saying were worried the local birds were much keener on the Yanks than us. Just messing about, you know, but it's true. Since they arrived . . . you know . . . well, they're a lot more popular.'

'What happened? Wiggins didn't like hearing that?'

'No. He went for me because I said that blonde woman who runs the laundry near Camp Knox had been quick to bag herself a Yank. We talk about her sometimes, me and my mates. She's quite a . . . a looker. I had no idea Wiggins was mixed up with her or I'd never have said it.'

'The blonde woman who runs the laundry? Quick to bag herself a Yank?'

'Yes. Anyway, he immediately loses his rag and starts asking what I mean by that and I blurt out that I've seen her with a GI. Then he goes completely berserk, starts calling me a liar, and before I know it I'm lying in the road and the bastard's giving me a right belting.'

'You saw Vera with a GI?'

'Yes. We sometimes pass her place on our way out here and one morning this Yank was all over her. It was obvious he was just leaving. I didn't dare tell Wiggins that or he'd have murdered me. So I tried to say it was an honest mistake but by then the police had arrived and he went nuts and ended up trying to take them on and all. He went completely berserk, poor sod, so they took him away.'

'Are you sure it was her?' asked Thorson. 'That it was Vera?'

'I'm positive. We'd been talking about it. About what a looker she was. But I had no idea about her and Wiggins. The boys from Camp Tripoli told me he was crazy about her, always tied to her apron strings, doing whatever she told him to. Helping her with her laundry. Sorting all kinds of stuff for her.'

'But you saw her with a GI?'

The soldier lit a cigarette and nodded. 'He was a lot flashier than Billy Wiggins, that's for sure.'

41

Jósep had come to the attention of the police for a series of minor offences including vagrancy, drunk and disorderly behaviour, shoplifting, egg theft and the illegal hunting of eider ducks. Flóvent didn't know how often he had been picked up, since such minor offences weren't always recorded. There were two brief police reports under his name and in one of them, which was fairly recent, Flóvent saw that Jósep had given his sister's name when asked for his current address. Flóvent drove over there, only to discover that Jósep had never lived with her; in fact, they very rarely saw each other, though the sister, whose name was Albína, was able to tell him that Jósep sometimes stayed at the Citadel, a hostel run by the Salvation Army. Curious to know what the police wanted with her brother, she was politely insistent that Flóvent come in, and before he knew it he had accepted her invitation to coffee. Although it was late in the day, her husband wasn't home yet. He worked in the offices of Eimskip, the

Icelandic Steamship Company, and lived in a state of constant anxiety about the fate of the company's vessels in these dangerous times.

'What's Jósep done?' Albína asked with a worried frown. Flóvent had explained who he was straight away, and she was quite unused to receiving visits from the police.

'Nothing, as far as I know,' Flóvent reassured her. 'I think he may be able to help me. You see, I'm trying to trace a man he may know, or may have known at one time. It might sound rather an odd question, ma'am, but does he ever talk about his schooldays?'

'I'm afraid we don't have much contact, and we were never close. Never really knew each other, to tell you the truth.'

'You didn't grow up together?'

'No, we didn't. I'm five years older than Jósep, and I was fostered by a couple from Akureyri when I was three. Later they adopted me.'

'Do you mind my asking why you were fostered?'

'It's never been a secret.'

Albína had a decided manner. She wasn't embarrassed about discussing her family. She had been taken away from her parents because they were judged unfit to look after her: they were both drunks, and she only had the haziest memories of them. When she was older, her adoptive parents had talked to her about them: they didn't hide anything from her. But they never had any contact with her parents in Reykjavík. It wasn't considered wise, they told her. Best to cut all ties. So she hadn't learnt of her brother's existence until she moved south with her husband, a few years before the war. She had decided to look up her birth parents, only to discover that they were both dead. Jósep was their only child, apart from her. He'd had a tough upbringing, to put it mildly.

'I was an adult when I met him for the first time,' she said. 'I looked him up, and it was heartbreaking to see the state he was in. He'd succumbed to drink. Our parents lived in a slum.' After a brief pause, she added: 'I suppose I was lucky. He's had a wretched life. I've no idea whether he brought it on himself to an extent, but I can't imagine he got much support from our parents. And he ended up treading the same path as them. Isn't that often the way?'

'I daresay,' said Flóvent.

'You mentioned that you were looking for some school friends of his,' said Albína. 'Have they done something wrong?'

'We don't know yet,' said Flóvent, anxious to be honest with her. 'He was at school with a boy called Eyvindur, who was recently murdered here in town. Maybe you heard about it?'

'The man who was shot?'

'That's right. Jósep was also at school with a boy called Felix Lunden. We're looking for him in connection with the murder. Not necessarily because we believe he's guilty, but because we're hoping he can help us with our enquiries. Has your brother ever mentioned either of these men?'

'You don't think Jósep's mixed up in this . . . this shooting?' the woman asked incredulously.

'No. We have no reason to think that.'

'How strange that you should ask. Jósep came round here a couple of weeks ago, and I gave him a meal and some of my husband's old clothes. He said he was pretty well set up and couldn't complain, but it was clear that he'd been drinking. I don't think he's often sober, poor boy.' She gave Flóvent a sharp look. All of a sudden she seemed to feel she had to leap to her brother's defence. 'I can assure you that Jósep's a good man, though he's had a very rough time of it. He's a dear soul, really.'

'I don't doubt it,' said Flóvent.

'He told me he'd met one of his old school friends recently. I don't think he mentioned his name or I'd have remembered it, but he told me they'd been reminiscing about the old days, about things he'd forgotten all about.'

'Did he mention anything in particular?'

'Yes, something about medical examinations. He talked about a nurse – somebody Hólm or Hólms – who looked after them.'

'Brynhildur Hólm?'

'That could be it. Miss Hólm, he called her. Apparently she used to keep a close eye on the children's health, especially those who came from bad homes and were neglected, like him. She used to ask all kinds of questions, and sometimes there'd be a man in a white coat with her, who used to prod them and pinch them and look down their throats as if they were cattle. He put some kind of measuring instrument over Jósep's head too.'

'Could this man's name have been Rudolf?'

'Jósep didn't say, but he reckoned there was something amiss about the whole thing. That's what his old school friend told him – that it had been part of an experiment they weren't authorised to carry out, and I think he said the doctor in charge was German. Could that be right? Could he have been one of those Nazis? Is there any truth in what he said?'

'Was this the first he'd heard of it?' asked Flóvent.

'Yes, Jósep had never given it any thought, had forgotten all about it. The doctor – the man in the white coat – he had a son who was involved as well, and Jósep didn't have a good word to say about him. He was sitting here at my table, reliving the past, but I couldn't really follow what he was talking about.'

'Was his name Felix? The son?'

'Yes, Felix, that's right. What was it Jósep said? That he was sly, or something. At any rate, Jósep didn't like him, didn't like any of it. He got quite worked up when he thought back to those days. Then he left and I haven't heard from him since.'

The volunteers at the Citadel turned out to be well acquainted with Jósep, though they hadn't seen him for a while. They said he dropped by from time to time, especially in the depths of winter, for a square meal and to get some warmth into his bones. To be taught that God was good to all men and that God's blessing was extended to him as well. Flóvent was tempted to say that God didn't seem that well disposed towards Jósep, given the state he was in, but stopped himself. They admitted that Jósep didn't really take part in the singing, unless it was 'Onward Christian Soldiers'. They saw less of him at the Lord's citadel in the spring and summer, when he slept outside in the open air. In gardens, or sometimes in boathouses, or net sheds, he'd told them.

Flóvent thanked them. On his way out he encountered a tramp who had slipped into the entrance hall, and he thought to ask him if he knew Jósep. There was a throat-catching stench from his filthy rags, and it took all Flóvent's self-discipline not to hold his nose, for fear of offending the man. Not that he looked the type to be easily offended.

'Jósep?' the tramp croaked in a shrill voice. 'Why are you asking about him?'

'I need to talk to him,' said Flóvent. 'Do you know where I can find him?'

'Are you his brother?'

'No.'

The tramp shot him a sideways glance. He had a matted beard, a battered, brimless hat pushed down over his filthy hair, and his hands were black with dirt.

'Can you spare five krónur?' he asked.

Flóvent produced three krónur from his pocket. The man tucked them away in his clothes.

'I haven't the foggiest where Jósep's living,' he announced and continued on his way inside the Citadel.

'But . . . ?'

'You can try the yard behind Munda's place on Gardastræti. She sometimes has leftovers.'

It was only a short step from the Salvation Army hostel to Gardastræti. Flóvent walked round the corner to the street where a woman by the name of Ingimunda, popularly known as Munda, had started up a small kitchen called The Little Inn at the beginning of the war. Her daily specials were fried cod in breadcrumbs, and meatballs in gravy, Danish style, and she was run off her feet. She was a small, thin woman, past her prime, very brisk in her manner, and had little time to attend to Flóvent. Yes, she said, Jósep sometimes came round to her kitchen door asking for scraps, and she had been known to slip him leftovers because her heart bled for down-and-outs like him. She'd known hard times herself, though business was booming now, thanks to the war.

'He was here a couple of days ago,' she said as she formed Danish meatballs for the evening rush. 'Said he was dossing in the west end. In one of the sheds on Grandi. Told me he was expecting to come into some money soon, so he'd be able to settle up with me. A bit muddled, he was, the poor lad. I told him he didn't owe me anything. Not a brass farthing.'

42

Thorson drove up to the laundry. White sheets were flapping on the lines behind the house, and there was an empty tub lying in the grass. He got out of the jeep and walked over to the washing, taking in the view over Faxaflói Bay, the white summer clouds over the sea, remembering how captivated he had been by the scenery and the light when he first came to Iceland. But it was the silence that really drew him, the tranquillity; you could feel it as soon as you left town, even here on the outskirts, where the sheets fluttered under a blue sky.

There was no movement near the house. He knocked at the door, then went inside and called out, but there was no answer. He stood there at a loss, surveying the piles of dirty washing and thinking that Vera had her work cut out. Presumably she wouldn't be gone for long. Just then he heard a noise overhead and saw her descending the steep ladder, pausing halfway to peer down at him.

'You again?'

'Excuse me,' he said. 'Is this a bad time?'

'Yes . . . no. I was just so tired all of a sudden that I went for a nap.'

'I'm sorry, I didn't mean . . .'

'It's all right,' she said, glancing back up towards the attic before continuing her descent. 'What do you want? I thought I'd answered your questions. I don't know anything about what happened to Eyvindur, so there's no point asking me.'

'I realise that,' said Thorson. 'I came to tell you that you can plan the funeral if you like. The doctor has finished his examination. I know you'd left him but . . .'

'Oh, I see. I don't know . . . perhaps his uncle could . . .'

'Yes, well, I guess you'll be hearing from him.'

'Yes, I suppose so.'

'Have you heard from your friend Billy Wiggins at all?' Thorson asked, looking around the laundry.

'Billy? Why? What about him?'

'May I ask if you two are close?'

'Close?'

'Would that be a fair description of your relationship? And that you're engaged to be married?'

Vera gave him a long look, as if trying to work out why he was really here, why he was asking about her relationship with Billy.

'Billy and I are very good friends,' she said. 'I don't know what you want me to say. We haven't discussed marriage. Was that what you wanted to know? Why are you asking about Billy anyway?'

'Of course, you haven't known each other very long. A few months, maybe? It would be a little premature to talk about marriage.'

Vera dug out a packet of cigarettes from among the piles of washing, lit one and blew out smoke. They were an American brand, though that wasn't necessarily significant.

'Why don't you just get to the point?' she said. 'What are you doing here? I've told you everything I know.'

'Have you?'

Vera stared at Thorson, smoking her cigarette, not saying a word.

'Did you know that Billy has been sent up to Hvalfjördur for a few days?' he asked.

Thorson had learnt that Billy's unit had been sent with two others to work on the construction of barracks and harbour facilities at the naval base in Hvalfjördur. He hadn't yet made up his mind whether to send for Sergeant Wiggins.

'Yes, he told me,' Vera replied.

'Did Billy also tell you that he recently got into a fight at Hótel Ísland because of you?'

'Because of me? No. It's the first I've heard of it. What happened?'

'He met some young soldiers – a couple of them walk past your house every day. And he took offence on your behalf. You see, they said you were friendly with a GI.'

'That's a lie,' said Vera. 'People will say anything. You shouldn't listen to gossip. I don't know any GIs. People are forever spreading rumours in this town. You don't mean you actually took it seriously?'

'Well, the fact is that Eyvindur was shot with an American military pistol. Of course, anyone could get hold of a gun like that if he wanted to. There's a black market in that kind of thing around the defence force. All the same, I wanted to ask you if it's true – if you've started a relationship with one of the new arrivals.'

'Of course not,' said Vera. 'What a load of rubbish.'

He saw that it took her a moment or two to work out the connection. Work out what he was insinuating. Her reaction appeared genuine. Yet he had gone out east to her old stamping ground and learnt that there was nothing particularly genuine about her.

They locked gazes and he could tell the instant it dawned on her.

'What . . . You're not seriously suggesting Eyvindur was killed by some American soldier that I'm supposed to know?'

Thorson didn't immediately answer. He thought of the blacksmith and his encounters with her in the smithy, and although his own interests didn't lie that way, he could see why the man had fallen for her. How she'd got Billy eating out of her hand. Why it wouldn't take her long to hook a GI, fresh off the boat, if she had a mind to. Everything she did was on her own terms. The only question in Thorson's mind was how far she'd be willing to go to get what she wanted.

'Isn't that what happened?' he asked at last.

'Are you crazy?' said Vera. 'Are you completely off your rocker?'

'What about Eyvindur?'

'What about him?'

'Wasn't he holding you back?'

'I left him,' said Vera. 'He wasn't holding me back. I don't understand what you mean. I got tired of him. That's all. I left him. There's nothing more to say.'

'Like a thief in the night,' said Thorson. 'Didn't say a word to him. You'd found yourself a British soldier and had been seeing

him while Eyvindur was away. Wouldn't it have been more hon-
ourable to come clean?'

'No doubt. Look, I just couldn't live with him any longer. And
I'm not . . . I didn't know what to say. What was I supposed to say?
That he was never going to amount to anything and it took me a
while to work it out? That it had been a mistake – the whole thing
between him and me? That I'd regretted it from the moment I
moved in with him? Eyvindur couldn't bear to hear the truth –
never could bear the truth – so I decided not to tell him.'

'But he tracked you down anyway?'

'Yes.'

'Came to see you here?'

'He wouldn't let it drop, though he knew perfectly well it was
over. That it never really meant anything. Because I told him as
much.'

'Then what? Did he leave you in peace?'

'What do you mean?'

'You wanted to get rid of him.'

'Get rid of him? No. I *was* rid of him. I'd left him.'

'How did Wiggins take it?'

'What?'

'His coming here? Harassing you? Begging you to move back in
with him?'

'He didn't know.'

'Maybe it was Billy's idea,' Thorson suggested.

'What?'

'Did you talk Billy Wiggins into going after Eyvindur?'

'What are you on about?'

'Or did he come up with the idea all by himself? I hear he's a
jealous man. Hot-headed. What did you tell him about Eyvindur?

How did you describe your relationship? Did you tell him that Eyvindur wasn't going to let you go? That Billy would need to get him out of the way first, before you and Wiggins could be together?'

'Where did you get all that? I don't know who you've been talking to. What do you take me for? A moment ago you were saying I'd got some Yank to shoot him! Why don't you make up your mind? You've got some nerve, coming round here accusing me of this rubbish.'

'I know a man who's suffered thanks to you,' said Thorson. 'He lives in the countryside. Alone with his dogs. He warned me about you. How you twist men around your little finger. He told me not to believe a word you say.'

Vera stared at Thorson. 'Who are you talking about?'

'Oh, I think you know. You're familiar with his little smithy.'

'You went to see *him*?' she asked, dumbfounded.

'He says he still thinks of you sometimes,' said Thorson. 'In spite of everything.'

43

Suddenly Vera was like a cornered animal. She was visibly shaken by Thorson's reference to the blacksmith. Grabbing a tub of clean washing, she hurried outside as if she couldn't bear to be trapped in the laundry a minute longer. Thorson followed her and saw that she had started pegging out the wet clothes. The sun had begun to cast a golden glow on the sky in the west.

'How is he?' she asked.

'Not good,' said Thorson. 'Not good at all.'

'What . . . what did he tell you?'

'You didn't come out of it well.'

'What did he say? Just tell me what he said.'

'He told me how you used him. That you dreamt of escaping to the city and that he'd been nothing but a means to an end. You seduced him, and he was too slow to realise what was going on. You had a bad reputation out there and –'

'Who gives a damn?' she interrupted. 'Who gives a damn what those peasants think?'

'Why do you talk about them like that?'

'Because they're forever running me down.'

'That's strange,' said Thorson. 'If anything, it seemed to me like they felt sorry for you.'

'Why do you think I wanted to leave?' asked Vera. 'I was suffocating there. I never wanted to be a farmer's wife, frying doughnuts and milking cows. As if that's all life has to offer. It's crazy. As if women shouldn't be allowed to do anything else. Just work their fingers to the bone like skivvies. Wait hand and foot on some old sod. Churn out children and never dare to dream of any other fate.'

'Yet you were engaged to a farmer?'

'He used to feel the same. He wanted to leave. We talked of nothing else. But it turned out he didn't mean any of it. He kept dragging his heels about selling the farm. Kept making all kinds of excuses. We quarrelled. We were always quarrelling. When it became clear that he'd never had any intention of moving, I said I was leaving him. "Well, good luck," he said, "because you're not going anywhere. I won't let you leave." He always talked like that: I won't let you. *I* won't let you! As if he could tell me what to do!'

'So you decided to do something about it?'

'It was . . . I wanted . . .'

'To show him that you made your own decisions?'

Vera dropped the shirt she was holding back into the tub and turned to face Thorson, who was standing by the laundry door.

'I don't know what he told you, but I never meant to hurt him,' she said. 'Never. I know that's what happened, and I know what he thinks of me – what they all think of me – but I never meant it to turn out that way. I don't deserve all the blame. He had just as big a part in it as me.'

'He says you played with him. Played with his feelings. Used him to get back at your fiancé, then tossed him aside like a piece of rubbish.'

'Are those his words?'

'He says you deceived him.'

'Isn't that because he wanted to be deceived?' said Vera. 'And when things didn't turn out the way he wanted, it was all my fault? I was to blame? He knew I was with another man. He knew I was cheating on him. That didn't put him off. That didn't stop him. I'm not saying my behaviour was beyond reproach. I'm not . . . I was angry. I wanted to get back at my fiancé, I admit it. I admit my conscience isn't exactly clean, and I certainly could have done things differently. But who was deceived? What's all this talk of deception? He knew what he was doing. How do you know he wasn't just waiting to be deceived? Dreaming of it? I bet you didn't grill him about that!'

Vera stood facing him squarely, and when Thorson looked into her eyes what he saw above all was her strength of will. He wondered if it had been this strength of will that the blacksmith had found so impossible to resist. Thorson also detected a growing anger, directed at him, but it didn't even occur to him to try to placate her.

'He believes you ran away from the whole mess because that was always your plan,' he said. 'When you'd finished. When he'd served his purpose. You took off without warning. Just like you took off and left Eyvindur. Just like you'll leave Billy Wiggins.'

Vera had heard enough. The self-control she had shown up to now snapped and she spat right in Thorson's face.

'Shut your mouth,' she snarled.

Thorson knew he had provoked her, but he hadn't been expecting quite such a violent reaction. He wiped his face with his sleeve.

'You think I don't know?' she hissed.

'Know what?'

'What you're trying to do? What you're trying to achieve? You think I can't see?'

'What? What am I trying to achieve?'

'You'd better leave me alone.'

'Or what?'

'I've done nothing wrong. Nothing.'

'What did you say to Wiggins?' asked Thorson. 'Did you complain that Eyvindur was standing in the way of your relationship? That he wouldn't take no for an answer? That he wouldn't leave you alone? What did you say? That he should take Eyvindur out fishing and come back alone? That accidents happen? Was that pretty much how it went?'

Vera shook her head. 'My friend certainly didn't pull his punches.'

'No,' said Thorson. 'He doesn't have a lot to say in your favour.'

'You're talking rubbish,' she said. 'A load of bloody rubbish.'

'Was Wiggins happy to help?' Thorson went on relentlessly. 'Did you sit there talking about all the ways you could get rid of Eyvindur? Was it your idea or his? Did Wiggins tell you his plan? Or was it up to him? All you had to do was lay your cards on the table and he'd take care of the rest?'

Vera burst into mirthless laughter. 'Now you're just being ridiculous.'

'Am I?'

'Do you think I don't know what you are? Do you think I can't tell?'

Thorson didn't immediately grasp her meaning.

'Women like me . . . we can sniff it out,' she said and smiled her crooked smile. 'We sense it straight away. I'm right, aren't I?'

'What?'

'About what you are, who you are. You're not interested in women, are you? Never have been.'

Thorson was left momentarily floundering.

'Is that what this is about?' she said, coming a step closer. 'Did he get under your skin, there in his smithy? He's not a bad-looking fellow for a boy like you.'

Belatedly it dawned on Thorson what she was insinuating. She saw him flinch, though he tried to hide it, and she knew that she'd touched a nerve.

'You hinted didn't you?' he said. 'You hinted that you could get rid of your fiancé if the two of them went out fishing together and he came back alone?'

'Why won't you answer me?' she asked. 'Don't you want to talk about it? Are you embarrassed?'

'Women like you,' Thorson said, 'sniff out nothing but trouble. I get that you wanted to escape the countryside. And that you like soldiers – that they seem like your ticket out of poverty and a life of drudgery. I get that you want to be independent. Lots of women feel the same. But they don't all go about it like you. They don't need to play any little games. All they need is to be themselves. Women like you . . .'

Thorson didn't finish the sentence. He'd said what he'd come to say. It wasn't for him to judge her, and he'd already begun to regret his words, even if Vera had been needling him. But then he had deliberately provoked her. He had come here to get a better sense of who she was, to discover what she was capable of. He had got his answers.

'If you and Wiggins had something to do with Eyvindur's death, we'll find out.'

'We had nothing to do with it. Can't you get that into your thick skull? Don't you dare try and pin it on me. Don't you dare!'

'OK,' said Thorson. 'We'll see what Wiggins has to say, then you and I can have another little chat.'

'Get the hell out of here,' she snapped. Turning her back on him, she started pegging up the pristine washing again.

44

One of the welders at Daníel's Shipyard recognised the description of Jósep. The man pushed his goggles up on his forehead and told Flóvent that Jósep sometimes came round to the shipyard to scrounge a coffee. He was always terribly polite but not very talkative. The welder was glad of a break and happy to tell Flóvent what he could about Jósep, saying he didn't like to see a man that young in the gutter. He was a harmless creature who used to pass through on his way to or from the centre of town. His life consisted of nothing but aimless loitering. The man pulled down his goggles and went back to welding his joint.

The workers at the newly opened shipyard couldn't keep up with the flood of orders for repairs and refitting. Flóvent contemplated the grey British and American naval vessels anchored in the outer harbour; they were interspersed with Icelandic freighters and fishing vessels, everything from small open motorboats to trawlers. The Icelandic fleet had not emerged unscathed from the dangerous task of plying the oceans in wartime. U-boat attacks were becoming increasingly common and that spring dozens of Icelandic sailors had lost their lives as one boat after another was hit. Most recently the freighter *Hekla* had been torpedoed off the southern tip of Greenland on her way to America, taking fourteen men down with her. Every time a ship left port people knew the voyage could end in disaster. Flóvent had read that, following the sinking of the *Hekla*, Icelandic crews were insisting that all trips should be made under the protection of an Allied convoy.

As he walked along the side of the shipyard, towards Grandi, a British motorcycle unit passed him with a great roar of engines, vanishing in the direction of the town centre. A little further on he came to a ramshackle bait shed where a small, heavily bearded young man, wearing a much-patched winter coat but no hat, was bending over a tattered blanket. He had been trying to beat the dirt out of it by banging it against the shed wall. Flóvent asked if he was Jósep. The young man was startled and reluctant to confirm his identity. He seemed wary of talking to Flóvent, perhaps under the impression that he was the owner of the shed. He relaxed a little when it became clear that he was mistaken. Flóvent explained that he just wanted a little chat and they spoke for a while about the ships in the harbour and the dangers of sailing these days. The talk turned to Daníel's Shipyard, and Jósep said he had friends there. Flóvent asked if he was hoping for a job at the yard, but Jósep said he hadn't given the matter any thought.

'But why . . . How do you know who I am?' he asked, when it finally dawned on him that Flóvent was addressing him by name.

Flóvent explained as succinctly as he could that he was from the police and had come to speak to Jósep as part of his enquiries into the death of a man called Eyvindur, whom Jósep might remember from his school days. Flóvent noted the tramp's alarm when he said 'police' and hastened to reassure him. He just wanted to ask if Jósep could be of any help to them in their hunt for Eyvindur's killer.

'No, no chance,' said Jósep. 'I know nothing about it. Nothing at all.'

'You know he's dead, don't you?'

'Yes, yes, but I know nothing about it. Honest.'

'When did you last see Eyvindur? Was it a long time ago?'

'I don't remember,' said Jósep. 'Can't help you. Can't help you at all. Why don't you leave me alone? I sleep here sometimes, but I'm not in anyone's way and –'

'It's all right, Jósep. I'm not here to arrest you,' said Flóvent, seeing how nervous the man was. 'I only want to talk to you. You're not in trouble. Really, you have nothing to fear. It's just that I spoke to Munda, who offers you meals from time to time, and she told me you were planning to pay her back soon for all her kindness. Can you tell me how you're planning to do that? Have you got a job? Where are you going to get the money to pay Munda?'

'Did Munda say that?'

'Yes.'

'I haven't got any money,' said Jósep firmly. 'I've never had any money. I don't know what you're on about. Please, mate, just leave me alone.'

'The thing is, Eyvindur said he was expecting to come into some money as well,' said Flóvent, 'but no one knows where it was supposed to come from. Can you tell me anything about that?'

'No, I can't help you.'

'When you last met Eyvindur, did he tell you about the experiments you were involved in at school? Do you remember?'

'No, I don't.'

'Do you remember the experiments?'

'No,' said Jósep flatly.

'Are you sure?'

'Yes.'

'You don't know which experiments I'm talking about?'

'I can't remember any . . . any experiments. I don't remember.'

Seeing that he wasn't getting anywhere, Flóvent decided to take another approach, though it went against the grain. All he wanted was for Jósep to cooperate.

'You're not making it easy for me, are you, Jósep?' he said. 'I thought we could have a chat just the two of us, but now I might have to take you down to Pósthússtræti and put you in a cell. See if you're more talkative there.'

Jósep didn't react.

'It seems as though Eyvindur heard about these experiments from one of your old schoolmates, Felix Lunden. Remember him?'

But Jósep had stopped cooperating altogether now that the threat of being thrown in the cells hung in the air.

'His father, Rudolf Lunden, was in charge of the experiments. And a school nurse was involved too. Maybe you remember her. She was called Brynhildur Hólm. The headmaster, Ebeneser, was also mixed up in the affair. Did Eyvindur tell you all this?'

Jósep shook his head.

'Eyvindur had started asking questions about what went on. It seems he found out.'

Jósep avoided Flóvent's gaze.

'What did your father do, Jósep?' asked Flóvent, reaching into his breast pocket for the photograph taken long ago in the school grounds.

Jósep kept his eyes lowered.

'I did a quick check. Your fathers knew each other, didn't they? Your dad and Eyvindur's. They did time together. Isn't that right, Jósep?'

'Yes,' muttered Jósep, so quietly that Flóvent could barely hear him.

'It wasn't the only time he was behind bars, was it?'

'No,' whispered Jósep. 'He was a . . . bastard.'

'Did Eyvindur tell you that Felix and Rudolf Lunden had committed a crime and that you were one of the victims? That you could try and blackmail them?'

Jósep shook his head.

'This is an extremely serious matter, Jósep.'

The young man seemed tormented by the barrage of questions, but Flóvent had no alternative but to keep up the pressure.

'Did you write a letter to Rudolf, threatening to expose him unless he paid you a substantial sum of money? Did you tell him to leave the money by the cemetery gate on Sudurgata?'

'Not . . . it wasn't . . .'

'Did you or did you not write that letter, Jósep?'

'Eyvindur told me to do it,' Jósep whispered. 'He didn't dare do it himself. He was always such a coward. He said I had to do it and fetch the money and all the rest. I just did what he told me. He was going to give me half. He promised. But the money didn't come. Then . . . then he got killed. But it wasn't my fault.'

'What did he say, Jósep? What did Eyvindur say to you?'

'He needed money because of that . . . that woman,' said Jósep, still staring at the ground. 'He thought he could win her back if he got hold of some cash. She'd walked out on him. He said we could

298

squeeze some money out of those people. He told me what to write, and I took it round, but . . . nothing happened.'

'Was he going to talk to Felix, do you know? Eyvindur had a key to Felix's flat. Have you any idea how he got his hands on it?'

'He stole it. In the West Fjords. When Felix was plastered.'

'What was he planning to do with the key?'

'Break into his place and . . .' Jósep didn't finish.

'What?'

'He thought Felix kept money in his flat.'

'Why did he think that?'

'Because he was working for the Germans. That's what Eyvindur thought. He was going to find proof.'

'Then what? Was he going to blackmail Felix? Or expose him?'

'I don't know. He was sure Felix was a spy. He spied on us and now he was spying for the Nazis. Eyvindur said he was a bloody Nazi.'

'And Eyvindur was going to prove all this by breaking into his place?'

'Yes.'

'What did he tell you about the experiments?'

'He said they were illegal – done in secret. Those people didn't want anyone to find out about them; Felix had let the cat out of the bag. Eyvindur said Felix used to spy on us when we were kids and tell his father everything. He wasn't our friend; he only pretended to be. So there was nothing wrong with making them pay. They owed us. Owed us a load of money. Specially . . .'

'Specially what?'

'Specially Rikki's mum. Eyvindur told me to write that in the letter. He told me to mention Rikki specially.'

'Rikki? Who's Rikki?'

Jósep went silent again. Flóvent waited, but when no answer was forthcoming, he held out the school photograph and asked if he recognised the people in it. At first Jósep kept his head turned away, but when Flóvent pushed the pamphlet into his hand, Jósep finally looked at it. He was quick to avert his eyes again, but then he seemed to pull himself together and held the leaflet up for a closer look.

'What happened to Rikki, Jósep?'

Jósep hesitated a moment longer, then put his finger on the fourth boy in the picture.

'That's Rikki,' he said. 'Felix was always bullying him. Saying he was skinny and had a small head and that he was thick . . . That was nothing new. He was always saying stuff like that to us.'

'About how thick you were?'

Jósep nodded. 'Felix was always trying to impress his dad. We talked about that, Eyvindur and me, after he found out about those experiments. How Felix's dad had ordered him to behave like that because he wanted to see what Felix could make us do.'

'What sort of things did he make you do?'

'Felix gave Rikki a pill that he said came from the doctor. Told him it was the latest scientific development. It could make people fly. Specially little boys, like Rikki, who didn't weigh anything.'

'What happened?'

'Rikki believed him.'

45

Billy Wiggins tapped his fingers on the table in front of him as he smoked, cool and unconcerned. Thorson had decided to have him recalled from Hvalfjördur where he was working on the construction of the naval base at Hvítanes. The sergeant hadn't offered any resistance but had reacted with surprise and wanted to know why they were taking him to Reykjavík. They asked him to be patient; all would be explained in due course, so he accompanied the two military policemen out to their jeep without any fuss and sat quietly in the back seat all the way to town.

Once there he was taken to an interview room that the military police had at their disposal in the detention camp at Kirkjusandur. He accepted a coffee, and someone gave him some cigarettes, as he had finished his own on the journey to Reykjavík. He was stubbing one out when Thorson entered the room and sat down in the chair opposite his. Wiggins recognised Thorson from his visit to the laundry but didn't seem at all surprised to see him, just grinned, straightened up in his seat and flapped away a cloud of blue smoke.

'I guessed as much,' he said. 'Are you going to tell me what this is all about?'

'What exactly did you guess?' asked Thorson.

'That I'd bump into you again,' said Wiggins. 'Did you really have to drag me all the way back from Hvalfjördur? Was it really that urgent? Or were you just trying to embarrass me? Get me into trouble? There were plenty of people around when the police picked me up.'

'That was unavoidable,' said Thorson. 'We need to wrap up this investigation, and we believe we're onto something. Your name has cropped up more than once in connection with Vera and Eyvindur, and I wanted to talk to you –'

'Are you arresting me?' Wiggins interrupted. 'Am I under arrest?'

'No, you're not under arrest. Can you tell me more about your relationship with Vera? What are your plans for the future? Have you discussed them at all?'

'I didn't touch that bloke. I thought I'd made that clear the last time we met. I didn't know him. Never met him. It was Vera's decision to leave him. These things happen. I was more than willing to help her move out. We had nothing to do with his death. Couples do often break up without killing each other, you know.'

'Sure,' said Thorson. 'And Vera has a pretty impressive record. Has she told you about her fiancé? The man she was with before she met Eyvindur?'

'I'm not interested,' said Wiggins. 'I don't care about her past.'

'So you don't know what she did? How she got even, when he went back on his word?'

302

Wiggins shook his head, apparently indifferent to Thorson's question.

'Do you want to hear?'

'It's none of my business,' Wiggins said.

'She has a history of manipulating men,' said Thorson. 'Men like you, Wiggins.'

'I don't doubt it for a minute. A woman like her. Christ, they must have been queuing up.' Wiggins bared his teeth in a grin.

'Is she planning to go to England with you when the war's over?'

'What kind of question is that? Why don't you just get to the point? What we do or don't plan to do – it's none of your business. Why don't you just get off our backs?'

'Can you tell me about the time you –?'

Wiggins leant forward across the table. 'The fact is, you've got nothing on her,' he said. 'You've got nothing on us. That's why you're asking all these stupid questions. Because you don't have a bloody clue. You're up to your neck in it, and you're trying to claw your way out. Well, you're not getting any help from us, I can tell you that. Why don't you just leave us alone and concentrate on doing your job?'

'Can you tell me about the fight outside Hótel Ísland?' Thorson went on, unperturbed. 'I gather you didn't care for a remark some soldiers made about Vera. Can you tell me what they said?'

'I'm leaving,' said Wiggins angrily. 'I haven't got time for this bollocks.'

He stood up and waited for Thorson to say something or try to stop him. Thorson sat tight, watching him. Wiggins shook his head in disgust and made for the door.

'Wasn't it something about her hanging around with a GI?' said Thorson. 'I understand you weren't too pleased to hear that.'

Wiggins halted by the door and swung round.

'That's a lie,' he said. 'A bloody lie.'

'If it's a lie, I expect you heard the truth from her,' said Thorson. 'That must have been a relief for you. Unless she . . . no, surely she wouldn't lie to you? Why wouldn't you trust Vera? Are you sure you don't want to know how she ended it with her fiancé?'

Wiggins hesitated by the door, as if unsure what to do. Thorson, aware that he was the jealous type, had set out to needle him, and reckoned it was working. Finally Wiggins came back, put his hands on the table and bent over him.

'There was no Yank,' he said through clenched teeth. 'I know exactly what you're doing. There was no Yank. Do you hear me?'

'Her boyfriend was killed with an American pistol, a Colt .45. It's standard issue in the US Army,' said Thorson, trying not to show how unnerved he was by the British sergeant's threatening proximity. 'Do you think she asked someone else for help? Someone she'd met recently? A GI, maybe?'

Wiggins glared down at Thorson, his face dark red. 'There is no Yank,' he snarled.

'I suppose it would be pretty easy for you to lay your hands on a weapon like that? Maybe you even have one yourself.' Thorson said. 'Why don't you take a seat?'

'I haven't got a Colt .45,' said Wiggins.

'You mean you couldn't get hold of one if you wanted to? I know the defence force has a pretty robust black market.'

'What would I have shot the bloke for?' reasoned Wiggins. 'She'd left him. He didn't matter. Why the hell would I have risked my life for something so pointless? You tell me that.'

'Maybe she told you Eyvindur would never leave her alone. That she'd never be truly free. You tracked him down, followed him. You thought he lived in the basement flat because he opened the door with a key, so you took your chance. You shoved him inside, made him kneel on the floor and shot him. Only he didn't live there: he was visiting an old friend. Of course, there's no way you could have known that, but it came in handy when the murder was pinned on his friend and it looked like you'd got away with it.'

Wiggins dropped back into his chair. 'For Christ's sake,' he said. 'I didn't touch the bloke. I didn't do it. She only got together with him because she needed somewhere to live when she first came to town. That was the only reason. She wasn't in love with him. She said as much herself. Then one thing led to another, and she moved out. They weren't in love. It wasn't like that.'

'Of course you didn't necessarily do the dirty work yourself, so even if you have an alibi – and we're checking where you were at the time – that doesn't really tell us much.'

'What are you on about?'

'Maybe you're friendly with a few GIs. Knew someone who might be willing to do you a favour. For money, maybe. Or maybe one of your British pals owes you a favour. The possibilities are endless.'

'I can't understand why you won't leave us alone. We haven't done a thing.'

'We'll see about that,' said Thorson.

'We haven't got any secrets from each other. It's the real thing. Our relationship's got nothing to do with "the Situation" or anything like that. It's real and I don't like the way you talk about her. You ought to be ashamed of yourself.'

'What do you mean, you don't have any secrets?' asked Thorson.

'I know all about her fiancé,' said Wiggins. 'She told me herself. I don't need you to tell me. I know why she left him. She had every right.'

'Oh?'

'He treated her badly,' said Wiggins. 'Used to knock her about. Was always putting her down, followed her everywhere. She did her best to please him, but he only got worse, so in the end she left him and moved to Reykjavík. She told me the whole story. We haven't got any secrets. So don't try and run her down. Because it won't work, you hear?'

'Why do you think we suspect she was involved in Eyvindur's death? Why do you think we brought you all the way back from Hvalfjördur?'

'Because you're making a mistake.'

'She was engaged and cheated on her fiancé, then suggested that her lover go out fishing with him and come back alone. See why we're interested in you two? See why we're interested in her?'

'But that was understandable,' said Wiggins. 'Can't you see that?'

'What do you mean?'

'She was asking for help. It was a cry for help. And I'm not surprised, considering how the bloke treated her. Not a bit surprised. I understand her. I'd have done exactly the same in her shoes.'

46

The Pólar was a slum on the outskirts of the town, just to the south of Snorrabraut. The buildings had been hastily erected during the Great War to house families in need, but now more than two hundred people lived there in squalor and poverty. Although the wooden buildings had recently been supplied with electricity, there was no mains water and the houses were flimsy, badly insulated and freezing cold in winter. The slum consisted of four rows of tenements enclosing a small courtyard, which had originally contained latrines. Flóvent had often visited the Pólar in his time on the beat, since things could get pretty rough there at night and at the weekends, with all the drinking and brawling that went on. This was where Jósep and Rikki had grown up and, as far as Jósep knew, Rikki's mother still lived.

In the courtyard a man directed Flóvent to a woman sitting outside her front door, in a cloud of feathers, plucking a chicken. She paid no attention to Flóvent as he stood watching the deft efficiency with which she worked. Only when he decided to interrupt and ask her name, did she glance up from her task. She was a plump woman of about fifty, dressed in a threadbare housecoat, wearing rubber-soled shoes and woollen socks, with a headscarf knotted under her chin. The evening sun was behind Flóvent so she couldn't see him properly. Squinting up at him, she asked who wanted to know. Her face was wizened and she had wide gaps between her teeth. She returned to plucking her chicken.

'I see you're busy, ma'am,' he said. 'I won't take up too much of your time. I was just –'

'Eh? Oh, no, that's all right,' the woman said. 'I'm going to boil this ruddy thing,' she added, as if to explain what she was doing. 'Dússi gave it to me. His chickens won't stop breeding. Do you know Dússi? He keeps a big flock of hens over Nauthólsvík way, and sells the eggs to the British. Makes a packet out of them.'

Flóvent said he wasn't acquainted with Dússi, but he had just been talking to a man called Jósep, who used to be at school with her son. Did she remember him?

'Jósep? I should think so,' she said. 'I sometimes see him wandering around town, the poor lad.'

'I'm told he knew your son Ríkhardur. He was known as Rikki, wasn't he?'

'Yes, him and my Rikki used to be mates,' said the woman, brushing some of the feathers off her lap. Then she turned the chicken over and continued with her task, unconcerned by the presence of this stranger, looming against the evening sun. 'He was looking rough the last time I saw him,' she said. 'Hit the skids, hasn't he? Used to be such a clever boy too.'

'We were talking about Rikki,' said Flóvent. 'About their school. And Rikki's friends from the old days.'

'Oh, were you now?'

'He told me what happened to your son. In his last year at school.'

The woman paused in her plucking. 'Why was he telling you about my Rikki? What for?'

Flóvent explained that he had come to see her because another boy who was at school with Ríkhardur had been found dead in a basement flat in town, shot in the head. His name was Eyvindur, and Flóvent was investigating his murder on behalf of the police. He had spoken to various people who had known Eyvindur at different times, including during his school days.

'A policeman?' she said. 'Come to see me?'

Flóvent nodded. 'Do you happen to remember Eyvindur?'

'No, I can't say I do. The man who was shot – was he at school with my Rikki? All I know is what I heard on the news, like everybody else. Has it got something . . . something to do with my Rikki? I don't understand how that could be possible.'

'No, we don't know for sure,' said Flóvent.

'What did Jósep say?' asked the woman. 'The poor boy's in a wretched state, isn't he? I know only too well what drink can do to a person, how it can drag you into the gutter. I reckon the lad's in a hell of a mess. He didn't look at all good the last time I saw him. No better than a tramp. He's a lovely bóy, though, Jósep. Always says hello and stops for a chat, never tries to beg for money.' The woman sat pensively for a while, her hands busy with the chicken again. 'Yes, my poor Rikki,' she said at last.

'It must have been hard for you. Losing him.'

The woman didn't answer, just carried on with her task, her mind far away. The air quickly turned chilly as the sun went down, but she didn't seem to notice. Flóvent buttoned up his coat.

'Of course the Pólar kids were always picked on,' she said. 'Teased for being poor and dressing in rags that stank of mildew, and for having parents like us. The dregs of society. All the kids from here ended up in the dunces' class. Of course I realise we . . . I don't remember ever making him a packed lunch. It's terrible to think of. And I don't suppose his clothes were up to much. If there was any money in the house, it all went on booze. His sister took more care of him than I did. It was . . . it wasn't a happy home and Rikki was a terribly sensitive boy. He had ever such a tender heart, my Rikki. Do you have kids yourself, mister?'

'No,' said Flóvent, 'I don't have any children.'

'His dad was a bloody waster. A thief and a bum. Stole from Dússi and plenty of other people too. Broke into summer houses around here. Was mixed up in smuggling, and used to hit the bottle hard. Did time. Kept bad company.' The woman ceased her plucking. 'Not that I was any better. I was . . . I was on the booze too in those days. It's all a bit of a blur, to be honest. It wasn't until Rikki died that I gave up the drink. Haven't touched a drop since. Not a drop.'

'Could you tell me what happened? Jósep remembered parts of the story, but he suggested I talk to you.'

'Rikki suddenly stopped turning up at school. I knew nothing about it. He didn't tell me. He still left home every day. Always at the same time, heading towards the school. Then one day . . . I was standing out here one morning, where you're standing now, when a man appeared. He'd been sent by the school to ask where Rikki was. He hadn't been going to his lessons for several weeks. It turned out he'd just been wandering around town during school hours, playing on the beach, trying to kill time, and hadn't told anyone. He was never happy at school, especially not that last year, so he just decided to stop showing up.'

'Do you know why?'

'It was that boy . . . that doctor's son my Rikki used to go about with. That's what they told me – Jósep and his friends – so I went round to his house, to "the German house", as the boys used to call it. I wanted to speak to the boy, ask if it was true what they said, that he'd turned against my son. Ask him why he'd done those things. Why it had happened. After a lot of pleading I managed to speak to his father. He claimed not to know anything. By then the boy was in Denmark – he spent the summers there, he told me, and wasn't due home any time soon.'

'Did you tell his father what you'd heard?'

'Yes, I did, I repeated the whole thing. He came across all surprised and of course he tried to make excuses for his son, but I could tell he knew exactly what I was talking about. Knew how cruel his boy was. Didn't need me to tell him. But by then it was too late. My Rikki was gone.'

'Jósep told me he fell off a roof at a building site on Eskihlíd.'

'That's right.'

'He says the doctor's son persuaded Rikki to jump.'

'They said he thought he could fly. That boy was with him at the time. And Jósep, and another boy who was there too, they said they'd heard him egging Rikki on. Daring him to jump off. Goading him. He'd been bullying him unmercifully all winter, never left him alone, called him such ugly names that in the end Rikki didn't dare go to school any more. Disgraceful behaviour – you can't call it anything else. I don't know why he hated Rikki so much. Maybe Rikki was an easy target because he came from the Pólar and couldn't stand up for himself. The other kids sometimes used to call him a dunce. And then there was the smell of mould and the poverty and his ragged clothes. Maybe Rikki thought it would never end. The police said it was an accident – just boys mucking about. They wouldn't listen to me. Wouldn't lift a finger.'

The woman sat without speaking, the dead chicken abandoned on her lap, as if she couldn't face dealing with it any more. The sun had gone down and a cold wind came creeping through the Pólar.

'But I soon came to my senses,' she said. 'I was in no position to moan about other people's behaviour. Who was I to start blaming anyone else? I knew I hadn't a leg to stand on. We weren't there when he needed us, you see. He never got any support from us. I was pissed when I heard the news, didn't know what was going on. That was all the support he got from us. What a pathetic cow I was. All he got from us . . . My poor, sweet boy.'

Flóvent saw that the woman was finding it increasingly hard to choke back her tears, her impotent rage. She stood up in her distress and the half-plucked bird fell to the ground. She took no notice. Instead she scowled at Flóvent, her eyes full of accusation, and he regretted that he had upset her so much. He should have thought out what he was going to say, taken a different approach perhaps, been more considerate.

'What do you care about my Rikki?' she said angrily. 'No one cared about him while he was alive. Why are you asking about him now? Why did you have to rake the whole thing up?'

Flóvent wanted to express his sympathy, to explain, but she waved him away and told him to get lost, she had nothing more to say to him. So he left her there in the cold wind with her unbearable grief and a world of misfortune in her tired eyes.

47

Flóvent learnt about the broken window later that evening, when he phoned the police station on Pósthússtræti to check whether they'd had any reports of unusual goings-on in town. They told him that the policeman who responded to the incident had concluded it was nothing serious. Someone had thrown a stone through the window, but it could hardly be described as a break-in. It wasn't the first time a window had been smashed there. Two months ago a similar report had come in. Probably just kids messing about. That's what happened when properties stood vacant for long periods. Sooner or later the little blighters would start chucking stones at the windows. The police wouldn't have bothered to investigate if it hadn't involved this particular house.

A quick phone call to the hospital established that Rudolf had been discharged and taken home in an ambulance. He had insisted on it, and the doctors had seen no reason to keep him there under the circumstances. Flóvent gathered from the nurse he talked to that Rudolf had been helped by his maid, who was going to make sure that he didn't lack for anything. Flóvent assumed this must be the girl he had spoken to at the house.

Flóvent also put through a call to the prison on Skólavördustígur. Brynhildur Hólm had received two visits since he last saw her, from the same lawyer in both cases. She had taken his advice about hiring one.

It was late, and Flóvent was alone in the Fríkirkjuvegur offices, thinking about the broken window, when he heard a sound outside in the corridor. He stood up and was about to step out to investigate when a man appeared in the doorway. It was Arnfinnur, his old colleague. As they shook hands, Flóvent was privately astonished by the visit. Arnfinnur had never come to CID before. He was a tall, lean man, with a face tanned by the summer sun, and a firm handshake.

'I saw a light in your window,' he said, 'and thought I'd look in.'

Flóvent recognised this at once for a lie but didn't call him out on it. Lying didn't come easily to an honest man like Arnfinnur, and Flóvent wondered why he didn't simply tell the truth: that his business was of the sort that required a clandestine meeting after hours. He suspected that it was connected with Winston Churchill's possible visit. Arnfinnur could have rung but obviously regarded it as risky to discuss such matters over the phone.

'Are you making any headway with your investigation?' Arnfinnur asked, taking a seat and surveying the office.

'We're following up various leads,' said Flóvent. 'And gradually making progress.'

'I heard a rumour that this man you're looking for – this Felix Lunden – may be a spy. Is there any truth in that?'

'It's possible.'

'What, so he's been supplying the Germans with information about the defence force? About the construction of the base in Hvalfjördur? About Icelandic shipping?'

'We can't rule it out. We haven't found a radio transmitter yet, but it's possible he's been passing on messages to German U-boats off the coast. It's all part of the investigation. But tell me about Churchill. Is he coming here?'

'Why haven't you arrested the suspect – this Felix – yet?'

'Because so far he's evaded capture,' said Flóvent, omitting to mention that he had come within an inch of nabbing him at Rudolf Lunden's surgery.

'I hear you're detaining a woman from the Lunden household.'

'The housekeeper, yes, that's right. We're putting pressure on her, but it's not clear how much she knows about Felix Lunden's activities. However, we do know that she's been helping him since the murder. Hiding him. Mind you, I'm pretty sure she's doing it out of loyalty rather than anything more sinister. They kept his father, Rudolf, in the dark. Or so she claims.'

'If,' said Arnfinnur, 'the visit you mentioned happens – and I should stress that we know nothing about it – would Felix Lunden pose a threat to the safety of the visitor?'

'No, I don't think so. There's nothing to suggest that. Are you worried? Have you heard rumours?'

'No,' said Arnfinnur emphatically. 'I just wanted to check with you. Have you had any contact with a man called Major Graham from the US intelligence department? I believe he'll be in charge of security. If the visit happens.'

'Thorson – who's working alongside me on behalf of the military police – has been in touch with a Major Graham at the Leper Hospital.'

'Well, he's to be informed the instant you lay your hands on Felix. Will you bear that in mind?'

'Have they been leaning on you? Graham and his men?'

'We're always being leant on, Flóvent, you know that.'

Arnfinnur rose to his feet. 'They're extremely anxious for this man to be apprehended, and from what I hear they're poised to intervene at any minute.'

'There's absolutely no need.'

'Maybe. But they think you're not getting anywhere. They want to take over the investigation themselves – and start getting pretty heavy-handed. They want a house-to-house search. More people arrested and interrogated. Radio transmitters tracked down and communications intercepted. They're getting increasingly impatient. You'd better bear that in mind. They don't believe we can handle the case. They think we're bumbling amateurs, especially when it comes to investigating cases of espionage. They point out that we have no experience with the latter.'

'Fortunately, in my opinion.'

'Yes, perhaps. I'm guessing they're jittery in case the visit actually comes off. The last thing they want is for the Germans to get wind of it. They're afraid for the great man's safety. You're to keep them informed.'

Flóvent watched Arnfinnur leave and was about to head home himself when the phone rang. It was Thorson, calling to tell him about his conversations with Vera and Billy. He had no grounds to request their detention as there was no direct proof that they had plotted to kill Eyvindur. Flóvent told him, in turn, what he had dug up about a boy called Ríkhardur who had been at school with Felix, and the news that Felix might have played a part in the tragic accident that led to the boy's death.

Flóvent was just about to hang up when he remembered the broken window. They discussed it briefly, then agreed that they had better look into it and arranged to meet at the scene.

A few minutes later they were standing outside the German consulate on Túngata, looking up at the round window. Thorson still had the keys from their last visit. The broken pane was in a small cellar window round the back of the building. It had been reported by the people who lived next door. As soon as they shone their torches on it, Flóvent and Thorson realised this wasn't a case of kids throwing stones: there had been a break-in.

'The lazy so-and-so,' said Flóvent, 'he obviously didn't bother to investigate at all.' He examined the traces by the cellar window: the obvious footprints and signs that someone had lain down by the window and squeezed through it.

'You mean the police officer who was sent to check this out?'

'If he even bothered to come round,' said Flóvent, peering in through the window.

'See anything?'

'It looks like the boiler room. There's some rubbish on the floor.'

They walked round to the front of the house and Thorson unlocked the door. They entered the hall, then headed straight down the stairs to the cellar and found the door of the boiler room open. A mattress had been dragged inside and placed next to the old coal-burning boiler, with a Nazi flag and curtains serving as bedclothes. There were some leftovers – stale bread and raw potatoes – on the floor. But they couldn't find any clue to the identity of the mysterious visitor who had been living in Werner Gerlach's cellar.

'Could it be a tramp?' asked Flóvent, peering round the room. 'No one's keeping an eye on the property any longer.'

'Maybe,' said Thorson. 'Someone might have been camped out here for a while. Made themselves at home.'

'Wouldn't we have noticed all this the last time we were here?'

'I guess.'

'And shouldn't there be old *brennivín* bottles lying around if it's a tramp?' said Flóvent. 'Or meths . . . or bottles of baking essence?'

'You're saying it's not necessarily a vagrant . . . ?'

Flóvent prodded at the Nazi flag with his toe. 'It looks more like a hideout than a tramp's dossing place. Don't you think?'

'A hideout? You mean . . . ?'

'I don't know, but it's possible.'

'You think Felix Lunden broke in here?'

'It's no worse a hideout than anywhere else,' said Flóvent, picking up the flag. 'Felix doesn't have many places to turn. Perhaps he reckoned on this being the last place we'd look for him.'

'Do you think he could still be in the building?'

'Perhaps we'd better check.'

They embarked on a systematic search of the consulate, starting with the cellar, then the ground floor, opening the doors one after the other, peering into every cupboard and storeroom. They did the same upstairs and in the attic, but it appeared that the uninvited guest had kept to the cellar: they found no trace of him anywhere else in the house.

About half an hour later they were back where they had started, standing by the mattress in the boiler room. Thorson shone his torch into every nook and cranny and eventually the beam caught something in the narrow space behind the boiler. Getting down on his hands and knees, he reached into the space and pulled out a metal tube of toothpaste. Thorson got up again and showed the tube to Flóvent.

'Isn't that the brand he was selling?' Thorson asked.

Written on the tube, which was squeezed flat in the middle, were the words *Kolynos Dental Cream*. Flóvent unscrewed the lid and sniffed at the toothpaste.

'Do you think he carried a tube with him?'

'Why not?' said Thorson. ' "For whiter, brighter teeth".'

Flóvent smiled.

'Who else could it be?' Thorson went on. 'Surely Felix has been hiding here.'

'We certainly can't rule it out,' said Flóvent, screwing the lid back on the tube and putting it in his pocket.

'You're right. He must have thought it wouldn't ever occur to us to look for him here,' said Thorson.

'He must be getting pretty desperate,' said Flóvent. 'If this was the only place he could find.'

48

Brynhildur Hólm still couldn't sleep in her prison cell, so she was awake when the guard opened the door and escorted her out to the interview room, explaining that she had visitors. Waiting for her in the room were Flóvent and Thorson, who apologised for disturbing her at such a late hour but said they felt their business was too urgent to delay. Brynhildur took a seat facing them, an apprehensive look on her face, and they told her about the break-in at the German consulate and how they believed Felix had been hiding there since he'd fled from his father's surgery. An unobtrusive police guard had now been posted at the consulate in case Felix returned. They wanted to ask her if she knew where else he could be hiding.

'No, I have no idea,' Brynhildur said.

Flóvent removed the tube of toothpaste from his pocket and showed it to her. 'Was he carrying this with him? Do you know?'

'It's possible,' replied Brynhildur. 'I didn't check his pockets.'

She reached for the tube in order to examine it, but Flóvent withdrew his hand.

'For goodness' sake,' she said indignantly. 'Did you think I was going to eat it?'

'We found it at the German consulate,' said Flóvent, putting the toothpaste back in his pocket. 'He'd been camping in the cellar. I repeat, have you any idea where he might go next? Where else might he think of taking refuge?'

'I can't help you with that,' said Brynhildur. 'I don't know of anywhere else, except . . .'

'What?'

'There . . . Some years ago Rudolf bought a hut on the coast at Vatnsleysuströnd with the idea of converting it into a summer house. Then he had his accident, and he's never been back there or done anything with the property since. Felix . . . I don't know . . . perhaps he's hiding there. But I really have no idea.'

'Flóvent tells me that you knew Felix was working for the Germans,' said Thorson. 'That his uncle, Hans Lunden, recruited him.'

Brynhildur nodded. 'Felix has a high opinion of Hans, and I'm fairly sure they discussed spying and that Hans provided him with contacts in Germany and Denmark. But when I asked Felix, he refused to confirm or deny it. I know he's always been a committed Nazi. Like Ebeneser and Rudolf.'

'But they abandoned the faith, didn't they?' said Flóvent.

'Yes, but Felix didn't. His attitude hardened, I think, when the Germans started overrunning one country after another, though he kept his thoughts to himself.'

'Do you believe his stint as a travelling salesman was merely a cover for his spying activities around the country?'

'It's possible. But I'm not the person to ask about such things.'

'He didn't tell you why there was a price on his head?'

'No. I assume it's because of his "activities".'

'Did he offer any hints as to the identity of these people?'

'No, he wouldn't tell me who they were.'

'But you said he had other theories about the murder. Wasn't he telling you something about Eyvindur's girlfriend – that she may have wanted to get rid of him because she was mixed up in the Situation?'

'Felix felt he couldn't rule that out,' said Brynhildur. 'Really, he was as mystified as you are.'

'Who would have wanted to eliminate Felix?' asked Thorson. 'If we work on the basis that he was the target. Had he given himself away? Had someone here got wind of the fact that he was a spy?'

'That was one possibility he was considering, but he wouldn't talk about it. Wouldn't say who these mysterious people were or why they were after him, but it didn't seem that far-fetched to me – that he was frightened of something like that. He thinks they're out to kill him – there's no question of that. That's why he's on the run. That's why he won't turn himself in.'

'You mentioned that he talked about some "outsider" being hired – when Eyvindur was killed?' said Flóvent.

'Yes, but sadly I couldn't get any more out of him,' said Brynhildur. 'I've no idea what he meant. But I did get the feeling that he was terrified of someone here in the garrison. Maybe even someone he was in contact with, who provided him with information. At least, I get the impression that someone was feeding him information. But Felix was very vague. He wouldn't tell me anything. He was deliberately evasive, just started stammering.

But that was my impression after I pressed him about the matter. That he was terrified of someone in the defence force.'

'Let's move on to the letter Rudolf received about the experiments, the blackmail letter.'

'What about it?'

'Didn't you say you thought it might have had something to do with Eyvindur's death? That he might have gone to put pressure on Felix but the visit ended in disaster?'

'Yes, I have wondered about that,' said Brynhildur reluctantly. 'That's true.'

'That Felix might have shot him?'

'Yes.'

'Do you think he'd be capable of that? Of shooting a man in the head?'

Brynhildur hesitated. 'I'm in no position to judge,' she replied after a moment. 'It's impossible to answer a question like that.'

'Is it?' said Flóvent. 'Is it so impossible? Didn't you say he had inherited a cruel streak from his father's side? From Hans Lunden?'

Brynhildur didn't answer.

'Do you remember a boy who was at school with him and Eyvindur and Jósep, a boy called Rikki? You ought to remember him. He's in the photograph.' Flóvent took out the leaflet and laid it on the table in front of her.

Brynhildur held Flóvent's gaze silently for a moment, before dropping her eyes briefly to the picture, then looking away to study the tabletop.

'Why don't you pick it up?' asked Flóvent. 'Take a better look?'

'I've seen it often enough.'

'Do you remember what happened to the boy in question?'

Again, Brynhildur didn't answer.

'I expect you have at least a vague recollection,' said Flóvent. 'He was one of the boys Felix focused his attentions on, befriended for a while. The doctor's son, no less, deigning to visit the boy from the Pólar, where the dregs of society lived, inspecting his living conditions, observing his drunken mother and his violent father who used to hit her, and his sister who was mistreated. Observing Rikki himself, who did his best to please Felix.'

Brynhildur kept her eyes lowered.

'Jósep here,' said Flóvent, pointing to the photograph, 'told me about Rikki and his family. He also told me that Felix had a strange hold over the boys he got to know. He was more intelligent, from a stable home, his father was an important doctor and so on, but there was something else about him, something captivating, almost dangerous, which they'd never encountered before. A certain charisma. They were ready to tell him anything he wanted to know, obey any orders he gave them. They held nothing back, which was how he managed to learn their inner secrets: their thoughts, their fears – and test how easily they would bend to his will. He was their leader. They did everything he wanted. Jósep shoplifted for him. Eyvindur killed a kitten by bashing its head against a rock – because Felix told him to.'

Brynhildur bowed her head, and Flóvent leant across the table to try to see her face.

'And Rikki jumped because Felix gave him a pill, which he'd acquired from his father, and told him he'd be able to fly.'

Brynhildur didn't say a word during this speech.

'Did Rudolf give Felix the pill? Was that part of the experiment?'

Brynhildur didn't answer.

'Wasn't it all part of the experiment? The blind faith they put in their leader?'

'Rudolf never thought . . . he thought Felix would stop the boy before he could jump.'

'Never thought . . . ? Was he never struck by the irony that the only boy in all these bizarre experiments who turned out to be really dangerous was his own son? Little Felix Lunden?'

'Felix put the blame on Ríkhardur . . . on Rikki himself. On his naivety. His stupidity. Rudolf has never got over the shock. Of course he was responsible. It was part of his research. He pushed his son. Encouraged him. Felix told him all about the boys, and Rudolf directed Felix. He didn't wake up to the consequences until it was too late. The study was never mentioned again. He blamed Felix and sent him to live with relatives in Denmark. He avoided him. He's never really made it up to him, and their relationship has never recovered. When Felix came back he was restless, neglected his studies, then left college without taking his exams . . . He'd been to stay with his Uncle Hans in Germany and seen the rise of Nazism first-hand and was swept away by enthusiasm for everything he saw and heard. He latched on to the Nationalist Party here but felt they didn't go far enough, weren't ambitious enough. "A bunch of nonentities," he called them.'

'Were you aware that he had started sending information to Germany? Did you help him?'

'No, I didn't.'

'But you didn't report him?'

'Don't try to put the blame on me for . . . You . . .' She broke off, and they could see that she was angry now. Burning with resentment at the questions, at the accusations, at the way she was being treated – which she felt was entirely unjustified. Suddenly it seemed she'd had enough, that she had finally decided to place all her cards on the table.

'Aren't you overlooking the obvious?' she said.

'The obvious?'

'Why do you think Felix wasn't sent to Britain after he came home? There he was: half German, related to Hans Lunden, a known Nazi. And why do you think Rudolf, a personal friend of Werner Gerlach, wasn't immediately deported? Why do you think father and son aren't sitting in internment camps in Britain right now?'

'What do mean?' asked Thorson.

'Use your heads,' said Brynhildur.

'Rudolf's a sick man,' said Thorson. 'The journey would have finished him off. The old man wouldn't have posed any real threat. You said so yourself: he'd turned his back on Nazism.'

'Don't be so naive,' said Brynhildur. 'As if they'd have cared a damn if Rudolf had dropped dead on the voyage to Britain. It would simply have meant one less Nazi to worry about.'

'Then what are you . . . ?'

'Instead of arresting Felix and deporting him, they decided to make use of him,' said Brynhildur.

'Make use of him?'

'Felix is convinced that the British have been using him to transmit information they wanted the enemy to know. I don't know how he came to this conclusion, but he thinks somebody exposed him. And that the person in question is based in Germany and is vital to the British. That's why Felix is so terrified. Why he thinks Eyvindur was shot with a bullet that was meant for him. That's why he's gone into hiding and is afraid to give himself up.'

'He thinks the British are after him?' asked Thorson.

Brynhildur nodded. 'Those were his words,' she said. 'He doesn't know how many people are involved.'

'And you believe him?' asked Flóvent.

'I'm not sure,' said Brynhildur. 'I don't know what to believe any more. Felix has said a number of things that I can't begin to understand. He's very isolated and paranoid and his ideas are becoming more and more outlandish because he doesn't know exactly what's happened or why it's happened or where to turn or how he's ended up in this mess. But there's one claim he's made consistently, right from the first, and that's about Eyvindur.'

'That he was shot by mistake?'

'Yes. That Eyvindur took a bullet intended for him. He's desperate for it to be known that he didn't harm Eyvindur. He wants his father to know that.'

'Do you know where Felix is?' Thorson said once more.

'No,' said Brynhildur. 'I don't. You could try asking Rudolf. But I don't know if there's any point. They . . . they have rather a tricky relationship, as I've said before. Felix hates his father, but it's as if he longs for his recognition more than anything else in the world. And Rudolf may have turned against his son to a degree, but, on the other hand, there's no one more concerned about him. That's the only suggestion I can offer. Otherwise I can't help you. You'll have to find him for yourselves.'

They sensed that she was genuinely uncertain of his whereabouts.

'I don't know what to make of Felix,' she went on after a moment. 'I have to admit. The thing about him is . . . I pity him and I want to try to understand and help him. I thought I could do that by hiding him. I could tell how frightened he was and believed that he was the victim of circumstances beyond his control. But, on the other hand, he can be . . .'

'Cruel?'

'Ever since he was a boy, Felix has been involved in a struggle with his father that has poisoned his life. Whether it's a struggle for understanding or affection or recognition, I don't know. I have a feeling he would go pretty far to earn his father's regard. And he has no qualms about tricking or betraying people to get what he wants. I expect being a salesman suited him. He's extraordinarily good at convincing people of his worth. No one's more cunning when it comes to selling himself than Felix Lunden.'

Flóvent stood up.

'This is all very well,' he said, 'Felix's fantasies, your attempts to protect him. But I believe the matter's much simpler and that you know it. I believe that everything you say is a deliberate attempt to deflect our attention from one simple fact: Eyvindur was going to expose the Lundens, and Felix decided to get rid of him as a favour to his father.'

49

When they emerged from the interview room, Thorson was told that he was wanted on the phone in the prison governor's office. A fellow MP was on the line with news of Billy Wiggins. The sergeant had been released after his interview with Thorson earlier that day, but while waiting for a lift back to Hvalfjördur he had got into an altercation outside Hótel Borg and been arrested for drunk and disorderly behaviour. Later, once he had calmed down and promised to clean his act up, the police had driven him back to his barracks at Camp Knox.

'Is everything under control now?' Thorson asked the police officer. 'And if so, what's the reason for the call?'

'They said he'd mentioned your name when he started going nuts.'

'My name?'

'He kept saying he wanted to kill you, but the boys didn't take any notice because he was crazy drunk. Called you some pretty ugly names. I'm not going to repeat them out loud, but apparently he threatened to rip your head off. The boys are starting to regret that they didn't make him sleep it off at the station. They said he was pretty wild at first. Then he calmed down, and they took him back to his barracks. They just wanted you to know.'

'Thanks,' said Thorson. 'The trouble outside Hótel Borg – what was that all about? Who was he fighting?'

'Some GIs. He starting calling them a bunch of poofs – faggots, you know – and they went for him. Some British soldiers intervened and brought him in, so luckily it didn't turn into a serious incident. We're all supposed to be on the same side.'

Thorson relayed the news to Flóvent and asked if they were going to do anything more about Felix that night. Flóvent said probably not, but he was going to drive by Rudolf's house on the way home, just to make sure all was quiet.

'What's the matter with Wiggins?' asked Flóvent.

'He's a goddamn fool,' said Thorson. 'What did you think of the stuff Brynhildur just told us? Is she trying to be straight with us now?'

'It looks like it. If her suspicions are correct, then Felix has got himself into a serious jam. That's probably as good a reason as any other for why he's gone into hiding and daren't show his face. But I can't work out what's true and what's not. All this stuff about spies and assassins and traitors. We're just not used to that kind of thing here. We've never dealt with an investigation on this scale.'

'Let alone engaged in espionage yourselves,' said Thorson.

'Quite,' said Flóvent. 'I suppose that's why Felix has got himself into such a mess. He doesn't have a clue what he's doing. And he's in way over his head.'

'You're probably right.'

'This is more your department than mine, Thorson. You'd better talk to your people right away.'

'Yes, of course. I'll see to it.'

'Mind you, if there's any truth to what Felix told Brynhildur – if he's considered a risk to someone within your ranks – perhaps you shouldn't go talking to just anyone. You'll have to watch what you say and who you speak to. It'll be almost impossible to keep a story like this under wraps. Supposing it isn't just some fantasy and there really is a man using Felix to feed the Germans false information, it would be a big deal for your people.'

'That's for sure,' said Thorson. 'It's just a shame Felix is so slippery. I don't know if we can believe a word he says.'

They parted company, and Thorson decided to drive out to Camp Knox before going to bed, just to check that everything was quiet in Billy Wiggins's hut. He wasn't too worried about Wiggins making good on his threats: that was just the booze talking. Although Thorson didn't like the guy, he wasn't particularly scared of him. He had requested a background check on the sergeant to see if he'd ever had a brush with the law in Britain or had a record as a troublemaker in the army. Thorson was also anxious to find out if he was married, maybe even a father. He wouldn't be the first soldier to tell his Icelandic girlfriend that he was a bachelor when the truth was very different.

The Nissen huts, with their semi-cylindrical roofs and small windows, stood in rows along muddy tracks named after places at home. Thorson already knew which one was Billy's. As he passed the hut, he saw two soldiers smoking under the large outdoor light over the door. Thorson hadn't seen them before. This part of the camp was reserved for NCOs, and the huts were roomier and more comfortable than the privates' barracks. Thorson couldn't see Billy Wiggins anywhere. He halted the jeep, switched off the engine and said good evening to the two men.

'That didn't take you long,' one called, as Thorson jumped out of the jeep and walked over to them.

'Long?' queried Thorson, unsure what the man meant.

'To get here.'

'Get here?'

'I've just come off the phone to police headquarters,' said the man, grinding his cigarette butt under his heel. 'I don't know where he went, but he was blind drunk. He didn't stop after you lot brought him round. Didn't go to bed. Just got hold of a bottle from the hut next door and carried on drinking and cursing the bloody Yanks. He was pissed out of his mind when he stormed out of here.'

'Who are you talking about?' asked Thorson, suspecting the worst.

'Billy, of course,' said the soldier. 'Sergeant Wiggins. I just stepped out to take a leak and he scarpered.'

'He's not here?'

'No, that's what I'm trying to tell you. He's gone. I wouldn't have troubled you, only I think he's armed. I can't find his gun. I checked because he was making all kinds of daft threats. I know where he usually keeps it, and it's not there now. I'm afraid he's planning to do something bloody stupid.'

Thorson raced back to his jeep. He had to find Billy Wiggins before he got too far from the camp.

'Any idea where he was heading?' he called back to the soldiers.

'No, I don't know if he was going back into town to find those Yanks or to meet a woman or . . .'

Thorson leapt into the jeep and gunned the engine.

'A woman?'

'I dunno . . .'

'What woman?' yelled Thorson. 'What woman was he talking about?'

'The girl he's been seeing,' shouted the soldier. 'The woman who takes in washing. He was pissed off about something she'd done and kept ranting on and on, saying that he'd sacrificed everything for her.'

'Do you know what she was supposed to have done?'

'No, but the bastard was hopping mad. Beside himself with rage.'

Thorson slammed the jeep into gear and scanned the camp, looking west towards the sea where Vera's laundry stood. There was a faint light in the upstairs window, and he was overwhelmed with the horrible sensation, familiar from his nightmares, that however fast he went, he'd be too late.

50

There were no lights in the windows of the pebble-dash house when Flóvent drove up. He assumed Rudolf must be sound asleep and couldn't decide if he should disturb him now or wait until morning. He walked softly up the path to the house but wasn't aware of any movements around him. The street was quiet. All the neighbours seemed to be in bed, and there was no traffic to break the silence. Flóvent found the front door locked. He stole round the side of the house and noticed that the back door was slightly ajar. There was no sign of a forced entry, no damage that he could see in the dark. It appeared that someone had simply failed to close the door properly behind them.

Flóvent dithered for a moment, then warily pushed at the door. It opened noiselessly to reveal a small passage leading to the kitchen. He strained his ears but could hear no sounds in the house, so he tiptoed towards Rudolf's study and peered inside. There was a figure silhouetted against the paler rectangle of the window. Flóvent immediately recognised the outline of Rudolf's wheelchair.

'Rudolf?' he whispered.

'Who's there?'

'The garden door was open. It looked as if someone had broken in,' Flóvent said, in an attempt to excuse his presence. 'It's Flóvent. From the police.'

The wheelchair creaked and to Flóvent's astonishment the man stood up, walked over to the desk and switched on a lamp. The light bathed his face in a warm radiance. Flóvent had only seen him for a split second before, but he knew immediately who he was. Their paths had crossed once before in the old surgery on Hafnarstræti.

'Felix!'

'I hope you've recovered after what happened in the surgery,' said Felix. 'I didn't know who you were and thought I might have to defend myself so I just grabbed the first thing that came to hand and hid in the wardrobe.'

'Are you armed?'

'No. I don't have any weapons on me,' said Felix, raising his arms as proof. 'I'm not going to cause any trouble. I'd been planning to give myself up after I'd had a chat with my father. You've nothing to fear. I'm the one who should be afraid. How did the police know I was here?'

'We didn't know you were here.' Flóvent walked over to the desk. Felix didn't protest when the detective frisked him for weapons. 'I just wanted to check on Rudolf. Where is he?'

'Asleep,' said Felix. 'I was about to go in and wake him up when you appeared. I wanted to say goodbye. I'm not sure I'll ever see him again.'

'After you're tried, you mean?'

'Something like that.'

'Do you really think someone is trying to kill you? Brynhildur said –'

'I'm not sure she's in a position to tell you much,' said Felix.

His calm and collected manner was at odds with Brynhildur's description of a man descending into neurosis and paranoia. Flóvent guessed this was because he had made up his mind to surrender. Perhaps he was experiencing a certain serenity now that he'd decided to let go. His voice was tired, he looked pale and haggard in the lamplight, his eyes were dull and his thick dark hair was unkempt. He had a long face with small, slightly prominent eyes, thick lips and dark stubble covering his jaw. He was dressed in dark clothes and wore a thin jumper under his jacket.

'She's told us what she can – about you and your theories about what happened,' said Flóvent.

'I didn't shoot Eyvindur,' said Felix. 'You've got to understand that. It wasn't me.'

'Then why didn't you come forward and tell us that instead of going into hiding?'

'Do you think it's that simple? I've no idea who to trust any longer. For all I knew, they could have planted evidence against me. I don't know what Brynhildur's told you, but we discussed it a great deal and she . . . she helped me, but she hasn't done anything wrong.'

'Who could have planted evidence? What are you talking about?'

'They're working against me,' said Felix. 'Trying to make me look suspicious. You've got to understand that.'

'Who?'

'The people who've been using me all along.'

'Who are they?'

'I thought I'd got lucky,' said Felix bitterly. 'I should have been more careful, but I didn't realise that until it was too late. Someone must have shopped me. Someone who knew what I was doing. Someone ostensibly on our side. Someone in the German secret service.'

'German . . . ?'

'What has Brynhildur told you?'

'Who do you think shopped you?'

'It wasn't . . .'

'Have you come here to ask Rudolf about that?'

'No, it . . . he knew absolutely nothing about it.'

'Was it Eyvindur, then? He worked out that you weren't just a travelling salesman but something else altogether. Felix Rúdólfsson. Did he hear you use your alias? Was that why you shot him?'

'I didn't shoot Eyvindur.'

'Did you kill him out of revenge?'

'I didn't touch him,' said Felix. 'It wasn't my fault. I'm completely innocent.'

Flóvent suddenly remembered his conversation with Rikki's mother. 'Isn't that what you said when Rikki died?'

'Rikki?'

'Don't you remember Rikki?'

'What's he got to do with this?'

'We know about the research your father was doing behind closed doors. We know about the boys he was observing. We know about your role in the whole thing. About Eyvindur and Jósep and Rikki. How you and your father tormented Rikki until he threw himself off a roof. You had some kind of hold over those boys, and you deliberately exploited their weaknesses and their miserable family circumstances to humiliate or flatter them, according to your whim.'

'Have you been talking to Jósep?'

'He doesn't paint a very pretty picture of you.'

'You know Jósep's a drunk who tried to blackmail my father for money? Him and Eyvindur. You should take all that with a pinch of salt. Rikki didn't need any help from me. He was stupid enough to do it all on his own.'

'You told him he could fly. For all Jósep knows, you may have deliberately pushed him. He can't say for sure. He doesn't know if you meant to take things that far, but the fact is you lied to Rikki and dared him to do it. Just like you dared the other boys to do whatever you wanted them to. You goaded him until he jumped. Perhaps he didn't need any help from you, but he certainly got it.'

Felix's face betrayed no emotion.

'Was Rudolf behind it?'

'You shouldn't –'

'He abandoned his research straight afterwards. He packed you off to Denmark, desperate to get you out of the way as fast as possible.'

'Did Brynhildur tell you that?'

'Then years later, when you bumped into Eyvindur on your sales trips, you couldn't resist. Maybe he got on your nerves. Maybe you were drunk. But you couldn't resist, could you? You talked about the experiments. About Jósep and Eyvindur and Rikki and the other boys, who you described as your father's guinea pigs. You blurted it all out, doubtless to humiliate him. No change there. Eyvindur talked to Jósep. They remembered what had happened to Rikki, so they wrote your father a threatening letter. He was so upset that he burnt it.'

'It was so easy . . .' Felix shook his head. 'Of course, none of them were very bright,' he said. 'None of them. And I soon discovered that I could make them do whatever I wanted. It's a unique sensation. To have that kind of power over people.'

'What did you give him? A hallucinatory drug?'

'I didn't think he'd do it.'

'Was it –?'

'Look, I'd rather not talk about it, if you don't mind.'

'Was that why Eyvindur came round to see you? Because of the letter? Had you arranged to meet? We know Eyvindur was boasting about coming into some money. Were you going to pay him off? Talk to your father? Make it all go away?'

'Eyvindur was in the wrong place at the wrong time,' said Felix. 'Typical of him. He wasn't the one they meant to shoot. The British made a mistake. The man they sent round to my place couldn't tell us apart. That's how professional they were. I expected better of them.'

'We've heard that excuse as well,' said Flóvent. 'Anything to deflect the blame. Just as you shirked all the blame over what happened to Rikki.'

'Excuse? What are you talking about?' asked Felix.

'We've heard your tales about spying. That your time as a salesman was just a cover. That you sent the Germans regular reports about the military build-up here. Reports on shipping. The number of troops. The locations of military facilities around the country. The developments in Hvalfjördur. We heard that your uncle, Hans Lunden, put you in touch with the German secret service. That you're working for them.'

'Did you hear that from Brynhildur as well?' asked Felix. 'So she believes me, then?'

Flóvent shook his head. 'I think she's trying to help you,' he said. 'She told us you'd found out that you were no more than a pawn. An errand boy. But she also knows just how manipulative you are. She doesn't know what to think any more. And if Brynhildur doesn't believe everything you say, why on earth should we?'

At that moment they heard a sound from the hall, as if someone was trying, with great difficulty, to shift a heavy object across the floor. Felix's face remained impassive, but Flóvent went out to investigate. He got a shock when, through the darkness, he made out a man in a thick dressing gown dragging himself painfully towards the study on a pair of crutches. It was Rudolf Lunden.

51

Rudolf warded Flóvent off when he tried to lend a helping hand. He was astounded to see the policeman in his house and demanded to know what he was doing there. Flóvent said he was talking to his son. Rudolf heaved himself forward on his crutches.

'What did you say?'

'Your son, Felix. He's in your study. He came here to speak to you.'

Rudolf stared at him blankly as if he couldn't take in what he was saying. Then he waved Flóvent away again and struggled into his study, subjecting his son to a look of such fury that his eyes seemed to shoot sparks. Hobbling to the wheelchair, he collapsed into it, threw down his crutches and turned the chair to face Felix who stood motionless behind his father's desk.

'What are you doing here?' Rudolf asked, his voice thick with rage. 'What the devil do you want?'

'I came to see you,' said Felix steadily, as if he were accustomed to dealing with his father's temper and no longer let it upset him. 'I wanted to tell you –'

'No, I have nothing to say to you,' interrupted Rudolf. 'Nothing! Just go with him,' he ordered, jerking his head towards Flóvent. 'Go with him and face your charges and try to act like a man for once.'

'I wanted to tell you that I didn't kill Eyvindur,' said Felix. 'It wasn't me. I wanted you to know. To hear it from me.'

'There is no point in listening to a word you say. There has never been any point. Get out of here. Both of you – get out of here this instant!'

Rudolf made to propel his chair back out into the hall, but Felix came round the desk and blocked his way. Flóvent hung back, taking no part in their quarrel. His eye fell on a telephone, and he began to edge his way towards it with the idea of ringing for assistance. Felix was focused on his father. He took hold of the arms of the wheelchair and shook it so hard he almost lifted it off the floor.

'Listen to me!' he yelled. 'For once in your life, listen to me. Then it's over.'

Rudolf's jaw dropped. He gaped at his son, stunned.

'I haven't killed anyone,' said Felix. 'It's important for me that you know that. They'll try to pin it on me, and they'll tell all kinds of lies about me, but I wasn't the one who shot Eyvindur. I want you to know that.'

Rudolf was glowering up at Felix now, the gleam of fury back in his eyes. 'Get out!' he shouted.

Felix was still gripping the arms of the chair, towering over his father.

'The man who shot Eyvindur was sent by the intelligence

department at the Leper Hospital. He was sent by the occupation force. I'm convinced of that. He was meant to kill *me*. That's obvious. He's after me because I went too far. I know it's my fault – I made a mistake and brought down an assassin on my head.'

Felix had succeeded in rendering his father speechless.

'I've been sending the Germans information ever since I came home from Denmark. I had to do it. When Hans suggested it . . . I didn't think twice. And Uncle Hans's recommendation was all it took. They trusted me implicitly. They provided me with a secret code and a small radio transmitter that they'd hidden here before the war. I sent them pretty low-level stuff about the occupying army's movements. They advised me to become a salesman, that way I could travel round the country, gathering information, without rousing suspicion. One evening, after I sent them a report, there was a message waiting for me at home. An unmarked message that someone had pushed through my door. I was told to go to a certain spot at a pre-arranged time and there would be a message waiting for me there. I did as I was told and found an envelope. It contained a typewritten sheet about the construction of a port for large ships in Hvalfjördur and the laying of a submarine barrier across the fjord. All very simple. All very clear. I passed on the information.

'I was supposed to return to this same spot regularly and check if there were any new messages from my contact. Sometimes there was an envelope, sometimes nothing. I grew curious. I started watching the place in the hope of seeing who dropped off the messages. Of course, I didn't tell anyone. It was a private initiative. And one day I saw him and shadowed him back to where he worked. He went to the Leper Hospital, which could only mean one thing: British intelligence.'

343

'So he was working for the British?' asked Flóvent.

'I assumed either the Germans had planted him there or he'd decided to go over to the Nazis.' Felix had relaxed his hold on the wheelchair. 'I must have rattled someone when I followed my contact, because next thing I know I stumble across Eyvindur lying in a pool of blood. I knew I'd lost my key, but I didn't realise Eyvindur had it until I saw him lying there. I've no idea what he wanted from me. It was probably something to do with those experiments of yours. Maybe he just thought I was being malicious. He called me a Nazi whenever I bumped into him in the West Fjords. I insulted him – told him about the experiments. Perhaps he was looking for incriminating evidence or was planning to rob me. I have no idea. All I know is that the moment he opened the door with my key he was a dead man. I fled. I knew Eyvindur didn't matter to them. I was the one they were after. I'd gone too far. That bullet was intended for me.'

Felix loomed over his father, who was still glaring up at him without saying a word. Flóvent had picked up the telephone receiver and dialled the number of the police station on Pósthússtræti and was now waiting for someone to answer.

'It was typical of Eyvindur to blunder into a situation like that,' Felix continued. 'I don't know ... I heard his girlfriend had ditched him for a British soldier. Perhaps Eyvindur thought he could win her back if he got his hands on some money. Perhaps that's why he sent you the letter and broke into my place.'

'Who was the man?' Rudolf interrupted, suddenly finding his voice. 'The man who was feeding you information?'

Someone finally picked up the phone at the police station, and Flóvent requested assistance at Rudolf's house, saying it was urgent and telling the duty officer to get a move on. After replacing the receiver, he walked across the room, closed the study door and positioned himself in front of it.

'It doesn't matter,' said Felix.

'Did you begin to suspect that you weren't on the same side?'

Felix didn't reply.

'What did you do, Felix?' asked Rudolf.

'Nothing.'

'What did you do?'

Felix didn't answer.

'I know you. You couldn't resist the temptation to contact him, could you? What did you say? What did you say to him? Why did he have to get rid of you?'

'I expect the whole intelligence department was behind it,' said Felix with a grimace. 'I expect they wanted it to look as if they were sending a message to other spies – that they could expect the same fate.'

'Answer me! What did you say to the man?'

Felix faltered, as if unsure how to go on. As if he had lost track of what he had already said and how it would fit with what he intended to say next. He hesitated, confused, as his father demanded answers. Demanded that he reply to his accusation. Demanded that he drop the charade, the lies, the half-truths. Stopped trying to pull the wool over his eyes.

'What did you say to him?' Rudolf shouted at his son. 'Why did you make contact? Why were you set on finding out who he was?'

'Why are you so outraged?' Felix countered. 'Tell me. Why do you hate me so much?'

'What did you say to him, Felix?'

'It was you yourself . . . Have you forgotten that it was you who taught me to snoop . . . you who made me spy on the other boys and report back to you, pose as their friend, tell you all I knew . . . It was you —'

'I bear no responsibility for what you have done.'

'Oh no, you've always had right on your side, haven't you?' Felix said, raising his voice in turn. 'I've never been able to do anything . . . never been able to please you. Whatever I do, however hard I try. I tried to win your . . . to win your . . . I told you about the boys and Rikki and you . . . you've never . . . I disgust you . . . but it was you who . . . you who used me . . . you used me . . .'

'Why did you make contact, Felix?' Rudolf went on relentlessly. 'Were you planning to blackmail him? Did you threaten to expose him? Was it money you wanted or were you merely trying to seem important?'

Flóvent caught the flash of headlights as the police turned into the drive.

'You didn't need to say anything,' said Rudolf.

Felix shook his head. 'Don't think —'

'You did not say anything, did you?' whispered Rudolf.

Felix was silent.

'You alarmed him simply by making contact with him, didn't you? He must have felt threatened. Afraid that you would blow his cover. He sent a man to your flat who lay in wait for you and killed Eyvindur instead.'

'I don't know . . .' said Felix. 'I . . . the whole thing went disastrously wrong . . .'

'Who is it?' asked Flóvent, interrupting. 'Who is this contact?'

'Of course it was childish of me,' said Felix. 'The thing is . . . the thing is I'd started to suspect that he wasn't . . . that maybe he'd given himself away and they were using him – the intelligence people – using him to send selected information, some of it deliberately false, like the business with the submarine barrier at Hvítanes. It wasn't exactly where they said it was. I checked it out. And there were other examples – little inaccuracies that could be important. So I started wondering what was really going on. I thought I was just a pawn and he was running me – that we were on the same side, at least. I wanted to warn him about the little inaccuracies, so I started watching him to see if I could make contact. It didn't take him long to work it out. I thought he'd kill me. He was furious and said the game was up and that I was putting both our lives at risk. We'd have to stop what we were doing.'

Felix paused. He stared at his father.

'His reaction . . . It was only then that I realised how badly I'd miscalculated. What a . . . Of course it wasn't him they were using to send misinformation. It was me. I . . . all of a sudden I realised, and he saw. Saw that I'd worked out the truth. I was such a bloody fool. That's why they didn't touch you, why they let me move around as I pleased. The last report I sent was about Churchill. That he wasn't stopping over here. Which means he must be coming in fact, because they've been feeding me lies all along.'

'Felix . . .'

'They must have decided to dispose of me before I could send my next report and warn the Germans that all the information I'd sent before had been worthless. Their response was so swift. So . . . rushed. It's the only explanation I can think of. I didn't dare go near the radio transmitter – I was sure they were watching it . . .'

Someone banged on the front door. Flóvent was about to go out and open it, but hung back. A second car had pulled up outside.

'Someone must have betrayed me to the British, and they decided to use me to disseminate false information. Someone within the German secret service who's working for the British must have given me away, told them I was spying for the Germans in Iceland. The British are afraid I'll blow his cover. But I have no idea of his identity. All I know is that he must exist.'

'Felix,' said Rudolf, 'don't –'

'I won't let them catch me.'

'Don't do anything foolish, Felix. You cannot get away. Try to be sensible.'

'They'll send me to Britain,' said Felix. 'They'll hang me. I'm done for.'

He gazed imploringly at his father and Flóvent saw that he was close to collapse.

'I want you to know that it wasn't me who killed Eyvindur,' he repeated, bending down to whisper something to his father or perhaps to say goodbye. Flóvent didn't know which. Rudolf raised his arms in rejection, his face full of angry contempt. Felix immediately straightened up again, saying something in a low voice. Flóvent couldn't catch the words. He turned his back on the father and son and headed towards the hall to let his colleagues in. Two had already found their way in by the back door, and he was just gesturing to them to go and open the front door for the rest when he heard an anguished cry from Rudolf.

'Felix! Felix! What are you doing?'

Thinking Felix had attacked his father, Flóvent spun round to come to Rudolf's aid, only to see Felix clasping his own neck and sinking to the floor.

'Water!' shouted Rudolf. 'Fetch water! For God's sake, get some water down his throat! Felix! Felix! Spit it out. Give him water. Felix! Don't do this. Felix!'

He tried to rise from his wheelchair but fell back into it, watching helplessly as his son writhed on the floor.

A rattle came from Felix's throat and foam appeared at the corners of his mouth and began to run down his cheeks. He was groaning in agony. His eyes rolled, his head jerked back and forth and his ribcage reared up in violent convulsions that gradually subsided until he slumped down lifeless, and his groans gave way to silence. He lay still, staring up at his father with glazed eyes.

52

The jeep skidded on the gravel outside Vera's laundry and came to a halt in a cloud of dust, a hair's breadth from the wall. Thorson grabbed his gun and leapt out. He had never used it except for target practice and had always wondered when he would first have to fire it in earnest.

Holding the gun down by his side, he ran for the door behind the house. When he rounded the corner, he saw white washing hanging from the lines, billowing gently in the breeze. The door to the laundry was open as before and in the dim light that spilled out Thorson noticed that the washing wasn't all clean, although it had been hung out to dry.

'Vera!' he called, pausing by the lines. 'Vera, are you there?'

There was no answer.

'Billy!' he shouted. 'Billy Wiggins!'

He gripped his gun more tightly and was about to start inching his way towards the house, unsure what might await him there, when his gaze fell on the rows of white sheets hanging on the lines. There was no question about it: they were soiled. Either the washing machine had failed to remove the stains or something had brushed up against the sheets after they were pegged out to dry.

Thorson edged closer and, taking hold of one of the sheets, saw that it was covered in dark smears. He ventured further into the rows of sheets and saw that something had definitely brushed up against them. He had already begun to fear the worst by the time he stumbled on Vera lying on the ground.

Tearing the washing aside, he saw that she had fallen against a sheet and brought it down with her as she fell. She lay there in a tangle of bloodied white linen. Blood trickled from her head. She appeared to have another wound in her arm and a third in her chest. Clearly, she had tried to flee but had got caught up in the washing until, in the end, she had sunk lifeless to the ground.

Thorson heard a noise behind him and turned to see Billy Wiggins emerging unsteadily from the laundry and staring in his direction with a gun in his hand. Thorson was unprepared. Their eyes met, and for a moment it looked as though Wiggins was going to raise his weapon, but then he flung it away in surrender.

'I didn't mean . . .' he faltered, gazing towards the spot where Vera lay. 'It was . . . she . . . I didn't mean . . .'

53

The meeting between Thorson and his commanding officer, Colonel Franklin Webster, was brief. Thorson had been sworn to secrecy. First, they dealt with the incident involving Billy Wiggins.

'Extremely regrettable,' said Colonel Webster.

There were many other words Thorson could have used to describe Vera's fate, but he chose not to comment.

'I understand it was motivated by jealousy,' said the colonel. 'A crime of passion.'

'Apparently she had started seeing an American,' said Thorson.

'Extremely regrettable,' repeated Webster, and Thorson told him that Sergeant Wiggins had been arrested and was now awaiting deportation to Britain.

'Yes, of course,' said Webster, seeing no reason to waste any more time on the matter. 'Anyway, I have had several meetings with our friends at the Leper Hospital,' he continued, 'and although they've been accommodating, they're not giving much away. Of course we have to respect the fact that they can't go public about their operations. They had no choice but to dispose of the man. They had their reasons and although things went very wrong, there's no need to pursue it any further. It seems like the man chosen to carry out the execution was one of Ballantine's team. He's no longer in the country. His negligence is Ballantine's problem. Hopefully Graham'll learn from this.'

'Yes, sir,' said Thorson. 'I understand Intelligence were prepared to intervene in our investigation if necessary.'

'There's more at stake than that, Thorson. Though they didn't tell me straight, they hinted that they'd only narrowly prevented the exposure of a major counterespionage operation on the Continent. They've gone to great lengths to protect their people. This Felix almost upset the applecart. An amateur, I'm told. A dilettante.'

'Yes, he doesn't seem to have had much training. Though he did figure out that he was being used to pass on false information, and he was intending to warn them.'

'I'll give him that.'

'I heard he was fed information about Churchill's movements.'

'Of course, that information is confidential; it's none of our business,' said Webster. 'They say that their operations were at risk of being compromised, and we have to take their word for it. There wasn't much time, so they had to act fast, though granted they could have planned the assassination better.'

'They sure could.'

'But a necessary sacrifice like that is of little significance when you consider the big picture. The Icelandic government has agreed that the matter should be classed as a military secret. It's nothing to do with them, anyway: the Icelanders aren't involved in this war.'

Thorson didn't see any point in arguing.

After the meeting, Thorson went round to see Flóvent, who was sitting in his office on Fríkirkjuvegur. In spite of being sworn to secrecy, Thorson judged it safe to confide in his Icelandic colleague about what he had learnt from Colonel Webster. Brynhildur had been released. No official explanation had been given for Felix's death: his suicide was being treated as a family tragedy. Flóvent had found the radio transmitter he had been using hidden in Rudolf Lunden's dilapidated summer house on the coast at Vatnsleysuströnd.

'And Eyvindur?' asked Flóvent after they had talked over the case yet again. They had discussed it endlessly in these last few days, always getting stuck on this same question.

'There's a war on,' said Thorson.

'Is that supposed to make it all right?' asked Flóvent.

'Officially the case remains unsolved, whatever happens further down the line. I guess there'll be nothing to stop someone revealing the truth once the war's over.'

'And the swastika on his forehead?' asked Flóvent.

Thorson shrugged. 'I don't know how these people's minds work.'

'A necessary sacrifice?' said Flóvent, making a face.

Thorson said nothing.

'I wondered if they were more jittery than usual at the Leper Hospital because of the visit,' Flóvent said.

'Visit?'

'Apparently he's on his way.'

54

Quite a crowd has gathered along Laugavegur. Men in hats, women wearing coats or jumpers over their light summer dresses, children running around their legs and out into the street. Police officers shoo them good-humouredly back onto the pavement and tell them to stay there and behave themselves. Some people are waving Union Jacks, others Icelandic flags, as if it was the first day of summer when the townspeople traditionally celebrate the end of winter. British soldiers are patrolling the crowd, keeping their eyes open. There is a rumour that he will drive along this route on his way to Parliament House, and the crowd has been waiting patiently for hours, excited at the prospect of catching a glimpse of the great man.

A girl of about twenty hurries up the road from the Shadow District and finds herself a vantage point on the corner of Klapparstígur. She's wearing a smart coat and a pretty hat, and is carrying a two-year-old girl in her arms. She's adjusting the child's sunhat when she hears a murmur further up the street and knows something's starting to happen.

The swell of excitement reaches her, and she spots the car at the front of the procession. The people around her start frantically waving their flags and break out in cheers as the vehicles approach and finally drive by. Daringly, the woman steps out into the road and holds up the child so she won't miss anything. As the procession drives past she sees a fat, round-faced figure with a peaked cap on his head, leaning forward in one of the cars. She beams and waves at him and he waves back, and their eyes meet for an instant before the column of cars crawls on down Laugavegur and vanishes from sight.

penguin.co.uk/vintage